HIDDEN STEEL

BOOK 2 IN THE JOHN STEEL THRILLERS SERIES

STUART FIELD

All characters in this publication are fictitious and any resemblance to real persons, living or dead, is purely coincidental.

STEEL AND SHADOWS © Stuart Field

Layout design and copyright © 2019 by Next Chapter

Published in 2019 by Terminal Velocity – A Next Chapter Imprint

Edited by Marilyn Wagner

Cover art by Cover Mint

The right of Stuart Field to be identified as the author of this work has been asserted by him in accordance with the Copyright, Designs and Patents Act 1988.

All rights reserved. No part of this book may be reproduced, stored in a retrieval system, or transmitted in any form or by any means, electronic, mechanical, photocopying, recording or otherwise, without the prior written permission of the copyright holder.

Dedicated to

The fine men and women of Law enforcement, the military, and emergency services.
Who do so much but receive little reward.
But are ready to pay the price with little regard for their own safety.
We thank you.

ACKNOWLEDGMENTS

I want to thank Next Chapter for giving me this chance.

I would also like to thank my fantastic wife and my brilliant daughter for believing in me and pushing me on.

Thank you to my brother and sister for just being part of my life.

Thank you to Sarah, Dick, Candy, Tina, for your support.

PROLOGUE

A colossal blood moon hung in the midnight sky and shone as brightly as a winter's early morning sun. Below, the ocean reflected the Luna giant causing each wave to sparkle, like the lights of a big city. There was a whoosh of spray, and a mighty steel leviathan cut through the tranquil waters. A cruise ship of immense size – a city of the ocean, cruised by, its destination set, but it ran silent and dark, no music or signs of life. Aboard, it was as still and as dark as the grave.

Below, in the bowls of the floating city, a group of passengers stood huddled together in fear in the darkened depths of the ship. Sparks flew down from broken power cables like bright orange raindrops. Intermittent flashes from bursts of electricity lit up the darkened lower sections and the faces of the scared passengers. Their wide-unblinking eyes were glued to the electronic counter as it flickered with every change of the countdown. A man knelt in front of them. Even though he was dressed all in black, his broad-shouldered back was made visible by the emergency lighting above the doorway and the internment flash of blue light from the broken power cables. The man as he used his hands to search for a way to switch off the timer, in case there was another way other to switch off the device.

"Can you stop it?" Asked a tall blonde woman. The man

remained silent, lost in his task, the rest of the world was oblivious to him, as though he were the only one in the room.

"Hey, the lady asked you a question," barked a large American, but the man knew it wasn't personal, the American was scared but acting bravely, mostly for the sake of the ladies – or himself.

"Please, Mr Black – can you stop it?" The women asked again, the man they all knew as Mr Black stood up and walked towards them. Mr Black was tall, and his rugged features seemed more handsome as the flashes of light illuminated one side of his chiselled face. He wore all black, and he wore it well.

"I need the code, but we have time" he lied – hoping it would reassure the people. He turned and looked at the timer that read 04:45:36. "I have to find the actual device and hope to stop it from there." He turned and started to walk away but stopped. He half turned towards them and waited for a moment, as if pondering his next move. "Oh, and by the way, the name isn't Black its Steel, Detective John Steel." There was a large burst of sparks from the cables, making them shield their eyes. As they looked back to where Steel had stood, they saw only the empty passageway.

ONE

FOURTEEN DAYS EARLIER.

The rain came down heavy and hard, with raindrops the size of peas hammering against every surface, making dull thuds with each impact. The streets became like lakes, drains bubbled, and fountains of water spewed from the draining systems, as they were unable to cope with the watery onslaught. The sky above the Southampton port loomed with grey mountainous clouds that crackled and flashed as a storm brewed within. It had been several weeks since John Steel had arrived back home in Britain. The trip he had considered to have been most productive and fruitful in many ways. He had spent some time at the office of the company his family had founded some many years ago, to speak with the chairman of the board, to ensure everything was running smoothly, but mostly to make sure he wasn't needed to be there. Steel wasn't a businessman, that had been his father's domain. Steel was a soldier – a detective, not someone who was meant for a desk job.

He stood in the departure lounge and gazed out through the waterfall that was cascading down the thick glass of the waiting lounge window. A huge plate-glass screen was as big as the wall itself. He watched the ships in the harbour as they were rocked about like toy boats in a bathtub. There was a flash of lightning that lit up the sky, followed instantly by a crack of thunder. As the light show faded, the outside grew darker once more, and John Steel caught a glimpse of his reflection. He's tall broad-shouldered frame was clad in a black suit, a black shirt and maroon tie. A pair of mask-like sunglasses hugged the contours of his rugged good looks. John Steel looked like a million bucks, though, he was going for the two million look. The joys of undercover.

As he lifted the cup to his lips, his face winced at the smell and taste of the strong brew. He smiled as thoughts of the Homicide Department back in New York came flooding back to him. A couple of weeks before, Steel was attached to the NYPD on a case. It had been a triple homicide, which had been masking a massive arms deal, set up by a criminal organisation. It was meant to be for just for one case, but he had the feeling things were not over - not yet, so he would remain there for a little while longer. Besides, he was having too much fun getting under their skin, especially the lead detective – Detective Samantha McCall.

The lounge was full of families, tour groups, and people who just had to get away from it all. He did not fit into any of those categories. They were there for relaxation; he was there for answers. As he looked around at the happy couples who were laughing, and the children were running about with excitement. Everything seemed to slow down. His mind drifted to images of his wife. The memories rolled like an old film, real into his mind: her smile, her beautiful face. The locations appeared blurred in the background, but it didn't matter. As he watched memories unfold, the image was of his wife laughing and smiling, and they were running on a beach somewhere, their time together reeling off like he was watching a home movie in his mind. The image changed, she lying in their bed and rolling over to face him, she smiled as he touched her face, his heart froze as the image distorted, and her eyes became cold and empty. Steel went to cry out her name, but a sensation stopped him, something was yanking at his leg. Reality crashed through the daymare like a brick through a windowpane. Steel looked down with a startled and confused look on his face at first, but a warming smile replaced it. A little girl, who was no more than six years old, was tugging on his trouser leg, with not much force, but enough to get Steel's attention. The girl had a look of that tender innocence and inquisitiveness most have at that age. For some sweet and amusing, and others found it annoying after a while.

"Hey Mr, why are you so sad, are you scared of boats?" she asked, in a squeaky voice. Her rosy cheeks masked her freckled face, and her mousey-coloured hair was tied up into pigtails held together by bright pink hairbands with bobbles that looked like fat ladybirds. As Steel smiled at her, he looked up in time to see a woman rushing towards them; she knelt and grabbed her daughter, embarrassed at her daughter's intrusion.

She was tall, blonde and beautiful. A black dress hugged her body, revealing every fake curve she had – but she made both work well for her.

"I am so sorry; I hope she didn't disturb you?" Her voice was soft, with a hint of an East London accent.

"Not at all." Steel replied, smiling back at the woman. Steel noticed her ring finger had a white band, which indicated a divorce and, judging by the whiteness of the band, a recent one at that. Steel smiled and thought if she was on this cruise, the whole thing must have ended with her on top.

"It's fine; really, I was just daydreaming, that's all." Steel said, readjusting his sunglasses. Eyewear that he had found to be perfect to look at people without them noticing him, as well as having other unique benefits. As Steel gave the woman and the rest of the room a once over, as he did, he caught her gaze. A full, wide-eyed look, like the cat who was staring at the fishbowl look. It was obvious she liked what she saw – especially the lack of jewellery on the wedding finger, or the hint that there had been any for that matter. As she stood from the kneeling position by her daughter's side, the woman straightened out her dress, ensuring to push out her chest and flicked her long blonde locks.

"Are you travelling alone Mr…?" She reached out a hand to start the formal introductions and inenviable friendly interrogation. Steel smiled and, taking her hand, laid a gentle kiss on the knuckles of her trembling hand.

"Black, Antony Black, and yes I am travelling alone, a bit of a business trip mixed with pleasure," he smiled; as he watched the woman became flushed, "And you are…?" The woman slapped back to reality by her daughter pulling at her mother's dress and giggling.

"What – sorry, I am Miss Wade, but you can call me Julie and this little madam is Trish." She dug her fingers into the top of the child's shoulders, causing her to giggle and struggle out of the tickle grip.

"Would all passengers please make their way to the promenade ready for boarding, thank you," came a voice over the Tannoy. A tall, thin, grey-haired steward placed back the handset and stood next to his female colleague as the preparation for the mass of people began.

"I hope we run into each other again, Mr Black" Steel smiled, broadly.

"Oh, something tells me that will be inevitable," he bowed slightly with his right hand over his chest. "Madam" Trish giggled and returned the bow, "Madam" Julie smiled, and her tanned cheeks blushed as she made for the desk, entirely dazzled by the display.

Steel stood back and watched in wonderment at the cascade of people pushing through the reception in an almost manic need to be first, and he knew it would be the same for disembarkation, the same people would be first off, and he smiled to himself and shook his head as he finished his coffee.

As John Steel made his way outside and towards one of the three gantries, he caught the full view of the massive floating city, the whole walkway had been covered by what appeared to be a long marquee to ensure the seven thousand five hundred passengers wouldn't get wet before they started.

The massive wonder held twenty-three decks and lay 3,800 ft long; the floating colossus was a remarkable sight; its white gloss walls gave way to the glass balconies of the apartments and the yellow lifeboats housed below the living quarters. As

Steel entered the vessel, he saw a long-carpeted corridor which then opened out to the main floor. Large open brass-coloured elevators with seating carried the passengers to the upper floors, as well as grand staircases that led to the next deck. There were potted plants, a fountain in the centre of the room which held a large bronze statue of the ocean god himself. Steel took the stairwell – choosing to take in the breath-taking view of the open-plan floors. Reaching the next level, he noticed it opened out into a massive auditorium. Red and gold marble tiles lined the floors while grand stone pillars held up the next floor, which gave it a grand appearance – with its maroon wallpapered walls and paintings in gold frames. Chesterfield furnishings were arranged in groups across the marble floor. Steel was impressed at its mixture of old grand and modern, bright lights and entertainment. The white marble information desk, crowned with brass fittings that curved around the sides, and a polished oak top was placed against the right-hand wall.

The ceiling rose up to around eight feet, the room itself had an abundance of touch screen information boards, large potted plants, and palm trees. Steel looked at the information pack he had received at check-in, which was more like a flight check-in than that of a cruise.

He was in one of the suites on deck seventeen; he stood for a moment to get his bearings. Steel watched the masses rush here and there, as though the whole ship was about to close in five minutes. He chuckled to himself at the fact that these people had fourteen days to explore but felt the need to see everything now.

"Can I help you, Sir?" Asked a steward in a white uniform. Steel turned and showed his key card, displaying his room number. "You're on deck seventeen Mr – Black; elevators are just over there." Steel thanked the man and made his way through the chaos towards the safety of the glass elevator. As Steel headed passed a brass post, he caught the reflection behind him, the steward was on his cell and watching Steel as he headed away. He thought nothing of it and just put it down to his soldier paranoia.

Standing in front of his door, he drew out the key card and slipped it into the slot, a green LED flicked on, and a click signalled he could enter. The room was large with a king-sized bed and furnishings fit for a five-star hotel, at the far end of the room, a blaze of sunshine showed the sliding glass doors to his balcony. Throwing his suitcase onto the bed, he approached the two sliding doors and pushed the blue and white curtains to the side. Outside looked cold and miserable but the warm climate inside made it feel very much snugger. He turned and crashed onto the bed; he bounced slightly, meaning it was a good mattress – for him anyway. The bed was comfortable and inviting possibly too inviting. He shot up off the bed, "No" he thought, "I got to unpack." He opened the suitcase and blew out a large breath to wake himself, "First unpack, and then check out the ship."

JOHN STEEL AWOKE WITH A START. There was a blast from the horn of the ship, followed by another as the ships bid its farewell to the port. Steel scowled, annoyed at the interruption to his nap.

"Cheers for that you bastards," he yelled, as though anyone could hear him, he looked at his watch – it was half-past two in the afternoon, he'd only been asleep for half an hour, but it had been a nice half-hour. Sliding himself off the bed, he silently cursed himself for giving in to the comfort of the mattress, but as he finally unpacked, he gave a self-indulging smile.

AT HERBERT WALKER AVENUE, two large, long buildings lay next to the River Test. Their white walls housed the arrival and departures of the large cruise liners. Surrounding the buildings were a series of long-stay car parks and container storage for the large cargo ships. The clouds above gave a menacing bon voyage to the floating city with crackles, low rumbles of the electrical storm within.

With a roar of power, a blacked-out Land Rover raced into

the parking lot next to the cruise terminal and, with a screech, came to a halt, the vehicle was parked side on to the water. Slowly the back window wound down, the sound of electrical gears assisting its decent. A pair of binoculars crept out and scanned the vessel, only the sound of the hum from the engine, and the raindrops impacting with the metal of the vehicle, broke the silence of the moment. As the ship pulled away down the river towards the mouth of the ocean, the car remained until it was no longer visible by naked eye or binoculars. As the massive ship became a dot on the landscape, the window wound up, and with a spit of gravel, the car sped away.

TWO

Detective Samantha McCall sat at her desk in the Homicide Department of the NYPD. Even though she was tired from a full day of investigating a homicide downtown, her youthful good looks held fast. McCall gently brushed the hair of her fringe away from her eyes as she proofread an arrest report she'd just finished typing. Her blue eyes scanned the document; satisfied the content was accurate; she filed it. Picking up her coffee mug, she sat back in her chair and took a mouthful of the dark liquid. Her eyes wandered to the empty chair next to her desk and stared at the void. Detective Joshua Tooms spotted her powerful gaze upon the chair.

"You miss him, don't you? Go on admit it." he said, his voice deep and gravelly, like a brown bear would sound if it could talk. McCall looked up at him, still holding the same open-eyed expression, then McCall blinked.

"No, I am trying to move the chair with my mind, jackass" McCall shot him a fake grin, which suddenly soured. "But if you ever tell him I'll hurt you," she said, with a friendly growl.

"Yes, of course, OBI-WAN," Tooms said, backing off with his hands up, wearing a playful grin. McCall scowled back at him as he sat down in the chair. Tooms's large frame hunched over the desk as he started to check his cell for messages. The phone seemed small in his large black hands. The guy had the frame of a quarterback and the haircut of a Marine.

"So, no word from our boy, huh?" Tooms asked, taking note of her gaze at the empty chair. McCall shook her head with a worried look on her face.

"Don't fret girl, he's probably been busy bustin' some bad guys over there and shooting everything" she smiled. "Or on a beach somewhere with some supermodels or something," Tooms added - chancing a glance out of the corner of his eye and smiling as he saw her murderous look.

"Ok, are we done for the night? I am beat, and if I don't make it home on time, I am a dead man walkin'," Tooms said, standing up and placing his cell away into a jacket pocket. McCall shook her head, suddenly confused for a moment, then a look of clarity shone through.

"Oh god your anniversary, go, man, go, and give her my best," McCall said, shooing him out with a guilty smile. Picking up the file, McCall headed towards Detective Antony Marinelli, who sat at his desk, looking uncomfortable.

"Thought you would be heading out too?" She asked, somewhat confused until she saw the napkin on his desk. It was from a diner. As well as having the diner owner's monogram; it held a phone number scribbled in blue ink and what appeared to be red lipstick in the shape of a pair of luscious lips. Smiling, McCall sat on the edge of his desk and looked down at him, looking back at her. Tony smiled and held up the napkin.

"Did you call her?" McCall asked, with a searching look. Tony looked scared but forced a smile.

"Not yet," he replied, feeling like a school kid again. McCall laughed and picked up the receiver of the phone.

"Call her – hey what's the worst thing that could happen, right?" Taking the receiver in his hand, he froze for a moment. McCall laughed aloud, making Tony give her a hurt look.

"My god Tony, you chase down murderers, you've taken on drug gangs when you were a NARC and done several tours in Iraq, but in the face of a pretty girl, you crumble. Sad, but sweet." Tony laughed, knowing she was right.

"Call the girl, make a date, then get out of here," McCall said, as she winked at him and left him to talk. As she sat at her desk, McCall put down her coffee mug after taking several large mouthfuls; then turned her attention to her e-mails. There was a weird silence that made McCall look up and around the room. The bullpen was nearly empty, she sat back and blew out some air from her pursed lips. Her cell vibrated to life, the blue glow from the display showed that it was Steel calling. At first, she was reluctant to answer as he had not called or written for weeks. Hesitantly, she picked it up and answered.

"Steel wow, long time, how's it going?" McCall said, trying to cover the bitterness of her tone. Steel could make out the cover of her voice, and he felt terrible, but she would understand.

"Hi McCall, sorry I haven't been in touch or anything…" Steel started, still feeling he had left it too late to call.

"No, it's fine, you have been busy, I get it," her voice wobbled, and he noticed it, but he did not have time.

"Look something has come up and well…." He hated to ask, but this was important. "Can you check something for me?" She looked at the cell phone, stunned; she wanted to smash the phone to pieces, but just hearing his voice again gave her a warm feeling.

"Yeah sure, what is it?" She felt a lump in her throat swell, but she fought back the emotion. "Can you check on a company called *Callan Industries*," she jotted it down on a post-it and stuck it to her monitor. McCall heard a loud horn blare in the background.

"Steel, where are you anyway?" she asked, with a curious tone ringing in her voice.

"Uhm – I'm on a cruise ship at the moment," his voice sounded awkward and somewhat embarrassed at admitting to his location, knowing she would get the wrong idea.

"Wait – you're on a cruise, and you want me to look something up, are you friggin' kiddin' me?" She was stunned and angry at the same time.

"McCall – Sam it's important, I hate to ask, but you know I

wouldn't if I didn't have too." The line went dead, McCall had hung up or shot her phone, he couldn't be sure. Either way, he knew she was pissed. McCall threw the cell across the desk and screamed to herself.

"Wow, that must have been Steel; how is he?" The sudden voice from behind her made McCall jump. McCall spun around slowly in her chair to see Doctor Tina Franks standing there, her arms crossed and looking like she was on the way to a party.

"No word for weeks then he calls to get me to check on something, do you believe the balls on the guy?" McCall growled through her teeth.

"I'd love too, and I really think you'd love too as well, but for now, get your jacket "WE" are going out, and "WE" are going to have some fun." McCall gave Tina an *I can't really* look. But Tina grabbed McCall's coat and held it out for her to put on. "Come on, get your sexy ass outta that chair," Tina ordered.

"On the menu tonight my girl is fun, fun, fun," Tina said with a purr in her voice and a wicked smile. Reluctantly, McCall stood and put on her coat like a six-year-old going to the dentist. "Come on, Sammy, smile; it will be fun…you remember fun, don't you?"

McCall could remember fun, and it was running around on a case with John Steel.

THREE

The cruise ship cut through the waves, it's massive bulk unaffected by the chop of the sea. The view of the dock was long gone, and they were underway to the next port on the list. After finally unpacking his suitcase, Steel decided to take a walk and try to get acquainted with the layout of the vessel. Something was going to happen, and this ship or someone on it had something to do with it. Deck 8 was a massive expanse of shops, bars, coffee shops all lined up with white tiled floors and neon window signs. There was a central reservation with seating and palm trees and plants, which gave the whole place a feel of being in a big city, rather than being on a ship. Passengers rushed about, taking in the sights, excited at their new surroundings. Steel looked around, in awe of the ship's interior and size. He wandered around a little longer before his mouth became dry – he needed something to drink. Steel smiled to himself. Next to a gift shop was an Irish Pub, with old-style seats and tables outside the entrance and alongside the wall and window. Steel chose a seat next to the window, he had a full range view of the area, and his back was to the wall.

After a short time, a waitress came to take his order. She was short and petite. Her long black hair was tied up into a ponytail which bounced as she walked. She had a round face that sported a large mouth with a red lipstick smile. As she spoke, she gave a broad smile, causing her to squint – hiding her beautiful large brown eyes. Steel ordered a large Balvenie and a beer – feeling the need to blend in was excuse enough to start drinking so early in the day. He watched the people and wondered how he was going to find a target in all of this, he had over seven thousand suspects – and that was just the passengers. Plus, he didn't know what they were suspected of doing? Hell, he did not even know what he was doing there, one thing was sure, if it were nothing, Steel knew the others wouldn't let him hear the last of it when he got back to the precinct.

Steel's mind drifted back to the meeting with Darius Johnson at Battersea Park in London. Darius was an old friend of the family. Steel's father had given Darius a job after he'd left the army, back in the seventies. The man was in his late fifties, an average-sized Jamaican, but he had the strength of an ox, he was strangely handsome with his short hair that had flexes of grey and a trimmed beard that made him look more like a professor. Darius often dressed in loud shirts and baggy jeans which seemed to be two sizes too big for him.

The two men sat at one of the chess tables that were set up, so the public to come and enjoy a quick game. Of course, the half-empty bottle of wine between them told many that the two men had been there awhile.

"Looks like I beat you again Jonny," the man said, as he moved his queen into the checkmate position. He grinned with pleasure as he knocked over Steel's King. "You must learn to concentrate my boy," his accent was heavy with a Caribbean tone. Steel just smiled and sat back in his chair.

"Concentrate, with that shirt?" Steel laughed. Darius looked down at his shirt and pulled the bottom forwards, the multi-patterned shirt screamed with colour.

"What's wrong with my shirt? Your problem is you have no style." They both laughed.

"It's good to see you again, old friend," Steel's voice sounded calm and refreshed, Darius returned the smile.

"So, what brings you home, last I heard you were a Detective in New York," Darius said, with a curious wink.

"I still am, Homicide Department" Steel replied, picking up the small bottle of mineral water and taking a quick mouthful. Darius's eyes widened and gave a carp-mouthed nod.

"Homicide, well, well. Funny, I remember you used to make the bodies, and ironically you now detect them, "Darius laughed and took a sip from the plastic wine glass. "And what about THEM?" Darius's voice sounded bitter, and his expression was sour.

"I get to hear a lot about THEM, don't worry," Steel replied, as he took another hit from the bottle. Darius nodded as he reset the board.

"You always did make the strangest moves for the right reasons; I can't believe you suck at chess," Darius laughed.

"Too many rules, if you change the rules it confuses your opponent," Steel shrugged with a broken smile. Darius nodded in agreement.

"Ok, so what rules are you bending now?" He could feel Steel's eyes on him. Steel was silent at first as he moved his pawn into the middle of the board.

"Leads in New York have gone silent, so I thought I would try back here," Steel replied. Darius's eyes looked up without moving his head.

"Uh-huh, you know something, like I say, you don't just do things without reason, so what or who are you after?" Steel smiled, and leant back in his chair and breathed in the fresh air.

"God, I miss this sometimes," he looked around at the people as they went about their day to day, enjoying the morning sun.

"London, Britain or suckin' at chess?" Darius laughed. Steel just gave him the finger as he readjusted his sunglasses at the nose bridge.

"A woman named Teresa Benning," Steel said, leaning back after moving a pawn. Darius thought for a moment, then shook his head.

"No, don't know that one," Darius admitted, with a shake

of his head. Steel smiled, which made Darius feel very nervous, very quickly.

"What?" Darius asked, looking up from the board and sitting back in his chair. A look of mistrust covered his face.

"Don't worry; I know roughly where she is," Steel laughed. Darius gave Steel an uneasy look.

"Cool, where is she?" He followed Steel's gaze to a woman playing on one of the other tables. She was pretty, with long red hair, large blue eyes, and a set of full pouting lips.

"So, what do you need me to do?" Darius asked, suddenly figuring out that him being here was no coincidence.

"Nothing much, just you know talk to her, keep her busy for a while," Steel said, with a slight shrug of his shoulders. Darius chanced another look over his shoulder at the redhead.

"And you will be…?" Darius turned around to find an empty chair where Steel had been sitting.

"Man, I hate it when he does that," Darius growled as he grabbed his drink and stood up.

HER APARTMENT WAS a minute's walk away from the park, the place itself was set above a small grocery store, the entrance was a red door at the side of the store, through which a staircase led upwards to the apartment above. As Steel approached the front door of the apartment, he checked for signs of cameras or alarms but only found graffiti and spiders webs. Picking the lock took seconds as the bump key found its mark, and with a click, he was inside.

Pulling the door slightly ajar, Steel took out a dentist's mirror and scanned for an alarm. He almost seemed disappointed at how easy this was, Steel thought for a moment the information he'd acquired was false, but he had to check it out nevertheless. The flat was homely and tidy with potted plants in nearly every room. The long corridor ended with the kitchen at one end and the sitting room at the other; in the middle of the wooden-floored hallway lay the doors to the bedroom and a bathroom. The walls of the corridor had been painted terracotta, and the ceiling was white with Victorian-style edgings, the doors to each room were glossed white as were the skirting on the floor – giving the effect that the room was longer than what it was. He started in the kitchen - this had a brown marble effect vinyl floor, the surrounding pinewood cupboards, and work surfaces stood out from the white walls. Steel carefully looked through draws and paid particular attention to the photographs and postcards magnetically pinned to the refrigerator door. The cards had been sent from various locations – and all from a couple named "Stewart." Steel took one last look then proceeded to the bathroom, the white-tiled room gave nothing up, and with a shrug, he entered the bedroom. The pink coloured walls clashed with the brass bed and the white furnishings, her clothes hung arranged in almost military fashion, Steel smiled at the thought of the phrase knowing most military people were not the tidiest of people. He started to have a bad feeling as he left the bedroom and entered the sitting room – so far, he had found nothing.

As he looked around, Steel noticed that the apartment had been correctly set out, maybe too perfect. The sitting room was long, with a large window at the opposite side of the room to the door. A fireplace with a dark wood surround was situated in the middle of the left wall – the flooring was the same as the hallway, and so was the paintwork. In the middle of the floor, facing the fireplace, was a black, cloth couch, and near the window on the right wall, there was a computer desk, proudly. Steel took his time looking at the room as he made his way to the desk; he did not want to miss anything. Sitting in the swivel chair, he turned on the computer; he knew that the computer would be password protected. Steel smiled, true enough the screen asking for the password. Steel began to search through draws at the desk for a clue to the password. Soon he found her passport – typing in her date of birth, he pressed the ENTER key, but only got a resounding "Ding" for failure. Then he remembered on the refrigerator she had put up many types of post-it as a reminder for her, regarding shopping items and who had called. He smiled.

"Could she be that obvious?" Steel thought. He tilted the keyboard, and a disappointed look came over him. There at the underside was a piece small piece of paper sellotaped with the words *UNITY1*. Steel frowned and typed in the code, the screen opened. Steel looked at his watch, he knew that Darius wouldn't be able to stall her forever, he had to hurry. Her folders drew a blank, so Steel went for emails, she had several spams from weight loss companies, dating agencies the standard stuff that clogs up the inbox, but then he saw several letters from "The Stewarts," he clicked on to the latest one, his eyes widened.

"*Dear Teresa,*

Hope you are well and everything is going well at work.

We have found the perfect trip. Also, Daddy says that NEPTUNE is good as gold.

Don't forget to pick up the goods and speak to Callan reference the industrial cleaner.

All the best,

The Stewarts"

He closed down the computer and stepped back to think. Steel had an uneasy feeling.

"What the hell is Neptune?" His words faded into a whisper, he had to go and find Darius, he was a wealth of information, and his memory was almost computer-like. Darius remembered every fact he came in contact with; if anyone would know – it was him.

Darius sat outside a local pub, sipping tea. The pub was just around the corner from her apartment – meaning it was possibly her local watering hole, not that Darius was interested, his mind was on other things.

"Damn it, Jonny, where the hell are you?" Darius said, studying his watch. He had waited nearly ten minutes after she had left him at that very pub. They had played chess and talked until she noticed the time, then insisted she had to go to work. Darius had walked her this far before she kissed him on the cheek for his gallantry and left. Darius looked behind him to see if Steel was approaching from the street behind. No luck, he cursed under his breath, thinking the worst. Images of her coming home and finding him there flooded into his head, but Darius knew Steel was too slick for that. He shook the thought from his head and turned back round to take another sip of the tea.

"Jesus" he cried out at the sight of Steel sitting in the chair opposite. Darius's yelp had caught the attention of a plump barmaid, and she made her way over. She had a cute smile, her black hair matched the colour of her skirt and waistcoat of her uniform, her white blouse straining to hold her large breasts, and her black stockings stretched over her large short legs.

"What can I get you, gents?" She asked, chewing gum as she spoke, Steel looked up at her and smiled, her face was round but pretty.

"Just a coffee, for now, thank you," Steel replied, with a winning smile. She blushed and returned the smile.

"Man, what it is with you and women?" Darius groaned, and shook his head. Steel sat back and looked innocent.

"OK, Casanova what did you find at her place?" Darius took another sip after blowing on the fresh brew.

"Don't know, there was something to do with NEPTUNE, I found an email from a friend named

"The Stewarts" but that was certainly a cover for something" he shrugged, and picked up the menu card.

"Have you heard of anything called NEPTUNE on your travels or someone called Callan who might be linked to the organisation?" Steel asked, as he checked out the steak and ale pie on the menu. Darius shook his head.

"Neptune, mmm," Darius said, stroking his beard. "Other than the Roman god and several ships and spacecraft, what can I say?" Darius said, taking out a pipe from his pocket and filling it with tobacco from a pouch.

"As for Callan, that could be CALLAN Industries?" Darius, said lighting up his pipe.

"What do they do?" Steel asked, curiously.

"Mostly bio tech and shit, weapons for the government, or anyone with the right cash," Darius laughed. Steel knew that asking him about Neptune was a long shot, but he had to try.

Steel's gaze fell on the table opposite theirs, and to a man reading the daily paper. As the man lifted it to put the pages back to their original fold, Steel caught a glimpse at the front page.

He waited until the man left, leaving the tabloid on the table, Steel shot up to grab it before anyone else had a chance. Steel held the paper up, hiding his face.

"Hey man, do you want to share with the rest of the class?" Darius barked impatiently, knowing his friend had found something. Steel folded the paper down; Darius saw the huge grin of satisfaction on Steel's face.

"What you won the lotto, not that you need the money?" Darius smiled. Steel turned the paper round, so the front page was in full view. *The new ship launched* read the headlines, *New flagship of the ocean travel group launched today, THE NEPTUNE is the largest passenger ship ever built at 3,800 feet long and able to hold over 7,500 passengers.* Darius's mouth fell open.

"Do you think that…?" Darius went to ask, then saw Steel nodding wildly with a childish grin.

The barmaid brought Steel his coffee; he smiled up at her and thanked her.

"Well my friend, I think I better ready for a trip," Steel said, taking a sip from his black coffee. Darius sat back and put his cup down.

"You got a feeling about this boat?" Darius asked, with a curious look on his face. Steel nodded and sipped his coffee. "Well, I hope the fuckers have got insurance?" Darius laughed.

FOUR

Steel snapped back to reality as a Tannoy message announced they were about to enter international waters. Steel looked around – seeing what had changed since his daydreaming had interrupted his observations. To his left sat two elderly gentlemen, playing chess, Steel smiled and headed off towards one of the restaurants. Finding a spot in the corner of the room by the long glass window, he settled himself, picking up the menu card he perused its contents, but studied the outside world with more interest. There were over nine thousand people on the ship or, to be more precise, over nine thousand needles in one hell of a big haystack. Steel needed something, anything that would give a clue as to what he was doing on the ship. He didn't have a plan as such; he never did – plans go wrong, but sometimes they help. There had been a reason this ship was so important but for why? Whatever the reason, he had to find it and fast. A smiling Asian woman came over and took his order.

"Just a coffee thanks", Steel could feel her eyes on him. She was attractive with long black hair that had been pinned up to hold at the back; she had a slim figure and curves in the right places.

"Maybe something later then, sir?" Her voice was sultry.

"Yes, maybe later," his reply was equally apparent as her

question, as she turned and walked away. Steel smiled to himself, thinking about Darius's remarks about him and women.

The restaurant was half-empty, except for families with screaming children - too excited to eat or take a nap, couples who looked happy to be away from their everyday life. Outside the restaurant, people moved about slowly – almost without purpose, the excitement of being on the ship had finally subsided, and they had come to realise there was no place to rush too. Steel looked over at the doorway just as a couple entered the restaurant. The woman was mid-twenties with only her man's cash in mind. Her long legs put her at around six-foot-tall, and her long blonde hair was styled – possibly by some guy with a fake French accent who charges too much for too much hairspray and calls it the latest fashion. She wore a red and white checked dress that hugged every curve of her body – purposely leaving little to the imagination. The woman's peach-shaped ass seemed to balance out her large breasts. Steel chuckled to himself, the man was around five foot six with thick-rimmed glasses, and a pensile moustache, his face was round and held a nervous look. As a waitress seated them not far from his table, Steel could not help but smile at the massive difference between them.

"Ah, L'amour," Steel said, with a smile. In the far corner of the room, Steel noticed a man sitting alone at the bar, he usually would not stick out as lots of people were sitting unaccompanied, but something made Steel nervous, something about him was off. Steel watched the man as he made out he was watching the football on the large television on the wall, Steel couldn't make out the man's height due to the fact that he was slumped at the bar – as if he was trying to make himself smaller or not visible. He had shoulder-length brown hair which nearly hid his square-jawed face. He was in his mid-thirties and had the start of a tan which Steel thought may have been from Middle Eastern or African sun. Steel watched intently as the man scribbled in his small notebook, only looking up to take note of his surroundings. Steel broke his gaze; he emptied the contents of his coffee cup, and stood up, this trip was fourteen days long, and he needed to find why this ship's name was so essential, the problem was that Steel didn't even know if this was the right place, all he knew was that the name NEPTUNE was important.

* * *

AT THE 11TH precinct New York City, everything seemed like a typical day. The phones never stopped ringing, and uniforms brought in suspects for questioning, or people cued to speak to a detective or the desk sergeant. The crime rate that year had been strangely low – possibly due to the constant rain showers. Captain Brant of the Homicide Department had a theory that the warm weather made everyone nuts, so the cold, wet weather was a blessing. Unfortunately, some of the criminals didn't share the same view and broke his law of criminality far too often. He sat in his office, going over the latest directives from 1PP – the Mount Olympus of the Police Department in New York, where the commissioner and the rest of the powerful suits sat and made decisions before a round of eighteen holes. A place he never fitted into – and would possibly never see as a workplace and that suited him just fine. Brant was a big man – broad shoulders filled out a white shirt with thin blue stripes. The first black man in his part of town to make it through college, served in the military in the Marines and after twelve years of service, joined the police department.

He had seen most of his friends end up in gangs, then later making the front page because of a gang shooting. He had decided to make something of himself. He had served in Grenade and the first gulf war. He'd seen enough death to last him a lifetime, or so he'd thought, then he got posted to Homicide.

Brant slammed down the paperwork and rocked back and forth in his chair. The government wanted to make more cutbacks and budget cuts. How were they supposed to keep order with fewer police and solve murders with fewer detectives? Overtime had gone out of the window last month, and at least ten good detectives had been asked to take early retirement. Brant had the feeling with any more cuts they might be looking at closing precincts next. Budget cuts, ha, they had plenty of cash when it comes to paying for a presidential visit. Brant stood up and looked out through his window and out onto the bullpen. He smiled as he saw McCall sitting at her desk. She was a good cop – captain material if she'd pull her finger out. She'd already done her sergeants exam and was waiting for confirmation. Probably wouldn't get it with these cuts, *shame* he thought, waste of a good cop, a good detective. With her was her best friend and also the police pathologist – Tina Franks. Brant walked back to his desk and grabbed his suit jacket from the back of his chair. He was going home. No reason to stay, bad guys would still be there in the morning; besides, there was no overtime.

"Good evening doctor," Brant said, with a smiled greeting.

"Captain," she responded, returning the expressional greeting.

"Sammy, don't leave it too late, remember you'll be working for free if you do," he joked, but his voice held a bitter tone.

"Goodnight Captain, don't worry, I'll be off soon, just need to finish off the paperwork for the Collins case," she replied, pointing to the computer monitor.

"OK, see you in the morning," he said, slipping on his jacket, and headed towards the elevator. As he stepped into the elevator, he heard his phone ring. He was tempted to go back and answer it – but he knew it would be someone from downtown asking him what he was doing about the cuts. He let the doors slide shut. As they did so, he gave a wink to McCall and put his finger to his lips. She smiled and shook her head. *He was out, at a meeting or something*, was the only thing she could think of if her phone rang and the people Brant was avoiding called her. *Try again tomorrow, dickhead*; she continued to think. She smiled and shook her head. *Possibly not those exact words*, she thought with a wicked smile.

McCall sat at her desk, sipping her coffee and looking out of the window at the far side of the room as the rain came down in sheets. The Cascades of water streamed down the misty panes, obscuring the view out of the window. Flashes of light clung to the rivers of rainwater and distant rumbles of thunder became lost in the melody of the New York traffic below.

Mountains of files filled the corner of her desk, but she had no lust for the hours of paperwork, the adventure with Steel had given her insight into a darker but more exciting side of the job, and she wanted that, now. She looked over to the empty chair next to her desk and smiled softly; she almost jumped out of her seat when the phone on her desk rang with the electronic bell tone.

"Detective McCall, Homicide" she listened while grabbing a pen and noting down an address on a pad of post-its that lay next to the phone. As she stood up, Tina Franks looked over towards her.

"What's up?" Tina asked, with a disappointed look on her face.

"We got a fresh one," McCall said, with a broken smile. "No fun tonight I'm afraid Tina, better grab your stuff," McCall said, handing her a copy of the address. As Tina left, McCall spotted Detective Jenny Thompson coming from the coffee room "Jenny, get your coat, your riding with me." The fresh-faced detective nodded eagerly. Jenny walked over to McCall just as she had opened her desk drawer.

"Have you heard anything from Detective Steel?" Jenny asked, with a concerned look on her face. McCall looked up and shot the young woman a look that left her cold.

"He is on vacation, on a cruise ship," McCall said, slamming the drawer, and shoved the small notebook into her jacket. A post-it sailed gently down to the floor. As Jenny quickly turned, she knocked the piece of paper under the desk, as it flew under the words *STEEL. CHECK CALLAN INDUSTRIES*, disappeared from view.

FIVE

The rain poured down relentlessly onto McCall's faded blue Mustang as they turned onto Madison and headed north. As Detective Samantha McCall drove, the wipers on her '66 Mustang worked overtime to clear the windscreen of the pounding rain. They soon arrived at the hotel on East 56th Street; the rain had kept many of the New Yorkers off the streets. Unfortunately, the people who had stayed home on East 56th had abandoned their vehicles rather than parked them. Between the poorly parked cars and UPS vans making deliveries, parking would be a nightmare on any day of the week, let alone a day when it was full of police cars and the ME's wagons.

Eventually, McCall found a parking spot next to a dry cleaner's, its red and green sign seemed brighter as the rain streamed down the front window of the store. Both detectives made for the hotel. Rushing from the car, they entered the large brass front doors of the building, the lobby of the hotel was quite dark, even though the walls were a mixture of white paint and mirrors, the highly polished floor mirrored the small lights encrusted into the ceiling. Before them, stood a uniformed officer who directed them to the second floor. Not far behind them, Tooms and Tony came through the entrance, dripping on to the polished floor.

"What the hell are you guys doing here?" McCall asked, with a scowl.

"We got the call as well," Tony said, waving his cell phone. "Besides, the date sucked, she preferred the waiter," Tony shrugged.

"Speak for yourself, I was havin' steak tonight man, friggin' steak and they call me in," Tooms growled. McCall shot him a confused look – not understanding where his priority's lay, it was his anniversary, and he was worried about steak?

They took the elevator to the third floor. The small box shuddered to a halt, and the doors opened. As they stepped out, McCall noticed the hallway was full of uniform officers making door to door enquiries, to try to get some information on the victim or hopefully, the murderer. They moved up, passing officers in the hallway until they reached room 208. The room was large with a double bed that had been placed in the middle of the room against the right wall, the only light came from the bedside and a lamp on a dresser which was opposite the bed. Next to the large window, a standard lamp illuminated the corner. Two armchairs had been placed in front of the window with a small coffee table nestled between them. Thompson oozed with pride as she passed the uniforms. She had gone through the ranks quickly, some thought too quickly, but she did not care. As they stood in the doorway, they could see Tina examining what appeared to be a woman on the bed. Before entering, the detectives put on the blue plastic booties, they had found next to the door, and a pair of blue gloves.

"Ok guys, don't touch anything, CSU hasn't been in yet," Insisted Tina, they all nodded in agreement. McCall was a thorough cop, a good cop; she insisted that the other detectives carry at least two things - a notebook and a camera. Some thought the camera was unnecessary, but she had learnt from her dad that sometimes, memories are not enough on a case. McCall walked up to Tina, who was noting the body temperature.

"Hey," McCall said, greeting her friend. Tina looked around at McCall.

"Hey," Tina said, returning the greeting with a smile. "Well we got a Caucasian female around late thirties, early forties," Tina said, as McCall took notes. The victim was wearing a red dress which looked more evening wear than as if she were going shopping, possibly for a night out or rendezvous with someone special. The woman had been pretty once McCall had thought, noting the photographs of the woman that were on the woman's cell phone.

"So, I guess she sat on the edge of the bed and took out the .45, put it underneath her chin and…?" McCall said, mimicking the action with her fingers. The team took note of the massive blood splatter on the ceiling and most of the back wall; there was also a blood pool on the bed where she had fallen. The woman lay there, staring upwards into nothing with her grey, lifeless eyes. In her left hand, she held a nickel-plated snub-nosed .45 revolver – her fingers wrapped loosely around the pistol grip and trigger. McCall moved in closer to get a better look, behind her the CSU had arrived and were taking photos. McCall turned to see a small woman in CSU coveralls holding the SLR camera fully laden with flashes to get the perfect shot.

"Sorry," McCall said, moving out of the technician's way. "Can I get copies of those as soon as possible please?" McCall asked.

"Sure, Detective," the tech replied as she took another shot. McCall watched as another tech removed the pistol from the woman's grip, and clicking the chamber open, he removed the cartridges one at a time, checking them and placing them inside a clear self-sealing evidence bag.

"One round fired," he said, holding up the empty brass case, then bagging it separately. McCall leaned in and looked at her face, studying the features. Thompson stood next to her and noted the expression on McCall's face.

"What's wrong?" she asked, inquisitively. McCall stood up and began to take her photos of the body. McCall's face winced as she watched Tina try to separate the woman's blood-sodden head from the bedclothes.

"What do you see?" McCall asked Jenny. Thompson gave McCall a confused look.

"What do you mean?" Jenny asked, suddenly feeling as though McCall was picking on her. Ever since she had moved up, McCall had been hard on her, or so she thought – did McCall feel threatened by her? She couldn't say.

"Jenny tell me what you see," Thompson studied the scene, she felt like saying "A dead chick on the bed," but she knew that would go down like a lead balloon.

"White female, possible suicide," Jenny started to explain, then she paused.

"Go on," McCall said. She smiled as she could feel the tension building in Jenny.

"I…I don't know." Jenny suddenly barked. "What is this? Are you testing me or something?" with that, she stormed off. Tina looked up at McCall and gave her a sympathetic look.

"Ok, Tina, have you got a T.O.D?" Tina looked at her clipboard, "Well till I get her back I can't be sure, but you're looking at around twelve, twelve-thirty last night." McCall thanked her before turning, and went looking for Thompson. McCall found Jenny in the hallway, leaning on her knees, gasping for breath.

"You ok?" McCall asked – her look was unsympathetic, emotionless even. Jenny looked up and gave McCall a bad puppy look, which caused McCall to smile.

"Look, yes, I am testing you, but I am also training you. I need to know what you know and well – fill in the blanks." McCall said, recalling her own experience as a new detective. Working the street is one thing, but McCall had soon learnt it wasn't like the movies or books. Jenny stood up and blew out a gut full of air.

"Ok, we're going back in, and you tell me what you see, but don't speculate, just what you see," McCall said, extending a hand so Jenny could pull herself up. Jenny nodded, and they went back in. The metallic tang of dried blood filled the air – along with the stench of perfume and hairspray. Jenny walked over to the body and McCall waited close by, giving the rookie detective space to observe.

"White female, possible suicide," Jenny said, moving her head around the body to get every angle possible.

"Why possible?" McCall butted in.

"It's an assumption to say one way or the other without proof of anything suspicious, or the ME's results," Jenny answered with a serious face.

"Go on," McCall smiled. She was learning.

"We found a purse, but it's empty so it could be she didn't want to be identified, she comes from money judging from the clothes and jewellery, also looking at the way she looks, we could rule out working girl." McCall nodded in agreement.

"Anything else?" McCall asked. Jenny's eyes strained, and McCall could see this was a determined look, rather than an observing look.

"Ok, that's good, so would you say murder or suicide?" Jenny knew, either way, she would have to explain.

"Suicide," Jenny said confidently. "The note, the door was locked from the inside, the position of the wound," McCall nodded and walked around the body to the other side of the bed.

"I am going for murder," McCall said. Jenny suddenly looked confused. What had she missed?

"The note was written by a left-handed person, which was obviously faked. Plus, if you're going to the trouble of being unidentified, you don't kill yourself where you can be found," McCall explained, Jenny nodded as she took in the deduction. McCall had a point, something she had missed, more out of trying too hard than a rookie mistake. She was better than that; all she had to do was chill out.

"How do you know it was faked?" Jenny asked, inquisitively.

"How do I know she was left-handed?" McCall asked, hoping her question would answer Jenny's.

"The watch! She wore it on her right wrist" Jenny smiled as an idea washed into her mind. McCall nodded in agreement.

"Well done. However," McCall started to say, Jenny's

expression dropped, "If you look closely, you can see a white line on her right wrist, a tan line." Jenny leant in to observe, "No, she was killed, and the watch put on after, in hope to throw us off." McCall explained. She turned to the CSU tech.

"You done with the body?" McCall asked. The tech nodded as she put some sample bottles into an evidence bag and labelled it. McCall turned to Tina and nodded confirmation that she was good to remove the body. As the orderlies came with the gurney, McCall moved towards Thompson.

"You're doing well but it's my job to make you better, look you have a lot to learn. Follow the body to the morgue and get the report, ok?" Jenny nodded and went with the coroner's crew. McCall spent a while studying the room; nothing was out of place apart from the fact that she had no luggage. McCall bit her bottom lip as she concentrated, making pictures in her mind as to how the whole thing must have gone down, but the noise of too many people about broke her concentration. No, she would have to come back later; instead, she would settle for a hundred shots of the room with her small camera. Tooms walked over to her.

"You will be shocked to know that nobody saw anything, let alone knew our vic," Tooms said, flipping his notebook shut.

"Why am I not surprised?" McCall cracked a smile. "Wouldn't surprise me if our vic didn't pay for the room either," she said, heading for the elevator, Tooms followed close behind.

"Only one way to find out." he shrugged.

SIX

As the sun was setting, the great fiery orange ball looked as if it was melting into the ocean itself. As it sank, it was leaving glowing splinters of itself resting upon the waves. Steel stood outside on the balcony of his room; the cool breeze of the evening air cut through the black golf ball shirt of his tuxedo. He watched the last slither of light disappear into the horizon, leaving a deep purple horizon. Steel smiled at the beauty of it all, then returned to the comfortable climate of his room. Steel walked to the dresser and took out a small contact lens holder and cracked open the lid. Taking them out one by one and slipping them over his eyes to change them to blue. He blinked several times to get used to the feel of them. Usually he wore his unique sunglasses, but he thought it might look a little strange for the evening – he was after all undercover, so he needed to blend in. Steel looked into the mirror at his new light blue eyes.

"That will do," he thought to himself. Picking up his tuxedo jacket, he finished dressing then headed for the captain's dining room. Tonight, he would be dining at the captain's table along with several other guests. As Steel walked the many corridors, he hoped tonight might reveal something, the days were getting shorter, and he was fresh out of ideas.

Steel walked towards the entrance of the impressive dining hall, the carpet was a deep red with gold patterned inlays, the dark wood walls stretched up to the three stories of the dining room, and a magnificent chandelier hung down the centre, illuminating all three levels. He made his way through the crowds of people and found the table in the centre of the room; it was large and sat twelve people. The majority of the tables were round, seating six to eight guests, with white linen tablecloths and wine red linen napkins which were folded into something that resembled a bishop's hat, that had been placed neatly on the crockery plates. Crystal wine and water glasses were placed at a forty-five-degree angle to the placemats, and the shining metal silverware glinted in the light from the enormous chandelier.

The whole room had a turn-of-the-century feel to it rather than a modern-day one. As Steel looked around, he could understand how the captain loved this room. The moment Steel walked into it, it was as if he had been transported back in time. Steel had done his research on the captain before boarding and found he was an old sea dog. The man had been on ships all his life. The captain had been born on one in the early forties. The man's family's history was full of sailors dating back to as far as Steel could find.

Captain Tobias Long was a large man with a barrel chest and a white beard anyone would associate with the captains in the galleons and frigates of old. To look at him, he appeared as everyone envisaged a ship's captain should appear to resemble. Steel made his way to the large table where some of the guests had already taken their places.

Steel observed the name cards as he moved round to shake the hands of his fellow passengers, Steel smiled as he noticed that the names were on both sides of the place cards. *Very clever,* he thought to himself. A simple but useful way to ensure that nobody would be embarrassed about forgetting anyone's names when it came to conversation. His introduction was more to get the "Up close and personal" look at the people than it was politeness. Along with Steel and some other single people, there sat three couples who could not have been more different from each other if they tried.

First, there were the Dawsons – Mary Dawson was a large plump woman with a pretty face and a beaming smile, her long black locks had been arranged in an Audrey Hepburn style bob and she was wearing a stunning white dress that complemented her large frame. In fact, at first glance, Steel would have sworn she was an opera singer because of the way she looked and held herself.

Her husband Ronald was of average height, and his large frame was a mix of body fat and muscle - he also had thick dark black hair with streaks of grey on the sides. The man grinned as much as his wife and with good reason, As they talked, Steel found that, after spending twenty-five years running a small shop in Yorkshire, an Aunt of Ronald's had died and left a small fortune to him.

Next to them sat Susan and Alan Metcalf. She had long, thick, wavy auburn hair that clung around her bare shoulders; she was tall with a slim frame which was complemented by her electric blue dress. Alan was of the same height and build; his side-parted hair was brown and glistened with hair products. They both had a slight tan and had a healthy look about them. Susan was also an heiress – her mother had died when she was quite young, and her father passed around three years ago, leaving her the shipbuilding family business and a fortune in Florida.

The Texas oil king Albert Studebaker and his wife Missy sat to the left of the Metcalfs . He was a massive bulk of a man with shovels for hands – even though he was nearly sixty, he looked fit and strong as an ox. His tanned skin looked leathery and made his white hair and goatee appear whiter than it was. Missy was younger – by around twenty years, but just by looking, anyone could tell she was in it for him and not his money. She was once a supermodel and still retained the figure, even after retiring several years after their marriage. Missy's hair was blonde, and the sides cut short. The fringe was long and covered part of her face, making her blue eyes to glow in the shadow that the fringe cast upon her perfect facial features. Her silver strapless dress hugged her natural curves like a second skin.

They all chatted for a while as they awaited the others and of course the captain, who was busy on the bridge. As Steel sat, a waitress came to take his drink order. He looked up to see it was the waitress from before, he smiled both curiously and joyfully to see her again.

"Can I get you anything, sir?" she asked her eyes, not leaving his.

"A large Lagavulin if you have one," he smiled, as she turned slowly and walked away, her head still trained upon him till the last moment.

"God damn boy, what aftershave you wearin'?" Albert laughed out loud. Steel turned to the large Texan and shrugged innocently as they all laughed.

"So, I guess this is all of us then?" Missy looked around as she spoke, "Or not" she corrected herself on seeing the approach of what appeared to be two couples. Steel stood up and pulled the chair out for the gorgeous long brown-haired woman who was to be at the place setting next to him – her red one strap dress hugged her hourglass figure, and her dark eyes sparkled, reflecting the surrounding lights.

"Thank you, kind sir," her voice was soft but had a roughness to it. As she spoke, Steel could feel the hairs on the back of his neck tingle with excitement. After everyone had reintroduced themselves, Steel learnt that the woman to his right was called Tia May and that she worked at a small art gallery in New York. She had gone on to tell how she was born in Hawaii, her father had been in the Navy, and her mother was a local girl. After college, she got an art degree and found work in the gallery.

Retaking his seat, Steel noticed the others, the pair who had taken the places to his front were called the Stewarts , Steel's interest grew at the sight of their nameplate, *could it be?* He thought to himself, *No, too easy;* he shook the thought. Bob and Jane Stewart were both in their forties and somehow dressed similarly, almost as though she was the female version of him. They both had short blonde hair and pale complexions; Steel could not help but think *Body snatchers* or *Village of the damned*.

This brought a small smile to his face, the Stewarts came from Long Island and worked as accountants for a large firm there; as odd as they seemed, the Stewarts smiled and told amusing stories about their work. Then Steel laid eyes on the twelfth guest – it was the man from the bar, he seemed different from before, calmer and he also smiled and joined in the jovial conversion, his name card said he name was Jonathan Grant, he was in property in LA and was here to celebrate a massive deal he had just closed. Steel's eyes searched the group, and he found it strange, the array of different backgrounds at the table, sure it made for brilliant conversation but Steel, being Steel, read more into it. *Nothing happens by chance* he thought.

As the captain entered, the room stood in respect. He casually waved a fond greeting, and as he sat, so did the guests. No sooner had they taken their seats, when two waiters came around, each carrying a bottle of red and white wine. The captain asked them all what they thought of the ship and the facilities. As expected, the response was a pleasant one. The conversation then turned to the guests; who they were and what they did for a living. The captain showed massive interest in their stories.

"So, Mr Black, you have been quiet all evening," Albert bellowed, Steel could tell that the giant American was about to start a "friendly" interrogation.

"What exactly is it that you do?" his tone was as Steel expected, distrustful and insinuative. Jonathan Grant looked up instantly - his fork full of the prawn cocktail starter poised, waiting for Steel's reply. Steel put down his fork and dabbed the side of his mouth with the linen napkin. Then he took a mouth full of the water to wash down his food.

"A bit of this and a bit of that really. I spent some time in the Army and found, after a while, I needed a carrier change," he watched their eyes as he spoke of some tale to satisfy their lust for knowledge. "As for now I don't really do much. My parents passed on a while back and left me some money, so I pretty much travel around and pay attention in people, who knows, I may write a book one day," Steel took another mouthful of water. "My life is quite boring really, not like yours of course." The large American sat back and grinned at the compliment.

As the evening wore on, Steel spent most of it examining the room, trying to catch a glimpse of someone suspicious, but so far, the only odd people were the ones right in front of him. Jonathan Grant was also observing the room, but most of the time, his gaze was fixed on the characters at the table, especially Steel.

Steel, after some lengthy banter, and listening to each of the couples play, which was worth more, he had concluded that most – if not all - the people were not who they said they were or had a hidden agenda for being there. Either way, he was at the table of lies.

All through the night, the captain told stories of his days in the Navy, and aboard fishing vessels before that. He held his audience captive as he told a good tale, Steel could not make out how much was true but all the same, it did not matter. Steel also noticed something was bothering him; now and then, he would stare into nothingness, his look vacant and lost. Steel's appetite was getting aroused – he was looking for something or someone on the ship, for what he did not know, the people in front of him all had big secrets that they were running away from. Steel could not be happier; *the only thing missing was a dead body*, he thought.

The band snapped Steel back to reality as they started to play a slow dance, with that Steel stood up after dabbing his mouth with the napkin and turned to Tia.

"May I have the pleasure of this dance?" Tia grinned as though she had been waiting all night for him to ask. He pulled out her chair slightly, and he got a waft of her perfume as she rose.

As they danced close and slow, Steel couldn't help but notice how intoxicating her perfume was, he felt almost drunk as he breathed in her sweet scent, but that is precisely what he needed – a reboot. Steel's brain had been subjected to hours of mystery after mystery, and this little getaway was all he needed.

The dance ended and he returned Tia May to her seat. While they were gone, Steel had found the conversation had continued as the captain told another one of his fantastic tales.

"So, Captain" Grant spoke with a joyful tone. "The maiden voyage of a new ship must feel bloody marvellous."

As Steel returned to his seat, he eyed the captain for his reaction. The large man put down his wine glass and smiled proudly and looked around.

"Did you know, Mr Grant, that this ship was designed to be how the Titanic would look if it had been built now instead of in 1912?" the captain said, proudly. Grant shook his head as he took a small mouth full of the creamed dessert. "This ship is 3,800 feet long and weighs over 246,000 tons; it has 30 lifeboats, each designed to carry around three hundred and fifty passengers. The ship itself carries over 7,500 passengers, this Sir, is the largest cruise ship ever designed, so yes it feels bloody marvellous," the captain grinned from ear to ear. Steel felt a little uneasy at the thought of the ship being referred to as "The Titanic of the modern age." Steel felt the mood turn sour as everyone had the same idea.

"So, Captain Long, where are we off too next?" Steel asked, knowing the captain would not just stop at a simple explanation but would go into a fully detailed description of the Spanish port, Vigo.

As the night drew on and Steel could feel that the travel and the fullness of the magnificent meal had taken their toll on him, he rose from his seat and excused himself for the evening. As he ventured out onto one of the decks, he looked out onto the vast expanse of water, the cold breeze felt good against his warm skin. He needed fresh air and quiet, so his brain could sort through the events of the evening, who was who? Was anyone at that table honestly who they said they were? Tomorrow he would find out. On checking out the ship, he had noticed it had an internet lounge, would he find the answers there? The night was black except for a half-moon that shone just as brightly as if it had been full, casting light upon the gentle waves below. The view was breath-taking, and the silence more so.

Venturing back to his cabin, Steel reflected on the evening and also the waitress. Maybe it was a coincidence, but something deep down told him otherwise, though he was still none the wiser. What was so special about the ship? Who were the "Stewarts" from the e-mail? A good night's rest would help clear some of the fog, he thought, walking towards his door. Stopping he noticed there was a light on in his cabin, and shadows moved from side to side, giving away signs of a visitor. He thought about inserting the card key slowly, but he knew the "Click" would alert whoever it was, so he decided to play it casually. There was a loud "Click," as the door lock was released.

He walked in as though he had no idea someone was there. On his bed with only a sheet to cover her, lay Tia May. Steel stood in the doorway for a moment, utterly dumbstruck by what he had stumbled on to – but played it casual and cool. As Steel looked around the room, he saw her dress lying upon a chair in the corner. He looked again at the room number on the door.

"Well one of us is in the wrong room," His words were playful. As she got up, she glided towards him with the sheet clasped in both hands hiding her nakedness.

"You better shut the door, there's a draught coming in," her voice was soft and sensual; closing the door behind him Steel walked towards her, his eyes mapping her perfect body. Her eyes, lustful and longing; her mouth, glistening with red lipstick, was partially open, showing her white teeth.

"Well, Mr Black, whatever shall we do now?" He moved towards her and took her into his powerful arms.

"Yes, what indeed," as their mouths joined in a passionate kiss, she let the sheet fall to the ground, she wanted him as much as he wanted her. Moving slowly towards the bed, he flicked off the lights, stripped off the tuxedo, and as the lights in his cabin dimmed into darkness, the liner effortlessly cruised through the ocean.

THE NEXT MORNING, Steel awoke to find Tia had gone, his eyes still blurred from the long sleep. As he sat up and stretched, he noticed a note on the dresser. Steel Slipped out of the warm, comfortable bed; his muscular naked body swayed with the motion of someone who is not fully awake. He smiled as he read the short, hand-written note. *Thank you for a wonderful night. Hope to see you at breakfast.* Steel refolded the note and lay it back onto the dresser. As he headed for the bathroom, he stopped as instinct kicked in. Reaching into the front pocket of his suitcase Steel, produced a small torch. Switching it on, the blue light it emitted showed the grease particles on his hand. He closed the shades on the balcony door and searched the room, knowing the key places he would look – he started with the safe.

"Let's see who's been a naughty girl then, shall we?" Steel said to himself. Knowing that every time he had touched something in the room was of importance, he wiped it clean of his prints. Steel smiled as the buttons on the wall safe lit up, smudges on the raised buttons indicated they knew the numbers, but not the order they were in. Steel punched in the correct code and opened the safe; he checked everything was there. Steel locked it up satisfied everything was in order and punched in a new code. Steel's suitcases had clip locks – which also lit up, showing smudged prints. Switching on the main light he checked his wardrobe, the clothes remained on the hangers but were out of place as though someone had been through his clothes. It was clear someone had been searching for something, but for what? Had someone figured out who he was? Putting down the torch, he moved to the bathroom to shower and freshen up. Today would be another long day, but he had things to do. The passengers at the table last night had struck a note with him, something didn't sit right, and he wanted to know what.

SEVEN

McCall sat patiently in the ME's office, awaiting the arrival of Tina. McCall looked at the clock on the wall – it was around quarter to eight, and she knew Tina was always in at half-past. As she lifted the coffee cup to her lips, the doors burst open and Tina danced in. McCall watched intently as her friend fluttered about, getting her stuff together as per normal, but she was on cloud nine. Tina did not notice McCall sitting on the edge of her desk, watching her display. To McCall's surprise, Tina began to sing and then McCall knew that last night had been a good one. Tina spun around as if she were giving a music concert and looked up, straight into the eyes of McCall; Tina froze in position as her friend walked forwards, holding two coffees.

"Morning," McCall said, holding her composure and trying not to laugh, or make her friend anymore embarrassed – well for now anyway.

Tina took the cup from her friend, and after taking a small sip, she got ready for the day-to-day. "So…." McCall started, only to be interrupted by a guilty-looking Tina.

"I know, I know it was the first date, but he was soooo –?" Tina saw McCall's eyes widen with confusion and interest.

"Oh, you want to know about the case?" McCall gave a

friendly shrug as if it meant nothing, but in truth, McCall would have preferred to have heard about Tina's date.

"Well, our Jane has no tattoos, no marks, or moles," McCall looked disappointed. "However, what she does have is contacts to change her eye colour, and her hair has had at least three changes in the last six months." Tina lifted a small piece of microscope glass, inside was a hair. "She has gone from black to red and finally blonde," at that point, McCall had a bad feeling.

"Did you get prints?" McCall asked, hoping for a hit. Tina held up the digital fingerprint scanner and smiled.

"I was just about to do it; want to help?" McCall walked around and lifted Jane's left hand, as Tina went to use the thumb first on the scanner she stopped as the skin on her thumb seemed to attach itself to the scanner's screen.

"What the hell!" Tina said, looking up as McCall leaned forward to get a better look, "Her skins coming off!" Now McCall had a horrible feeling. Tina put the woman's hand down along with the scanner. "Pity Steel's not here, he would love this," Tina said with a smile – one which soon faded when she saw McCall's angry expression. "Still not heard anything since the last call?" Tina asked. McCall picked up her coffee and drank.

"Oh yes, didn't I say, he's on a cruise," McCall growled. Tina's jaw dropped, "The lousy bastard goes off to England on a goose chase, doesn't phone for weeks and goes on a cruise," Tina felt her pain.

"Forget him, girl, tell you what, I have got a friend whose brother is perfect for you, trust me," Tina said with a wink. McCall scowled, the thought of a blind date.

"Ah, what the hell," McCall said with a shrug. Tina grinned and, taking off her gloves, went into her office to make the call, leaving McCall with an open-mouthed expression, as her friend's sense of priority seemed more that of the dating front than the mystery of a fake fingerprint.

Using a key card, Alan Metcalf entered a darkened room on the second deck, a shard of light cut through the thick curtains displaying a chair just in front of him.

"Hello, are you there?" he whispered.

"Close the door you idiot and sit down," the voice was that of a woman, her tone was soft but held a powerful attraction to it. Closing the door, he edged his way to the chair, making sure he did not fall over anything en route.

"How did it go, did you find anything?" Alan asked, as he sat in the beige fabric chair. His words were nervous and excited at the same time.

"No, he is not the one; he did not have it," she spoke slowly as if she was thinking of something. Alan felt disappointment at her omission, but he savoured every word nevertheless. The room was clad in darkness which enhanced his imagination at what she must look like, images of a tall, long-legged woman with long black hair that went all the way down to her pert pear-shaped ass, slipped into his daydream as she spoke.

"What now?" his words were a whisper, but he seemed distracted, and the woman picked up on this.

"Don't worry, I will find it, besides we are on a ship, where can it go?" she said with a confident tone. Alan's mood lightened slightly.

Suddenly the silence was broken, the muffled sound of a vibrating cell; he knew it was not his, as he had not brought it.

"You must leave now, if I need you, I will get word to you," he got up slowly and made his way back to the door that had a chemical stick glowing brightly to aid his withdrawal from the room. As Alan opened the door, he heard the woman answer the phone.

"Yes sir, I am aware of the deadline, no we don't have it," there was a pause as she listened to the caller. "Not yet but it's close, I can feel it. Yes sir, understood." Alan closed the door quietly, rivers of sweat ran down his forehead and back, he smiled at the plan in his head, if he found the device first, HE would be the one in the shadows, HE would be the one in charge, not some sultry sounding bitch.

. . .

After a small continental breakfast at one of the smaller restaurants, Steel decided it was time to try to find the others from the table that night. The ship was massive, so finding them would be a feat in itself as the sun rose, further under the blue, cloudless sky, hordes of passengers gathered in their droves to find that perfect spot on one of the many plastic loungers that lined the sun decks, packing themselves in and lying like great seals on ocean side rocks. The ship had a water park on the upper level with water slides and pools, and inside there were gaming halls as well as a casino. There were five large-screen cinemas as well as an opera house and theatre. Entertainment on the ship didn't seem to be a problem. However, these things did not interest Albert and Missy Studebaker, not entirely. They sat in the casino on the tall, brass legged velvet cushioned stools, putting coin after coin into the slot machines in front of them. Bright flashing light and the never-ending electronic chimes signalled games going on or won — beads of sweat accumulated on the top of Albert's forehead as he played.

"We need to lay low; we can't afford …," Missy's voice trembled with fear.

"Now calm yourself, nobody knows us, besides, like it or not we have to be here, so enjoy it," Albert's face appeared from the other side of her machine as he leant over on his chair and smiled at her with a childish grin.

"I know, but what if somebody…?" his grin melted away and he scowled at her.

"Nobody is going to find out anything, besides even if they do, it will be too late," Albert said, before he disappeared back around to face his machine and said nothing more. In the corridor next to the games room, Steel stood with his back against the wall, pretending to listen to music on his cell which he had conveniently held in the doorway, the phone held a small microphone which picked up the conversation. Satisfied, he smiled and put the device into his pocket and left, he had heard enough…for now.

EIGHT

McCall crashed down exhausted into her desk chair, looking at the pile of folders on the edge of her desk, she knew it wasn't going to get easier. Stacked up on the end of her desk were hosts of homicides that uniforms had written up quickly and which required investigation. The four files were a mix of robbery gone wrong to accidental electrocution. All these were recent, and the crime scenes still taped up. She leant back in her chair and looked for enlightenment, none came. McCall forced herself out of the chair and headed for the coffee room, "I need coffee," she mumbled to herself. As she marched in, she saw Tony and Tooms sitting at the small table, sipping on their fresh coffees and discussing what Steel might be doing on the cruise.

"I am telling you, man, he's probably got all the ladies……" Tony's words cut short at the sight of McCall at the doorway. "Oops," Tooms grinned. "Oh, hey Sam didn't see you there," Tony said, suddenly wanting to disappear into a deep hole somewhere.

"No, it's fine I hope he is enjoying himself while we do all the work," she was bitter, but they could tell it was not because of the workload. She walked in and poured herself a coffee from one of the half-full jugs. She lifted the jug offering a fresh top up, and the two men put their hands over the mouth of their cups to signify that they were good.

Back at her desk, McCall spread out the files, deciding to choose which one first. She shook her head, thinking it was unprofessional. Picking up the first file she read the cover name, it belonged to a Donald Major, fifty-two years old and he had been an electrical expert who accidentally plugged himself into the mains, McCall's face winced as she read the report how apparent faulty wiring in the ceiling lights may have caused his death.

The next was Karen Greene, a thirty-four-year-old woman who was involved in a mugging gone wrong. McCall exhaled deeply to try to wake herself up. She looked up at the two detectives and smiled. Walking over to them, she held two files:

One was Bill Foster a possible suicide – Bill had been an import and export dealer for a large company, until one day the pressure was too much and he shot himself.

The other was John Barr; he had been a crane operator for the docks until he took the quick way down, foregoing the steps from his cab, which was thirty feet up.

"Here you go," McCall passed to files to Tooms. "We have two cases each, divide and conquer." Tooms looked at the files briefly.

"And, what about Jane Doe," Tony asked, leaning over to take the files from Tooms.

"We wait for Tina to get something we can work on, but for now we have these," she looked at the files in Tony's hand.

"These people need closure too," Tooms smiled in agreement.

"OK, what's the plan?" he asked as McCall headed for her desk.

"Plan!" she stopped and turned, "Plan is what it always is, do our jobs quickly but do it right," McCall said with a stern look. Jenny Thompson came out of the coffee room, blowing on the hot tea she had just made. "Hey, Jenny, you're with me." Thompson turned around to look at McCall in surprise "What…oh, cool,"

Thompson oozed with enthusiasm. Even though she had only been a detective for less than a few weeks, she was learning the ropes but too slow for McCall's liking. McCall could understand the transition between uniform and detective was somewhat of a big step, and McCall understood that some adapted quicker than others at the change of rank. She looked at Thompson as she got herself ready and smiled. *She'll be ok,* she thought to herself.

"What's the case?" Jenny asked, as she sat in the empty chair next to McCall's desk. McCall felt a brief moment of anger – as if Jenny had been sitting in a forbidden place. McCall composed herself and passed her the file so she could get the ins and outs for herself. McCall would be assessing her, she knew that, and she was OK with it.

McCall waited until Jenny had finished reading before asking, "Well Detective, what's our first move?" Jenny thought for a moment.

"We go see his wife, get to know the victim and his lifestyle, see if anything pings," Thompson saw the side of McCall's mouth raise in response to the assessment of the situation.

"Ok, let's go," McCall got out of her chair, and they both headed for the elevator, "See you later guys ," McCall shouted back towards Tooms and Tony, who looked up at McCall as she said their farewells just before the elevator doors slid shut.

STEEL WALKED into the Irish Bar and found a booth that presented a decent view of the door and the bar area. As he slid himself over the fake leather cushioned seats, Steel took out a brochure that had a map of the ship from his pocket – cursing himself he had forgotten to get a tablet or another internet device. As he studied the plan of the cruise and the decks, he looked up to see a waitress approach; it was the same girl from the dining hall.

"Can I get you anything cold or maybe something HOT?" her eyes almost purred at him with passion.

"I'll have a single malt and a mineral water, thanks," he replied, leaning back in the chair, casually. She took down the order and left. Steel laughed to himself then sneaked another look at her as she made for the bar. She was attractive, sure, but maybe too attractive for a cruise ship. He had to admit he had never seen an ugly waitress or salesperson on any of the ferries or cruises he had been on, but she had supermodel looks, and somehow that did not fit with him.

The cruise would be a simple two days at sea before reaching the first port in Spain. After which there would be a further eight days of ocean before arriving in New York, he figured he had time to search the ship and get to know as many passengers as he could, especially the ones from the dinner the other night. Whatever the reason the ship was mentioned. Steel knew that it could not be good, not if THEY were involved.

His drinks arrived, but Steel noticed that another girl who had brought it; she was much shorter than her colleague was, and her round face held a pretty smile. Her short hair was a deep red, almost maroon in colour. Steel smiled to himself as he noticed that her uniform was, either by choice or from some plan of the owners, a bit too tight in areas of her buxom figure.

"Will that be all, or can I get you something else?" he smiled at her and told her he was fine for the moment. As she moved back to the bar, he wondered what had happened to the other girl.

As he sat and enjoyed the Malt, he heard two familiar voices from a booth on the other side.

Steel cursed himself; he had been distracted and had failed to see them come in. He knew the voices but failed to put a face to them, moving carefully so the people in the next stall did not see him.

He slipped to the other seats opposite his in order to get a better listen. Taking out his phone and activating the recorder, he placed it on the top of the divide. The man's voice was deep and authoritative, even as a whisper.

"Look it's all arranged, so there is no going back."

"Look, it's too dangerous, what if…?" the second voice was weaker and panicked.

"What if what, look the plans in motion, the end. Look, you

have been well paid so shut up and stop your whining." There was a creek of artificial leather and Steel knew, whoever they were, they had left and had disappeared into the crowds. Steel's interest grew, his only regret was that McCall was not here to be a part of this great mystery.

Steel needed more information on his quarry; he knew that the ship had the internet lounge and that had been his target since this morning, he would go online and try to get as much information on the other dinner guests as he could. These were all prominent people so the internet should be full of pages on them, or so Steel thought. He finished his drinks then made for the exit. As he passed the barkeeper, Steel placed a ten-pound note onto the counter without losing a stride. "Keep the change," he said coolly, then made his way to lose himself in the mass of people.

There were bars, toy shops, perfume shops, shops with over-priced sunglasses. There were magazine shops, clothes shops, even a chemist. As Steel walked through the crowds, he couldn't distinguish whether he was on a ship or walking through a small town. As he made his way through the crowds, Steel couldn't shake the feeling he was being shadowed. In front of Steel was a large window of a restaurant which reflected as well as a mirror. There, in the crowd, at least ten feet behind Steel, was Jonathan Grant, trying to blend in. Steel smiled at the thought that someone was following him, where normally it was he that was doing the following. Steel knew he could just slip into the crowd and disappear – he could, but as he looked back at the determination on Grants face, he thought that this was much more fun. Steel let Grant follow him for a while until he saw that the internet lounge was near. Looking back at Grant, who was pretending to look at a pair of sunglasses, Steel knew that he could not let Grant know what he was doing. A group of scantily clad women rushed past Grant, and his eyes followed them for a second, realising his mistake, Grant's gaze shot back to where Steel had been walking, only to find his mark had disappeared. Grant swore to himself for his stupidity and looked around in hope of catching a glimpse of Steel, but he was gone.

From the inside of the internet lounge, Steel smiled as he watched Grant angrily rushing all over, trying to pick up Steel's trail. The internet café was large with sofas for people who were waiting for an opening at the small booths with desktop computers. The lighting had a strange orangey yellow illumination that was soothing on the eyes, rather than bright strip lights. Steel found a machine that had a clear view of the doorway and sat on the swivel brown leather chair. He pressed the enter key, the machine flickered to life, and the search engine appeared. Looking up from the monitor, Steel saw Grant again, this time he was looking through the window to try and see what Steel was doing. Grant had found Steel either through luck or powers of deduction. Whatever it had been didn't interested Steel, all he knew was that Grant was becoming a pain in the ass and Steel had to sort it out now.

Grant stood at the window wondering what his next move was; a few feet away a mass of screaming excited children ran through the deck with freshly painted faces.

As Grant watched through the glass, a wave of six-year-old kids almost knocked him off his feet. Grant laughed as he watched the mass of little terrors disappear. He had only turned for a second, but as he looked back over at Steel, he found an empty chair, fear poured over Grant.

"Who the hell was this guy?" Grant growled to himself, as a sudden need for alcohol came over him. Panicked at the thought of losing the mysterious Mr Black, Grant made his way to the nearest bar, all the while looking over his shoulder as he went. Grant butted into people as he hurriedly made for a bar. Grant found a gloomy looking place next to a sports wear shop. The bar was almost empty, only a few people were scattered about the room. The bar was dimly lit apart from some blue and red neon lights above the bar and on the support pillars around the floor space. The floor had dark wood tiles that reflected the brightly coloured illuminations. The bar stretched against the back wall with a mirror backdrop hidden behind glass shelving; the shelves displayed a selection of bottled hard liquor. Finding a spot at the bar, Grant crashed himself on to one of the wooden bar stools.

"Give me a double whiskey" Grant didn't really drink the stuff, but it was booze.

"Any particular brand or year, sir?" asked the Italian looking barkeep as he polished a large beer glass.

"Does it look like I care?" Grant growled, not in the mood for questions. All he wanted to do was get drunk. The barkeep placed down a shot glass and filled it, Grant grabbed it, and with a cringe in his eyes, he downed it in one. For the next five minutes, shot after shot the barman kept pouring, and Grant kept drinking. Suddenly, distracted by another soberer customer, he left Grant to his mumblings.

"Yes sir, what can I get you?" He smiled hoping Grant would forget he was there,

"Two coffees – black, Thanks," Grant turned to see who had stopped the drinks from coming. On seeing Steel sitting next to him, he fell off his stool, causing the barkeep to smile in the mirror. Steel saw the barkeep's smile and tried to contain his own. Grant looked up in fear and pointed to Steel, "You," his finger waved about as if searching for the real one of the three that he saw in his drunken state.

Steel carried Grant to a booth, and the barkeep followed with the coffees.

"Just keep them coming will you and a large bottle of still water if you would, thanks," Steel asked laying a twenty-pound note on the bar. The barkeep nodded and smiled. Falling on to the long-cushioned seat of the booth, Grant fell on to his side.

Steel immediately sat him upright. Steel needed answers, and he hoped Grant could give some; it was obvious to a blind man that Grant was tailing Steel because he thought that he was somebody important. After the third coffee and the fifth glass of water, Grant was sober enough to talk but still drunk enough to spill his guts.

"So, why are you following me, Mr Grant?" The drunk looked disappointed at the question, was he really playing this game?

"I know who you are, Mr Black," Grant said, waving an index finger at Steel – who was suddenly knocked back at the accusation, how the hell did he find out and who was he working for?

Steel, not wanting to show his hand, just on the off chance that Grant was either bluffing or had got the wrong person entirely, Steel decided to play dumb.

"So, who do you think I am, Mr Grant?" Again, Grant waved his finger, and all Steel could think of doing was ripping the damn thing off his hand.

"You're with THEM aren't you?" Grant said, after beckoning Steel forwards, so he could whisper, Grant stank of alcohol so much it must have been coming out of his bones.

"Sorry, Mr Grant you have lost me, who are THEM?" Grant's face soured.

"You know, THEM, the organization, forgot what they called themselves, strange name." Steel could see Grant's mind heading off to another direction.

"Sorry, but I am just here on a cruise; I am not with anybody apart from American Express." Grant's jaw dropped as did his hopes. Steel could see the desperation in his eyes, he knew something, and the only way to get it out of him was getting him on his side.

"Oh god, I have the wrong person?" Grant drank another mouthful of coffee.

"Do you want to talk about it?" Steel asked. Grant shot him a suspicious look.

"About what?" Steel could see he was deflecting – which was bad as Steel realized that Grant was now sober enough to shut up.

"Hey, you started this, maybe I can help or something?" Steel said with a shrug, then sipped his coffee. He could see Grant's mind working on the proposal, his eyes almost fully closed as he squinted to try and make out whether Steel could be trusted or not. Even though he had those damned sunglasses on, there was just something about him that Grant felt he could be trusted.

Ever since he saw Steel in the lounge, he had a feeling this man was trouble. Maybe he was wrong, but that did not change the fact in his mind that he was still alone in this.

"Thanks for the offer, Mr Black, but I am afraid this is my problem and mine alone," Grant said, as he went to stand but, his drunken legs forbad it, and he fell back onto the chair. Steel smiled at his bold attempt to leave.

"Look, Jonathan," Steel started. Grant looked up at the sudden change in familiarity,

"I know people…I have worked with the NYPD for a while, helping them on cases, so if they can trust me why can't you? Look you are obviously on to something big, so let me help."

Grant could see Steel's point, and he was right he was alone; would it be a massive mistake?

"Ok – Antony," Grant smiled, as he threw the first name term back at Steel. "What you have to understand is what I have is merely circumstantial," Steel nodded that he understood. "Well about three or four weeks ago a cargo ship in New York was sunk just as it left the harbour," Grant leant forward as he told the tale.

"The Eisen Wolff," Grant's eyes lit up as Steel mentioned the name. "Yes, I read about it in the papers, so what about it?" Grant's face was an explosion of delight that he was able to tell the tale.

"Well, apparently the NYPD swat stormed the ship and stopped a major Arms smuggling operation headed for the Middle East," Steel wanted to put him straight about the matter but why burst his bubble?

"Please, continue," Steel tried to sound interested.

"Now this didn't spark my interest until a friend of mine had an accident one night," Grant used his fingers to signify exclamation marks, " after he was investigating a slaughter at an English manor house around ten years ago. Some Lord, his family and friends, had some homecoming for the son, who by the way went missing." He gave Steel a drunken wink or as good as he could.

"So, they suspected the son?" Steel asked, curious about his opinion.

"Na, apparently they found a load of dead guys in tactical gear, the thought is that the son came home, Oh FYI, the son was Special Forces or something. Anyway, the police reckoned he came back and took most of them out." Behind his sunglasses, Steel's eyes burned, but he could not cry, for some reason he had never cried, most thought him heartless, but he found other ways to vent his emotion. Grant took another gulp of coffee, his eyes looked excited so much they moved from side to side, Steel would have put it down to a coffee rush, but it was probably just a rush from telling his tale.

"And then?" Steel enquired as he could see Grant's mind wandering to another plane.

"What! Oh yeh," Steel smiled, as the man twitched and looked around as if he had come back into his own body. "Oh yeh, right so after my buddy's ACCIDENT" Grant made the motion with his fingers once again. "I decided to find out what was going on," Steel leaned forwards, his chest rested on his hands, his fingers interlinked.

"There is a group, they are not terrorists, well not as we know terrorists. No these are organised, and I really mean organised, almost like an organisation. To them terror and stuff like that is more of a business than a way of life," Now Steel was very interested. Grant banged a clenched fist against his own forehead. "For the life of me, I can't remember the name Brand told me," Steel looked puzzled

"Your friend who died?" Steel asked. Grant looked up at him. lost in his own confusion.

"What...yeh, Brand Hemming that was his name," Grant's eyes wandered again, and Steel knew that this Brand Hemming was more than a friend.

"Well, I found a trail that started at the English estate and traversed around the world to New York, a source of mine told me about someone in London and, from the information I got from them, I made it here." He raised his palms and wore a smug grin on his face to show off his achievement, but Steel could see he was keeping a lot to his chest.

"So," Steel began "What's so special about this ship?" Steel had a theory he may be able to fill in the blanks; Grant shot him a suspicious look.

"Besides its maiden voyage, can't say, I just know it has something to do with THEM. So, what's your interest Mr Black, why are you here?" Steel had had a feeling all along about Grant, and his reaction just confirmed it, the man was a reporter.

"Like I said at the dinner, just a guy travelling through life, not much to tell," Steel smiled.

Grant went to stand up realising he had said too much to a complete stranger who, for all he knew, was working for the people he was after.

"I will see you around Mr Black, be sure of that," Grant said, and, using the first two fingers of his right hand, made the "I am watching you" gesture and as he left, he kept on pointing.

NINE

Below, deep in the bowls of the Titanic ship's hull, long passageways gave way to crew quarters, storage compartments and of course the beating heart of the leviathan – the engine room.

The steady thump, thump of the engine echoed the long white corridors as the monstrous engines powered the turbines. Apart from a couple of engineers heading to and from their shifts, all was clear. The newest addition to the engineering crew was young Walter Norris, a tall black haired boy, freshly twenty years old, his thick hair covered by a baseball cap that had the ships name embroidered on the front. He had started as part of an apprenticeship made by the company a couple of months back, and Jim Dockett had taken him under his wing. Jim was an old school sailor and ships engineer who had been on ships all his life. The man was average height but had broad shoulders that held a round face with a raggedy white beard.

The lad was keen and full of passion, and that is what old Jim loved about the boy, every time he looked at his smiling face Jim could see himself thirty years ago. Jim would teach the lad as much as he could about the old ways, almost as if he had found someone to keep the tradition going. In the restroom, Jim's large frame entered and sat down on one of the chairs that nestled by a small square table.

STUART FIELD

"Come here boy," he bellowed at Jim – who was busy tidying some cups away. Jim turned, and with a grin, he rushed over like a child to his grandfather. As he sat, the old sailor pulled out of his jacket a diagram of knots.

"Right then boy let's see how many you can get, shall we?" His face alight with pride as he knew this would be no problem for the young lad. Just they were just starting when a tall, thin sickly-looking man approached, his blonde hair thick with gel.

"Oh, goody its grandpa hour," said the man, his voice sickly sweet and full with violent screeching tones, like nails on a chalkboard. The two men looked up at the man and immediately shivered just at the sight of him, Walter could not take his eyes off the man's obscure features, his face was long with a wide grinning mouth, and the dark rings around his eyes and the redness of the exterior enhanced the paleness of his blue eyes.

"Now," the strange man started, his gaze fixed on the boy. "I need you to take something to the captain, Ok?" Walter did not answer at first, but his gaze was transfixed on the man's hypnotic eeriness.

The man looked for a moment then quickly shot forwards, "Boo", Walter jumped out of his skin, causing the man to clap his hands together and put them towards his mouth as he giggled. Then he stopped, smiling he drew closer to Walters face, almost nose to nose. "I want you to take something to the captain, OK, capiche, comprende?" Walter nodded slowly, fear oozing out of him.

The man shot back to his former position with the grin back on his face as though nothing had happened.

"Good, here you go," he presented Walter with a small back box around six inches square, the sides smooth and no visible signs of how to open it. Walter grasped the object, but the man held it fast with one hand, Walter was shocked at how much strength this spindly man possessed. The man's grin drew to a scowl. "You will go directly to the captain and return back here; you will not go anywhere else, just there and back again, do you understand?" Walter nodded, slowly. "You will not open it you will not speak to anyone; I don't care if you see your grandmother, understand?" Again, Walter nodded, beads of sweat cascading down his brow. Then without a word, the man released his grip, and the sickening grin grew back. "Oh good, right off you pop." Walter could not travel fast enough out of the room and to the upper decks just to get away from the man. As he made his way past the white coloured walls and heavy looking doors of the lower deck, he had noticed on the storage room had a sign placed upon it. The square notice was around eighteen inches in diameter, and red letters stuck out from its white background. The words simple *KEEP OUT NO ADMITTANCE*. Walter stood for a moment and wondered when that was put on, it had not been there when they had arrived in Southampton, but fearing the man was behind him, he thought nothing more of it, he just ran.

THE CABIN of Tobias Long was on the 24th deck, so he was close to the bridge. The room was set out with dark wooden floorboards and turn of the century furniture, making it look more like a museum than a cabin. Tobias Long sat at the dark wood desk as he filled the brandy glass; his red leather-bound captain's chair creaked as he changed position to lean over his desk. Reaching over, he picked up a picture of a woman. The photograph seemed as though it had been taken in the last couple of years. The woman, who was almost certainly his wife, was in her late fifties, and her short hair was brown with hints of grey. Behind her was a park or a garden. He reached forward with a shaky hand and gently picked up the silver-framed photograph.

A smile came to his brandy moist lips, raising his glass he saluted the woman and downed the contents of his glass "To you, my love." Three knocks to his door made him turn; a look of fear twisted his features as his eyes glared at the entrance to his cabin.

"Y…. yes, who is it?" his hand tightened around the whiskey glass – breaking it under his vice-like grip.

"Crewman Walter Norris sir," the captain's eyes burned as his heart rate calmed, he did not look down at the piece of drinking glass on the floor, his gaze held steady at the door.

"What do you want crewman?" His voice sounded exhausted but somewhat relieved; his face held the vision of his voice.

"Sorry sir, I was told to bring you …. uhm…. something," the boy yelled back through the door. Tobias's eyes crept up from the floor, and the look came back as his eyes reached the peephole.

"W…what kind of something, answer me boy?" his fear had built up once more, and it was being masked by his anger, Anger at the boy. *Don't shoot the messenger*; he suddenly thought, trying to calm himself.

Walter nearly jumped out of his skin as the door was suddenly yanked open, and a red-faced captain stood in the doorway, his eyes large, and his chest heaving as though he had just been for a run around the decks.

In his left hand, he held a photograph in a silver frame, and the right hand was hidden from view as Tobias held the door open from the other side.

"What do you have for me son?" His voice was calmer as he saw the cowering boy; Tobias smiled, relaxing the boy slightly.

"A man gave me this for you," Walter raised up the box in both hands, Tobias looked at the strange gift and sighed like a man who was so far gone it did not matter anymore.

"Ok son, that will be all," Tobias's words sounded worn out as he took the box from Walter's hands. The door closed slowly and, as it shut, Walter heard the sound of the deadbolt being slid on.

With his task done, his journey back was somewhat slower as he was in no rush to see the man again. Climbing into the elevator, he pressed for the third floor and waited for the doors to close.

Down in the depths of the ship, Walter made his way back to the restroom to inform the man his task was complete, in the distance he saw a figure trying to get into one of the rooms.

HIDDEN STEEL

Walter yelled after them causing the stranger to run off with Walter in pursuit. He had gotten so far then stopped and rested his hands on his knees for support, his first thought was how unfit this job had made him, but as he stood upright, something to his left caught the corner of his eye. Turning slowly, he noticed the door with the sign was slightly open, every alarm in his body told him not to go in, that was until he heard the low moan as though someone was injured. Without a thought, he entered slowly.

"Hello" he whispered, "Hello is anyone there?" Silence was the only response his ears registered in the darkness. As the door was open, it allowed in enough light to see the mass of container boxes and crates piled upon one another. Moving further on past the wall he stopped. In a far corner, a red glow lit up the adjoining walls behind whatever was being concealed under a tarpaulin. Reaching down, he lifted it slightly, but dropped the canvas and backed away slowly; the pulsing red light illuminated the look of his utter fear.

His gaze did not leave the corner until he backed into something. First, he thought it was the wall until, as he turned, he looked straight into the maddening eyes of the strange man. Walter yelped and jumped backwards, falling to the ground as he went.

"Oh dear," the tall, thin man closed the door behind them, and the light was enveloped by the darkness. A blinding light made Walter shade his eyes as the man switched on the room's lights.

"Well, you know what curiosity killed don't you?" The man was walking from left to right, not looking at the scared boy on the floor but in the air.

"T... The cat sir," the boy answered, his voice trembling with fear. The man spun around and clapped as a look of utter delight came over him.

"Oh goodie, yes you got it," he reached down and, grabbing the boys hand, helped him up. Walter froze as the man did not release his grip but pulled him closer. "But unfortunately, in this case, curiosity killed the..." His grin changed from happy to a callas unforgiving evil, "The kid." As he finished the sentence, his voice dropped to a baritone. Walter had a mini second of fear before the man stuck the taser into the boy's neck and activated it, they both jiggled about as the current passed through them both. The man relaxed the *on* switch and Walter fell to the ground, motionless. The man danced around singing and waving his arms. He stopped and walked up to the unconscious boy.

"I don't know what the problem was really," he said, circling the boy like a vulture searching for a meal. "Don't go anywhere I said, come straight back I said." He was now shouting at the boy, "Simple I thought, but no you had to make it difficult."

He reached down and stuck the taser into the boy once more, his motionless body convulsed as the volts coursed through his body, smashing his head against one of the crates, "Oops, mind you don't bump your head," laughed the thin man, the hideous cackles echoed through the steel corridors of the lower decks.

THE MAJOR'S home was in a nice neighbourhood; the buildings were clean and free of graffiti. McCall and Thompson walked up to a door that displayed a large wooden plaque on the wall. The plaque was a cut from a medium-sized tree and displayed the rings of its life through the lacquer. The inscription was simple *The Mayors*. McCall stopped and touched the plaque with her gloved hand and smiled, thinking how much this reminded her of her home before her dad's murder.

"You ok?" Asked Jenny, somewhat puzzled by the display, McCall looked over to Jenny Thompson, the smile disappearing.

"Yes, fine, ok let's do this." McCall reached out and pressed the polished brass doorbell. The familiar *ding-dong* chime resounded through the house. They waited for a moment, listening for any signs that someone was there, but heard nothing. As they turned to leave, the door opened slightly. McCall and Thompson stopped and looked back to see a girl no more than five years old standing in the doorway. McCall smiled and walked slowly towards here.

"Hi, my name is Samantha, I am a detective…." the door was slammed shut and the sound of tiny feet running on a wooden floor echoed through the hallway. McCall stood up and looked at Thompson who just shrugged and raised her hands as if to say, "Don't ask me."

Slowly the door opened again, and a woman stood before them, she was average in height and build with long scraggily mousey hair, her eyes red from too many tears and her nose looked raw from too many tissues. McCall had seen this too many times, first time was with her mom.

"Hi, I am Detective McCall, and this is Detective Thompson," McCall said, showing her shield and ID. The woman did not respond; she just hung on to the door and stared as if they were not even there.

"Are you Mrs Erin Major?" The woman's eyes met McCall's, and she just nodded. "We are investigating your husband's death, can we come in?"

Stephanie Major said nothing just walked away from the door and headed for the kitchen, Thompson closed the door behind her as she followed McCall in. There was a large floor space that opened up to the sitting room to their right and a set of stairs on the left-hand wall leading to the bedrooms. Beyond that was the sitting room, a door next to a breakfast bar. Following Stephanie Majors lead they followed towards the kitchen. The sitting room was quite large with a sofa in the middle of the room and a flat screen on the wall above a brick fireplace.

The house was modest and cheerful; pictures hung on the walls of a once happy family. On entering the kitchen, they found Stephanie starting to make three coffees as if an automatic instinct of being a good host had kicked in. As she poured the coffee into the mugs, her hands were shaking with shock and adrenalin.

"Here, I'll do that for you," McCall said, taking the clear glass coffee pot from her. Stephanie Major smiled and wiped her eyes with the sleeve of her bathrobe. "Do you mind if we sit down somewhere, it might be easier?" McCall suggested.

As they returned into the sitting room, Stephanie beckoned them to take a seat on the long sofa while she placed herself on another armchair which was opposite the other.

"I don't understand. I already spoke to the other officers about it" McCall smiled, sympathetically.

"I know but, sometimes things get missed or left out by mistake. We have to find out what happened to your husband" Stephanie Major took a sip from the coffee mug and stared at the chair opposite.

"Ok Detective, what do you want to know?" Stephanie took a deep breath and composed herself. McCall reached into her pocket, took out a small Dictaphone, and placed it on to the table, McCall always carried one – she found it easier and quicker than taking notes, plus she could listen to the way the people spoke long after the fact.

"Just start from the beginning, how the day started," she could see Stephanie think about that day, and a little smile came over her face.

"I don't know, we all had breakfast, I had to get Jilly ready for kindergarden," she turned and pointed to the small girl cowering around the corner of the sitting room, holding a stuffed rabbit doll.

"It was a normal day. He had finished a big job a couple of weeks before, and he had a new one in the city, that's all I know really." Stephanie explained, her tone was almost drowsy, as if she had taken too much medication, or she was just in shock from losing her husband.

"Who did your husband work for?" McCall sat back into the sofa as she listened.

"He was an electrician, he worked for ULTRA-TRONICS, they are a specialist firm, and he did alarm systems, cameras sensors. All sorts of high-tech stuff," she replied. McCall took out her notebook and took down the name of the firm.

"At any time did he seem occupied, nervous? Not himself?" McCall asked. Stephanie shook her head.

"No, he was his normal happy self." Stephanie broke down, but no tears came as if she could not cry any more.

"This big job you mentioned, what was it?"

Stephanie shrugged, "Don't really know, it's the only job he didn't talk about, but I know it lasted for around two months." McCall had a puzzled look.

"What do you mean the only job he didn't talk about?" Stephanie took another sip from the coffee; her eyes began to clear slightly from the red haze.

"He normally bored us to death about how he had done this job and that, but this one, well it was if he could not talk about it. I wish he had now."

Stephanie Major looked into McCall's eyes, picking up a familiar stare.

"Have you ever lost someone, Detective?"

McCall nodded. "Yes, my dad. He was killed in the line of duty, a sniper shot him."

Stephanie smiled, thankful for a kindred spirit.

"He had finished the big job, and this smaller one came up, in the store. They said it was bad wiring or something that caused the accident, but he was too much of a professional to let anything happen." McCall sensed she thought it was not an accident. Stephanie leant forwards, her eyes now telling a different story, and this one was of mistrust.

"Detective, my man worked twenty-five years and didn't even blow a fuse, so you tell me, was it an accident?" Stephanie growled, her eyes red from too many tears and anger. McCall had to agree, if the man was that cautious how this happened, her gut turned, and that for her was a bad sign. The sign of this picture getting bigger.

McCall had good instincts, and they were saying, "You have enough for today." McCall could see that the whole ordeal had been a strain on Stephanie and the kid. She picked up the recorder and switched it off, as she put it away in her jacket pocket she stood, and Thompson followed her lead.

"Mrs Major, if you think of anything else, please call me,"

McCall took a small business card from her notebook wallet; Stephanie Major gave her a curious look.

"I know that I should say sorry for your loss, but I think you have heard it enough times from people who felt they had to say it. I will say it when we have answers for you, and you can put this to rest." McCall said with a stern look on her face.

A tear rolled down Stephanie Majors pale face; she knew then that someone would find the truth and not just write him off as an accident. Now she had hope.

TEN

Steel had returned to the Internet café and resumed his search for the people at the dinner table the evening before. If they all showed up to be who they said they were well, so be it, but that would mean that he would have to search again, and time was running out. However, his gut told him that some – if not all - had something to hide, and he had to find out what.

All the time at the dining table, he could not shake a feeling that last night's meeting was more than coincidence.

After hours of searching and several cappuccinos later, he had gathered a large pile of information. He sat back in the chair and finished the rest of his cold coffee. Steel had printed off volumes of data to look at later in the comfort of his cabin. If something did not add up, he would find it.

Gathering his notes, Steel made for the exit, as he did so he caught a reflection, in one of the monitors, of a man rushing for the terminal Steel had just used. He smiled at the predictability of it all. Naturally, he had cleared the search log and looked up all sorts of other junk before he closed down; he'd had a gut feeling, and as normal, his gut was right. Stepping out into the bustling crowds, a woman with arms full of shopping bags collided with him, sending both their wares crashing to the floor.

"Are you ok?" He asked, as he helped her gather her belongings.

"Yes, I am fine, sorry it was all my fault," her voice sounded flustered by the whole affair. As Steel stood there with her bags in his hands, he watched as she gathered up the large amount of paperwork that was strewn across the polished floor.

"Here, let me get your papers," she said, gathering them up and handing them over to him, while taking her shopping back. As she stood there with arms packed with shopping bags, Steel was able to get a better look at her. The woman was tall with a long light blue wrap-around dress that tied up at her left side; darkened sunglasses with overly large lenses covered her eyes and almost half her face. A large wicker summer hat bowed slightly to one side of her face.

"Are you sure you are ok?" his words meaningful but his thoughts were sceptical. He knew she had done this to see what he had been researching, all this to get a look at what he held! As she gathered her belongings, she quickly scurried away. He smiled to himself as he looked down at the mass of paperwork in his hand and as he flicked through the articles on diving, prices of hotels and flights to exotic corners of the globe and scratched the small of his back, where the true articles had been digging into his back and tickling the bare flesh.

Steel headed back to his room; he needed the solace of his cabin to think. He looked down at his watch, the luminous hands on his Tag Heuer read ten to five in the afternoon, dinner was at seven, so he knew he had time. As he entered his room, he made a quick study of his surroundings, it all seemed normal, possibly too normal, given the past circumstances. He reached into his inside pocket and found the small blue light, "No" he thought, if someone had bugged his room, he had to find them without looking like he was looking for them. He thought for a second then smiled as he walked calmly into the comfortably sized bathroom. Steel stared hard at his reflection in the mirror and ran some water to quickly splash over his face; the water was cool, and refreshing as it met his warm skin. Reaching over, he found a towel on the heated rail and dabbed the water away. Looking into the mirror, his gaze fell upon the shower unit; he smiled like a schoolchild. Reaching in, he turned the dial until it was on to the full heat setting and he left it running, the sound of the water hammering against the safety glass like a bad rainstorm faded as he closed the bathroom door behind him.

Steel stripped the clothes from his muscular body; if they wanted a show, he would give them one. Taking a bathrobe from the back of the door, he covered himself with a grin as he could feel the eyes on him. He needed to freshen up before dinner, yes, the dinner. He hoped that there would be fresh faces at his table, but not actually knowing which table that would be. *First things first*, he thought to himself, he needed to find the bugs and hopefully who had installed them. He poured himself a large whisky from the bottle of Johnnie Walker Black label. The smell of mixed malts and spices tickled his nose and prepared his mouth for the smooth taste. Taking a small mouthful, Steel just let it linger, letting his mouth warm the golden liquid before slowly swallowing the rich taste. As he raised the glass to take another heavenly shot, he noted the smoke detector had a small hole opposite the small red LED light.

"That's one," he noted, his eyes made a quick search of the room. There would be others, to that he had no doubt. Steel put down his glass and opened the door to the bathroom, as he had hoped, a billow of steam flooded out of the enclosed bathroom, filling the living area for a short moment but long enough to see the small dot of light from dresser mirror. He entered the bathroom, and sure enough, he saw another small spot on the bathroom mirror, which the steam had not been able to consume.

He smiled as he ran the water into the sink, ready to get rid of his twelve o'clock shadow. Part of him wanted to put shaving foam over the small point, but he resisted the urge. Instead, he swept away the condensation from the mirror and lathered up.

After the cool shower, he sat on the small couch that stood against the left wall of the room, the soft bathrobe felt good against his tight muscular body. Reaching for the paperwork that lay on the seat next to him, Steel studied the portfolios of the group of people he had encountered the night before.

He looked over to the clock on the bedside cabinet; the electronic counter told him he had around thirty minutes before dinner started. He stood, and then walked to the small wardrobe; on the door was a full-length mirror. He dropped his robe and stared at the fake tattoos that covered his upper body, the elaborate artwork covered the six entry and exit wounds from where he had been shot so many years ago, his fingers ran over the small markings stirring faint flashbacks of that day at the family home, the day he lost everything. The day he died.

As he dressed, he used the long mirror to chance a gaze at the smoke detector, he smiled to himself as he tied the bow tie, then he stood still and inspected his dress. He wore a black golf-ball shirt underneath his black tuxedo, using both hands he pulled his tie tight and brushed down the arms of his jacket. He was ready.

McCall and Thompson returned to the station to find that Tooms and Tony had already set up their own murder boards for their first victim – John Barr. The man had been a dock-worker, a crane driver until his apparent accident a couple of days ago. The file had crossed to Homicide just in case something was off. McCall stood in front of the board; her hands rested on her hips as she took in the details.

"So, what you got?" her eyes never left the board as Tooms ran through the information on his notepad.

"John Barr aged forty-three, ex-wife Helen now lives in Queens with their two boys John Jr. and Sam." McCall nodded as she took in the information.

"So, what happened to Mr Barr?" her voice calm, her words slow and distant, as though she had a million other things on her mind.

"Well poor Mr Barr took a tumble at work," McCall shrugged, Tony spoke as though it should have meant something.

"So, people trip every day." Her words sounded tired. Tony placed a picture, on the board, of a large pool of blood and what used to be a man.

"Yes, unfortunately he was a crane operator at the docks," everyone moved in for a closer look, as morbid curiosity took hold of them.

"The poor SOB, came out of the cab under the unit, tripped or something and fell," Tooms said, moving his hand in a downwards curve. McCall had that *bad feeling thing* again.

"Ok, interview the family, check financials." She said, looking over to Jenny, who was getting their murder board ready.

"You mean the usual things?" Tooms joked, he could see that McCall was a million miles away and she hoped it was not about Steel. "Are you ok?" he asked in a concerned tone. McCall nodded and came back down to earth with a smile.

"Yes – yes. I'm fine. It's just all this after the last case just seems…." Tooms smiled.

"Mundane, yeh I guess it does a little, but hey be careful what you wish for," he placed a reassuring hand on her shoulder.

"Anyway," Tony butted in. "We already did some digging on our skydiver and it appears he had a bit of money trouble," McCall's eyes widened.

"Apparently after his divorce he was up to his neck in debt, until he borrowed some money," Tony took a picture from the file and placed a colour photograph on the section marked *SUSPECTS*.

The man was in his late forties, his black hair greased back over his pointy-head. His face was long with a long thin nose that protruded from his pale face. The man's top lip was thin with large two front teeth that seemed too large for his closed mouth. His eyes were dark, as though there were no eyes in the sockets.

McCall's jaw dropped, and her gaze went from the picture to Tony.

"He looks just like a …."

"Wessel, yes I thought that as well. Freaky isn't it?" Tooms laughed. McCall nodded, her mouth tightened so as not to laugh.

"Meet Joshua Newton, aka, the rat," Tony said, pointing at the photograph. Now McCall was struggling to keep it in. She turned away from the photograph and composed herself.

"Ok bring him in, let's find out what he knows." Her gaze fell to the empty chair next to her desk. Jenny looked back with pride at her layout on the glossy white board. McCall joined her and looked once more at the crime scene photos; her eyes met with the close-up of the victim. His eyes were wide open, as well as his mouth. Almost as if, he was calling out. He lay on his back with his arms outstretched as if trying to grab hold of something to prevent the fall. McCall could not get the look out of her head, the look of pain.

The other photographs were taken from different angles, but all centred on to one point – the victim. His body lay next to a self-supporting stepladder, which lay on its side, from the ceiling, two cables stretched down, almost as if they had been yanked down with force.

McCall's concentration was broken as Jenny brought her a fresh coffee; she thanked her as she took the mug. The smell of the coffee was intense.

"What the hell is this?" She barked putting the cup down.

"We ran out of the other stuff and Steel forgot to mention where the coffee came from," Jenny said, with a shrug and an apologetic look. McCall shrugged and took a sip, hell it was coffee and she needed it.

"ME's report said it was "Death by electrocution," McCall read from a file as Jenny sat on the edge of the desk next to McCall.

"What are you thinking?" Jenny asked, suddenly, noticing the familiar look on McCall's face when something did not add up.

"Did CSU dust for prints?" McCall asked, a tone of suspicion hung in her voice. Jenny picked up another beige coloured file and flicked through the notes.

"Yes, a couple of partials, but those belonged to the manager, why?" McCall frowned at the reply.

"We need to see the crime scene; has it been opened yet?" Thompson shook her head.

"No, it's still locked down." McCall smiled "Come on, we got some hunting to do."

THE STORE WAS A LARGE 7-11, the police tape stuck tightly on to the doorframe preventing entry. McCall took out a key from a small clear bag and placed it into the lock. The beams of their torches cut through the darkness of the store. The large room was filled with empty shelving and cardboard boxes stacked up on and around the counter along the back wall. The room was square with windows on the entrance wall. Shelving ran down sideways, so the shopkeeper had a perfect view of all the aisles.

At the far-left side, in the corner, was a door leading to the upper floor, backdoor and under the stairs, the breaker box. As McCall moved slowly towards the white outline of a man, she stopped and knelt, her tight backside rested on the back of her boots. Using the flashlight, she mapped out the scene in her head.

"Seems like an accident, don't you think?" Jenny asked. McCall looked up at Jenny and stood up.

"Things are not always as they appear, Detective," McCall's tone was sombre, and Jenny knew that meant lesson time.

"Ok, tell me what you see?" Jenny paused for a moment; her eyes gathered information.

"The cables there suggest that was where the current came from." McCall nodded in agreement.

"So, why was there power, surely a veteran electrician would have all the power switched off?" Jenny added, her gaze following the cables, then back to the scene. McCall grinned and walked towards the breaker box which was tucked under a stairwell. Under the stairs, everything had a thousand years' worth of dust on it, all except the handle to the breaker.

"Did CSU check this for prints?" Thompson opened the

file, and with the small Maglite in her mouth, she flicked to the CSU report. "Yes, but they came up empty."

"What no prints on the breaker?" Jenny shook her head in reply. "Ok Detective, so accident or murder?"

Jenny grinned, "I'll have an M for Murder please Bob."

ELEVEN

Steel had studied the plans as much as he could on the vessel, and his head began to hurt. This truly was a city; he walked to the balcony of his room to get some fresh air. The cool breeze felt good on his warm skin as it penetrated his black golf-ball shirt. Taking a deep breath, he could smell the fresh saltiness of the ocean, and then ventured back to his room, all the while he could feel the eyes on him. This trip was starting to be more tantalising than he thought, hidden cameras, strange rich people that stuck out. No, this was more than he could have hoped for, but he had a job to do and not much time to do it. Checking his appearance once more in the full-length mirror, he smiled confidently to himself.

"Ok, let's do this." He knew tonight he would be at a different table and sitting with different people. He was running out of time and had far too many suspects. He prayed something would happen to bring them out. As he made his way down the well-lit corridor, his eyes caught a glimpse behind him from the polished framework of the wall to his front. A man in blue overalls entered Steel's room using a card key, Steel smiled. He knew the people who had him under surveillance were near – he just didn't know just how near they were.

. . .

THE DINING ROOM was full of people in tuxedos and gowns. This was the chance for the rich to parade like peacocks and show who had the money, who had the power. Steel found a quiet place at the bar and quickly snatched a glass of champagne from the waiter's tray as he strolled by – the silver drinks tray balanced on the palm of his hand as he held it aloft. The whole place smelt of money, and it was intoxicating. Couples strutted around as if they were royalty, while laughing false laughs, greeting one another with false platitudes. As he stood at the bar, Steel looked around; his eyes searched for someone new, someone he had not yet laid eyes on, who may ring the alarm bells as much as the group from the previous night.

As Steel took a sip from the fluted glass, he looked around and thought how familiar this was, the same faces as the other evening. He grunted to himself with disappointment. His theory was, if someone was going to do something it would be in plain sight, they would not stand out in this room – the ordinary Joe. Steel knew that if there was something going to happen, it would be the guy in the cheap seats. The man who would stand out more as a terrorist or killer because he looked the part or fitted all the criteria laid out by the NSA, FBI or Justice Department. Captain Long had been right; this was like the Titanic, them and us, rich and poor divided by decks. Who would suspect a millionaire, the police would not give it a second thought, and Steel just hoped his theory was right?

Steel raised the glass once more to his lips, he paused as everyone was ushered to take their seats. Downing the rest of the golden liquid, he placed the empty glass on the bar and hunted for the table plan. A large red velvet-backed board showed five round circles, each of which held twelve names, these represented the five important tables on the dining floor. If your name was on a table, you were one of the lucky few. The centre table was naturally the captains. As Steel looked, he was surprised to find he was on the main table again, but this time there was a new name *Martin Goddard*.

As he approached the empty seat, Steel noticed that a round man, with short black hair and a sweaty disposition, had replaced Jonathan Grant at the table. Steel looked down at the tag, which confirmed the man's name, or at least what he wanted people to think his name was.

"Good evening," he greeted the others as his hands rested on the back of his chair; almost in unison, the others reciprocated his friendly words. Looking around, Steel found the stunning face of Tia May; she wore an electric blue dress that clung to her stunning body like a silk glove. She looked up at Steel and smiled a childish grin; her eyes followed him as he took his seat in between Missy Studebaker and Ronald Dawson.

Steel felt the presence of another person behind him. As he turned, he saw it was the waitress from before. As she approached, he noticed the glass of whiskey on the metal tablet. A smile broke from the corner of his mouth at the thought, had he made that much of an impression? As she lifted the glass to put it before him, he held up a hand gently to stop her.

"Thanks, but I thought I would go for something new." Her eyes seemed stunned, but her face tried to crack a smile.

"Very well, what would Sir like?" the waitress smiled.

Pausing for a moment, Steel grinned. "Vodka martini, two shots of Bombay gin, and a hint of lime with a lemon peel and stirred, not shaken." He could see that she had made a disapproving mental note of his order and left, leaving everyone a memory of the tight-fitting skirt on her gyroscopic hips. Everyone gave him an inquiring look.

"I just saw a spy film, and I thought I would try it," his voice was boyish. The others laughed at his childlike attitude, all except Tia; she was giving him another look altogether. He smiled and looked around at the familiar faces until his gaze rested on Martin Goddard. The large man was pale, and his large head sported a clean-shaven face and large blue eyes that did not seem to blink.

As the volume of conversation got louder, the table suddenly fell silent as the waitress brought Steel his drink. The waitress placed it in front of him, ensuring he got a good look at her ample breasts through her open top as she moved away. As he looked up at the table, he saw approving smiles from Alan Metcalf and

Albert Studebaker. Steel shrugged until he caught the disapproving look of Tia May, but he just casually took a sip from the slightly cloudy concoction and stared into nowhere in particular.

"Actually, it's not bad; I wouldn't go as far as saying I would drink them all the time but." Steel nodded to himself and put down the full glass on to the cotton tablecloth. Steel's eyes glanced up at their new addition and smiled.

"So, you must be Mr Goodhart?" Steel asked with a tone of interest. The large man did not respond; he just sat there drinking his water. Everyone stopped talking amongst themselves and turned towards the man, suddenly he felt all eyes on him, and he shook as if woken from a dream.

"What…. oh, yes, that's right, Goddard, Martin Goddard, and you are…?" Everyone smiled falsely and continued with their chatter. Steel got up and walked round to shake the man's hand.

"Sorry old man, Black, Antony Black." Steel's grip was tight enough to feel a pulse. However Goddard's grip was limp and sweaty. As he returned to his seat, Steel wiped his hand with his napkin. He had the feeling something was off about this man. First – he didn't know his own name or at least he had not had the false one that long he did not respond to it. Sure, Steel had said it slightly wrong. However the guy never corrected him. And second – secondly there was something else, but he could not put his finger on it.

For the next few minutes, as the courses came and went, Steel just sat back and observed the crowd giving the same introduction to Martin Goddard as they had received the night before, and then it struck him. It was the exact same speech as the other night – none of their stories changed. Steel smiled at the smell of lies from the table.

"Fine," he thought, "They may have told their life stories so many times it was almost like script, but people add things to make themselves look better to certain people, no one's stories are so exact." his thoughts became excited. However, Martin just sat there and nodded and smiled, but gave nothing back in the way of conversation. Steel noted how uncomfortable the man looked; the streams of sweat cascaded down his forehead and ran down into his collar.

"So, Mr Goddard – or May I call you Martin?" asked Susan Metcalf. Steel looked up, as he was just about to take another mouthful of the Beef Wellington. His eyes darted from Susan back to Martin who too had a mouthful of food. For a brief second, he looked panicked and stopped chewing. The look of shock subsided as he relaxed, and just bowed slightly to confirm that she may. Susan smiled at the gesture and continued; her eyes transfixed on the large man that was eating as if he had not eaten for days. Her words were broken in repulsion as she watched him devour the meal.

"So, Martin what type of work are you in?" The table fell silent, and all eyes fell upon Martin once more. He swallowed the mass of food he had been chewing on, then took a quick mouthful of the water to force it down.

"Well," he started, sticking a fat digit into his collar to try to widen it. "I am a computer programmer for a large international firm. I mostly write software for the military and so forth," he explained, as everyone nodded falsely, as if they understood every word he had said. Steel smiled at the false expressions around the table.

"Oh, that sounds…. interesting," Susan said, almost sounding sincere. Steel smiled to himself as her words crumbled, as did her interest in further conversation.

"Are you working on anything at the moment?" Steel asked, just before he enjoyed a small helping of the main course. Before he replied to Steel's question, Martin looked up from his plate and a curious, even evil, grin crept across his pale, sweaty face.

"Yes, it is a complex binary clock," Steel felt uneasy, as Martin began to explain his project, each word held a sinister tone. "It counts down rather than showing present time."

"You mean like the clock in Times Square?" Missy beamed excitedly; everyone sniggered behind their napkins at her

STUART FIELD

childish remark – all but Steel, he was too transfixed on their new guest.

"Yes, in point of fact, very similar." As Martin smiled it was more of appreciation of her remark; Martin was a genius, this was true, but he found her innocence refreshing. To him she was not like the rest at the table, they neither understood nor wanted to for that matter, all that concerned them was their money and how good they looked in public. Steel saw something in his eyes as he spoke to Missy, there was something gentle, but that slipped away when one of the others spoke. The gentleness turned to contempt and loathing, even if he tried to conceal it in a false smile.

"Well I wish you all the best on your project," Steel raised his glass to the man, as if proposing a toast; Martin smiled at Steel, giving a small bow in genuine appreciation.

"Thank you, Mr Black, I know it will be a real blast when it is completed." Then Steel saw the cruel smile as Martin observed everyone else at the table.

Steel knew he had to get Goddard alone and question him, mostly on why he was there – and it was damned sure he was not there for the holiday. Martin patted his lips with the napkin and slowly pulled out his chair and stood.

"Well, if you would excuse me, nature calls, but please continue." Everyone smiled fake smiles as he walked towards the men's room. Steel knew that maybe this was the only chance he would get and so he took it.

"You know," he started, as he stood up and placed down his napkin to the side of his plate.

"Oh, why Mr Black, I would love to dance," Steel looked shocked, but faked an instant smile as Tia rose from her chair and offered her hand. Taking her hand, he pulled her towards him in a violent motion almost ripping her from her feet to dance a tango, which had just started. He felt it appropriate because it would mask any rough movement during the dance.

What was she up to? he thought. *Why did she not want Steel near Goddard?* It was obvious he had missed his chance with Goddard for now, he wanted to know why. Tia leant in and bit Steel on the earlobe; his eyes rolled at the feel of her breath on his neck, god she smelt good. His thoughts began to cloud again.

"Last night was soooo good," she purred, her words soft and inviting and the feel of her warm fantastically-shaped form almost made him forget his purpose.

"Oh, it wasn't too bad I guess," his words sparked a shocked look on her face, that made him smile, *a bit of revenge for making him miss his quarry* he thought.

As the music tempo raised, he flung her away gripping her hand tightly and drew her back just as roughly.

"Why Mr Black, pity you weren't this rough last night," she held a cat-like stare with bedroom eyes, the blue of her eyes was even more beautiful as they captured the candlelight, drawing him in, almost trying to make him forget.

"Well maybe we could make it just as good, say my place after dinner?" she smiled again, causing her ruby lipstick to glisten.

"Maybe we can ask your friends next door to me, they seem very fit, darting in and out of rooms, don't you think?" Steel said with a smile. She suddenly tried to back away, but he just pulled her close.

"We need to talk, don't you think?" his words bitter, as she looked up into his eyes, she saw something, she did not see the travelling millionaire, no this was darker.

"Not here, after dinner." Now she was nervous and less confident, but she masked it well.

The music stopped, and everyone clapped, applauding the orchestra, who stood slightly in appreciation. Steel led Tia back to her seat just as Goddard returned from the restroom. Steel noticed fresh droplets of water on his forehead from where he had obviously just splashed water on his face. Martin Goddard took out his handkerchief and patted away the moister, laughing nervously as he did so. For the next two courses, the conversation became dull and uneventful, the other guests twittered on about their lives and "How marvellous things were."

Steel was now torn, he had to find out what the hell Tia and Martin Goddard were involved in. These two held answers, and he hoped, to the same question. It was more than obvious that Goddard was up to something; hell it did not take a detective to figure that one out, but Tia was something else, his gut told him CIA, FBI or some other three-letter agency, but what was not clear was why she was here!

He would wait till after dinner then take her back to his room. It was question time, and she may loosen up, knowing the cavalry was next door, just in case. He looked at his watch, the luminous hands of his Tag Heuer watch told him it was nearly Ten Thirty, not really late but late enough to be sitting around, listening to the same conversation.

TWELVE

As the evening sun began to set upon the New York City skyline, the fiery orange glow reflected in the labyrinth of glass, stone and steel. The populace rushed about at their usual pace as most headed home after a long, productive day, while others made their way to meet friends at restaurants or one of the many watering holes.

The city was alive as it always was, regardless of the time of day, it truly was *The city that never sleeps*.

McCall sat at her desk and stared at the murder board, its shiny white surface masked by photographs and writings in several different coloured markers. She stared hard as if it would reveal something the more she looked, but the more she looked, the more it made no sense. The murder of Donald Major made no sense; McCall stood up and walked about, her hands cupping the back of her neck as it tilted back in frustration. McCall knew she was missing something, but she feared it was something she had not yet found.

McCall turned to see Tony and Tooms return from their venture down at the docks; they were not smiling, but then they did not look mad either. That meant they had found something, and it was not good. Tony headed for the coffee room while Tooms headed for his desk; Tooms slammed down in his chair and leant back, stretching off. McCall walked over slowly but caught his eye as she travelled to him; she smiled sympathetically but did not really know why. It was more a gut reaction to his look.

"Bad day?" He raised an eyebrow at her question, "Worse, our jumper didn't jump, he fell." McCall stood there for a moment with a puzzled look on her tired face.

"He fell?" she sat down on the edge of Tony's desk just as he came through holding two cups of coffee "Yeh, CSU did a reconstruction using computers and found that, if he had jumped, the body would have been further away, but the computers say he fell, so he fell." He announced, as he handed Tooms one of the cups.

McCall drifted off in thought, her face blank, as if she were in another place entirely.

"What you thinkin' McCall?" Tooms knew that look well; it was the look that meant long hours and apologetic dinners for his wife. McCall stood up and walked to her desk again, her heels tapping on the floor as she walked with purpose. True, Tooms had struck out on the weasel-faced loan shark, he was busy collecting from someone on the other side of town, and pushing a guy off a crane, to make it look like an accident, does not really send out a message to discourage others. No, this was someone who wanted him out of the way. She looked through the notes on the *ACCIDENTAL DEATH* of Donald Major as the Officer had quickly put in the report. McCall threw the file onto the desk, reached for her coffee cup and placed it to her lips. She stopped as she saw the stained white bottom of the empty cup; slightly annoyed, McCall stood up and headed for the coffee room, her taste buds still yearning for that last drop of coffee she thought was in the bottom of the cup.

As she filled the cup, she looked over at the clock above the elevator; the black hands against the white backdrop told her it was nearly seven. Tomorrow was another day, and they couldn't really do anything till morning anyway. It was time to go. Tomorrow she would go and see the owner of the store and Thompson would have to get her feet wet. Everyone had a case and she would have to pick up the Karen Greene mugging. However, tonight, she needed to be somewhere else.

McCall walked into the crowded Italian Restaurant. She wore a black dress that hugged her curves but was loose enough if she had to run after someone. She was wearing make-up and her hair was styled and held fast by a can of hair spray. As she entered, she looked around as if looking for someone and met the gaze of a short grey-haired man, standing at a dark wooden podium. He smiled at greeted her with open arms.

"Samantha, so good to see you again," his face soured slightly. "why don't you come over anymore, huh?" he laughed, and they embraced once more. "Sorry, Sal, Things have been kind of…" he raised his hand.

"You don't need to apologise for nothing, so how's your mom?" Sal led her to a nice table away from the bustle and pulled the chair out for her.

"You still drinking that cheap red stuff?" McCall shot him an innocent look, and he just laughed and walked off, jokingly cursing in Italian.

McCall looked nervously at her watch; it seemed like an age since the last time she was on a date, any date. She patted her sweaty hands with her cotton napkin. Sure, she was slightly panicked; this was a blind date which Tina had set up with one of her Doctor buddies. Why should she be nervous?

A young waiter brought over a bottle of wine and presented it to McCall as if to ask if it was correct, she just smiled politely and pulled over her glass; all McCall new about wine was that it had grapes in it – and it either tasted good or not, the end. The waiter filled her glass and retired to the back, after leaving her with a menu. She checked her watch again, it was eight o'clock, and she was early.

After around ten minutes the waiter returned, he smiled the usual smile that most of the high-end restaurants require.

"Would madam wish to order?" McCall had finished all of the breadsticks while she waited.

"Actually, I am waiting for someone," her smile was filled with hope that there would be someone and she would not leave alone. The waiter smiled this time with a feeling of understanding. As he headed back to the bar, she checked out his tight behind and thought bad thoughts. One way or another, she was leaving with someone.

McCall looked at the half-empty bottle and sighed; she could not believe she was being stood up. She had stopped looking at her watch around ten minutes before so not to look desperate. As she picked up the glass to down the rest of the contents, she heard a deep, gravelly voice. She looked up hoping he was worth the wait. Her eyes crept up his form until she reached his broad shoulders that displayed what must have been and five-hundred-dollar suit; He was tall – at least six four and was healthily tanned. The man displayed a square jaw and dashing good looks. His shoulder length hair was a mousy colour with a left side parting; she gazed into his dark brown eyes and just melted.

"I am David, David Haynes and I hope you are Samantha, or this is going to be really embarrassing?" McCall stood up and shook his large masculine hand. "Sorry I am late we had an emergency and Tina never gave me your number." McCall just giggled like a schoolgirl with a crush and filled his glass to cover up the half-drunk bottle. They talked for what seemed hours, she learnt he was a doctor at the county hospital in the E.R, and he did volunteer work with the services overseas.

She felt guilty about the instant attraction but then Steel never really showed any interest, she did not know why, but then that guy had so many issues, a shrink would not know where to start.

As he sat down, the waiter came over with some menus and a new bottle of wine. The soft music and candlelight set the mood. They both ordered small portioned meals, more in hope of how the evening would end, rather than politeness. Nobody wants to have passionate sex on a full stomach. The conversations were about anything but work – an agreement that had been set earlier. She didn't want to think about work, and he didn't want to seem as if he was showing off. The air was tingling with emotion as they looked into each other's eyes, and to them, no one else was in the room.

"Shall we?" he asked, standing up and moving to assist with her chair. As McCall stood, she felt him behind her as he offered her coat. McCall slipped her arms into the sleeves of the coat and he brought it forwards and slipped it over her shoulders. Now she could smell him, the intense mix of aftershave, deodorant and male pheromones almost brought her to her knees, *god he smelt so good* she thought.

The night air was warm even though it was a cloudless sky. A billion stars shone brightly and, here and there, a shooting star sped past, leaving just a slither of a tail. They walked through the quiet streets with nothing but the sounds of the city to keep them company, not really paying attention where they were heading. Their conversation full of laughter as though they had known one another forever, she had felt the spark between them, and she hoped that he felt it as well.

McCall stopped outside a building realizing it was her apartment block, still not knowing how they had gotten there after walking for what seemed a pleasantly long time, and they walked up the steps to her buildings front entrance. Then came the awkward moment, the intense moment when neither wants to make the first move in case it was the wrong one.

"Well, this is me," McCall laughed the words, all the time picturing him tearing her clothes off.

"Right – nice place," his words were small talk to try and figure out what to do next, his arms waving back and forth in an uneasy rhythm.

"Would you like to come up for a coffee or something?" McCall asked. He backed off slightly with a shocked look on his face.

"Look, I had a really great time and everything, but I think we are moving a little fast, after all we have only just met." McCall shot him a disappointed look.

"David, if I wanted that I would have said do you want to come up for sex not coffee," she tried to sound insulted, but she was more angry that he had just burst the bubble. He smiled and went a nice shade of red; she slapped him on the arm and opened the wood and glass door.

Inside, he walked round, checking out the many photographs on the walls and the box shelving next to the large window, McCall was busy in the kitchen preparing the coffee machine and placing a couple of cups on the counter.

"Cool place you got here," he shouted over the sound of the machine as it began its loud metallic howl, McCall's head appeared round the doorframe.

"Sorry, what did you say?"

"Cool place you got here," he repeated the compliment; she just smiled at him and beckoned him to take a seat on the couch.

Moments later, McCall brought in a small tray with the two cups of coffee, with it a small jug of milk and a small porcelain bowl full of sugar.

"I didn't know how you took it, so I brought everything," she said, with an awkward smile. He smiled and took the tray from her as she sat down. She thanked him and smiled; she had lied that she had brought him up here not for coffee but to have a mad night of passion. They sat next to one another but with a comfortable space between them, McCall leant forwards to finish making his drink.

"So how do you like it…. your coffee I mean," she suddenly corrected herself with a giggle. She turned towards him and her smile turned into a lustful look as their eyes met.

"Damn it, I want you." His words were as if a weight had been lifted from her soul.

"Thank god for that," McCall flung herself towards him, their lips met and they kissed as if they only had a moment. McCall pushed him down flat on the couch and slipped her black dress over her head. David smiled with satisfaction as he looked at McCall's tight body, her ample breasts held by the black lace bra.

She leant down, and they kissed again but this time she was playful and teased his lips with her tongue while her fingers unbuttoned his shirt slowly. She moved down his chest, kissing the bare muscular flesh as she went. David's eyes rolled back as he ran his fingers through her hair. As she reached his belt she stood up, a grin, like that of the Cheshire cat came over her face as she made her way to the bedroom. Tonight, would be a night to remember, she would make damned sure of that. David sat up, mesmerized by her sexy, athletic form; how she moved purposely, all she had on was her stockings and the little black thong. McCall reached the bedroom door and stopped halfway in, just so that her back and her sexy tight ass showed, she looked back at him with bedroom eyes and purred.

"So, you are coming in or would you rather have coffee?" With that she disappeared into the room. David scrambled off the couch, tripping as he went, attempting to take off his trousers on the move.

On entering her dimly lit bedroom, he found her lying on the bed with her head resting on her angled arm, he stood there for a moment, taking in her hourglass form. As he moved on to the bed they embraced in a passionate tumble, their breathing heavy in the heat of the moment, McCall threw him onto his back and started to kiss her way down his body. Her tongue following the contours of his muscles, he gasped as she bit gently into his erect nipples and flicked them with her tongue.

She moved down slowly, and then reaching his shorts removed them, dragging them inch by inch still kissing his bear flesh as she went.

"Well, no need to ask how you like this," she said with a pleasurable grin. As she climbed up his body like a stalking cat, McCall straddled him and felt his pleasure.

Their bodies became sweaty with passion and entwined in the heat of each other, as they grew closer to the inevitable climatic end, they both cried out together, holding each other close until collapsing onto the messed-up sheets of her bed. McCall just lay on her back and looked up at the ceiling, which at first seemed to be spinning. She was panting as if she had just run a marathon, beads of fresh sweat cascading down her tight skin.

McCall had no idea where that had come from but she did know she felt good, alive. She had no idea if this was the start of something, but whatever was to happen later would happen later, for now she had just enjoyed great sex and for the now, that was enough.

THIRTEEN

The Neptune cut through the water calmly and steadily, the massive ship's deck lights could be seen for miles across the great expansion as this floating city cast a glow on to the horizon.

Steel sat with the other guests listening to one of the captain's tales of when he was a merchant shipman off the coast of Africa and how pirates had boarded, looking for goods. Steel had to admit his tales were gripping but felt that was all they were, but then it didn't matter, he was a good host and entertainer.

Tia May looked up as she saw a grim-faced man in a white officer's uniform head directly to the captain's chair. Steel also looked up as the man crouched down with his back to the guests to whisper something to the captain. As the officer spoke, the captain shot bolt upright and went pale, his look was of horror and concern. Captain Long stood up and wiped his dry lips with the napkin.

"I am sorry ladies and gentlemen; something has come up that requires my attention. If you would excuse me, but there is no need for alarm, it's just a routine thing." Steel saw through his charade, it was obvious he was lying, but about what. He waited until the captain was a fair distance away before he stood up and made some excuse about needing the rest room.

Steel knew he had to move quickly and without being seen, both of which he had mastered over the years. He followed them from deck to deck, but he noticed that neither one spoke during the fast walk to the elevators. As the two men reached the glass elevators Steel stopped at the corner next to a large potted mini palm, but he was close enough to see they had pressed for deck four. He thought for a moment and realized they were going for the engine room.

Down in crew's area, the maze of white walls gave home to sleeping quarters, crew restaurants, and storage areas for heavy cargo and food items. At the end the engine room, Steel could hear the pounding heartbeat of the colossal machine driving the city through the watery depths. Sticking to the corners, Steel saw the men enter the engine room as the heavy iron door opened the noise became deafening. He used the noise to cover his footsteps as he ran forward to small storage room full of mops and other cleaning utilities. He knew he had no chance of hearing a conversation through the heavy door, but he hoped, due to the loud hammering, all their talking would be outside of the engine room.

Moments later, the door swung open and four men carrying what appeared to be a tarpaulin with something heavy within it. Soon after, the captain and two other officers came out, all holding their mouths as if trying desperately not to be sick.

"Make sure that the body goes to cold storage, the coroner can take a look when we get to the next port." the men nodded to the captain's order and shuffled off.

"What the hell happened, Jarvis?" Yelled the captain as an engineer slammed the compartment door shut and engaged the holding bolt. A tall well-built man in his mid-thirties shook his head.

"Don't really know sir, one of the men found him whilst doing a routine inspection, the lad had somehow fallen from the top area whilst carrying some cabling, it must have gotten snagged and as he fell, he was hung." The captain shook his head in disbelief at the tragedy.

"Such a waste of a young life, funny I only saw him this

morning when he brought me…." he stopped, realizing he was thinking aloud.

"He brought you what sir?" The Captain raised an awkward hand.

"It was nothing, now, we say nothing to the passengers, ok? God knows the press would have a field day with this, agreed?" The other men nodded.

As the men left to return to their duties, Steel came from the darkened room, he had heard everything. Looking that the way was clear, he headed for cold storage; he had to see the body of the poor crewman.

A cloud of cold mist filled the preparation room as they opened the large steel door of the cooler. Grasping the latch handle, one of the men pulled at the freezer door, there was a sucking noise as the rubber seals released the vacuum and the door swung open. "Jeez," exclaimed one of the engineers who had opened the door, he felt the cold bite his skin, making him back away with his arm raised to shield his face. Inside, large halves of pork and beef swung freely as they edged past, carrying their shipmate.

"I tell you one thing, Joe; I am never eating meat on this tub again." The small stocky engineer held the feet end of the tarp with tall thin engineer. As they backed in, they found a suitable place in the corner, away from prying eyes, or the meat. As the four men placed their colleague onto the cold floor, they removed their caps and left.

"Right you lot, come on we still have work to do." The last man closed the door to the large walk-in freezer and replaced his cap. Slowly the door to the preparation room opened and Steel walked in, he had managed to procure a chef's white coat and hat. He knew he had no chance of knocking out the surveillance cameras without suspicion, so disguise was the next best thing. Casually, he entered the freezer and made his way to the back. He figured the men wouldn't want their colleague anywhere near the meat, so the back seemed the perfect place. Steel found the remains of Walter, still a sickening, twisted stare on his face. Steel opened up the tarp to check the body. He started at the neck, sure enough the deep marks round his neck showed he must have been there for some time or was he assisted by a great weight? Moving down Steel checked his pockets and uniform. Disappointed to have found nothing, he began to wrap poor Walter back up. That's when he saw them. Six parallel marks like small burns on his left arm. Steel stopped and looked closer, the marks were in pairs around two centimetres apart, but each pair held no pattern, more randomly placed. "A taser" Steel thought out loud. He had seen such marks before, but not so many in one spot. It was if the boy had been tortured. Steel rewrapped the body and left, things were starting to get interesting, Steel knew then that this was the right ship but he had a bad feeling, what was about to start?

Tia May had waited for what seemed ages at the dining table. She found it curious that no one paid any heed that neither the captain nor Mr Black and returned. Tia stood up and said her good nights, everyone smiled and returned the false pleasantries, she was glad to be away from the table. Their self-gratifying talk had made her feel ill. As she made her way to her room, she could not help but feel she was being watched. First she thought it was the knock-out dress she was wearing, but the faces on the men didn't seem to send out the usual signals. Quickly, she used the key card on the room door, a red LED flashed; she tried it a second time, again the red LED flashed. Tia looked down the long corridor to see a large man standing with his arms crossed, waiting. She tried it again, again the red LED flashed at her.

"Come on you stupid thing, open," Tia looked round to see the man approaching. Tia took out the card and wiped it on her dress then slowly pushed it in. Green light and a click brought a smile to her face; she looked round to see that the man had vanished. Tia shook it off as just being her imagination.

On entering her room, she stopped, it was dark, why the hell was it dark? The last slither of light faded as the door shut behind her. She turned to run, but someone grabbed her and threw her hard. Tia landed on something soft which she could only imagine to be the bed, a cool breeze tickled her face and she knew whomever it was had come through the balcony window.

"Who do you work for?" Growled a voice; it was a man's voice, deep and rough, probably from too many cigars and whiskeys. From the accent she made him out as a Scotsman. Tia struggled, hoping to get a punch or a kick into her attacker, then she felt something long and cold on her skin, it was a blade. Long, thick and sharp.

"Now if you don't settle down, I am going to have to make this slow and bloody." She froze. He repeated the question after slapping her across the face hard.

"I work for the New York Gallery," she spat blood with every word.

"Don't lie to me woman, who do you work for and what are you looking for?" he growled, his breath stank of unbrushed teeth and whiskey. Tia went to speak but felt her legs been parted and felt him between her legs, her face cringed at the thought of this monster anywhere near her. She felt his whisky sodden breath on her face as he grew near to her.

"I will only ask you one more time and then if I don't get my answer, I will ride you like the lying whore that you are." Then she felt his fat wet tongue lick the side of her face. She wanted to scream but she knew it would be no good. Tia knew it didn't matter what answer she gave, he was still going to do what he set out to do anyway. She opened her mouth to scream only to have a cloth shoved into it.

"Now, now sweetie, let's not spoil the fun shall we?" Tia was terrified and also puzzled, how the hell could he see?

A tear rolled down her face as she felt him undoing his belt.

"I am going to enjoy this," his voice growled with pleasure and anticipation of what he was going to do. Tia held her breath and waited for the inevitable.

"The thing about night vision goggles is that they react really quite badly to light, for instance," said a familiar voice. Suddenly, the room lights came on causing the attacker to scream and rip the device from his face. Dazed and confused, the attacker stumbled around. blind from the light shock. Tia shot up from the bed and landed a direct kick into the man's balls.

"Bastard," she screamed as the man dropped to his knees holding his damaged goods. Tia grabbed the small stool from the dresser and was about to put it across the attacker's head when Steel grabbed it and pulled her away from him. "Tia, go to the bathroom and cool off, we want him alive so we can figure out what's going on," he gestured for her to go. Steel turned as the man rose from the floor, the thick blade in his hand and a grin to match. The assassin was an average sized man with a shaven head and covered with tattoos. His face was square with thick lips and badly grown teeth. On his long chin, he had a deep ginger goatee. His nose was fat and crooked from too many fights.

"I am going to cut you up, but I won't kill you till after you have watched me pleasure the girl," the assassin grinned. Steel didn't have time for the games he just wanted answers. The man lunged forwards swinging the blade, hoping to catch Steel, but Steel was too fast and just leapt backwards then bringing down a smashing blow to the man's face. The assassin stepped backwards, sensing this was no average guy, he reached into his Army style jacket and pulled out a taser.

"Now then pretty boy, let's see how you dance shall we?" blood streamed from the man's nose. The assassin was crouching slightly, finding his balance for the next strike, his blade held tightly in a vice like grip, the knuckles on his large hands white. The assassin span, the blade slicing the air almost nicking Steel's midsection as it went but Steel had stepped backwards, pre-empting the attack. As Steel came back, he placed a well-aimed kick to the man's right knee causing him to buckle.

Steel watched and assessed what the man may do next. Rising from the floor he stared at Steel and smiled.

"Funny, no one has ever given me this much trouble before, be a shame to end it but orders are orders I suppose." Just as Steel predicted, the assassin lunged with the taser, hoping to catch a body part to immobilize Steel. He grabbed Tia's leather jacket from a coat rack, and tossed it over the taser arm, then spun with his back to the assailant as the man rushed in, Steel grabbed the man's wrist of the outstretched blade arm and with a quick twist, broke it. There was a loud, sickly snap, like a branch breaking, and the blade fell to the ground. In the same motion, Steel brought his head back, smashing the man in the face. There was a muffled cry as the assassin stumbled backwards and fell over the bed. Steel quickly turned, ready for what may come.

"Ok, who do you work for and what do you want?" Steel asked. The assassin struggled to get to his feet. Blood flowed freely from his mouth and nose. Steel repeated his question, his eyes fixed firmly on the broken man who just smiled, raised his middle finger of his left, and then jumped off the balcony in to the night. They both stood and stared at the open balcony door.

"Well," Steel said with surprise, walking over to the balcony door and closing it. As he did so he noticed bloody print on the door. Steel took out his cell and photographed it.

"Well – Mr Black, what do you mean, well? Well, how did that maniac get into my room, or well how the hell did you get into my room?" Steel smiled as he sat on the bed wondering how long this was going to take. "Or maybe, well, how did you learn to fight like that?" Steel got up and kissed her to shut her up, he felt her melt in his arms as he pulled her close, they drew away slowly still looking in one another's eyes.

"Actually, what I was going to say was, well I could do with a drink, coming?" Steel brushed himself off and headed for the door. "See you in the Irish bar in ten minutes?" he smiled as though nothing had happened. Tia stood watching him leave, her mouth open stunned at his coolness or coldness. Who was this man who had just fought an assassin, watched the guy jump out of the window and walk out like it was a normal day? She did not know whether to be impressed or scared.

In the elevator Steel sent a text to Tooms, it had the picture of the print and a brief explanation, he knew if he sent it to McCall, she may take her time opening it or just delete it without opening it just at the sight of his name on the caller ID. Things were definitely heating up and one way or another he was now a part of something. This was the right ship and he had to stop whatever was going to happen.

The hour was late, so by the time Steel had arrived at the Irish bar, most of the customers had left. Only a few hangers-on remained, nestled in corners, perched on bar stools holding on to glasses and bottles that they had clearly had clearly been cradling for some time. The air was full of the smell of stale beer and body odour. Years before, places like this would have been filled with cigarette smoke and loud music from live bands of a 70's style jukebox but times changed, some for the better others not.

Steel found a booth in a far corner, his back was to the far wall, next to him the large window, which was mostly covered by the bar's logo, was great to look out of without been seen yourself from the passers-by. From where he was sitting, Steel's seating position had both a perfect view of the entrance and he could remain unseen if he needed to. In the background, Irish music played softly from the overhead speakers mounted in the corners, a soft but sporty ditty. The sort of tune that stuck in your head and made you tap your feet without you realizing it.

As he watched people come and go, a waitress came over. She was tall and pretty. Her long copper-coloured hair was held tight in a ponytail, her eyes a piercing blue. She smiled and as she spoke, the illusion broke, her voice was high pitched, and toneless, Steel ordered a double Johnnie Walker Gold and watched her head back to the bar. With her figure she could have been a model but only for men's magazines. Steel shook his head in disbelief and grinned.

He looked up at the door to see Grant rush in looking all exited, his head darting all over, obviously looking for Steel or someone. Grant had a look of relief on his face as he saw Steel sitting in the corner booth; he rushed over and slid onto the cushioned seat opposite Steel.

"Good evening Mr Grant, to what do I owe this pleasure?"

Grant looked up at the waitress as she brought Steel his drink, she looked over at Grant and the smile dulled a little.

"Hi, what can I get you?"

Grant looked at Steel's glass, pointed to it. "I'll have the same please."

She smiled, and both men watched her walk away, swaying her hips as she went. "Wow," Grant kept his gaze on the pretty blonde while Steel waited patiently for him snap out of it and say why he was there.

"Grant – Grant," Steel tapped his glass on the table, bringing him back from his fantasy.

"What…oh yeh" Grant smiled sinisterly and leaned in. "I heard a whisper there was some trouble last night down in the engine room," Grant nodded and sat back as the waitress brought his drink. The waitress set down the drink in front of Grant, but her gaze was fully on Steel.

"Thank you," Grant's voice was just below a shout but slightly louder than normal.

"You're welcome." She turned and walked away; her hips moved like some kind of mating dance.

"What is it with you and women anyway?" Steel leant back and cracked a smile from the side of his mouth, he smiled, not because of what Grant had just said, but memories of Darius came flooding back.

"So, going back, you mentioned some trouble downstairs?" Steel said before raising his glass to Grant, so they could clink. Grant leant in again after looking round to make sure they were not being heard.

"It seems that some poor bastard fell off the upper gantry and hung himself." Grants eyes danced with excitement at the story. Steel wondered what he might do if he had learnt that the poor kid had been tortured first, and the hanging was just a cover up.

"Accidents do happen," Steel said almost coldly, as he took a sip from the whiskey, the strong aroma of the malt tickled his nose and the liquid had a pleasant warmth as he held it in his mouth before letting slowly flow down his throat. As he placed it down onto the table, he spun the glass slowly between his fingers.

"I don't believe it was an accident," Steel looked up at Grant moving just his eyes.

"Word is that the engineer went to see the captain that day to deliver something. And nobody in the lower decks saw him again after that," Grant sat back and took a large mouthful of the golden liquid; his eyes bulged at the burning sensation in his mouth.

"If you're going to spit it make sure it's in the glass will you, thanks," Steel smiled as Grant refilled the glass and pushed it away from him.

"So apart from you don't like whiskey what else have you learnt?" Steel waved the waitress over who, after seeing the display, knew water was in order. She placed the glass of still water in front of Grant and took away the refilled glass.

"Any ideas what it was he was bringing to the captain that day?" Steel asked, coolly. Grant shook his head as he drank.

"No, not a clue. But he was seen coming back through the decks he just didn't reach the upper decks." Grant said. Suddenly, he could see something was on Steel's mind.

"Mr Grant…. Jonathan, if I were to ask you to stop investigating this and let me handle it, would you?" Steel felt foolish asking, as he already knew what the answer would be, but he had to try. Grant looked at Steel suspiciously for a second.

"Why?" Grant's words were slow and cautious, almost afraid he had confided in the wrong person. "Why, what's happened?" Grant asked again. Steel's facial features didn't move. It was a deadly poker face, but Grant read this more as concern, for what? He didn't know.

"Jonathan, all I can surmise at the moment is that if you continue with this, you may come to some harm." Steel said, his tone was more of concern than threat. Grant thought for a moment, he could read something in Steel's words. He could tell Steel knew more, probably a lot more than he did, but his concern was with his well-being.

"I am afraid I can't do that Mr Black, I know there is a story here and I am going to find it with or without you," Grant's words brought a smile to Steel's stony face, Steel nodded in obvious admiration for Grant's decision – even if it was a foolish one. The fact was, Steel knew he would have done the exact same thing if the rolls had been reversed.

"Very well, we are to make port in Vigo Spain tomorrow. We need to know if anything or anyone new comes aboard," Steel said. Grant looked at Steel as he sat back in the seat of the booth. The fake leather creaked under the movement.

"So, what are you not sharing Mr Black?" Grant asked, with a suspicious look on his face. Steel smiled and took a sip from his drink.

"Jonathan, when I find out what is going on, I promise to sit down and tell you the whole damn story. But for now, I think it's better if only I know what I know," Steel looked over to the elevators and saw Tia step out into the almost empty promenade. "But right now, I would like you to leave if you would," Grant's face became filled with suspicion and contempt.

"Why, you got a meeting with someone special?" Grant leant back almost in an effort to signal defiance in being asked to go.

"Well, after last night I hope I am someone special." Grant looked up in surprise to find Tia May standing next to him, his mouth fell open at the sight of her tight Jeans and baggy T-shirt. She looked stunning, and she could feel all the eyes in the bar were on her, and she loved it.

"May I?" Her voice soft and gentle, leaving Grant with an open mouth and drifting thoughts. Steel put down his drink slightly heavier than normal, waking Grant from his daydream.

"What, oh, wow, uhm, sorry," Grant got up from the booth and allowed Tia to sit. His face glowed from embarrassment.

"How did you...?" Grant asked, completely gobsmacked by the whole affair.

"Oh, I just helped her take some garbage out once, that's all," Tia smiled as she watched Grant disappear, shaking his head.

FOURTEEN

The next morning, as the sun cast a pleasing burnt orange glow across the city skyline, McCall made her way to the electrical company where Donald Major had worked. The multi-story building's white walls were turned a fiery orange as they caught the new day's sun. The structure had a newness about it, large glass windows housed in large concrete plate walls encased by walls of small bushes and silver birches. McCall pulled up to the main gate where a security guard came out of a small booth. The guard walked up to her as she wound down the window to her faded blue '66 Mustang.

"Hi, can I help you miss?" He was a jolly, large built, black guy with gold-rimmed eyeglasses. McCall raised her badge.

"I am here to see Mr Brown, the CEO." She said, showing her ID. The guard smiled widely.

"Go straight in," He raised a large, thick arm and pointed to a parking lot to the left of the main building. "You can leave your vehicle there at the main building, you can't miss the entrance." McCall thanked him and drove up, slowing down for the precession of speed bumps on the way.

The parking lot was large and sectioned off alphabetically. Small signs stood at the entrances, each a different colour with a letter. As McCall drove past the mass of vehicles, she noted that this was to make easy for the thousand workers and the odd visitor. McCall found a shady spot underneath a small ash tree in one of the middle sections of the lot where only a few vehicles stood. She looked over at the sign and made a note of the sign, Blue *F*.

McCall entered through an automatic turnstile door. Inside, the entrance was large and bright with white marble tiled floor. Straight in front, embedded in the back wall, were three elevator doors, their polished surfaces reflecting the morning sun.

There was a long white marble reception desk to the far right and to the left a polished metal staircase curved its way down from the first-floor balcony. McCall approached the front desk and a tall woman who was sitting behind it, her heels making an echoing *tap, tap, tap* as she made her way across the stone tiled floor. The receptionist's black hair was tied up at the back in a chignon style, showing off her slightly pale skin. Hugging her form, she wore a black suit and a black tie with the company logo, which stood out above her white blouse. The woman, who appeared to be in her late twenties, saw McCall as she approached, her red-lipsticked mouth broke into a smile, showing sparkling white teeth. McCall looked around at the other women dressed in the same uniform who casually wandered around, they were all stunning, even from McCall's point of view which made her wonder if that was a publicity trick to get more clientele to visit? McCall smiled, feeling she was in a Robert Palmer video.

"Hi, welcome to The Tyler Corporation. How can I help you?" The woman's voice soft, sultry, and McCall thanked God that the other two were not there with her, she could just imagine their goofy faces, as they would have entered the reception, laughing and acting like a bunch of school kids. McCall lifted her badge that was hooked neatly on to the A4 leather bound conference folder.

"Yes, I am Detective McCall from Homicide. I would like to speak to Mr Brown," McCall said with a business smile. The woman raised an eyebrow and McCall could tell that this was going to be the most interesting day that the young woman had known in the place. The young woman picked up the chromed receiver on the cordless phone and pressed a button on the touch screen; McCall could hear it ring a couple of times before another woman answered. Smiling, the receptionist informed the colleague on the other end of the situation. After a couple of mumbled replies, the woman placed down the receiver and turned to McCall. "Ok, Detective if you take the centre elevator to the third floor, from there, turn left and then follow it to the end of the corridor. At reception, you will find Dawn, she is Mr Brown's PA." McCall thanked her and set off for the elevator.

THE THIRD FLOOR was full of offices behind long glass walls with rainfall effect etched into the thick pains. Dark wood accents covered the ceiling with small square lights that reflected on the sand-coloured stone floor. At the bottom of a long corridor of glass walls were two large glass doors with the building's logo etched into them, a large wooden desk had been placed neatly on a red-carpeted floor with a perfect view down to the elevators. Using the polished brass handle, McCall pushed one of the doors open and approached the woman behind the desk. The PA sat behind the perfectly organised desk; she was older than the others - somewhere in her late forties, McCall thought.

She wore a beige suit with a high collar and her dark brown hair placed into a bun at the back away from her slightly tanned skin. She looked up and glanced at McCall through her black-rimmed eyeglasses as the detective approached but carried on with her conversation on her phone. McCall noted that the PA was arranging a two o'clock meeting with someone named *Jonathan Hendricks*. The woman's fingers breezed across the keys on the keyboard while she spoke into the blue-tooth headset. McCall paced the waiting area to the left of the wooden desk, four black leather armchairs fanned around a thick, glassed-topped coffee table, behind them a large window with a breath-taking view of greenery.

"Sorry to keep you waiting, last minute business meeting for

Mr Brown," said the PA. McCall turned and walked towards the desk and the PA who held a smile, which seemed more polite than friendly. "You must be Detective McCall?" McCall showed her badge to confirm the woman's suspicion. Not that McCall needed too – she just wanted to.

"Yes, we spoke earlier; I am here to speak with Mr Brown," McCall could see the look on the woman's face was one of intrigue, something was up, and she wanted to know. McCall could just see the gossip flying round the canteen, something new in their enclosed, controlled lives.

"Can I ask what it is in reference to?" The woman asked, a small sinister smile cracked at the side of her mouth. McCall smiled inside, she knew this woman's type, facts or not, the story would be blown completely out of proportion until one greedy sap goes and sells some bull to the tabloids. No, she would keep this between herself and Brown, later he could calm the waters with the staff. She was here to solve a murder, not start some sort of squash chitchat.

"Sorry, that's between Mr Brown and the department, but feel free to listen in on the intercom which is what I know you'll do the moment I'm in there," McCall said with a grin. The woman shot a shocked look at McCall and pressed an intercom button on the desk.

"Sir, the – the detective is here to see you," she said, stumbling over her words from what McCall had said, was she that obvious? There was a brief moment of silence.

"Ok, could you send him in," McCall raised an eye-brow and pointed at the two large wooden doors to the left of the desk. The PA nodded and smiled, wishing she could see his face when McCall entered, watching his mouth drop open with embarrassment.

The office of William Brown was completely different from the rest of the building. It had the feel of a stately home to it, lots of oak furnishings and brown leather chesterfield armchairs. Waxed wooden floorboards were hidden underneath a large Persian rug. Red velvet wallpaper complemented the fine arts hung on the large surrounding walls. Even the windows with their high arches, were a scene from a country manor. In the middle of the room there was a large Victorian oak desk. Behind it, Brown sat in a high-backed red leather chesterfield office chair, but this faced the windows.

"So, what can I do for the NYPD?" The man's voice boomed but with no effect, McCall got the impression this man – this Mr Brown - was trying to seem intimidating; this was a man with a lot of power, and he loved to show it.

"Well, Mr Brown you can start by dropping the Bond villain act and turn your ass around and face me." His chair turned around swiftly, showing a startled little man, his eyebrow glistened with sweat, his tiny blue eyes wide with shock. McCall hated to admit she had enjoyed watching the man crumble. But she could tell this man worked on fear, but how could anyone fear him?

"I am Detective Samantha McCall and I am here investigating the death of Donald Major," McCall said, in a stern voice. William Brown nodded with a look of remorse.

"Yes, poor man, when we heard we were shocked, truly shocked," He stood up and walked round his desk to a Victorian drinks cabinet, the man was all of five foot six but held a good posture, his back straight and shoulders rammed backwards as if to make himself larger. "Can I offer you anything Detective? Water, coffee?" McCall shook her head and sat in one of the chairs in front of the desk, the creek of old leather and the unmistakable waft of aging and body soap filled her senses. He watched her sit. McCall was quietly, waiting for him to finish getting himself a drink then return to his chair. She could see he had become uneasy and that for her was a good sign. She didn't have time to go through any of the usual runaround, she just wanted the facts and them she would be out of his hair.

As William Brown sat down, McCall flicked open her notebook and switched on the small Dictaphone, his eyes watched her as she prepared for the interview.

"So, Mr Brown, how long had Mr Major been working for

you?" William Brown sat back in his chair and looked up at the ceiling, as though looking through a file in his head.

"Oh, around fifteen years now," His mouth fell open at the realization of how long it had been. "My god, fifteen years, I never realized until now." McCall noted it down.

"And what exactly did he do here?" McCall asked. William Brown smiled, but this was a fond, even proud smile.

"He was one of our best electricians. Now I am not talking fixing plugs and TV's, no, this guy was a genius at installation. He did all of our high-end things, surveillance equipment for homes, banks, even military establishments," Brown explained. McCall looked up, her mind picking up the key words, like military.

"He was a good worker, a good man, everyone liked him. Hell, even contractors asked for him by name, he brought in the business because everyone wanted him," Brown saw her eyes widen at the thought of a jealous colleague. "Now, Detective, I know what you're thinking, some of the others did something because of the work competition, but that would never happen, if Donald went on a job, he would get one of the others who didn't have a job at that time to help him out, just so the guy had some pay. Like I said, he was a good man." Brown's voice trembled slightly, McCall wasn't sure whether it was because his best worker had died or a good man had?

"Was he working on anything …special before he was killed?" Brown leant over to his computer and typed in Donald Major; a small icon spun round to signal the search. The screen opened into a calendar screen, showing all the workers and what they have and had been working on that year. Brown leant closer to the monitor and adjusted his glasses.

"Well for the past three months he had been working on a special project for some company, I would have to get someone to get the file for you if that helps," McCall nodded and genuinely smiled.

"That would be great, was anyone helping on that one?" Brown looked at the screen again.

"Uh, no. Looks like he did that one alone which is odd for him." McCall stood up.

"Can I talk to some of his colleagues, maybe see his office?" Brown stood up and wiped his gold-rimmed eyeglasses with his handkerchief.

"Yes of course, you'll find most of them out on jobs and the others in their offices. But he didn't have an office here he had a workshop somewhere downtown." Brown said with a crooked smile and a shrug. McCall thanked him and headed for the wooden doors, she stopped and turned.

"You said that was his last job," Brown nodded, a confused look came over his face.

"Yes, why?" Brown asked, confused. McCall tucked away the Dictaphone and her pen.

"Because he was found in a 7-11 installing lighting and if that wasn't one of your jobs, then who was he working for?" She said, mostly to herself than to Brown.

The door clicked shut behind her and she headed for the elevator. As she walked past the PA's desk, McCall noticed the PA had been crying, her eyes red and a handful for tissues lay in the waste basket next to her desk. William Brown had been right, people had loved him, probably some more than others.

FIFTEEN

McCall made it back to the Station House. She had spent most of the morning talking to co-workers about Donald Major. He was well liked and respected that was obvious, but someone had wanted him gone. As she passed the desk sergeant, she shot him a wave and a smile, "Hi Sarge." The white haired sergeant yelled over the commotion in front of booking.

"Hey McCall, you got a message from Tina." McCall raced over to take the note, *Sam, have something, meet me at my office A.S.A.P.* McCall stopped and looked at her watch. It was nearly two o'clock.

"Ok, thanks Sarge." McCall said with a wink. He smiled and shook his head. His expression faded as the next perp was brought before him.

Sure, she had stuff to do but she could do with some Tina time. Her plan – get some coffees, possibly a bear claw, on route and recharge her batteries with idle chatter.

As McCall walked down the long sterile white corridors of the ME's office, her phone buzzed signalling incoming text messages. Pulling her cell from her jacket pocket, she saw that she had several; one was from Tooms the others, Tony and Jenny, all sending brief messages on what they had found. She put back the cell into her jacket as she entered Tina's office.

Music played in the background, but it drowned out the office phone, its ring sounded impatient in the small room. McCall looked around but found she was alone. Reaching for the receiver, she answered it. On the other end, Tooms sounded surprised to find McCall there.

"Hey McCall, what you doin' there?" his voice boomed over the speaker. She smiled

"What can't a girl visit a friend, Tina sent me a message to come over, why, what's up?" A sudden feeling something was wrong washed over McCall. She took her cell from her jacket and pressed the speed dial for Tina's cell phone. McCall could make out a distant ring tone, she recognized it, and it was Tina's cell. "Tooms, can you hold on for a second, I just got to check something," McCall put down the receiver and walked slowly out into the corridor, her cell resting in her left hand and her right shadowing the grip of her Glock. Edging down the brightly lit hallway, the tune stopped, McCall quickly redialled. At the far end was the cold storage room and as McCall looked up from her cell her heart rose into her throat. McCall ran quickly towards the sound as it grew nearer. Tina was in the cold storage and McCall feared the worst. As she struggled with the latch handle, McCall banged on the door hoping for a response. Looking down, McCall noticed the cell phone on the tiled floor. Fear ripped through McCall as she tried the latch handle again, the handle stayed solid. McCall looked down with tearful eyes and, through her blurred vision, she saw the securing pin imbedded into the securing hole. She ripped it out and yanked the door open. There on the ground lay Tina, her body covered in a light frost. McCall reached down and checked Tina's pulse in her neck. Slow shallow beats, she was alive.

Tooms sat with his feet resting upon his desk, the receiver crammed between a large shoulder and his unshaven cheek, while he started to make a paper plane. All was quiet, just the gentle background music playing in Tina's office. Tooms hummed along to the tune playing in the distance.

"Tooms get your ass here now we got a situation, and get

the paramedics as well, Tina's been hurt." Tooms nearly fell backwards with fright at the sudden outburst down the phone. Tony looked over at his partner who was panicked and sweating.

"What's up man?" His voice trembled, his mind thinking the unthinkable "We godda get to the ME's now, Tina's been attacked."

The radio DJ announced the next record; his voice seemed to echo through the quiet stillness of the ME's corridor. A silence that was suddenly broken as the tactical unit burst through the double swing doors separating the departments.

"Clear, clear," their voices seemed louder in the confined space of the rooms. As Captain Brant rushed through, a pair of medics overtook him, heading for McCall and the half-frozen Tina. McCall sat on the ground, her back against the closed freezer door cradling Tina, as she tried to keep her warm. The medics ran up to McCall and Tina; another group with a gurney followed not far behind.

"Are you ok, Detective?" asked one, as they lay Tina down to make an examination. McCall nodded.

"Yes, I am fine; she was the only one in there," McCall said, with a harsh look of concern and anger. McCall watched as they lifted Tina onto the gurney and wheeled her away.

"Don't worry, she'll be fine." Said a paramedic. McCall smiled; she knew that she would be. She was strong, and she could not help but feel that whoever put her in there didn't wish her harm. They just wanted her out of the way.

"McCall, you ok?" Captain Brant asked, as he knelt beside McCall after the medics had taken control of Tina.

"I am fine, just a little shaken up that's all," Brant stood up and offered McCall a hand. She used it and stood up; her legs felt heavy from the cold.

"Who would want to do such a thing?" Tony asked, as he rounded the corner from one of the rooms. McCall shrugged.

"It's a morgue not a bank, who knows, sick joke gone bad?" McCall didn't have any answers only questions. The tactical team had done a sweep and found nothing, now it was down to CSU.

As McCall walked past Tina's "Cutting room", her eyes glanced in. All seemed normal, except for the blue sheet that lay on the floor instead of covering the body that should have been on the table. McCall stopped and rushed in, leaving a confused captain.

"Hey, McCall, something wrong?" He followed her in and looked round. "What's wrong with this picture?" She asked angrily. Brant looked down at the green medical sheet that lay strewed on the floor.

"Who was meant to be here?" His voice was calm but ragging. Tony picked up the chart from the end of the table.

"It was our Jane Doe, but why would anyone want to take her?" Tooms put the chart back, his voice puzzled.

"How about the people that killed her?" Brant growled. "I want this place ripped apart. I want to know how they got in and out. McCall you go with Tina, find out what she remembers, take a tech with you for trace, let's hope these bastards left something." Everyone shot away to start the canvas, this wasn't just a break-in to them, this was personal, one of their own had been hurt and that meant everything else stopped; this was number one priority.

McCall paced the floor outside Tina's room at the hospital. She had not been allowed in, only the female tech from CSU was aloud entry. McCall was angry, not with the doctors. She knew enough not to argue when it came to things like this - cross contamination - and she knew she would have to give up her clothes as well, just in case. No, she was mad at the people who had done this. The door opened and the young CSU tech walked out, on seeing McCall she smiled.

"Tina's going to be fine, but I'll let the doc explain everything," McCall lifted three clear bags containing her clothes.

"Thought you may want these," McCall said with an angry look. The tech nodded and took them.

"Guess you've done this before?" McCall nodded as she looked at the closed door to Tina's room.

"Too many times, but never for a friend," McCall took a deep breath and entered the room.

As she walked in, she was met by a middle-aged doctor. He was tall and had that George Clooney look about him. His brown eyes sparkled with the reflection from the lights above.

"How is she?" McCall asked, as she looked over to her friend who was gently sipping from a white porcelain mug.

"She's understandably shaken up, a minor case of hypothermia but nothing too serious. But we will keep her here for a while, just to make sure. Oh, one more thing, we found some small marks on her clothes I think she was knocked out by a taser." McCall smiled widely; her mind somewhere else for a second.

"Thank you, doctor, is it ok to talk to her?" McCall's knees buckled as he smiled back at her.

"Ok, but not too long, she needs to rest." As the door closed behind him, both women's jaws dropped in appreciation.

"The things you do to get attention," McCall joked; Tina smiled and rolled her eyes at the thought of the doctor. "You ok?" McCall asked, placing a gentle hand onto Tina's shoulder.

"Thanks to you I am, if you hadn't come in, god knows what would have happened" Tina took another sip of the hot coffee.

"Tina, I think whoever did this left us a note so we would find you, they wanted you found." Tina shook her head in disbelief.

"But why, there's nothing there just – well – dead people?" Tina said with a shrug. McCall nodded.

"Yes, Jane Doe to be precise, she's missing." McCall sat down on the end of the bed and took out her note pad and Dictaphone. Switching it on, she placed it on the over-bed table in front of Tina.

"You ok to talk about it?" McCall asked, with a sympathetic smile. Tina shrugged.

"Yeh, but I don't remember anything, it happened so fast." McCall wrote down some details in her notebook before proceeding.

"Just go through everything, no matter how small. Ok?" McCall said. Tina placed her cup down on the table and sat up slowly.

"Well, the day proceeded as normal until around twelve. I had some lunch in the office then brought out Jane." Tina picked up the mug and took another mouthful of the soothing liquid. "I went through the chart – you know checking for markings, pre and post-mortem." Tina stopped to think, something had slipped her mind before. "The delivery door," Tina said, almost shocked she had forgotten about it. McCall looked up.

"What about it?" McCall asked with interest. She could see Tina thinking.

"Someone buzzed the back door like they do to drop off," McCall's interest peeked.

"Who was it?" Then she saw the look on Tina's face, the look had gone from excitement to sorrow.

"I don't know, as I opened the door everything went blank, next thing I know, you're getting over friendly with the cuddles." McCall smiled, she was glad they had left a message, she would have hated to be the one who found her if it had been later.

McCall had texted the information about the loading bay to Tooms. Tony was in the security room getting the footage from that day in the hope of catching them, or at least getting a plate number. Every detective was busy on this. Some doing door to door of the buildings near the entrance, Jenny was getting the street cam footage. Captain Brant was back at the precinct co-ordaining the troops. He wanted whoever did this and they would pay. He looked out across the half empty room.

"God damn it Steel, why aren't you here."

SIXTEEN

Tia May sat on the seat opposite Steel. He sat back and grinned, remembering the look on poor Grant's face.

"Well Mr Black," Steel raised an eyebrow over his sunglasses. "I think we are passed that, don't you Tia?" She smiled back.

"Well Antony…." Steel's eyes darted from Tia to the waitress who was approaching. "Sorry I am I boring you?" Tia's words rang with a bitter snap, but her tone was like an angel's song.

"So, what can I get for you?" The waitress's gaze never left Steel.

"I'll have a coffee, black, no sugar thanks." Steel said with a flirtatious tone.

"And I'll have a Rum and Coke," Tia said loudly as the waitress went to leave, as though Tia wasn't there.

"Certainly," the waitresses gaze transfixed on Steel. Steel grinned as Tia growled her words.

"So, Antony, your trip is only about pleasure or have you another reason to be aboard this vessel?" Steel heard her words, but he was elsewhere. "Hey Antony, what's with you. If you want to bang the waitress fine, just wait till I have gone, will you?" she barked, feeling a little used. Steel turned back to Tia; he wore a confused look.

"What… I am sorry," Steel said, his thoughts in a million different places. Tia went to get up; quickly Steel grabbed her hand and forced her down. "That waitress was in the other bar before, when we first met, she has been serving at our table at dinner, and now she is here," Tia was too angry to see the point. She had had a long day, and she just wanted to sleep.

"So, she probably has an asshole for a boss; god knows I know what that feels like," Tia said, rolling her eyes. Steel looked over again. Tia frowned deeply.

"So why is she making our drinks while there are two bar staff doing nothing?" Tia looked over as she saw white powder suddenly being dissolved in the dark cola.

"Something smells funny, we have to leave - now!" Steel's voice rang with an urgent tone. Steel and Tia made for the door.

"Sorry, must have been the oysters. Got to go." Steel said, holding his stomach. The waitress shot them both an evil stare of disapproval as they raced past. "The elevator," Steel said, shooting a glace into the reflective surface of one of the shop windows. Behind them, two large men in black T-shirts were moving quickly through the small crowds. Steel made for a large group of drunken teenagers coming from the Neon bar. He smiled as he watched the two men being swept into the wall of screaming girls; each one grasping the men's shirts.

"Wahoo, take um off, take um off," The girls sang, trying to strip the well-built men. As Steel and Tia reached the elevator, she began pressing the call button, over and over. Steel looked down at her pressing eagerly.

"Does that help?" he asked, with a sarcastic grin. Tia just glared and continued to hammer the button, only stopping to turn around to see that the men had broken free and were now approaching.

"Any ideas?" She asked, panicked.

"Not really" he replied, pressing the other call button. Their pursuers growled as a welcomed *Ding* signalled the doors opening. As both doors opened, Steel reached inside one of the elevators and pushed for the elevator to go down.

"Wait, hold the door a second," he yelled, fearful she was going without him.

"Come on," she yelled, as the men broke into a sprint. As the doors closed, the larger man's face was right up against the glass door, his breath clouded the glass like an angry bull. As they began to climb, Steel just smiled slightly. They looked down, watching the figures grow smaller as they ascended.

"Ok?" Steel did not move; he just stood still, staring down "Who were they and why are people trying to kill you?" She stood, silent, so silent he could hear himself breathe. He turned slightly.

"What do they want with you, and what do your friends want with me?" She could hear the anger build in his voice but he strangely remained in control. She knew if he wanted to, he could have possibly taken those men apart. She stood still; her eyes fixed on the doors.

"Fine," Steel's tone rang with lack of interest. "Tell you what, next time you have a party don't invite me, will you?" His hand reached for the buttons to get off at the next floor, even though it was several levels below his. Her hand shot forwards and rested on his.

"Please – don't," Tia said, with tearful eyes. More out of fear than remorse, Steel thought. "Ok, we can talk in my room," she said, but Steel had already pressed for his floor.

"No, my room is better. That way your friends can hear what we chat about," Steel said, with a sarcastic tone.

STEEL ENTERED his room first and placed the key card into the slot next to the door to activate the room's power. The lights came on slowly, breaking up any darkened corner. Steel would purposely have the lights turned on before leaving his cabin, knowing that once the cardkey was replaced in the slot and power was restored to the cabin all the lights on in the room, so that he had no surprises. Tia stood in the doorway while he walked around his room, his eyes checking for anything out of place. He raised a hand and waved her in. Tia came in quickly and locked the door behind her before making for the bed. She sat on the cushioned mattress, her body cramped together like a child that was getting ready to be scolded. Steel walked to the selection of drinks on a small drinks table, picking up a glass he turned to the pale looking Tia.

"You want a drink? – I'll get you a drink." He poured two large glasses of Jack Gold and brought them over. "Here." Tia looked up at him.

"Sorry, I don't…." He just glared at her and thrust the glass forwards. She took the glass with both hands and drank as he sat in an armchair to the side of her. He waited for her to begin. He knew there was no point slamming into her. She was in shock. All that would do is button her up even more, and he didn't have time.

"So, who do you work for. CIA, NSA, FBI… Postal service?" Steel asked, his question seemed to ring with an ever-unanswered tone. Tia thought she could read most people. It was her job. However, she could not read the man who sat in front of her, this mysterious man who somehow would be in the right place at the right time. She swirled the golden liquid in the glass, watching it coat the sides of the crystalline glass. His demeanour screamed money, the way he held himself said good schooling, wealthy parents. However, there was something else, something dark, somewhat terrifying.

"Are we really going to play this game?" His voice was bitter. Tia looked over at him. She had a different look, a defiant look.

"And you Mr Black, who do you work for?" He smiled, as he saw the old Tia was back, not the shocked helpless girl from before. The strong-willed Tia.

"What do you mean? You know what I do." The dance was on, and he loved it.

"Oh, come on, I mean you get into my room, beat the crap out of some Irish psycho. Yes, you said you did some work for the police but come on. They don't train civilians like that," she said, with an unconvinced tone. He smiled as he could see her mind working, sure Steel was enjoying it, but as he looked at the bedside clock, he realised it was nearly morning and tomorrow they would dock in Spain.

"I am a private consultant for the NYPD." Her mouth fell open "You're a Private Dick?"

"Detective," he corrected her with a grin.

"No – I know what I was going for, and it suits you," she said, with a cheeky grin.

"Ok, I probably deserved that," Steel smiled, coolly. "Anyway, back to tonight's escapades. I want to know who and why?" She took another sip from the glass; the liquid seemed to tickle the back of the throat, making her cough slightly.

"I am afraid I don't really have any answers for you, not yet," he could sense she was more confused than he was. But she was holding something back, and he couldn't really blame her, after all, he was doing exactly the same. He thought for a moment, how did she know if HE was telling the truth, after all, he could be – and he was – lying his ass off, but she seemed at ease with it. Then it struck him, her friends next door would probably be checking as they spoke.

No doubt, they were scanning the Internet for his cover story – which he conveniently posted before leaving on the cruise. There was a bang on the wall from next door.

"Well, Mr Black…Antony, it seems you check out ok," Tia announced with a smile.

"And you Miss May…Tia. Who do you work for and why are people trying to kill you?" Her smile fell.

"Look, Tia, I just want to know what the bloody hell is going on." They both looked up at his door as someone knocked three times. Tia stood up and walked to the door. Steel heard faint voices in the background. As he downed the last of his drink, he heard Tia approach, but he didn't look up.

"What, did you order room service?" He looked up and saw the thin forms of Bob and Jane Stewart standing next to Tia.

"You have questions, Mr Black." Steel's mouth fell open.

"Well, I must admit I didn't see that coming." Steel said, sitting back in his chair with a grin.

SEVENTEEN

The body of Jane Doe was gone. CSU had found nothing. The area was clean. Whoever had taken her had done it cleanly and quickly, and that annoyed the hell out of Tooms. They had entered and left by the loading area, but after looking at the CCTV footage they came up empty, the footage hadn't been tampered with. However, the cameras themselves had.

One of the CSU had found a piece of a photograph that showed the loading bay; it had been placed over the camera lens to show an empty street. Whoever it was, they knew that getting to the feed would be impossible, so they went for the source.

McCall sat on the edge of Tony's desk as they all ran through what they had found. Tooms sat staring at the photo through the clear evidence bag.

"You know what I don't get? Why do this, why not shut off the camera?" He asked, his mind a million miles away.

"Who knows? Perhaps they thought a downed camera would bring too much attention – maybe they watched too many spy movies, fuck knows." McCall said. She was tired, hungry and she had a headache coming. McCall could see where he was coming from with the photo.

"Ok, so they plant the photo over the lens, but when and how?" Her mind exploring the options. "How did they know the angle?" Everyone looked puzzled for a second. "The camera angle had to be just right so how did they know it?"

"Well, they must have seen it somehow?" Jenny added, carrying a tray of coffees.

"Yes, but how? One key access secures the room. There is always a guard in there so no one can just slip in" McCall could feel her blood sugar race as her adrenaline began to build.

"So, someone got hold of the feed somehow, junction box or something," Tony said, picking up the hot cup, shaking off the some that had spilt onto his hand.

"Ok, they got hold of the feed, why the photo and not direct the feed to an external one from a portable player or something? No this was left on purpose." McCall said, standing up and heading for an empty whiteboard. Using a magnetic grip, she pinned the photo to the top left corner.

Taking a blue board marker, she wrote:
WHY PHOTO AND NOT RE-ROUTE FEED?
HOW DID THEY KNOW ANGLE?
HOW DID THEY FIX IT WITHOUT BEING SEEN?

"Ok, what else have we got?" They all flicked open their notebooks. "Well we know they didn't want to kill Tina," Everyone looked up, confused and shocked. "Look, if they had wanted to kill her, they would have. No, someone left two messages at the desk. One of them for me, the other for Tooms. Why?" Brant seemed intrigued.

"How do you know it wasn't Tina who left them?" Brant asked. McCall noted down a time on the board.

"I spoke to the desk sergeant, and he said he got the first call, which was for me at 10:15. The second call which was for Tooms," McCall slightly bowed towards Tooms, who returned the gesture.

"Came in at 10:20. He said the voice was male with a middle aged sort of voice. At first, he thought it was an orderly passing on a message, but when I checked, she has only had one, and that was two years ago." McCall looked back at the board. "No, someone wanted her alive." Brant took a large mug

STUART FIELD

from the tray; the black mug had newness to it and a large metal NYPD badge embossed on the side.

"So, what else we got, Tony?" Tony put his cup down and flicked through his notes "Well the tapes showed zip, and we know why. Nobody saw anything unusual …so in other words they saw nothing. CSU will send the report up as soon as they have something." Brant's face soured "So we got nothing, is that what you mean?" None of them wanted to admit it, but they hadn't.

"How's Tina doing?" asked Brant, concerned about the ME.

"She says she is fine, she's at home at the moment, don't worry I have a uniform outside just in case," McCall answered. Brant nodded, knowing he would have done the same but also feeling it was a bad idea leaving the hospital too soon. "I'll pop round later, see if she's ok," McCall said, feeling guilty she was not there now.

McCall thought for a moment. "Tony, you said that there was no change with the camera feed," He nodded while taking a sip from the coffee. "Nothing at all?" She could see his blank expression.

"What I mean is: Was there normal, every-day traffic, or was it empty like this?" McCall was on to something and Brant could see it.

"There was normal traffic until that morning," Tony said with a shrug. McCall smiled and moved to the board.

"Ok, so at some point from the last time nothing was seen till 10.00 that's when it was changed, Tony go back over it and find the last point, get us a timeline." Tony stood up and put his cup down.

"You got it." He was about to leave when McCall's cell buzzed to life on Tony's desk. Brant picked it up and read the caller I.D. It was Steel. Brant pressed the answer button and listened for his voice.

"McCall, It's Steel. Look…." Steel's voice sounded apologetic but rang with a hint of urgency.

"No shit" Yelled the captain.

"Look let me...." Steel tried to explain, but the captain had an axe to grind and Steel was getting it.

"Let you what? Look Mr, you wanted on to this team, and where are you? On a god damn cruise," There was a silence on Steel's end, he knew better than to speak, not yet. "Things are getting bad here and you're sunning your ass?" The captain felt like throwing the phone, but he knew it wouldn't achieve anything.

"What do you mean, where's McCall?" At that point, Captain Brant realized what must have been going through Steel's mind. Brant had answered McCall's cell, not McCall. Brant calmed slightly.

"She's fine, wait a minute," The captain pressed the button for speaker.

"Hi guy's," Steel's voice sounded shaken, McCall smiled, her heart skipped at the thought he cared enough to be worried.

"So, what's going on?" Steel's tone had changed. It was steady and calm. McCall knew he was probably crouched forwards, his hands on his temples ready for any input. She smiled at the image, one she had missed, him either lying on cars catching the days sun or sitting and just watching, letting his mind work.

"In the past couple of days, we have had a couple of strange deaths, five to be precise," Tony leant forwards, speaking louder than normal at the cell.

"So, it's New York," Steel sounded somehow lost with the lack of information.

"Also, someone broke into the ME's office and stole one of the bodies," Tooms's voice boomed over the distance to the phone making everyone back away slightly.

"Was anyone hurt – is Tina ok?" McCall smiled as his concern was touching, he almost seemed to care.

"Well she was locked into a freezer room, but she'll be ok, they say." There was a long pause. "Steel, are you still there?" McCall leant forwards, her mouth almost over the cell.

"What? Yes, I am just thinking, how far apart were the deaths?" everyone looked confused for a moment.

STUART FIELD

"They're not related Steel, bunch of accidents and suicides that's all," Laughed the captain, who knew what Steel was trying to put together.

"How far apart were they?" Steel repeated, his voice sounding angry and inpatient.

"Couple of days tops," Tony replied.

"So, what relates the deaths?" Steel's voice sounding calmer.

"They're not related Steel, didn't you hear what the captain said?" Another brief pause came from Steel's end.

"Ok you have five deaths in a short time, one body gets taken from a secure building, and Tina locked into the freezer. Ok so, why didn't they killer her? Easy enough, no witnesses," Everyone scowled at the phone not believing what they were hearing.

"Steel what's your point before I disconnect you?" yelled an infuriated captain.

"My point is they could have taken it when she was on call, or away for the weekend, but they chose to do it when she was there," Steel could feel everyone thinking down the line. "You said they were all accidents or suicides, are you sure?" Brant looked awkwardly at the cell.

"We were starting the investigation into all of them until this happened," His words softened by the admittance.

"Ok, look at it this way, if you want to stop an investigation into some deaths what do you do? First you scare the pants of the ME who would be doing the autopsy, and then you get everyone working on the break-in, leaving the others to go cold." Brant stood up from the corner of Tony's desk where he was sitting, he realized he had been played.

"Son of a…." He growled, throwing his prized mug across the room, the mug just slid across the floor, unbroken.

"Whoever did this knows you're short staffed, knows the layout of the ME's office and her schedule. What's today? Saturday, so finding a stand-in ME at short notice will take time, they know this. You're looking for professionals," Steel said, his voice sounding alarmed and disappointed. McCall knew he wanted to be there, but he wasn't. Brant walked round, his hands clenched round his head in anger.

"Bastards played me, I messed up and they played me," Brant growled, knowing his emotions had gotten in the way. McCall looked up at him as he circled the floor, the anger swelling inside of him.

"Captain Brant, you are a good man and you care about your team, that's what they were hoping for. Get everyone back on their cases, let robbery deal with the break-in," Steel suggested. And with that he was gone. Brant composed himself.

"Ok, everybody listen up, everyone stop what you were doing on the break-in, all those on the five cases move on those. I'll get robbery to take over, so have any notes you have ready for them. Ok let's go." He clapped his massive hands in a display of encouragement and sat back down.

"Ok people, we find a connection between the people. We find that, and we find who did this. Let's find these tricky bastards." McCall shouted from her chair.

EIGHTEEN

A blazing sun was just breaking the surface of the horizon, turning the calm swell of the ocean a deep orange. The clear sky was a fiery glow, with the cloud line rising like a distant mysterious land. A fresh sea breeze had a fresh chill to it and the tang of salt filled the senses. As the monstrous ship made its way towards the Spanish coast it would have to pass between the coasts of *Costa de Vela* and the small island of *Isla de Monte Agudo*. Steel sat up in his bed and stretched off the good night's sleep. It had been a short sleep, as his guests had not left until around three that morning. He looked over to the electronic clock on the other side of the bed. The electronic display showed it was almost half six in the morning. He groaned and collapsed back in the comfortable bed and moaned disapprovingly.

Outside, in the mouth of the *Ria de Vigo*, small craft darted here and there in front of the ship. As the land narrowed, mass structures and white beaches of the two cities came to view.

On the left was *Balea*, a hilltop farmland with a small, secluded bay full of small boats, rocky cliffs, and powdery white sandy beach. On the left was their destination, Vigo. This had a massive harbour area, called *Bouzas*, with warehouses and anchor points for large and small vessels. The city itself a bustling metropolis full of tourists.

On the bridge, all stood ready, awaiting the Second in

Command's orders for manoeuvring into the harbour. An overhead squawked the chatter of the port and the guiding vessel. The captain sat in his chair and watched, ready to jump in if he thought anything was amiss. But he had faith in his crew and his second. "Ok Mr Truman, take her in nice and steady as she goes." The pilot repeated the orders and set to task. Captain Long just sat and grinned, his mind wandering back to a simpler time of sails and a star to follow.

STEEL LOOKED out across the bay, the new day sun turning the cityscape a glorious orange. The sound of the ocean's spray against the ship's hull and the flocks of gulls above, swooping playfully, filled his ears. He took a deep breath of the fresh natural breeze. The city was alive and busy, small boats making fast haste into one of the many jetties. On the land, commuters in their cars and trucks hurried to their places of work. He smiled at the scene, after only a few days on the ship it felt less lonely, less as though they were the only ones on the planet.

He left the thick glass balcony wall and sat into one of the wicker chairs. Reaching over, he picked up the crockery teacup and sipped the steaming hot brew. The colour of the tea matched the burnt orange of the buildings across the bay. As he held the cup with both hands and went to bring it to his lips he stopped, his mind began to wander, calculating. Maybe the reason he had not found anything was that it wasn't here yet. When they dock, they would be bringing on new passengers and cargo destined for New York. He pondered the theory and took a sip from the tea. The steam vapour filled his nostrils with a hint of Earl Grey. He looked over at his cell that rested neatly buy the tea saucer. He needed to speak to McCall and find out what she had found out about the *Callan Industries*.

As the phone rang, he wondered what sort of greeting he would get. Their last conversation was a while back and that didn't really go as he planned, but he couldn't blame her really. As the phone continued to ring, he started to get an uneasy feeling. Normally she would have answered it straight away, if she were in interrogation, she would put it on voice mail. Something was wrong. The ringing stopped to signal someone was there. "McCall, It's Steel. Look…." He looked at the cell somewhat surprised to hear the captain answering it.

"No shit" Yelled the captain. "Look let me…." Steel tried to explain, but the captain ripped into, something was definitely wrong, sure, the captain was not what you would call social when he was mad but this was different.

"Let you what, look Mr you wanted on to this team, and where are you? On a god damn cruise."

Their conversation lasted around fifteen minutes and at the end, he had learnt nothing about what he had originally called for. However, what he had learnt just added to the puzzle. Somebody wanted those people out of the way for a reason, but why? Something was happening back in New York that was for certain. Then he remembered something Captain Long had said about the ship, how it was an Anglo-American venture. The ship was built in Britain and the electronics, fittings were done in the U.S. The hairs on the back of his neck stood up, and a chill ran down his spine. What if something was aboard and always had been, what if the whole ship was the reason he was here? He shook the idea off. It was stupid. In a few hours, the passengers would be released on to the welcoming city and the ship would be mostly empty. Empty enough for him to finally take a look at the lower decks.

He thought back to the dead engineer, had he seen something or heard something he shouldn't have? It wasn't until he was below decks that something had happened to the boy. Steel had too many questions and too few answers. As he looked out at the tranquil Spanish backdrop, he took another sip from his tea. He looked up as the ship's horn bellowed a deep tone, signalling its approach to the port. After today, they would be at sea for ten days, then final destination New York. If something were going to happen, it would be between now and then.

A knock on his suite door made him get up from the wicker chair that creaked from the change in weight. He finished the tea and left the cup and saucer on the balcony table. As he walked past the dresser table, he grabbed for the black suit jacket that hung from the back of the chair. He stopped and looked in the long mirror; he wore all black with a black silk shirt with the first two buttons undone. Picking up his black sunglasses, he placed them on his nose, then brushed down his jacket. With a self-confident smile, he headed for the door.

Steel opened the door and removed his key card. Tia May stood in the doorway. She wore an armless white T-shirt and beige shorts. Brown T-straps gripped her feet and the wooden heels boosted her height - not that she needed it. Large red-rimmed sunglasses covered her beautiful sparkling eyes.

"Morning Antony, trust you slept well?" Tia said with a warming smile.

"Good morning Tia, hope you didn't have any more visitors last night?" She smiled, widely.

"What if I said yes, would you be jealous?" A smile broke the corner of his mouth.

"Depends who they were, if there are any more crazy-arsed Scotsmen, they're your problem," Steel smiled. She stood for a moment and looked him up and down, taking note of his all black outfit.

"Don't you have anything with colour in it?" She asked, shaking her head.

"Only my life Tia, only my life." He replied, with a smile.

THE CROWDS of people herded themselves like needy cattle, heading to graze.

"So, Antony, what did you have in mind for today?" They walked slowly against the tide of people. Outside, the weather had the potential to be a fantastically sunny day, possibly even more reason to get off the boat for a while, but he didn't want to admit to it. Besides, he wanted to find out more about the boy's death. The ship was a giant puzzle. The problem was, he wasn't seeing the picture. The call to New York had gotten him thinking about things he shouldn't. If the ship and the deaths in New York were related, it would be a million to one chance. But then he had known bigger things having lesser odds.

"Oh, I thought I would check out the rest of the ship and you?" Steel replied. She didn't look up at him as she spoke, her attention was elsewhere.

"Oh, that's a shame, I thought we might go to this little café I have heard of in the town, it's meant to be really very lovely." Steel could feel himself been manoeuvred away from checking out the ship's lower decks. However, she and her friends knew something and this maybe a start.

"Alright, why not," Steel said, as he caught a glimpse of the two goons from the night before. If they were off the ship and they followed, he could at least have the advantage in an open space, also a lot less explaining to do if it came to blows.

NINETEEN

Alan Metcalf waited outside room 702, the key card tucked securely into his left palm. He waited until the corridor was clear before using the card and entering. The room was pitch black with only a handful of blue chem. sticks on the ground to mark the route to the chair. He had done this many times, on this and other trips and he found it tedious. He found the chair and sat down.

"Soon everyone will be in the city and then you can go back and look for it," His words rang nervous in her presence.

"How can you be sure it will be there?" Her voice deep, sultry, and full of doubt.

"Something happen yesterday, an engineer was killed." There was an eerie silence.

"So, what of it?" her almost cold response made him shiver.

"The boy delivered something to the captain that very day, and then…."

"And then someone shut him up, is that what you are saying?" Alan nodded.

"Yes exactly. I think it's what we have been looking for?" If she could have seen him, she would have seen Alan smiling. His eyes closed, imagining what she looked like. His fantasy fuelled by intrigue.

"Don't worry if it's there I will find it, don't you worry. And you Mr Metcalf, what will you be doing?" the woman asked.

"Oh, I have some personal business that needs my attention, been putting it off for a long time now." Alan grinned as evil thoughts filled his mind.

"Leave me, I must prepare." He stood and made for the door, his hands brushing against the door, searching for the handle. Finally, with a twist he was out, his back pressed firmly against the wall his head raised, gasping for air as though he had just run a marathon. Her words were like a siren's song to him, mysterious and deadly.

"Yes, I have some very personal business to deal with." As he headed for the elevators, he almost seemed to skip.

THE MORNING SUN felt warm on Steel's skin as he ventured down the gangway to the dock below. Beside him, Tia May with her arm interlinked into his like a new couple. At the dockside, the other passengers hurried along in a great precession. The sun was not fully up but its warmth had started to take the slight chill out of the air.

"So, Tia where do you suggest we go?" his words playful and somewhat suspicious. Why didn't she want him snooping downstairs? Taxis lined up on the streets, ready to drive the unsuspecting tourists round. Steel waved down one of the yellow cabs and opened the back door.

"Why thank you kind sir," she said, smiling. They drove through the busy street for what seemed hours. All the while, Steel took a mental note of bars, churches anything out of the ordinary he could class as a landmark. It was a trick he had picked up in his military career; pick a landmark so you can make a map in your head to get yourself home.

"So where exactly are we going?" She turned and smiled. It was a smile that said "Trust me." Nevertheless, he was in a strange land with a gorgeous but mysterious woman that he knew very little about.

"First, I have to meet with someone then we can have

dinner together, maybe take in some sights." She explained. They stopped outside the entrance to a small meeting area, with a lawn, restaurants, and a café. This circular centre was enclosed by five towering block structures, making a cylindrical shape. Each block consisted of a group of four to five different buildings, which had been constructed to make a singular structure that housed a hollow centre to the blocks.

Branching off from the large open spaced centre, five broad walkways broke up the enclosure. Steel looked round and became suddenly nervous, this wasn't a meeting place, this was brilliant for an ambush.

"So, which idiot picked this place?" His mind worked overtime on scenarios, best place to shoot from, escape routes if necessary. "Where are we meeting this guy of yours?" she stopped and looked at the pizza restaurant over the way.

"I am meeting him in there, you can come in, but you have to sit alone, got it?" He liked how forceful she tried to sound, but then with that face and that body she didn't really have to shout.

Steel insisted that they stick to the sides of the buildings rather than walking straight down the middle, sure there were plenty of people, but if Steel was right, they were dealing with people who didn't really care. The restaurant was small, but big enough for twenty to thirty people at the most, with a glass windowed front. It was early morning, so the midday rush had not set in yet, leaving plenty of seating inside. Outside, several tables and chairs were occupied by latte-sipping customers. As they walked in, a waitress approached and greeted them. "Buenos dias" the brown-haired waitress was short and slim; a brilliant white smile seemed genuine and welcoming. "Buenos dias" Tia replied.

"A table for two?" The waitress asked, picking up two menus, her English was good with a sensuous Spanish accent.

"Please" Tia responded, while Steel was busy checking out the exits and observation points from the buildings outside. He didn't like it one bit. They sat at a small square table in the middle of the room but against the left-hand wall. The room was quite spacious with the tables placed against both walls, leaving a sizable walkway down the centre. At the window there were two tables which were placed flat against the glass. Steel watched as a tall, well-built man entered and sat at one of the window seats, he wore all beige, a sweatshirt and chinos seemed new and out of place on the man. To Steel he would have been more comfortable in a black suit, white shirt and sixties style sunglasses. Tia got up and went to leave, Steel reached for her arm, grasping it tightly.

"You can't be serious about sitting there, surely?" Tia ripped her arm away and leant forwards to whisper in his ear.

"Don't worry darling, I have some angels watching over me." She said, giving him a friendly peck on the cheek. Steel moved forwards to an empty seat next to the entrance to the restrooms. Here he had a better view. Tia approached the man and sat down, Steel couldn't make out what they were saying, but then he had other things on his mind.

The two large buildings to their front appeared to be hotels, each one around nine storeys tall, of dull grey concrete, small balconies and dark grey tiled roofs. Each was no more than hundred feet away. Steel's view switched from the buildings to Tia and the stranger. Then he saw it, each block had an open window. It didn't seem much, but the curtains had been closed in both whereas all the others had closed windows and open shades. Steel didn't like anything that looked out of place and this stood out like clown to a funeral. He understood what she meant by *she had angels watching* but this didn't seem right at all. The open windows were near the top of the building and not lower down. Normally they would be in the centre unless anything disrupting the view. This was good for an over watch or a sniper's nest, but why were the windows open?

At the table opposite Steel sat an elderly couple, happily trying to decipher the menu. Steel noticed that the man had a pair of 10x42 binoculars on the table.

"Hi there, so sorry to bother you but do you think I could borrow your binoculars a second?" The couple looked blankly at him.

"What for?" asked the man, somewhat shocked at the request. Steel smiled and laughed.

"Well I just need to check those buildings to make sure there are no snipers in there you see." Steel smiled and shrugged as if it was nothing. Their mouths fell open and the man past Steel the matt plastic binoculars. "Thanks very much." Steel sat back down and scoured the buildings, inside one of the windows, he saw two men dressed like Mr Beige in the window. He continued to look along the row of windows and back again. As he moved back to the first window, he froze. Mr Beige had been replaced with a man in black tactical gear. Steel zoomed in as he thought he saw something in his hands. He did.

Steel rushed forwards and skidded flat on the floor, smashing into Tia's table. She yelped in panic as he pulled them to the ground. Suddenly there was the noise of glass being smashed and people screaming, as high-calibre bullets ripped through the restaurant and chewed up the tiled floor and walls outside.

"Who the hell are you?" The man asked, Steel smiled.

"Tell you what, let's get out of here first then we can discuss it, shall we?" Tia and the other man nodded. Steel knew that they would have little chance getting to the group of survivors at the back of the restaurant without a diversion.

"I hope you have a plan?" Tia's voice yelled over the noise of the bullets, as they chipped away at the building. Several aluminium trays lay on the ground from the up-turned tables. Steel looked over at the building to their front and saw the blazing sun creeping over the top of the dull dark grey tiles. He grabbed two of the round metal trays and gave one to the agent to his left.

"OK, use the trays to reflect the sunlight at the buildings, I'll take this one," Steel indicated by pointing at the building to their front with a nod, "And you take the other." The agent nodded. "OK, on three. One, two…. three." They raised the trays up casting a blinding light at both buildings, they waited for a moment, then ran for the safety of the back of the restaurant as angry 6.8-millimetre rounds zig-zagged up the building and over the top to the buildings behind. Steel and Tia kept low and ran swiftly to the others with her contact close behind. Steel looked around, confused. "Why are you still here, go out the back?" He insisted. A tall, thin waiter that Steel had seen earlier shook his head and pointed at the red-coloured back door. Steel nudged his way through the panicked looking people and listened at the door.

Outside, the voices of two men could be heard chuntering about not being in the action. Steel listened carefully; his left ear pressed fully on to the wood of the door.

"Think she got out?" Asked one, his tone was boyish, young. The other was deep and aged.

"Na, if they didn't come through here, the others would have got 'um." Said another voice. Steel stood there for a while trying to ascertain their distance from the door and each other. Braking away from the door, he looked around at the frightened faces and he smiled a fake non-confident smile.

"What did you hear?" Asked one of the survivors, the man's wife clinging to his arm as the middle-aged man spoke.

"Well it appears there are two more outside this door," Everyone gave a panicked muffled shriek. Steel waved his arms to try to quieten them. "Look, we will all get out of this, I just need everyone to be quiet and stand out of the way."

The back door was down a small corridor just off from the back of the restaurant floor. At the very end of the corridor was the office and a small storeroom opposite the back door. Halfway down the short walkway was the exit. All of the survivors cramped themselves into the office, apart from Steel. Steel waited at the back door, his ear pressed against the door, waiting for the right moment.

"This sucks man," Yelped the younger one.

"Look, we were told to stay here and make sure nobody leaves. Ok?" said the older of the two men, a short, stocky man in a loud Hawaiian shirt and beige shorts. The younger one marched around, the MP7 machine pistol clutched tightly in his grip, his bottom lip curled up like a three-year-old who had been told no more candy.

"Screw this, I am going in," said the younger man, boldly. The older man, who was somewhere in his late thirties, sat on a crate, the machine pistol resting next to him as he blew smoke rings from his thick cigar.

"Kid, sit your ass down and wait. We were told to stay put so guess what, we stay put." The kid kicked a stone and watched it disappear down towards the building behind. Their voices echoed in the enclosed space of the block structure, which made it difficult for steel to make a definite assessment. They could go up and try to get out through the roof but if they thought about a back door, they knew about the roof. Their only chance was to get the guards outside and take it from there.

"Ah screw this and screw you I am going in." the younger man said, spitting his words as he went. Steel smiled to himself as he backed into the storage room and switched off the light.

The young man edged into the corridor, his weapon grasped tightly in both hands. The machine gun fire had ceased but the silence was broken by the police sirens in the distance. The dining room at the end of the corridor was cast in shadows. He edged forwards; the tangy metallic smell of blood filled his nostrils. Before him, bodies shredded by the gunfire lay motionless on the tiled floor, covered in glass and brick fragments. Dust particles hung in the streams of sunlight that illuminated the dead.

"I would hate to clean this up," the boy swung round, startled by the voice behind him. All he saw was a man coming from the shadows before the darkness took him.

The older man sat happily on his crate. He smiled as he blew some more smoke rings. He was happy because there was no gunfire from the kid, which meant everyone was dead. There was no heavy gunfire which meant he hadn't ventured too far forwards and the over watch hadn't taken him out. He hummed to himself a little tune as he waited. He looked up as there was a loud crash from inside. Carefully, he got down and moved forwards. Reaching for the handle, he slowly opened the door, the weapon raised, and its extending stock pulled fully out sat deep into his shoulder. He edged around the corner, moving the top half of his torso first, the weapon fixed ready to fire. The green beam of its laser sight cut through the haze of floating dust. The silence was deafening, he began to breathe heavily, just to give his ears something to work on before he went mad. He knelt as he entered the beginning of the dining room. Using the red dot scope, he scanned the room for life, for anything. He froze as he saw the shadowy figure sitting in a chair at a table. The sun had not yet reached that part of the room and so the figure was immersed in shadow. The older man crept forwards keeping low, moving slowly and steadily. He stopped.

"Steve, is that you?" He looked round to make sure he was alone before moving forwards. The man crept forwards until he was at the man's back, then slowly stood up. He recognized the back of his partner and slapped him on the back of the head.

"Will you stop fucking around," he yelled. The boy slumped forwards then fell off the chair; he looked down in horror as he saw a mass of red round the boy's neck. He screamed like a girl and backed off slightly, but something was behind him, he turned to find a man all in black just standing there.

"Morning," Steel grabbed the man's machine pistol as he went to raise it. "Now, now, play nice. OK who sent you?" the man backed off towards the front door. Steel raised a hand to stop him "Uhm, you may want to stop there and come back before…."

Gunfire ripped through the building as the over watch acquired a target, they didn't care who it was. To them it was simple "Anyone in that building gets it." Steel dived for cover as the 6.8-millimetre rounds cut through the man – spraying the air with body parts and red body fluids. He rolled towards the back door and the office. Knocking three times the door was suddenly unlocked and the agent stood peering through the small slit between the doorframe and the door.

"Is it safe?" asked the beige clan agent, Steel looked down at the dining room.

"Not if you're one of them – no." As a group, they moved quietly across the courtyard to the building across the way. Steel had given the boy's MP7 to the agent and the other to Tia.

"OK you guys, get these people out of here," Tia and the agent looked confused.

"What you off to do?" Tia asked, somewhat terrified at his answer. Steel just grinned like a schoolboy and ran towards the other buildings.

"Who the hell was that?" Asked the agent, he watched Steel disappear into one of the buildings.

"You wouldn't believe me if I told you," She said with a smile, she shook her head in disbelief, then they set to work. They had to get the rest out and to safety.

Steel chose to take the nearest one first. This was in a larger block with red tiled roofs and white walls. The restaurant's roof was flat, but unfortunately, this roof was peaked, so it was more difficult to manoeuvre, despite this, Steel made it into the hotel unhindered. Guests ran out screaming, giving Steel perfect cover to get in if someone had been watching. He had noted the floor and rough location of the room from the restaurant. That was the easy part. Getting in when the guy was heavily armed was the problem. Steel reached the floor and the hallway of the shooter. He stopped and listened for any noise to give a location of the shooter. Silence hung in the hallway like an unwanted enemy. He froze just as he was just about to put the sole of his shoe flat on the ground. Drawing the leg back, he knelt in front of a room. The floor was littered with broken pieces of light bulb. Steel smiled "Sneaky bastards." His thoughts were cut short and his grin of admiration faded, as the door suddenly opened, and a large man stood in the doorway dressed in black tactical gear. Steel realized with anger he had seen this uniform before.

The brute was stunned to see Steel kneeling there. Quickly, he rushed for Steel, his large hands reached for him. Steel reached down and grasped the small rug in the middle of the floor. Then with both hands he tossed the glassy contents into the man's face. The man screamed and backed off into the room, his hands grasping his face. Steel rushed forwards and leapt, kicking the man full in the chest with both feet. The hulk stumbled backwards under the impact, slamming against the back wall.

The man shook off the attack and regained his footing. He reached down and pulled a blackened blade from a sheath next to his combat boot.

"Don't know who you are friend or what you were doing with the woman, but you have upset the mission and for that, I got ta gut ya." The man's accent was a mixture, like someone who had spent a lot of time in different countries. The man was tall – around six foot six. His short blonde hair had been recently cut close to the bone leaving just enough on the top. Steel could tell under all that gear he worked out – and judging by the silenced M249 SAW heavy machine gun that lay perched on its bi-pod, he needed to.

"I don't suppose we could talk about this?" Steel said, with an open-handed shrug and grin. He soon got his answer as the bulk ran at him like a quarterback. Steel rolled to the other side of the room and couched, ready for the next attack. "I guess not then," Steel said, bouncing on his toes. The brute smiled a hungry smile. Small scratches marked his face where the glass shards had made contact. Steel looked in the corner and found the other agent; his chest was rising so that meant he was alive. Steel realized he had to be, so that when the police arrive, they have their patsy. Down below there were shrieks of tires and loud screams, as orders were being past. Steel knew he didn't have much time. He needed answers, but this guy wasn't going to talk easily. He also had to get the other agent out. The hulk tossed the blade from one had to the other, grinning as he thought how he was going to gut this interfering man before the cops came. He lunged at Steel who rolled into the other agent, a loud grown came from the man who was semi-conscious.

"Get up you idiot," Steel yelled shaking the man with one hand as he kept a good watch on the brute.

"What the hell's going on?" the agent was stirring and half-awake, but Steel needed him fully awake.

"Get your arse out of here go and help your mate over the road, before it really goes south," Steel had no time or intention to explain, he just wanted answers from the hulking form. Steel ran at the bulk, as he did so the brute swung with the blade. Steel hit the floor and slid on the wooden flooring and grabbed the man's ankles as he passed between his legs and pulled. As the brute hit the floor, the agent ran, colliding off the door fame and walls as he went. *Good* Steel thought *He's out*.

Steel knew he had no chance at a fair hand-to-hand with the man. But Steel needed to know what the hell was going on. The large blonde Mercenary stood up; his massive barrel chest heaved as he sucked in the oxygen. His eyes red and maddened, he wanted blood, more specifically he wanted Steel's blood. Steel stood next to a dresser. There wasn't much on it, just a small, cheap, flat-screen television, some Spanish magazines and a mirror that was fixed on by a flimsy brass arm. Steel gabbed one of the magazines and rolled it up tightly with both hands. Now he had a weapon.

The brute lunged at Steel, his blade moving a deadly figure eight hoping to catch Steel in the mid-section. Steel sidestepped and pivoted on his heels, using his momentum as he landed a hit into the back of the man's head, just where spine meets skull. The brute let out a grown of discomfort as he carried on his movement forwards. Steel spun and crouched ready for the man. The brute turned and growled at Steel, he spun the blade on his palm and gripped the paracord-bound hilt tightly, so his knuckles became white. More sirens blared outside.

"They will be here soon," Steel thought to himself. He knew he had to end this one way or the other. "What's with the woman, who wants her dead?" Steel asked calmly. The brute just smiled.

"If you can beat me, I'll tell you." Steel shrugged as though there were a choice. Steel moved quickly, almost a blur to the massive mercenary's eyes. Steel barrel-rolled and caught the mercenary in the back of the knee, then in the groin. As he came down, Steel rolled to the side, just in time as the blade embedded into the floor where his head had been. The magazine baton impacted onto the man's wrist, a loud crack signalled the bone being shattered under the powerful strike. The man stood up screaming, holding his shattered wrist. Steel spun and using two fingers in a claw like motion, buried them into the fleshy area above his collarbone and pressed down.

"No more," gurgled the broken merc. Steel stepped back and let the man stand using the back wall next to the double windows as support.

"OK, what the hell is going on here?" Steel was tired, tired of not knowing and now he was about to get some answers.

"OK – OK," the brute said, nursing his wrist. "We were sent to get rid of the lady and whoever she was meeting, that's all I know, I swear." Steel could tell he was telling the truth, about that anyway.

"Who's your handler, who gives you instructions?" The man stood up straight and pointed to a black tactical bag in the corner. Before he turned his head to look, Steel noticed a small red dot creep up the man's vest. Steel screamed for the mercenary to get down, but it was too late. The window exploded and so did the man's head. Steel watched in horror as the side of the man's head disappeared, and the wall to the man's left became a deep red with the contents of his head. Arterial spray surged upwards from the wound, painting the wall and ceiling a deep crimson. Steel dropped to the ground for cover and crawled for the bag. He looked over at the corpse of the mercenary, who now lay on his side. His lifeless eyes just seemed to stare into nothingness.

A blood pool began to form as the red ooze quickly spread across the wooden boarding. Steel picked up the bag and ran out, making sure to take the magazine with him.

Down below, Steel could hear the Police tactical teams moving up. The roof was not an option, as he knew they would have that covered. His only chance of getting out was from one of the adjoining buildings. He made his way down the corridor, hoping to find a room left open on the left-hand side of the hallway. He needed a window that faced the courtyard and not the street. He made his way down, trying every door handle, his hand wrapped in a towel from the room, all the while the noise of the teams got louder. Finally, as he tried the last handle, it clicked open and he entered just as the first member of the Police elite was coming slowly up the stairs. The door clicked shut behind him. He had to move fast. First, he locked it from the inside to bide him some time, then he moved to the window. This room was somewhat larger than the other room. Steel opened the bay windows and carefully looked out onto a small brick balcony and the massive drop straight down on to hard cold concrete. He looked round at the other buildings. The hotel was the corner building of the multi-structure. The building next to it led straight across to the street on the other side, he had to get to that building.

The two buildings joined at a forty-five-degree angle and there was not much between. He looked up at the guttering, which looked new but unstable. Steel cursed as he heard voices shouting into radios and the muffled electronic answers. Soon the building would be swarming with police and forensic teams.

He needed to be out of the building and on that ship. All of the balconies had a metal railing that ran across the top of the brickwork. The last floor had no balcony, to deter intruders from getting any ideas.

Steel looked down. He was on the seventh floor and there were a lot of balconies inbetween.

He smiled as he thought of McCall, he could almost hear her now saying how he had to be completely nuts to even think of what he was going to do. Steel ran into the bedroom and brought out the double mattress, throwing it down he watched it sail to the bottom, landing just off the mark he had chosen. Leaning over, he let the bag fall, making sure it landed on the soft cushioning of the mattress. Climbing over, he let himself hang, then he dropped. A loud metallic bang rang out as he caught the first railing, his winded body hung for a moment, preparing for the next drop. Again, he let go, ensuring he wasn't looking down as he travelled. Another and then another. In his mind he had counted the number of seconds to the rail. He was on the third floor and his arms began to hurt from the impacts, he looked down at the mattress and smiled.

"Not that far now," he thought. He only had one more and then it was jumping time. He let himself slip as he counted the twelve seconds that it took. *BANG* as he hit the final balcony. He wanted to rest but he knew he had to get off the balcony and get into a cab as soon as he could. He jumped and rolled as he hit the mattress. He looked up to make sure he was clear then, dragging the mattress away, he disappeared into the other block.

The block had a drive-in garage and a utility room for people's unwanted junk. Steel stashed the mattress inside and headed out into the street. Outside people had begun to gather at the entrances of the walkways into the plaza, but they were been held back by police barricades and crime tape.

Steel smiled at his good fortune as he saw a tourist party from the ship. He did not stop, he carefully mingled with the tourist group that had stopped to film the commotion.

"Oh, look its Mr Black," the shrieking call of Missy Studebaker pierced the air. "Look, something's going on over there." They all looked with interest as the Grupos Operativos Especiales de Seguridad, or GOES, police teams brought out the body of the large mercenary. Steel stood confused for a moment: Who had shot him, his own man so he didn't talk? Or did the agent mistakenly do it to save Steel's life? In addition, what of the other shooter, had he gotten away or was he now in some dark room, having his fingers broken or his fingernails removed? The puzzle just kept getting bigger and he was tired and hurting. He decided his best bet was to stay with the group until they boarded. The tour group would be an excellent cover, as the police would most certainly be looking for strangers travelling alone.

He needed to get back to the ship. He needed to know Tia was safe, and he needed answers.

TWENTY

Tina had been released from hospital with specific instructions not to go back to work, but to rest up for a few days. Tina just nodded and smiled – she was going back to work.

McCall had received a voice message on her cell from Tina requesting: *Can you get me out of this hospital please, honey?* A short but precise message, one that McCall understood immediately. She knew Tina would want to get back to the office which was just off 1st Avenue – the offices of the Chief medical examiner. McCall had known the CME for some years – a nice man called Clements. He'd been the ME when her father had been on the force.

McCall had found her waiting outside the hospital on a bench with a double cream latte in her hand.

"Hey," McCall said, pulling up next to the curb.

"Hey," Tina returned the greeting. Tina got into the Mustang with a few moans and groans of discomfort. McCall said nothing – what would she say that Tina wouldn't tell her to politely shut up for?

"I take it we are going back to your office?" McCall asked, gently.

"You bet your ass, I got work to do, and I can't do that laid up feelin' sorry for myself," Tina barked. Her verbal attack was more anger at who ever had done this to her, and herself for being complaisant, but it wasn't meant at McCall, and Sam knew it.

"So, girl, how did your date go?" Tina asked with sudden interest. McCall smiled and shook her head. She was amazed at Tina's ability to switch a conversation to one about boys and gossip, it was like she had never left high school.

"It was – fine," McCall said, drawing out her answer, as if she didn't want to say too much too soon.

"Uh hu, I know what that means, you two did the nasty," Tina said, bobbing her head out of respect. "So, come on, details girl, details." Tina said with a nosy interest. McCall's mouth opened and shut like a bass, unable to know how to respond. She wasn't like Tina, who had to go into detail – sometimes too much detail, she was more thoughtful of the situation, a no kiss and tell girl.

McCall parked and they walked into the ME's building – a tall tower-like building of grey concrete and windows. As they approached, they saw the uniforms posted at nearly every door, Tina smiled.

"After the horse has bolted right?" McCall scowled at her, playfully.

"Captain wasn't happy when you said you were going back," McCall said, with a concerned smile. Tina shrugged.

"So, what am I meant to do, stay at home watchin' crap on tv for a couple of days? Uh, uh, that's not me and you know that." McCall sighed, she knew she would have – has done exactly the same on many occasions. . They entered the building, showing their ID badges at the posted sentries, making their way to Tina's office. As they went down the stairs, Tina stopped. The long corridor to her office seemed dark and full of shadow. McCall felt the gentle grip on Tina's hand on her arm.

"You good?" McCall asked, shooting her friend an understanding look. Tina just stared at the corridor that seemed to extend like in a nightmare.

"Yeh, no fear, right?" Tina said, looking over at her friend. McCall smiled and nodded.

"Right, no fear," McCall repeated the sentence as though they were special words of power.

TINA'S OFFICE was well lit with every light on. McCall had figured the techs had left it that way to show support for Tina. Tina smiled as she heard the sound of the coffee machine blubbing away to tell her someone had made fresh coffee for her return.

"News travels fast," McCall said, smelling the fresh scent of percolated coffee.

"In this place, you kiddin' me? These people know what you've done before you've done it, I tell you, gossip city girl," Tina said, as if she was innocent of any such behaviour. McCall smiled as she sat on Tina's desk.

"I guess I would have done the same, but still," McCall started. Tina shot her an angry look.

""But still," what?" Tina barked. Her arms folded across her chest; her scowl deepened.

"You could have called that guy from the other night to come over and comfort you?" McCall laughed. Tina smiled at her concern.

"Look, I am better off at work where I am doing something, not sitting around feeling sorry for myself. Yes, it happened, I'll live." McCall launched herself off the desk and walked over to where Tina was getting ready.

"So, you guys are carrying on with your other cases, cool, that's fine with me." Tina slapped on some blue surgical gloves and opened up the draw containing Donald Major. The sound of plastic rollers on metal slides echoed through the open spaced room. The body of Donald Major looked more serene after the rigger had faded and the chilling look of fright and pain had subsided. Mrs. Major had not yet come down to make a formal ID just yet, McCall and Tina had thought it was best she didn't remember him that way. His wallet contained enough ID to satisfy them for the time being. McCall thought back to when she and her mom had to go to identify her father after his shooting. He was a cop, a damned good one who took one in the chest from an unknown sniper. He had gotten a call from dispatch with news of a body in an old hotel room. It seemed an average call. Probably some meth-head OD on some stuff or some poor guy who couldn't take it anymore. As he entered the room, he saw a man sitting in a chair. The man sat, motionless and quiet. As he moved in to check, he ended up losing half his chest.

"You OK?" Tina asked, she had seen that look before on many occasions, but not for a long time now.

"Yes, I am fine. So, what we got on Mr Major?" Tina took out his file and opened the beige folder.

"Donald Major, fifty-two-years of age, no prior heart problems, blood work came back clean.

From what I could see, he was all-in-all a healthy guy. Unless you discount the whole being plugged into the mains' thing of course." McCall found it interesting how she always joked about stuff the harder or more stressful things were. She had heard it many times about troops joking about bad situations as a kind of release.

"So, it was definitely the electrocution that killed him?" Tina gave McCall a curious look.

"Why? You were expecting something else?" McCall was searching. She couldn't accept that this professional electrician had made such a mistake. Something was wrong, if there was nothing on the body, then it was at the crime scene.

TWENTY-ONE

McCall and the other detectives had resumed their cases as ordered. What Steel had said made sense, they had been blinkered by what had happened to Tina. However, now they were back on their cases, hopefully to the disappointment of whomever tried to derail the investigation. Robbery was now in control of the break-In. She and Captain Brant weren't happy about it but that was just the way it was, robbery was robbery, if someone had died that would be different. McCall stepped off the elevator and headed into the bullpen. She didn't want to be there, she wanted to be out on the streets finding who had done this to her friend. She wanted to be watching over her, making sure she was safe. But she wasn't, she was there trying to piece together a death that may or may not have been a murder.

McCall sat at her desk and logged on to her computer to check her emails. There was a lot of junk but nothing pertaining to the case. She turned in her chair and looked up at the murder board. She had a jigsaw and not enough pieces. McCall made a mental note to drop in and check out the crime scene again in the morning. She leant back and stretched in her chair, her arms stretching out to the sides. She looked up to see the smiling faces of Tooms and Tony as she realized her top had stretched over her firm chest.

"You guys were bottle fed, weren't you?" They just grinned and went back to work. Her eye caught a glimpse of the empty chair next to her desk and her mind wandered to another time. Flashbacks of the past came back to her. She smiled as she could almost see Steel sitting there pondering a problem, and those damned sunglasses. Her smile soured as she thought about him sitting on a deck chair or sunning himself at the pool when he should be here with her. McCall shook off the thoughts that started to cloud her judgment. She sat up and looked once more at the board. Her eyes squinted as though it would help. This was a happily married man. His colleagues respected him. He had no money problems, no priors. It made no sense. Perhaps it was an accident. But then, why was the fuse box wiped down and all the cameras down in the alley leading to the back door? More to the point, what was a top electrician working on a two-bit job? A favour for a friend, perhaps?

McCall looked over suddenly as Tony slammed down his phone back on the cradle.

"Great, another dead end." McCall got up and walked over to the two detectives who looked as stressed as she did.

"What's up?" She asked, her voice soft and calming. Tony sat back in his chair making it tilt on its hinge.

"The blood work just came back negative for anything." He growled with frustration. She could tell he was hoping the guy was on something to explain why the crane driver had taken the fast way down. McCall's mind began to work and Tooms and Tony could see her chew her bottom lip in concentration.

"Did CSU find anything on the crane to explain the accident?" McCall asked. Tony looked through the file.

"CSU never checked it, apparently the works accident investigations team checked it and it was classed as an accident," Tony replied with a shrug.

"Hope you boys aren't afraid of heights," McCall smiled.

McCall looked up at the wall clock. The hands told her that it was too late to be here. It was eight o'clock and they were all beat. They had been at it all day and what a day. All she wanted to do was get home, run a deep bubble bath and destroy that bottle of red in the kitchen.

"OK" McCall said, standing up and switching off her computer. "You boys go home, we can do more tomorrow. As for tonight, get some rest." She grabbed her jacket and made for the elevator.

After the usual chaotic drive home, she parked the Mustang and headed up to her apartment. With every step, the thought of the deep relaxing bath seemed even more welcoming. As she turned the corner on to her floor, she saw a welcoming sight leaning up against her wall, holding a bottle of red.

"I phoned the department, but they said you had…." She never let him finish. McCall pressed her lips against the doctor's soft passionate lips and sank into bliss. She wanted him and the closer she pressed against him, she knew he felt the same.

THE SOUND of reversing alarms from garbage trucks signalled the morning. McCall leant over and looked at the clock. The red LED read out five o'clock, she smiled wickedly. She still had time to spare and she just knew the right way to spend it. She stared at the handsome naked man next to her.

"Well I am awake now," She thought as she ventured down his body and under the sheets to give him a special morning call.

McCall skipped off the elevator and on to the shop floor. She made for the coffee room after grabbing her mug from the bottom draw of her desk. The smell of fresh coffee filled her nostrils. She stopped and realized the good coffee was back.

"Hey, Tooms, who found the coffee place?" He stood up with a disappointed look on his face.

"Well thank you very much. I am a detective you know. I feel insulted that you would imply…" She shot him a thoughtful look.

"Steel sent an order through, didn't he?" She smiled as Tooms sat down and hid his face in the computer pretending to work. McCall smiled and turned towards the coffee room. She stopped and turned.

"When did you speak to Steel?" she asked, curiously. Tooms looked up, his pen sticking out of his mouth like a cigarette.

"Uhm, he sent me something, asked if I would check it out. Nothing really," he turned away from her, quickly hoping she would brush it off.

"What did he send you?" her words intrigued and at the same time hurt, that he had not asked her.

"Just a print he wanted looking at," now she was more curious.

"Wait a minute, we are in the middle of a murder investigation and holiday boy wants you to check out a print? What was it some slut he made out with and he's checking to see if she's married or something?" She gave a look of disinterest and walked into the coffee room. Tooms and Tony got up and followed.

"We ran the prints and they belonged to a Shaw McKee," Tooms read from a small file. McCall snatched the file away from him. "It says here that this guy is a professional hitman out of Dundee, Scotland." She frowned, her thoughts in disarray.

"Why is Steel looking at this guy?" Tooms shrugged, "All I know is he asked me to do a search on a print and this came up. I don't know why, and I don't think I want to neither." Tooms held up his hands as if holding something away from him. She poured the coffee into her mug. The aroma filled her nostrils. It smelt so good.

"So, did you send off the results to him yet?" She filled the two empty cups on the counter for the two detectives.

"Yeh sent them last night. That's when I asked him about the coffee house," Tooms admitted. McCall leant against the counter and blew on the steaming hot brew. What was Steel doing on the ship?

"When you guys off to the doc's?" She watched Tooms check his wristwatch.

"We got a meeting with the doc's super at nine." His watch read eight o'clock.

"OK, I am off to see Tina. I'll see you guys later." She said, placed a black thermos lid on the metal travel mug and made for the elevator, leaving Tooms and Tony to finish up before heading uptown.

At the docks, a fresh morning breeze funnelled its way through the mass of steel containers. Cargo boxes that lay neatly stacked up displayed black lettering, some of origin and others of destination. The yard was neatly laid out into sections, a set of large buildings containing customs office, some restrooms and a control room. Massive towering cranes stood at the edge of the embankments, their skeletal structures reaching up from the light grey concrete. Tooms had arranged for them to meet with the foreman at the crane where John Barr had met his end.

As Tooms and Tony approached the crane, they saw a tall man in a white hard hat waiting at one of the cranes. The man was in his late fifties with thinning, short, black hair and a small, neatly trimmed moustache. He was talking to two other men. Each of the men was of similar height and build, one was blonde, and the other had brown hair. Both of them sported short hair and sunglasses. As they approached, the blonde man saw them and nudged the other. The other man didn't turn to see who was approaching, he just nodded, and they just walked briskly away. The foreman turned and put on a quick smile for show as Tooms and Tony were just feet away from him. Tooms noticed the beads of sweat on the man's forehead and knew it was fear and not the morning sun.

"You must be the two detectives, here about the accident, terrible tragedy, just terrible," His words sounded as false as his emissions.

"I am Detective Tooms, and this is Detective Marinelli you must be Mr Jackson, the foreman?" The two detectives flashed their badges to the man who just smiled and nodded.

"Well I don't know what to say, Detective, our sight crew took a look round and deemed it an accident." The man was hiding something, and it oozed from his aura like alcohol seeps from a person's bones after a heavy night on the booze.

"Well, sir we would still like to take a look if we may?" Tooms spoke coolly, he knew if he rattled the man he would button up and they would have nothing. The foreman stepped back and looked up at the towering mass of metal.

"Be my guest, Detectives." He grinned as he looked at their faces "Unless there's a problem?" the foreman laughed. Tooms could tell he was taunting them. Just the look on his smug face said, "I bet they don't go up.".

"So, where do we get some hard hats?" Tony said, as he smiled back. The foreman's grin dropped, and a look of panic gripped his pale face. The cab of the crane was attached to the underbelly of the structure. Above it, the long steel arms of the bridge-like construction supported the cab and crane unit. The long beams stretched out far over the murky waters of the Hudson below. As they ventured up, the wind began to pick up; Tony turned to Tooms who just smiled and egged him on. At the top, they arrived at a staging unit and the cab. Everything was encased in a medium height steel safety barrier. The two men walked around the cab looking for oils or anything to contribute to the *so-called* accident. As they met back at the stairwell, both men looked disappointed, and the foreman was wearing a smug grin.

"You see, no foul play – the guy must have jumped," the foreman said, with a crashing gesture with his right hand. Tony stopped as he neared the corner and looked up. Along the side of one of the metal walls of the cab, a slightly deep scrape angled upwards.

"Hey Tooms, come here a sec will ya?" Tony said, straining his eyes to get a better look at the metal. Tooms walked around and found Tony looking at the inch-long scrape.

"What you got man?" Tooms looked down and smiled as he pulled out his cell.

"You thinking what I am thinking?" Tony asked as he watched his partner dial for CSU, Tooms just nodded slowly as he put in the request. Tony walked over to the foreman, displaying a grin so wide it could have cut his head in half.

"Sorry, Mr Jackson this is now a crime scene I am going to have to ask you to leave. But please make yourself available for further questions." The man stormed off, but Tony noticed he was more scared than angry. Something was off – by a mile.

TWENTY-TWO

McCall entered the ME's building and headed for Tina's office – or the cutting room as she called it. McCall stood in front of the entrance and opened the double doors to Tina's office.

Tina sat at her computer, typing up some notes from one of the cases. Tina looked up over the monitor, and a pleasant smile crept over her pretty, dark-skinned face.

"Good morning," McCall announced, lifting the logoed coffee cup. Tina lifted a finger to signal she was busy typing and talking would put her off her stroke. McCall mouthed an apology and slipped into the cutting room. McCall wandered aimlessly around the brightly lit room while she waited for Tina to complete her work. The sound of keys of the keyboard rattled away in from the small office space. McCall placed down both coffees and picked up one file marked with Donald Major's name. She flicked through as if she was reading a magazine in a surgery waiting room.

"So, how did your second date go with Doctor Dave?" Tina asked, drawing out the words. McCall turned around suddenly, slapping down the file back onto the "To do" pile as though she had been reading something she shouldn't have.

Tina had a broad, cheeky smile as though she knew something McCall didn't. As she crossed over from the dark office, the bright ceiling lamps made Tina's red lip-gloss shine. McCall picked up Tina's coffee cup and offered it while holding a somewhat nervous smile.

"It was fine. Why?" McCall answered casually, as though it had been nothing. Tina took a sip from the welcomed coffee, but her eyes were still smiling. Now McCall was getting nervous.

"What did he tell you?" McCall asked, her eyes turned to slits as she gave Tina a searching glare.

"Nothing, he just phoned to thank me, but you have told me plenty, oh yes, plenty." Tina laughed. McCall jumped up on to the stainless-steel counter and took a sip from her thermos mug. A small self-indulgent smile broke the corner of her mouth and Tina clapped with joy.

McCall had spent around half an hour at the morgue. Tina had nothing new on Donald Major. There was no doubt he'd died from electrocution, but it was also evident it was no accident. Nevertheless, McCall had questions. Like why the fuse box had wiped clean and why the cameras in the alley were disabled. She always had the same questions, but they mattered. They were in her mind what separated this from murder and an accident. Now all she had to do was figure out who did it and why?

She looked over her notes again as she sat at her desk. Looking up at the whiteboard, she scanned every photograph every name and date. McCall leant back in her chair and closed her eyes for a second, then slowly opened them. What was she missing? She ran through the facts on her jotter pad.

Fact 1. Donald always used a partner, but not for the last two jobs. Why?

Fact 2. Why was a high-end electrician doing a two-bit job that was miles from his home and off the books?

Fact 3. The fuse box was wiped down and the cameras disabled which meant premeditation.

Fact 4. What was the big job that he had completed prior to the 7-11 job?

Fact 5. Where was his workshop? McCall stood up with a smile.

"His workshop," McCall thought aloud. Realising that was the piece she was missing. She grabbed her jacket and headed for the elevator, just as Captain Brant was walking out of his office.

"Where's the fire, McCall?" Brant laughed. McCall turned quickly to face the captain, shocked at his sudden presence.

"Donald Major had a workshop, and I think that may hold some answers," McCall said, excitedly. Brant nodded with a look of someone weighing up the options.

"Do you know where it is?" McCall shook her head with a grin on her face.

"No sir, but I know someone who would," McCall said with a twinkle in her eye.

"The wife?" Brant said with a broad smile, McCall nodded as she put on the leather jacket and headed for the open doors of the elevator.

THE SUN WAS HIGH, and the streets were as full as they could be for that time of day. It was just over a forty-minute drive out to The Majors residence in Yonkers. She took the FDR North and then onto the I- 87 North. The house was in a friendly neighbourhood with kids playing in the streets and folks watering the gardens. McCall smiled as she thought back to her old house before her dad's shooting. Now her mom lived in Boston in the house from her grandmother. The house was painted white with a small front yard surrounded by a white picket fence – the American dream. McCall found a place to park on the other side of the street just behind a UPS truck. It was four o'clock and the average Joe's day was about done. McCall stopped before entering the small pathway to the front door. She knew that, as soon as she knocked on the door, Mrs Major would be full of hope, if only for just a few seconds. She would be happy for a brief moment, thinking that McCall had some news about how her husband had died. Just some comforting news that he hadn't suffered, that he hadn't made a mistake, just something to hold on to. McCall knew that telling her she thought his death was suspicious was more than a long shot, possibly dangerous if she was wrong. She decided to go with "We are still investigating." McCall also knew that hopeless look as she explained that she was still looking, that they had nothing as of yet. She has been down that road too many times, and each time a little piece of her dies.

McCall raised a shaky hand, ready to knock. The door opened, and there stood Mrs Major. Her eyes raw from too much crying, her lips chapped from not enough fluids.

"Hi, Mrs Major, I am Detective McCall. We met the other day." Erin Major nodded and stepped to the side to let McCall enter. The house had been cleaned from top to bottom. Its floors vacuumed and the surfaces polished – something McCall had seen after her father's shooting, her mother turned into a clean freak to the point of being over obsessive. McCall figured she had done it to keep her mind occupied, just to do something and have no time to sit down and contemplate what had happened. Erin reached out a hand to offer McCall a seat on the long couch, which she took with a smile of comfort. Just seeing Erin Major and his need for something – anything to hold onto, made McCall rethink her decision to tell her about the investigation. Whether it was a good or bad decision to say to her, at least Erin would have some comfort.

"Firstly, Erin I want you to know I am treating this as a suspicious death, not an accident," McCall could see a small smile of relief on her face.

"You found something then?" Erin asked, with a broken smile. McCall thought for a moment before answering.

"There are just somethings that seem off. However, just because we are investigating it as suspicious, it still may not be, do you understand Erin?" McCall said, hoping that if it turned out to be an accident, Erin wouldn't be getting the lawyers involved.

"Yeah, I get it, but at least you are looking and not just brushing it off, thank you for that," Erin said with a smile. McCall sighed with relief.

"Your husband had a workshop I understand?" McCall asked. Erin nodded and wiped a lonely tear from her left eye. "I need to see it if I may, do you know where it is, and do you have a key?" Erin Major stood up and headed for a keypress that hung next to the back door in the kitchen. She soon returned with a bunch of keys and a piece of paper.

"The place is a small disused garage in Harlem; you'll need the code. The whole place is alarmed," McCall stood and took the things. As she did so, she smiled confidently at Erin Major.

"I promise I will find out what happened to your husband," Erin smiled and nodded slowly.

"I hope you find what you're looking for, Detective," Erin said, wiping away another tear.

"Sam, you can call me Sam." And with that, she left the house and headed for her car.

THE WORKSHOP WAS a small white-bricked building with a shutter door on the side – which was large enough to be used as an entranceway for vehicles. It was a little secluded place, which used to be a repair garage of some type, back in the day. The paintwork had faded or crumbled off with the years. Old weathered and torn paper signs clung to the sides, breaking up the paintwork with their faded reds and blues. McCall pulled up and got out of her car. A brisk crosswind carried the smell of diesel fumes and the local restaurants just down the street. The sun was still warm, but she kept her jacket on as if to cover her badge and pistol from view. The streets seemed oddly quiet with only the birds on the neighbouring trees to keep her company. The place its self looked as if it had stood empty for quite a while, with ankle-high weeds creeping from cracks in the concrete slabs and stylish graffiti that was more art than just some random statement. At first, she had tried the brass Yale lock. The key slid in halfway then it stopped. McCall fought with the key but to no avail. At first, she thought the keys she'd gotten from Erin Major were the wrong ones. After all, Erin was not herself. McCall thought for a moment. This guy was careful. He had a workshop that was disguised as a rundown disused place. His reputation was that of discretion, that's why he got all the secret jobs. "What if the Yale lock was also a fake?" She thought. It took McCall a while to find the correct key slot. The real lock had been concealed in the door under a piece of rubber that looked like a quick fix in the wood of the door panel. The key slid in effortlessly.

As she entered, McCall took out her small flashlight and moved in. There was a click from a pressure pad, and then a countdown beep boomed through some wall speakers. She rushed in. Erin had written down the location of the disarm unit which was behind a Playboy calendar. McCall moved it to the side and typed in the code on the piece of paper. There was another click, and then the lights came on.

McCall stood for a moment just looking around. Her mouth fell open at the contents of the room. As McCall entered into the ample space of the workshop, she felt as if she had been transported to another place. The outside looked run down and disused. Weeds grew from cracks in the surrounding flooring. The large metal chain-linked fencing was weathered and old. However, the inside looked like the drawing-room of the designers of the Starship Enterprise. Blueprints, workstations, computers. It had everything and more. "Wow" her eyes lit up with excitement. Shaking herself back to reality she looked around, hoping to find something on his last job. In the back was a small office which was filled with computers, their screens flickering as they booted to life. McCall had noticed the surveillance cameras on the outside and the ones that littered the corners of the interior. As the screens finished their start-up procedures, she saw the feed from the cameras. McCall took out her cell and dialled for the Tech Department of CSU.

"Hi, this is Detective McCall, is Brian there?" As she waited, she looked around the office to see if there were bits of information that might stick out reference the case. A man's voice came on the other end.

"Yo, McCall what's up?" She smiled at the greeting from the tech.

"Brian, I have a camera feed here, but it's not going to a hard drive my guess is it's an online server or something, can you run a trace for me?" She scrambled around for a phone number.

"Where you at?" She told him the address and waited as he did a search. McCall moved to the large workshop and looked through a filing cabinet in the left-hand corner next to a workbench that contained a coffee machine and a small refrigerator.

"McCall, this may take some time so if you leave it with me, I'll get back to you." McCall closed the cabinet and moved over to a large pinboard on the north wall.

"Thanks, Brian I owe you one." She could almost hear him smiling. "Bye Brian," she said playfully before he could come back with a funny comment.

McCall noticed a large blueprint that looked more like a rail plan than a plan for electrical cabling. Whatever this job had been, it was massive. She took it down and put it into an evidence bag. Taking out her small camera, she began to take photographs of the room and its contents. There was something important, but it would take the Tech Department to figure it out. However, she had another worry. If someone wanted him silenced, it was over one of his jobs. If that were the case, she had the feeling that this place was brimming with evidence. However, she couldn't risk calling it in, just in case someone was scoping the place. She had the blueprint, and later she would have the feed. If they could maintain the feed, the place would be as good as secure. If anything were to happen, it would be on film.

TWENTY-THREE

CSU arrived forty-minutes after the call – two techs – one male and one female. Tony and Tooms had seen them around before on different cases, so a quick "What's up?" was more than enough to pose as a greeting. The guy was a six-foot Hispanic. He was slim with short hair and a clean-shaven face. The guy was in his thirties and been on the job around ten of those. The woman was a slim petite redhead, she too was in her thirties but had been a cop before transferring to CSU after her kid was born.

Tooms explained the situation and what they had found. It was now for the techs to decide if it was just a scrape or something more sinister. Tooms and Tony had both served and knew the difference between a scratch and a bullet scrape, but better safe than sorry, they had thought. The last thing they needed was a false lead, not with other things going on. They left the techs to do their thing, but instead of returning to the 11th, they went straight to the morgue. They had heard Tina had gone back to work and wanted to check up on her – without making it look like they were checking up on her. The excuse was to see if there was any evidence that their victim had been shot. Tony called ahead to let her know they were on route, which was pretty much Tooms's idea, thinking she'd had enough surprise visits for one day.

They parked up and headed inside, past security, for the elevator. Tony pressed the call button and waited while Tooms made a careful check of the main lobby, both his cop and soldier instincts kicked in, checking the faces of the people, seeing if any looked suspicious. He knew it was improbable they would strike again, but he was in the moment. As the door slid open, they stepped inside, Tony pressed for the lower level – the morgue.

The brightly lit white corridors felt cold and uninviting – sterile. Soft music emanated from one of the rooms and the two detectives knew it was from Tina's workspace. A tall uniformed officer stood watch at the loading entrance; Tooms waved a greeting as they entered Tina's cutting room. The tall brown-haired officer returned the greeting as he watched them go in through the double doors. Tina stood over the remains of John Barr, which she had wheeled out especially for them.

"Hey, Doc," Tooms said with a crooked smile.

"Hey, you two," she replied, noting the look of concern on both their faces. She felt like a little girl with two older brothers looking after her. "and before you ask, I'm fine, still a little shaken, but fine," she smiled, feeling the love.

"That's cool, we were just passing and just wanted to –,"

"Come around and check on me, sweet, but unnecessary. We got damned security all over the place now, hell, I can't even take a pee without someone following my ass," she laughed. Tooms grinned. He had known Tina as long as he had known McCall, in fact they came in together. To him they were like sisters, so he felt some kind big brother sense of obligation towards them.

"OK, but you can't blame a brother for worrin'." Tooms smiled and went to give her a hug, almost forgetting she was wearing surgical scrubs with someone's bloody matter all over it. He smiled and backed away.

"So, you boys are here about your skydiver?" Tina said, with a cold humorous joke.

"So, what we lookin' at, Doc?" Tooms asked, a small

HIDDEN STEEL

lollypop locked into the side of his left cheek clattered as he spoke. Tina smiled and threw back the sheet. The two detectives reeled back as she lifted the blue sheet, revealing a tangled mess of flesh and bone. The body had been stripped of all clothing which made the sight that much more unbearable to keep eye contact with. The body of John Barr lay on his back. Shattered bone fragments stuck through bruised flesh. Both of his shin bones had snapped in two halves. Each one was now angled side on to each other as they ripped through the damaged flesh of his legs. His rib cage now stuck out through his sides. As he had landed on his back, every bone in his body had exploded like a crockery plate. His spine had disintegrated along with his pelvis. The impact had turned his organs more like liquid than matter.. John lay on a special table with drainage slats on the sides that reminded Tooms of gutters on a street. Just by seeing the table, the two detectives knew this was going to be messy. Tina looked up as she put on her protective goggles.

"You boys want to stay for this, or shall I call you?" Both men shook their heads, frantically, while holding their noses.

"We came down because we have reason to believe our vic here was shot before he fell," Tony said, trying not to lose his breakfast. Tina looked at the mangled remains. Starting at his feet she then moved up until she got to his left shoulder. She stopped and examined the hole where the collarbone had broken through. The hole was large – around the size of the top of a fizzy drinks bottle, pieces of shattered bone protruded out of the angry looking wound. The man's back was badly scarred and shredded from bone meeting hard cold concrete, so any evidence of an entry or exit wound had been lost. Tina picked up a magnifying glass and looked closer.

"Well, I'll be. Yep, this guy took a slug to the shoulder alright," Tina said, with a surprised grin. The two detectives' eyes lit up with excitement, their hands still over their noses. "If you look closely enough, you can see a large hole behind the bone," she looked up and saw the two giving her the thumbs up from a distance. "Unbelievable, the pair of you" the two men shrugged and got out, but not before Tooms gave the "Call me" signal with his thumb and pinkie.

TONY AND TOOMS made their way back to the 11th precinct and the comfort of their desks. By all accounts, it had been a productive but gruesome day. Tooms looked up at the wall clock and noted the time. He sighed, as it was only two in the afternoon. He turned to Tony, who was busy making the quick notes on what had happened at the dockyard.

"I am hungry, you want something?" Tooms said, holding his gut. Tony turned to him slowly.

"You're kidding me, right? After seeing crash test man, no, thanks." Tooms just shrugged and headed for the vending machines. While he was at the machines, Tooms's cell vibrated in his jacket pocket, he pulled out the cell as he slipped a dollar into the machine, and looked at the ID. It was from Steel. It was a simple message with an attachment. The message was a simple one.

"Please check this out. Urgent." He opened it to find a bloody fingerprint. Tooms heard the candy bar drop into the pull-out tray. His hand delved in and retrieved the bar, and he wrenched it open with his teeth as he bit off the end of the rapper, all the while his gaze fixed on to the print.

"What you up to on that tub man?" Tooms asked himself, then bit into the chocolate and caramel.

Back at his desk, Tony was going through John Barr's file. Nothing jumped out. He was an ordinary guy doing an ordinary job. He had an ex-wife and two kids, killing him didn't benefit her what so ever. In fact, she was just about to remarry so he would be off the hook for alimony. He didn't owe anybody money, so that was wasn't a factor plus, even if he did, killing him wouldn't get them their money back. No, if this was a murder, the simple answer would be some psycho.

Tooms walked up to the adjoining desks and sat down hard in his chair, the cell still in his hand. Tony looked over.

"What's up?" Tooms lifted the cell so Tony could see it.

"Does this guy attract trouble or just go looking for it?" Tooms shook his head out of disbelief and pushed the remaining part of his snack into his mouth.

"What is with this case?" Tony yelled, feeling helpless as he tossed the file back on the pile and stretched out. Tooms put his cell away and leant forward and rested his elbows on his knees.

"We wait for CSU, find out what they got. We know this guy was shot, that's a cert," Tooms said, pushing down on his left index finger as if he were counting. "What else we got?" he asked, hoping Tony had more.

"Nothing, we got no motive, no suspects, we got shit. All we got is a scrape on the crane that could be anything, a body that looks like a pizza and I got a fuckin' headache," Tony said, shaking his head. He looked tired and felt it. The past couple of days, since they picked up the cases, had seemed harder than any other.

Tooms picked up the beige file from his *In Tray*. It was one of the cases he had picked up – or rather McCall had palmed off onto him. Along with the precinct stamp, there was a dotted line and the name *Bill Foster* next to a case number. He opened it and read the report. It seemed a simple suicide, but after the past few days, he had the feeling this was going to be less than simple. Tony looked over at Tooms who was engrossed in his case file.

"Don't tell me you got a weird one as well?" Tooms shook his head.

"Nope, this dude decided to go to work, probably had a bad day, got fired or some shit like that, and removed the back of his head with a .45." Tony winced at the thought.

"Tell you what, I bet I'll be finished mine before you have finished the paperwork on yours," Tooms laughed as he watched Tony type with his two index fingers. Without looking, he raised the middle finger of his right hand as a signal to Tooms.

"Yeh, yeh – you know I am right baby," Tooms roared with laughter. Tony's thoughts were elsewhere. His thoughts were on the shooting of John Barr and if this was the beginning of something terrible.

TWENTY-FOUR

Steel had looked everywhere for Tia May but found nothing. He had hoped she had made it away from there OK and was at least on the way back from somewhere safe. Not everyone was back on board as of yet – it was too early. No, he would have to wait until final boarding at six and check with the loadmaster to make sure everyone was aboard.

As he sat in the Irish Bar, he watched the people wander past aimlessly, caught up in their own little worlds, smiles of complete bliss chiselled across their faces. They were happy, and why shouldn't they be? They were away from the chaos of normal life and were now lounging in luxury. His eyes searched the bar. *Strange* he thought, that the waitress was also not present. The waitress who was almost at every place he was eating or drinking. Sure, all the staff were working on this tub for the money, and she could have been taking on more work just for the extra cash. Then he remembered the other night with the two gorillas that followed Tia and him to the elevator. No, she was part of something, and he promised himself next time they met he would find out what. He looked up as the pretty young waitress brought him his coffee he had ordered as he entered the bar. She still wore that strange smile that made her eyes disappear into cute little slits as her broad smile pushed up her rosy cheeks. He smiled back and thanked her. Steel lifted the coffee cup and inhaled the bitter aroma of roasted Jamaican beans.

The smell was intoxicating. This was his first coffee of the day, and it was midday. Technically his second, but he never got the first one, as some silly sod decided to re-master the coffee shop with 6.8 SPC ammunition.

He remembered the bodies lying in a mix of plaster and broken glass, the floor covered by the blood of the innocent, and he wondered why it had happened and by whom? Sure, he recognised the one man's uniform. But why were THEY there? For him? Then Steel remembered what the shooter had said about "Being with her." They were not there for him, but for Tia and the other guy. She was the key, and he had to find out why.

Steel took the small aluminium spoon and placed it on the polished wooden surface. Holding the thin neck of the spoon between his thumb and index finger, he began to spin it slowly. His eyes stared forwards, but not looking at anything particular, just focused on a single point. Steel's thoughts were elsewhere. Suddenly he heard an unwelcome but familiar voice. His eyes focused as Jonathan Grant entered the bar. Steel looked up to see his grinning face approaching.

"Good afternoon Mr Grant, you look awfully pleased with something," Steel said, taking in Grant's broad smile. Grant sat down on the cushioned seat opposite Steel.

"This trip is turning out to be better than I expected," his voice almost trembled with excitement. Steel stopped spinning the spoon and placed it inside the empty cup.

"Do tell?" Steel asked, intrigued, but also anxious at what he may have discovered. Grant leant forwards, dropping his voice to a whisper.

"Last night an engineer was found hung, and then today two men shot up a restaurant in the town," He sat back, almost laughing with joy.

"Tell me more about the shooting," Steel asked. He did, of course, know all that there was to tell from his point of view, but he wanted to get the other half of the story, the fabricated account of the goings-on. The two men looked up as the waitress came up to them and smiled; her cute brown eyes disappeared into the slits of her eyelids as she did so.

"Hi, can I get you anything?" Steel pushed his cup forwards and smiled, She looked at him, and the smile changed to something else, something more of a dreamy-eyed look.

"Another coffee would be great, thank you," Steel smiled, as he saw her knees buckle slightly.

"Can I get one as well?" Grant asked, in a raised voice. She nodded but her gaze was fixed on Steel; even as she was walking away, she kept looking back.

"Unbelievable," Grant's words were bitter with slight jealousy.

"Anyway, you were saying?" Steel sat back in the booth; his arm rested along with the cushioned backrest.

"Yes, well it appears that some terrorists decided to shoot up a full restaurant in the town. Nobody knows why or who, just that the police took out one of the gunmen and the other got away," Grant explained. Steel smiled at the blatant lie that the police had told the press. Sure, they may have taken him down eventually, but he would have taken a lot of them with him.

"Sounds like you've been enjoying yourself," Steel said, his gaze switching between Grant and the world beyond the window. Grant nodded with a grin as he flicked through his notes.

"Any more news about what happened with that about an engineer?" Steel asked. Grant looked up from his notebook as the waitress brought their orders. She placed down the cups on to the wooden surface and left Steel with a broad smile. Grant grabbed for the sugar dispenser and measured out two teaspoons into the dark liquid.

"Oh yeh – so it turns out that one of the crew tripped or something and ended up hanging himself with the cabling he was carrying," Grant's words sang as though this was a trip of a lifetime for him, accidents, shootings, what was next? Steel just sipped his coffee and pretended to seem interested in the story, a story that he knew the truth about, but wasn't about to share with Grant.

"Sounds like you got the cruise of a lifetime Jonathan," Steel said. Grant nodded with a smile, as he looked down at his cup while he stirred in the sugar. Grant looked up; the smile had dissolved from his face as he felt Steel's questioning gaze upon him.

"Now wait a minute, you don't think for one minute I had anything to do with any of this?" Grant barked quietly so that few people could hear him. Steel placed down his cup onto the saucer and held the gaze. Even though he had his sunglasses on, Grant could feel those eyes burning into his soul.

"Do you think I orchestrated a shoot up in a restaurant and threw a man to his death, just for a good story?" Grant barked. Steel figured the outburst was more out of fear than feeling insulted. Steel mockingly stared upwards as if he was pondering the question, then leant back in his seat and smiled. "OK, I have heard of reporters doing anything for a story, but that goes a little too far, don't you think?" Grant smiled with a look of relief on his face as he realised Steel was messing with him. Grant drank a sip from the hot coffee and laughed.

"So, where is all this information coming from?" Steel asked, as he sipped his coffee.

"I have got my contacts here and there," Grant said, as he sat back with a smug look on his face. Steel nodded. Thoughts ran through Steel's head. Who could the snitch it be?

"Must be nice to have one of the crew in your back pocket I suppose," Steel smiled, hoping his fishing would draw something out. Grant looked up over his cup as he took another sip. At that moment, Steel knew one of the crew must have been present at both places. They had to have been. It was the only thing that made any sense. How else would they have known about both incidences? Just unlucky or right place right time? The captain had told all those present at the engineer's crime scene to tell no one, and as for the shooting, that wouldn't be common knowledge for some time. Grant looked at him puzzled for a moment.

"So, you didn't know anything about either occurrence?" Grant asked, with an almost surprised tone. He had thought this mysterious man had a finger on the pulse.

"Things have been a little slow here, I read a good book though," Steel said, with a sarcastic tone. Grant looked at Steel and his mouth dropped as he saw the side of Steel's mouth raised slightly.

"You were there?" Grant asked, his face almost pale with fear, "and the boy?" Steel scowled at Grant for even suggesting he had something to do with the boy's death. "Sorry," Grants eyes fell away from Steel's venomous expression in shame. "But the restaurant, you were nearby, you saw it?" Steel's eyebrows rose up even though the sunglasses were covering Steel's eyes; Grant knew the look. "You were in it when it took place. How the hell did you get out?" Grant thought for a moment then looked up at Steel, who had nestled himself in the corner of the booth. "The gunman, it wasn't the police that got him was it, it was you?" Suddenly Grant didn't know whether to feel afraid or safe. "What happened?"

Steel knew he wasn't going to get out of this, so he decided to humour Grant.

"Well, I heard about this nice square and excellent restaurant, so I decided to go, get some fresh air and culture," Grant watched him closely, his ears picking up the details of Steel's ordeal. "I went inside and enjoyed the view until some silly sod decided to redecorate with a heavy machine gun. A few others and I managed to get out in time." Steel paused for a second and looked at the people making themselves busy doing nothing. Steel's mood turned suddenly sombre. "Others were not as lucky." Grant nodded, only imagining what had happened.

"I can understand why you killed the gunman." Steel looked back at Grant and shook his head.

"I wanted him alive, however, someone else disagreed with that decision," Steel said, with an angry look. Grant put more sugar into his coffee and stirred the mixture.

"Did you see who it was?" Steel shook his head.

"No, but I got a feeling if I had, I wouldn't be talking to you right now." Grant nodded, with an understanding of the situation.

"Have you noticed how things are beginning to happen and they all revolve around this ship. There is a story here, and I intend to find it." Grant said, with a hungry look in his eyes. Steel sat up straight and leant forwards; his elbows rested on the dark wooden surface.

"Mr Grant…Jonathan, as a friend, don't go investigating anything, leave it to me, and I'll tell you everything when the time is right," Steel asked, his voice was low and held a tone of concern. Grant looked both puzzled and worried.

"Tell me Mr Black is there a particular reason you don't want me looking into things?" Grant asked, a look of suspicion crossed his face. Steel sat for a moment saying nothing. Grant could see him thinking.

"Look, I think that things may become…. troublesome," Steel said. Grant played with his cup handle; then he looked over to Steel who had a concerned look on his face.

"Tell me, Mr Black, do you look for trouble, or does it find you?" Steel looked over at Grant and smiled.

"Maybe a little of both," Steel smiled, thinking back to McCall and how she often asked the same question. Grant stood up and downed the rest of his coffee. He smiled back and threw down a five-dollar note on to the table next to his cup.

"Look, Tony, I appreciate the concern, but I have a job to do, plus I have been in sticky situations before. I'll be fine – really." Steel could see things getting a lot more intense, and he thought it would be best if Grant weren't part of the damage count. Grant had grown on Steel, even though he was a reporter. Steel had to admit Grant had been right, there was definitely something going on, and it did indeed revolve around the ship and Tia. Steel's eyes fixed onto a shop window as his mind began to wander. Why did Tia have to meet the contact there at that particular restaurant? As he looked out of the window, he couldn't help but notice the fresh faces, faces that had new excitement plastered on them which meant new passengers and ultimately new suspects. Once everyone was aboard, the ship would be at full passenger capacity, over seven thousand people on a floating city. Steel and Grant looked up as they heard the loud blast of the ship's horn signalling for all to board in the next hour or swim. Steel looked over to Grant.

"Look, Grant, you may be right but don't do any reports just yet, OK?" Grant thought for a moment, then nodded.

"OK, we do it your way for now but, at the first chance, you have to tell me everything, deal?" Steel smiled.

"OK, deal." With that, Grant turned and headed for the door. Steel sat alone for a while, his thoughts racing round in his head like a hamster on a wheel. He stood up and headed for the door. As he walked past the bar, he placed down a ten-dollar note without stopping. The barkeeper yelled an appreciative farewell as he watched Steel disappear into the crowds.

TWENTY-FIVE

At around eleven o'clock that morning, as the crowds of people hurried their way around the small town of Vigo, others decided to remain to watch a film in one of the five theatres or to just laze by the pools. The hallways and corridors seemed peaceful, less for the cleaning staff, making the most of the emptiness. Outside the temperature was rising. Even though it was early, it was in its high 70s. Inside it was a comfortable mid 50s for those who felt the baking sun was a little too much. A woman looked out of the massive glass panelled windows and surveyed the view of the port and the town beyond. She smiled confidently as she turned, walking down the corridor that had been behind her. She was tall and in her late thirties. Her maroon leather one-piece catsuit hugged her supermodel form. Her long black leather boots had flat rubber bottoms, which fell silently with each step.

Her shoulder-length black hair glistened like the pelt of a panther. The blue of her deep-set eyes reflected the overhead lamps making them sparkle. The woman stopped at the door and leant against the coolness of the wood panelling. She looked around and slipped the fake card key into the slot. A click as the bolt was disengaged made her grin. She opened the door and slipped inside. The cabin was dimly lit except for columns of light, streaming from the porthole windows. Inside the captain's room, she stopped to get her bearings. Moving around slowly, in the middle, she scanned the room for possible hiding places. *The safe,* she thought to herself. She shook her head as it was too obvious.

The woman moved with the grace of a ballerina as she walked across the wooden flooring towards his desk. Pulling out the draws, she reached inside the empty compartment to check for anything that seemed out of place. She frowned as her search had failed. For ten minutes she searched high and low for secret compartments and drawers, only to be disappointed again. Distraught, she sat in the captain's chair and swivelled around towards the desk.

"Where the hell have you put it, old man?" Her voice almost sounded impressed with his hiding place. As she moved around, her foot snagged a board under the antique desk. She froze and looked down, careful not to move her foot. Slowly she half got up and pushed the chair away – her foot solidly in place, as not to lose the spot she was marking with her boot. She knelt on to the other knee as she brushed her hand forwards to her foot. Using her gloved hand, she swept the floor, looking for an anomaly in the floor, as her hand moved over one board. The flooring seemed to be raised slightly as if it didn't sit quite right. She smiled and searched the desk for a letter opener or something with an edge. She felt the excitement build as she found the silver-plated opener on an antique office set. Finding the edge, she used the point to pry up the one edge of the board. The sound of wood against wood filled her ears as it came up with ease. Below, the hole was deep as though purposely made to hide something, she thought. Her hand reached in slowly, and the tips of her fingers nudged against something. She moved in deeper and retrieved the box that the engineer had given the captain before his accident. Raising it, she smiled, the image of her prize reflected in her eyes. Replacing the board and the letter opener, she stood up with her back to the doorway. She made a quick check that nothing was out of place then slipped the box into a small bag on her back. Her smug smile turned to a look of surprise as she saw someone standing before her, in the shadows.

"You – what are you doing here?" She was surprised to see the figure in front of her. "I got it; I was just about to…." Her body convulsed as the taser bit through her uniform as the attacker pressed the device against her chest. Her body hit the floor hard and began twitching as the nerves in her body sent her into neural chaos.

THE NEPTUNE WAS TAKING on fresh food and passengers. She was also taking on fuel and cargo. This was the last stop before the six-day ocean voyage, then on to New York for the presentation to commemorate its maiden voyage. The company wanted to name the ship *Titanic 2*, but due to bad taste and the slight superstition angle, it didn't seem appropriate. Besides, some billionaire had already created a replica of that fateful ship, and so the name seemed less worthy.

Steel had checked with the loadmaster (Mr Sing) who had confirmed all were aboard who should be. Steel sighed with relief that Tia had made it back on board the ship. As he looked out of one of the large plated windows, he watched as the evening sun was about to kiss the horizon. The sky bled a fiery orange with whisks of purple clouds. Behind him, weary passengers made their way back to their cabins after an eventful day ashore, laden with bags full of souvenirs they had bought for the people back home. He smiled as he watched them in the reflection. The ship seemed to be alive again. It was loud with conversation and children's laughter – or their cries about how tired they were. He closed his eyes and let the moment wash over him. Thoughts about being back in the city filled his mind - and her. He smiled fondly at the images of McCall.

Distant music made him turn around from his trance. It was oriental music. His eyes scanned the balcony and found, down below, in a glass-fronted room, a man was teaching Tai Chi. Steel leant on the gallery and looked down at the group of around twenty people, young and old following the man's every move. He was a Chinese man in his late fifties, Steel surmised, but he moved with grace and concentration. Steel smiled, and his gaze was blurred by memory, a memory of pain, death and rebirth.

The mists of time faded, and he was taken back to a dark place, an attic in his old family house in Britain. His ears filled with the sound of gunfire that rang like artillery guns. His body remembered the pain of each round as it passed through his body. He remembered looking down and seeing the life drain out of his beloved wife's eyes before he fell into the place of shadow. The shots were slow and aimed. His body wrought with pain as he fell onto the wooden flooring of the attic. The mixed sounds of screams and laughter filled his ears as Steel lay there on the wooden boards, he felt nothing but his life slipping from him, and he smiled. Voices screamed and argued, the words of one of them embedded in Steel's brain.

"Now you've done it you idiot, Santini will kill us all for this." The name branded into him like the wounds on his skin. "Santini."

He felt his body start to become cold and the muscles tight. He would be with his family soon, and that was good.

"Get up, you must get up," a voice filled his ears and a blurred vision of someone kneeling over him.

"Helen, is that you?" He raised a weary hand to try to touch her face. The voice was soft but had a sense of urgency to it.

"You must get up; we have to go; you must live." The world went dark again, but he felt he was been dragged. His eyes saw darkness, but every so often, small spots of light gave him something to focus on. He was being lifted up onto something; he felt cramped and small as if he had been put into a box. He moaned in disagreement and tried to fight. The voice again.

"Good, you have some fight left; use it." Steel felt panic as he had the feeling of going down.

"Was this it?" he thought "Am I destined for the other place, never to be with my family again." He wanted to scream but the movement stopped, and he felt himself being pulled again. His body hit concrete, and the pain brought him sight once more.

As he looked up, he saw the blurred figure taking him to a locked room in the basement. He heard the rattle of keys and the creek of old metal hinges. The world went dark once more, but he still heard the voice and …. music – oriental music.

"I need to close your wounds; this may hurt," the blurred figure said. Steel felt he was being put into a chair; his arms had been taped onto the arms of the chair. The darkness seemed to get darker; his breathing became more difficult. "I don't know if you can hear me, but if you can, be strong," the voice sounded different now, more like – Mr Lee, the gardener.

"What are you going to do?" Steel asked, his voice shallow.

"Have you seen Rambo?" Then it struck Steel what he was about to do. "Sorry, no time must do all at the same time, less painful that way." Before Steel could respond, a piece of wood was shoved between his teeth. "This will help with the pain," the old man sounded almost sorry about what had to be done. Then he felt his insides burn hotter than if he had gone to hell. It lasted but a second, but it was a second too long. Steel bore down on the bit between his teeth almost biting the piece of wood in half. Steel looked down at his body to see six flaming eruptions leaving his body through the exit wounds. The bit fell away from his mouth as he slipped away again into a strange, disturbing sleep.

Steel woke to the sound of birds chirping and children laughing. There was a smell of lavender in bloom and incense being burnt. The cheerful chatter of a finch sounded in the distance, and the smell of someone cooking filled his senses. Steel tried to open his eyes.

"Why the hell can't I open my eyes?" he thought. Steel raised a shaky hand to his face and found a damp cloth folded and placed over his clammy forehead. He lifted it off slowly; he groaned in pain. His body was stiff and uncooperative as he tried to sit up. He was disorientated and in pain. His body felt as if it had been run over twice. Steel looked around with blurry eyes at the room. It was around eight feet square with no windows; the only light came in a dulled stream from the half-open door. The door itself appeared to be made of wood

and brown paper. The bed was a futon that sat opposite the door against the back wall. The furnishings were sparse. He sat up on the edge of the bed and looked the place over, to his left an oriental dresser sat next to a small table with a crockery washbowl. On the wall above that, a simple mirror hung. Steel struggled to his feet, his knees felt weak and his legs like jelly. On the fifth attempt, he growled and stood up. Standing still for a moment, he moved over to the basin like a child learning to walk for the first time alone. As he got to the small table, he grasped the sides for support, his hands gripped them tightly and he just stood, looking down at the water. It looked cool and refreshing as the light from the doorway reflected in the pool before him. Steel thrust his head deep into the liquid and left it there. His burning brow seemed to cool in the fresh water. He pulled himself up. As the water ran down his body, he tilted his head back and let the soothing liquid cool him. Steel brought a shaky hand up to rub the water into his body but stopped and looked down at his fingers which lay upon a gnarly patterned wound in his right shoulder. His hand trembled as he touched each of the six exit marks. He gripped the table as images flashed before him, but he couldn't make sense of them.

Steel looked up at the mirror again. His body was stocky, with a bit of muscle, but nothing extreme, normal soldier physique from too much bad food, beer and the wrong sort of exercise to become the next Mr Universe. He looked straight into his eyes and gasped. His blue eyes had been a winner with the ladies; in fact, that's how he had landed the American Ambassadors daughter. He stared into the cold emerald green of his eyes. Where before, his eyes looked alive and happy, these were dead and uncaring – soulless even. He was a soldier born into the Aristocracy. His father had been Lord Steel, a prominent man in parliament and part of the Military Intelligence section in Whitehall. An Earl by birth, an honour bestowed to his family generations ago, before the time of Cromwell. Now he was alone; mercenaries had murdered his family – for what reason, Steel had no idea. As he stared hard into those cold eyes, his grip tightened on the sides of the small table. The wood began to creek under pressure.

"If you break it, you must buy it," Mr Lee said. Steel's grip relaxed as he saw the gardener in the mirror's reflection. Mr Lee was a short man – five foot six at the most, with a shaven head and a goatee which was showing signs of age, with streaks of silver amongst the black whiskers. His build was slight, and his clothes seemed too big for him. Steel had often wondered if his wife shopped for him and bought clothes, hoping he would grow into them. Steel had also wondered how this Chinaman got the job at the estate in the first place. A mystery he never went into, the stories in his imagination were far better. Steel was afraid if he asked he would find some boring story and his dream would be crushed.

"Where am I?" Mr Lee smiled and shook his head.

"It has been so long; it is no wonder you have forgotten my home. You used to sleep over in this room," Mr Lee said, suddenly shaking his head. "It is worse than I thought," the gardener said, tutting. Steel looked around; the room seemed unfamiliar to him. It had the same walls and furnishings as the other rooms, but this seemed new. Had the shooting caused him to lose his memory?

"I don't remember this room," Steel turned to face the small Chinese Gardener, a look of desperation crossed his face. Mr Lee smiled.

"Only joking, this room is new. Had it built last year," laughed the man Steel scowled at the man.

"That's just not funny," Steel said, holding the expression, but deep down was impressed at the joke. "How long have I been out?" Mr Lee went to answer, but a tall man in a black pinstriped suit answered for him.

"Nearly a week, give or take." The man was Doctor Edwards, the family's doctor. He walked in and put on his gold-rimmed glasses. His tanned face was large and round, grey hair mixed with the black in his receding hairline. Steel stood facing them; his backside rested against the table for support. Doctor Edwards looked at the wounds on Steels body and nodded somewhat pleased with the results. "Good, good. You're healing nicely." He stood up and looked into Steel's eyes by opening the lids widely.

"Why are my eyes like this?" Steel asked, the doctor opened his mouth to answer.

"You have the mark of the Phoenix, the born-again bringer of fire." The doctor turned to face Mr Lee, who was somewhat excited by the whole affair.

"It's probably a reaction to the medication, too much acids in the blood, or just some weird concoction this crazy bastard pumped you full of, should be nothing to worry about. It will be gone in a couple of days with the right diet," the doctor replied, with a smile. But Steel saw through the smile. He had no idea. *Great*, Steel thought, before nodding to signal he understood. But he knew that something had changed inside of him. "I'll come back tomorrow to check on you, don't worry, nobody knows you're alive – not yet anyway." Steel forced a smile as he watched the doctor leave. Mr Lee walked up to Steel and gave him some water that he downed in one. Steel handed back the glass but it slipped out of Mr Lee's hand. They both looked down in amazement as Steel had caught the glass between his two bare feet. Steel looked up at Mr Lee, who was now grinning.

"Good, good, now your training starts tomorrow," Mr Lee said, clapping his hands like an excited child. Steel looked puzzled.

"What training?" Steel asked, certain he didn't really want to know the answer. Mr Lee's grin widened.

"Training to be what you are, a ghost, a wraith." Steel swallowed hard.

"Don't tell me; you're not really Chinese, are you?" Mr Lee shook his head, a solemn look came over his face.

"I was born and worked in Japan. I worked in Japanese secret service for very long time. Your father and I worked on a case that nearly cost me my life and the life of my family. Your father saved us and brought us to Britain where I have carried out – shall we say services for both countries." Steel looked shocked for a second.

"You're a spy?" Steel felt he had to lie down before he fell down. He stumbled back to the bed and crashed down, unable to take it all in. He looked up at Mr Lee.

"So, what do I call you now?" The man thought for a moment, then he smiled.

"Mr Lee will do quite nicely," then he turned and began to laugh loudly and left the room almost dancing as he left. Steel knew this training was going to hurt more than his wounds.

STEEL AWOKE from his daydream and looked down at his watch. It was already half five. He thought about not attending the dinner but reconsidered, as there was always something to learn at the ghastly functions. He needed to know who was new on board and who had left out of the group. The one thing he had learnt about investigating was: Everything mattered. The minutest of details could be the breaker of a case.

He returned to his cabin and carried out the usual route of checking the locks on his suitcase and using the UV light on the safe. He almost seemed disappointed at the lack of attempt. He poured himself a large Johnnie Walker gold and stripped down to his underwear. The air con felt good against his bare flesh and he decided to just wander around like that for a while. He sat on the couch and flicked through the pages he had gotten off the internet about the dinner guests from the other night. Steel wondered how many more of the guests had false web pages. It was a proven fact that Tia and the Stewarts were fake. He downed the rest of the drink and headed for the shower. He reached inside the shower unit and turned on the water, keeping his hand underneath until it became the desired temperature. The washroom was suddenly filled with a small fog of condensation, and the mirror over the sink reflected no more. He stripped and folded his clothes, placing them on the small chair opposite the bed. The water from the shower felt soothing on his skin. The droplets came out hard and fast, almost like a jet wash. Steel stood with his hands against the wall and his head down letting the water massaged his stiff muscles. Today had been a hard day, and his body still ached from the drop from the building. He stood up straight and turned his back to the spray as he worked the soapy lather into his hard, taut muscles. He looked down at the temporary tattoos and wondered how much longer they would last before fading away. The tattoos had been a cover to conceal his wound just in case one of the Organization had been on the ship.

The Organization "SANTINI" was a criminal group responsible for the murder of his family. They were also responsible for hundreds of organised crime sprees around the world, including the case that brought him to New York and to the NYPD. Steel knew little about them, just things he had seen in his father's files, or information he had gotten from associates of the organisation – after some gentle coercion of course. In fact, Steel didn't know if Santini was the head of the organisation or just a pseudonym for the leader.

The water felt so good he didn't want to leave its embrace. Under the water, he had no cares, no worries. Under there he was alone with only the noise of the water against the glass. Rain, he thought to himself, he always found rain to be soothing. He smiled and switched off the water, then using his hands to brush off the excess water, he stepped out and towelled off. He looked over to the watch lying on the dresser. It was now nearly six. He smiled and sat down at the small coffee table and picked up the documents once more and flicked through. What was he missing? He threw them back down and stretched off. He looked at the paperwork lying almost fanned out for display. Maybe the reason he had not found anything was that it wasn't there at the time. They had just left port, maybe whatever or whoever it was had now boarded. After tonight, they would be heading into open waters, and after a few miles, he would lose his cell reception. He knew he would be alone on this and that was OK, he had worked alone before all of this. As the time ticked away, Steel knew he had to dress and attend another dreary night of dull conversation.

TWENTY-SIX

As McCall got off the elevator at the precinct, she saw Tony and Tooms sitting at their desks engaged in an argument about how to shoot someone who was in a crane, while Jenny Thompson sat at her computer, looking through some files. The air was abuzz with the feeling they were getting somewhere.

"Hi guys, what did you find out?" McCall asked, hoping for a short but sweet answer. The two detectives looked over at McCall as she approached. Tony picked up his notebook and flicked through the pages with a curious smirk on his face.

"Well, CSU confirmed the mark was a bullet strike," Tony said, rocking slightly in his chair, almost as if he was winding himself up for a big finale of bad news. "They used the laser to try and pinpoint the direction of the shot," suddenly McCall got a bad feeling at Tony's sudden pause. "Unfortunately, there was a problem," Tony said, his smirk widened. McCall looked confused as she sat on the edge of Tooms's desk.

"Why, what's the problem?" McCall asked, feeling the two of them were going to enjoy what they were about to reveal. Tooms smiled which meant she wasn't going to like the answer.

"It's in the middle of the Hudson River," Tooms said, still wearing his grin. She raised an eyebrow and nodded.

"Smart move, no worries about trace evidence and you

could just lose the weapon on sight and look like a normal fisherman," McCall looked at the pair and smiled. "But you guys already thought of that, do we have a calibre?" Tooms nodded as he leant back in his chair.

"CSU worked out where the round would have landed and found a .338 round with traces of our vic's blood on it." McCall looked at their murder board that was just as unrevealing as her own was.

"Has any potential suspect popped up?" Tony shook his head, a disappointed look on his face.

"No, the guy was clean, the ex is re-married to a rich guy, so no more alimony and his debt to the weasel was paid off in full," McCall looked over to Tony.

"How did he pay his debts off, sure he had a good job, but you said he was in debt up to his eyeballs, so where did the money come from?" Tony picked up the receiver and dialled for Financial Department. Yes, they had had his normal accounts, but maybe he had others?

McCall turned to Jenny, who was busy typing something.

"Hey Jenny, where are we with that mugging gone wrong?" Jenny stopped what she was doing and swivelled in her chair to face McCall.

"Well, her name was Karen Greene, she was thirty-four years old and lived in Greenwich Village. Karen worked as at a recruitment agency; she dealt with waitresses and bar staff for restaurants, aircraft and shipping." Jenny looked up at McCall, who was taking it all in as she stared at Tooms's board.

"The COD was exsanguination due to a gunshot wound to the stomach area, Tina is working on the wound and should be able to say what calibre was used." Jenny looked over her notes before continuing, "I asked around the neighbourhood, but of course, nobody saw anything. She was in a blind alley when it happened." She looked over at her notes that she had placed next to her monitor. Jenny had a bulldog clip placed in the crease to stop the pages folding over, so she could read it better.

"Tina has the TOD at around twelve o'clock, midday" McCall looked stunned for a second.

"That's probably why she took the alley because it was daytime. There's no way she would have taken that route at night" Jenny added. McCall weighed up the possibilities in her mind, making her head rock from side to side as she thought.

"Maybe, but why was she there in the first place?" Jenny stood up and walked over to the group.

"I asked her work colleagues, and they said that she had taken off to go to lunch because she had a date at the diner, just on the next block from her firm. I spoke to several of the staff, and they confirmed she was there with some guy, but the date ended badly" McCall smiled.

"Define badly" McCall felt the net tighten on the date. "He took off with another girl while she was in the restroom, he also left her to pay." McCall looked up at Jenny, fire in her eyes.

"Did you track down prince charming?" Jenny shook her head.

"Not yet, but I got a photo from the diners security cam, and I have passed it to uniforms and hotels, just in case." McCall smiled, Jenny had come a long way, and she was getting into the feel of being a detective.

"Nice job," McCall said, nodding. Jenny smiled at the compliment. McCall paused for a moment, then looked over at Tooms.

"Anything from robbery reference the ME's office?" Tooms shook his head.

"Nothing, no trace, and no prints. Even the security never picked anything up, almost like they weren't even there." McCall thought for a moment.

"What about the camera's server, was that messed with?" Tooms put down a file he was just going through.

"Tech's looking at that now, should have an answer by close of play today," Tooms said, taking a mouthful of coffee.

"OK, I am off to techs to see if they can track down the feed from Donald Major's workshop to see if that brings anything," McCall said as she headed for the elevator hoping that there was something in that feel to make headway.

She found Toby Lang, the Tech Assistant, in a small room with lots of monitors and computers, whose blue-lit cooling fans gave the dimly lit room an eerie glow. The tech was a young man in his late twenties with long brown straggly hair and red-rimmed glasses. Even though he was sitting, McCall knew he was tall. He had a thin, pale frame which was hidden by jeans and a grey t-shirt, on top of which he had a brown-checked shirt that lay open and unbuttoned. He sat at his workstation, going through the secure online accounts, looking for Donald Major's storage unit. McCall hadn't really found much at the workshop, but the tech was good at what he did.

"You got that address for the unit?" He asked, his body not moving from the position. It was almost as if he was afraid to miss something. She put a small post-it on to the workstation and then watched as his fingers flew across the keys like she had never seen anyone do before.

"OK just so I know, what are we looking for?" he asked, his gaze still locked onto the monitor. McCall smiled as she walked around the room, looking at the many different computers, each doing their own little task.

"Anything unusual really, someone else who may have access to his workshop or someone who may have visited." McCall shrugged, she wished she had more for him to go on, but this was a big box of straws and she was grasping.

"How far back we lookin' at?" He asked, as he started to do a little dance with excitement.

"Around two months ago to present, plus keep it open just in case he gets a visitor," McCall said, as she looked at a round fish tank that was full with multicoloured sand and strange rock formations and a skull which seemed to glow blue. This was set on a table next to a coffee machine and some bottles of water.

"I can put it on to stick when I find something OK?" He

said, with a confirmatory nod. She smiled and placed a grateful hand onto his shoulder.

"Thanks, Toby, you're the best," McCall said, walking away, but he didn't respond. The tech was in the zone and McCall thanked him and left him to him to his work.

As Tooms was waiting for the CSU report on the John Barr case, he looked over at Tony who was getting on with his investigation on Bill Foster. Bill Foster was a forty-two-year-old who moved from Boston to join the Cartwright Global organisation, a firm of import and export sales people that dealt with everything from butter to weapons. He had no financial problems, he was getting on well in his job, and he was making big money for the firm, so the one day he walks into his office and ends it all, by eating the barrel of a .45 revolver, made no sense whatsoever. Tony was getting ready to take off and go to the firm to talk to the co-workers and try to get a feel for the guy.

"Need a hand with your shooter?" Tooms said, tossing a baseball up in the air and catching it. He was leaning back in his chair with his feet on the desk, trying to look calm and in control of his case. Tony leant back in his chair and smiled, inquisitively.

"Why, you given up on yours?" Tony asked, with a grin. Tooms shook his head as he took a mouth full of water from the bottle on his desk.

"I am waiting for CSU to get back to us on the crime scene, who happen to be backed up, due to everything that has been going on, so 'till then, I am at a stalemate. Thought I could help you with yours; do my eyes good to look at something else for a while." Tony nodded, slowly.

"OK, let's go," He said, standing up and slipping on his short jacket.

"Where we going?" Tooms asked, taking his badge and gun from the locked top drawer of his desk.

"Lower Manhattan, place called Cartwright Global," Tooms slipped his coat on as the two headed for the elevator.

"So, I take it I am driving?" Tooms noted, as Tony tossed him the keys to the police Dodge Charger.

"You wanted it; you gotta pay the toll," Tony laughed. Tooms mumbled under his breath as the elevator doors closed behind them.

TWENTY-SEVEN

The offices at Cartwright Global were in Midtown Manhattan, on East 40th street. The tall mesh of concrete, steel and glass housed the masses of money-making opportunists and the lawyers to keep them out of trouble or find something on them. It was loud and bustling with life here. Taxis fought their way through the traffic while pedestrians tackled the oncoming crowds, it was organized chaos, but it held a feel that no other city possessed.

The two detectives parked and made their way into the lobby of the Grant building which housed many businesses and companies, within its twenty stories, to which Cartwright Global had the complete fifteenth floor. They rode the elevator up to fifteen and got off on to a bright and well-lit lobby full of people, moving quickly from office to office with purpose. To their front, lay a long sandstone-tiled floor with glass walled offices on either side that led down to the left, to their right there was a long, pine reception desk. The heavy-looking desk stretched around seven feet long and around five feet high, complimented by the white-walled backdrop. The smooth front of the desk had the companies name embossed in large brass lettering that caught the overhead lighting, making it almost glow. Behind the large wooden reception desk sat two women, both in their twenties and both wore black and white uniforms that resembled an airline rather than a global sales group. The two detectives made their way towards the desk, taking in their surroundings. As they approached, the two women smiled almost at the same time.

"Welcome to Cartwright Global how may I help you?" Their smiles faded as the two detectives opened their jackets, revealing the shining shields on their belts. One of the receptionists looked tearful, but held it back somehow, she had blonde hair and the face of a women who should have been in magazines rather than pushing paper.

"I'm Detective Marinelli and this is Detective Tooms, we're here about…"

"Bill Foster" She interrupted, before putting a handkerchief to her face.

"Yes, that right, I take it you were here that day?" He asked softly, she nodded whilst patting the tears away.

"She was the one who found him," said the other girl, giving the woman a comforting look.

"And you are?" Tooms asked, as he leant against the cool wood of the desk.

"I am Elisabeth Baker, and this is Susan Adams," replied the dark-haired colleague. Tony made a note of the names in his notebook before slipping it back into his jacket pocket. He wanted to see the room first before he started to question anyone.

"Susan, could you take us to his office, if that's OK?" She nodded in reply to Tony's request, then stood up.

"Who's in charge here?" Tony asked Elisabeth.

"Mr Shaw, Nathan Shaw," Elisabeth replied, Tooms noted that she seemed oddly nervous at just saying his name. Tony smiled, reassuringly.

"Could you let him know that we are in Mr Foster's office please?" Tony asked, Elisabeth smiled back and picked up the receiver and dialled one. As they made for the line of offices, Tony heard Elisabeth on the phone, explaining the situation to someone whom he could only surmise was this Nathan Shaw.

Bill Foster's office was at the end on the right-hand side, he had the sought after corner office. Tooms and Tony could almost feel the tension in the corridor about when the police tape was coming down and when the room would be free for them to fight over. As they approached, they saw a man standing in the doorway of an office, opposite the crime scene. He was short with round eyeglasses and slim build. His black hair had streaks of silver probably from stress, as he only looked thirty years old, touching forty.

"Hi officers, do you know when the office will be free?" Tooms glared at the skulking man.

"Seriously, you just want to just get in to another man's spot while the body is still warm?" The man smiled awkwardly, then shrugged, before looking round suspiciously, just in case someone saw. "That's cold man, real cold," Tooms growled, disapprovingly. "So, what's your name and where were you that day?" The man looked shocked for a second.

"Why…you don't think that I had anything to do with his death do you? I mean it was a suicide…wasn't it?" Tooms glared at the man, causing him to disappear into his office. Tooms shook his head in disbelief at the man's behaviour.

"Man, it's only a damn office. I mean what's so special about a friggin' office." As Tony opened the door slowly, he noticed Susan begin to back away. He turned and smiled at her. "It's OK if you don't want to come in." She smiled.

"It's OK, I am fine," her eyes looked red and sore from too much crying. Bill's office was large with two long windows that showed off a fantastic view of the Manhattan skyline. It had a modern and expensive look with a dark wood, "L" shaped desk, behind which an aged leather office chair sat proudly. There was a fifty-five-inch flat screen which was bolted on the wall, this was be used in conference calls as well as a TV or monitor. On the sidewall, a large dark wood cabinet held books and files as well as the odd photograph of family and holidays. A black leather couch had been placed between the windows, the wall holding the cabinet, and the TV. Tooms eyed it up and noted that it looked more comfortable than his bed did.

"OK, maybe I can see the hype on the digs, but to kill a man for it?" Susan looked shocked.

"No, he wasn't murdered, he did it himself, I saw it." Both Tooms and Tony looked round at her admitting to being there when he did it.

"So why didn't you stop him?" Tony asked calmly, so as not to seem he was implying anything.

"Well I wasn't in the room exactly, I was in the corridor at the time, heading back to the front desk." Tooms looked confused.

"So where had you been, this ends in a dead end, you could only have come from one of two offices?" Susan nodded, as she wiped away another set of tears.

"I had just dropped some files off at Brian's office," Tony looked back to the office door the strange man had come out of - "Brian?" Susan looked, confused for a second, then realized her mistake.

"What? – god no, Brian Fuller, he's also in the US – European sales team, same as Bill was," she explained. Tony nodded as he made notes.

"And then what?" He smiled as he asked, Tony could see it had a calming effect on her.

"That's when I heard the shot. I rushed in to find him just lying there in a pool of his blood, it was horrible," Susan's legs bucked as Tooms caught her and led her to a nearby office.

"It's OK, we can take it from here, and you just go back to your desk and have a drink of water," Tooms said. Susan thanked him and walked slowly back to her desk, every so often looking back at the door to Bill Foster's office.

Inside the two detectives moved around, trying not to disturb anything as they searched for any evidence that may support the idea he had killed himself or whether he was murdered.

TWENTY-EIGHT

With their blue sterile gloves on, they worked the scene. Tony took out his small camera and began to take photos just in case they didn't get the pictures from CSU or there was something they had missed, something on their sweep. Tooms walked up to the desk, its polished dark wood surface tainted by a massive dried blood pool in the centre. He stood in front of the desk and looked up at the wall behind and at the gory pattern of blood and skull contents that decorated the coat of white paint. Tooms moved slowly towards the thickly padded leather office chair and inspected it, only to find blood on the back of the chair, running down from the headrest.

"Hey man, come and take a look at this will ya," Tooms said, pointing towards the chair. Tony looked over to his partner and went to join him.

"What you got?" he saw Tooms leaning over to look at the rear of the office chair. Tooms stepped back to enable Tony to take a better look.

"Its blood, so what, the guy shot himself here?" Tooms shook his head.

"There's too much blood, like he'd been there for a while," Tony photographed the chair and made a note for CSU to take the chair away. Tooms could see that his partner looked anxious about something.

"What's up man, this getting to you?" Tony shook his head while wearing a strange look.

"We have lost two days of this case, one because we didn't get to hear about it till later and the second that thing at the ME's office." Tooms smiled.

"Sure, there was a mix-up, so we got the files late, but we got it now, and besides we have worked with less," Tony looked at his friend and smiled back, refreshed by his faith and confidence.

"Don't worry, we will get whoever did this, well after I've solved mine anyway, then I'll help you with yours," Tony disguised giving Tooms the finger by scratching between his eyes.

"Yeah whatever," Tony said with a grin. They span around suddenly at the sound of someone clearing their throat. There in the doorway stood a tall, well-built man in his late fifties, his tanned skin seemed darker by the grey suit and pinstriped shirt.

"You must be the detectives, I am Nathan Shaw," He stayed at the doorway as if not wanting to step inside for other reasons besides disturbing a crime scene, his massive stature almost made the doorway seem small. He stood around six-five with broad shoulders and a muscular face, his silver hair was styled and brushed with a side parting. Tooms and Tony walked over to him, and they all shook hands.

"I am Detective Marinelli, and this is Detective Tooms, we wondered if there was somewhere, we could talk?" Nathan Shaw thought for a second then beckoned them to follow him down towards the other corridor. As they left the room, they saw heads disappearing back into their offices.

"You will have to excuse my employees, gentlemen, and this is the most exciting thing that has happened to them outside their little worlds." Tony glared.

"A man taking his own life isn't what I would class as excitement." Shaw nodded in agreement at the suggestion.

"True Detective, however, you have to realise most people, if they are going to go, take it from the roof, last year we lost three top executives. The pressure you see." Tooms shook his head.

"Sorry I guess I don't, the man had everything to live for. Sorry, I don't get that, I don't get taking a .45 and painting the walls." Shaw stopped and looked around at Tooms.

"And believe me, Detective, I hope you never do, money isn't everything people say, but what if you suddenly lost a lot of money on a deal and the money belonged to average people who had saved for a lifetime, only to lose everything in a blink of an eye." Tooms looked even more confused.

"You buy and sell, what has banking got to do with this?" Shaw carried on walking towards the conference room at the end of the hall.

The room was long with a dark stained table in the middle with enough seats for around twenty people. To the left, a large window that showed off the other side of the city, to the right, on an almost empty wall, hung six monitors, each one around forty-six inches in size. Tooms and Tony joined Shaw as he sat at the end of the table next to the window. Tony took out his pad and a small tape recorder and placed them both onto the table. Shaw looked down at the recorder.

"What's that for?" His question sounded as if he were almost offended by the small device.

"It's for me, if I miss something or if my notes get lost, I still have this, so I don't have to bother you again." Shaw smiled, almost impressed by his ingenuity. Tony looked over to Shaw, who was calm and concise as he sat, leisurely in the black mid back leather chair.

"So, Mr Shaw, can you run through the events as you know them on that day?" Tony asked, his pen poised over his notebook, ready to take notes. Shaw looked down at the table, thoughtful for a moment, as though recalling that day.

"It was last Wednesday around twelve o'clock I think," Something crossed his mind which made him smile. "Yes, definitely twelve o'clock," Shaw said, with a nod.

"How can you be so sure?" Tony asked, looking up from his scribbling. Shaw had a twinkle in his eye.

"I was – let's just say I had a meeting in my office that required my full attention," Shaw's grin grew larger, and the two detectives got the point and hurried passed it quickly.

"OK, so you were…in a meeting," Tony ushered him on, his pen hand making small circles as if winding an engine.

"Anyway, it had been a tough week with a new client who was using the money from his firm to purchase something that would eventually make all the parties a handsome profit," Shaw watched as Tony made notes while Tooms just sat there and listened. "Bill was in his office all morning, tying down last-minute details, and he seemed fine until he went out for a short while." Tony looked up.

"Do you know where he went?" Shaw shrugged.

"Not really, he was gone, what, ten minutes at the most. But when he came back, he seemed shaken and upset." Tooms leant forwards.

"So, he could have just met someone in the main lobby?" Shaw thought for a second then nodded to concur with Tooms's theory.

"Sure, that's all he had time for really," Shaw said, with a shrug. Tooms sat back into his chair and made a mental note to check out the security tapes once they were done there.

"Please go on," asked Tony calmly, as he continued to make notes.

"Well he came back and went to his office, we were just getting ready for a meeting before lunch, and he was a no show, so I asked Susan to go and get him as she was off to deliver some papers to the office across from him." He paused for a moment to take it all in.

"That's when we heard the shot, we rushed to see what was wrong, but Susan was coming back as white as a sheet, screaming." Tony sat back in his chair.

"So, she saw him do it?" Shaw scowled at Tony.

"What are you implying that she watched and did nothing?" Tony shook his head.

"I am trying to get my facts here sir, if she witnessed him do it, we can work out if he was under duress or this was just, as you put it, another bad day at the office," Tooms said, Shaw looked confused.

"You don't think this is suicide do you, and you think that one of my staff did this." The man's brown face turned red with anger, and Tony raised a hand to calm him.

"Please, Mr Shaw I wasn't implying that at all, you said yourself he went downstairs and when he returned, he was different. We are only trying to establish what happened and who he met." Shaw sat back and opened one of the bottles of water on the desk.

"Forgive me, Detective, like I said it'd been a tough week," Shaw explained, wiping the sweat from his brow. Tony raised an understanding smile.

"You mentioned a new deal and something about losing a lot of money?" Shaw nodded as he took another sip from the water.

"Yes, the Callan deal, a small company who manufacture engine parts looking to spread their wings, they needed to launch abroad. So, all the workers pitched in everything they had to raise the capital it would cost to hire us. Quite a touching story." Tony tapped his pad with the blunt end of his pen.

"How did he lose the money?" Shaw's face fell at the thought of those very words.

"In this business, we provide a service of import and export of everything from elastic bands to heavy vehicles. A company wants something we get it, another company wants to sell something, and we find a buyer. We make it easy because we handle all the paperwork for customs and so forth." Tony looked at Shaw and smiled.

"So, you're like a smuggling eBay?" Tooms interjected. Shaw grinned and sat back into his chair.

"No Detective, everything we do is legal, and we have a customs officer on staff that checks everything in and out. In fact, what we have created has cut down a lot of illegal imports." Tooms cracked a smile as his mind wandered off.

"It's only as secure as you want it," he thought. "So, what happened?" Asked Tony, placing down the pen next to his notebook, Shaw's face became cold and angry.

"We do business with lots of firms some new some old. When we were looking up a buyer for the Callan sales, we came across one company that gave a generous offer, we dealt, and we lost. The company was bogus, and the engine parts lost." Tony still looked confused.

"But it was only engine parts, what's the big deal?" Shaw rocked back and forth on the back feet of his chair.

"These were prototype engines for tanks, all a company would need is just one, and Callan would be out of business. He went through a sales group in Britain, they seemed genuine enough, and they were not. Callan arranged for the engine to be sent over by ship for the company to test, a representative from Callan went with it, he must have been bought off by the company as neither the engine, nor the rep were never heard of again." Tooms looked at Tony who was wearing the same look of calculation.

"Who is in charge at Callan, and where can I find them?" Tony asked. Shaw reached to the centre of the table where one of the five intercom systems sat, he pressed the button and waited.

"Yes, sir?" Tooms recognised the voice that came over the loudspeaker as being that of the dark-haired receptionist.

"Elisabeth, can you get me the file on Callan please?" Shaw spoke into the intercom.

"Not a problem, sir," she answered before the line went dead. Shaw looked back to the detectives.

"If that will be all detectives, I have much to do. However, if I can help in any other way, please don't hesitate to ask." Shaw stood up and shook their hands before disappearing down the corridor to his office. Tony switched off the recorder and put it into his jacket, along with the notebook, as he pushed the chair back and stood up.

"What you thinking man?" Asked Tooms, who noticed his partner's concerned look.

"If this was a murder how the hell did they get out before everyone came in?" Tony said.

TWENTY-NINE

Steel poured himself a glass of the golden liquid from the half-empty bottle of whiskey. He had to admit that this had turned out to be one hell of a trip that was for sure. He picked up the glass between his fingertips in a claw-like grip, then moved to the balcony. The fresh ocean breeze made the delicate net curtains float like sheets on a line in a morning wind. This night was the first night of the six-day crossing, and he had nothing to show for it – nothing he had expected anyway. His suspects where definitely up to something but he felt it had nothing to do with a significant event. He still had the nagging feeling that what he had been looking for had not been on the ship until now, that's why he hadn't found it. As he took a sip from his glass, he looked out across the vast expanse; he gasped as the large and majestic moon rose over the horizon, like a morning sun. The ocean was calm and still, the night's air was crisp and soothing. Soon he would be back in the dining room, listening to more pointless stories from dull people. He hoped to be on the captain's table, but he knew there was a rotation that had to be done. He took another hit from the glass and closed his eyes as he sorted through the data in his mind as if he was sorting through the files in his office. Suddenly, his eyes sprang open and he finished the rest of his drink as he moved to the mirror to make a final check. He cursed himself as he had forgotten his coloured contacts, his dead green eyes looked deep and disturbing, even to him. He slipped into the bathroom and to an electronic contact lens holder. The device had the function of cleaning and powering up the special lenses that his firm had created. Just like the sunglasses, they weren't just eyewear. Steel put in the coloured contacts, then blinked several times then inspected the blueness of his eyes. A small smile broke the corner of his mouth as he remembered how he used to look before the incident at the family house. Steel took out his cell and punched a few buttons on the display. Slowly, he waved his hand in front of him, checking the special contact lenses were working. He smiled as if smiling to someone else, then turning on his heels, he left for the dining hall, ready for night's extravaganza.

The walk was slow and deliberate. He was taking his time getting there. As he walked inside, he noted new faces in the mix who were busy exchanging stories about what they had done onshore and the things they had bought. The orchestra was playing a slow waltz as guests made their way in to find their tables. Steel manoeuvred himself towards the safety bar. He perched himself on to one of the bar stools and looked out across the mass of people, but his interest was more for anything that stuck out rather than someone who would annoy. He was on the lookout for someone or something unusual, something to give him a lead on what was about to take place. He had gone over every theory he could think of what could be happening, some logical and some damn right strange.

"Good evening Mr Black, can I get you a drink?" Steel looked over to his left to find Grant standing there in a cheap tux.

"Good evening Mr Grant, sure why not," Steel replied. The two men shook hands and leant against the bar top, waiting for service.

"So have you learnt anything new?" Steel asked the reporter.

"No, not really, just we took on new passengers in Vigo as well as losing some," the men looked out across the passengers.

"And you, you get anything?" Steel shook his head and turned at the sight of one of the bar staff approaching. He ordered two whiskeys before turning back around towards the masses.

"No, but something better show up soon, or I am going to be disappointed," Grant smiled at Steel's comment.

"Yeh, I know what you mean." Steel took the two glasses from the bar and gave one to Grant.

"Well, here's to: "Be careful what you wish for"." Steel toasted, Grant raised his glass, and they both drank from the crystal glasses then headed for their tables before the captain arrived.

Steel was on the same floor as the captain's table, but Grant found himself on the floor above. Three friendly couples, one of which was in their eighties, joined steel at the table. Everyone talked mostly about life before the cruise, each having their own little tale to tell, but by far the elderly couple were the best. With stories of the war and the years after, even as he sat there, politely nodding and laughing, he could not help but wonder where Tia was. The loadmaster had assured him everyone was aboard and that she was one of them. Steel had the idea she was staying in her cabin lying low for a while, considering all the drama the past couple of days.

The captain's table had a new crowd to entertain him. It was evident to Steel that they had just boarded at Vigo, due to their look of awe at the decoration of the dining hall, and due to their look of awe at the decoration of the hall, and joy as Captain Long told of his tales upon the waves, tales of pirates, storms and sea monsters. Steel smiled as he thought back on the old sea dog tales and how outrageous they were, but fun; the captain was a true entertainer. However, he didn't seem himself tonight; he was more formal and serene; even his stories didn't have the same kick as usual. His mind was elsewhere, and that was probably where he wanted to be.

"So, Mr Black, what do you do for a living?" Asked the pretty red head who was sitting opposite him. Steel broke his concentration and looked round to see the longing faces of the others at the table.

STUART FIELD

"I am sorry I was miles away; what did you ask?" He smiled; the woman smiled back.

"I was wondering what you did for a living, everyone else has shared, I thought it polite to involve you," She had the smile of an angel and the body of a goddess, her dark red hair was long and full-bodied. She looked like a million dollars in her red sequined dress, and the man next to her knew it. He was a large, stocky man in his late twenties, the sort of guy you would expect to have played college football and been head of the "I don't like anything different" crew. His blonde hair was neatly trimmed, and the hair spray kept it nicely in place. The man was a jock, and she was a daddy's little girl. It was beauty and brains; the problem was that the man had neither. The more Steel looked, the more he came to think the man who's name card read *Brad Sherman* looked more like a 1930's mobster. Steel smiled to himself as he watched how Brad couldn't stop touching her.

"So you guys on your honeymoon or something?" Steel had already read the name cards, and her name was Lisa Hamilton as in the Boston Hamilton's. She shook her head and smiled with her eyes as well as her mouth.

"No, we're not married," she said in a sultry voice.

"Not yet anyway," Steel's smile faulted as Brad busted in on the conversation. Sure, he was a big man, but Steel knew he could have him on his knees screaming for his momma in one swift move. Steel had seen this arrangement before, and it never fared well for the woman; she was the money, and he was only around to make pretty and fit babies. He would probably end up in Daddy's Company screwing everything, and when daddy dies, he goes for half and dumps her.

"So, Mr Black, what do you do for a living? I can tell you're from money, sorry rich girl's nose. We are bred to sniff others out." Lisa laughed as she re-asked. Her ocean-blue eyes sparkled in the candlelight as she leant forwards, ready for his tale.

"Well, after I left Cambridge, I joined the army for a while. After I left, I decided to travel, see the world on my terms." Lisa sat with her head cradled in her hands and her elbows locked on to the table as she listened to the stories of his travels.

"Wow, did you become an officer or something?" Steel shook his head and smiled.

"No, I wanted to be one of the boys, I left at Sergeant," Steel admitted, recollecting his old life. Brad nodded with a smug look on his face.

"So what unit were you in, Infantry, Artillery – cook?" Brad laughed, but he was the only one.

"No, I was 22 Regiment," Steel replied then took another sip of water, he looked over to see the blank expression on Brad's face, and it felt good.

"What the hell is that, mechanics?" Brad laughed, with a shrug.

"The SAS you dumb ass, he was in the Special Air Service," The older man growled, annoyed at the jock's ignorance. Steel raised a glass to the older man who reciprocated the gesture. Steel grinned with delight as Brad's jaw dropped at the revelation.

"Oh, shall we eat?" Steel announced, as the waiters brought the first course. Lisa smiled at Steel, but this time, she had a different look in her eye, one he knew all too well.

The conversation became livelier as the evening progressed. Brad had relaxed and had joined in by telling some of his antics at college while he was on the team. All the while, Steel took time to scan the room without making it visible. He was looking for two things; first, for anything that seemed wrong, or out of place and second, he wanted to see if Tia was there. By the end of the evening, once coffee and cheese were served, Steel began to worry. He hadn't seen Tia, and Grant had taken his leave – suddenly skulking off after a phone call. Steel began to tire of the conversation and fake laughter. Suddenly, his inside pocket began to vibrate, he took out his cell and noticed it was a text message from Tooms telling him about the print he had sent. Steel smiled to himself as he stood up and excused himself, while he took the message. The others just waved him on and told him that he'd "better come back," Something he had no intention of doing. Steel made his way to a group of seats outside the restaurant in a large congregation area. He crossed the brown marble flooring and took a seat on one of the burgundy, velvet-covered chairs. Potted palms sat between the lines of back-to-back chairs. He looked down and opened the attachment he had been sent. As it opened it was a photograph and information on the assassin: The guy's name, background and rap sheet. Steel returned a text, thanking Tooms for the information, then slipped the cell back into his inside pocket. Steel looked at his watch, it was late, and so he decided to skip the conversation and hit the hay. What he needed now was peace, quiet and heat. He looked over at the wall and found the interactive map board, displayed on a forty-inch touch screen, he looked at the diagram of the ship and pressed the options button, as he touched it a menu came up with places and activities on the ship. He scrolled down with his finger and searched for saunas and gymnasiums. The screen blinked, and it showed three gyms onboard, each with a sauna. He pressed the icon of the one on the top floor, it seemed quiet, and out of the way, Steel knew most people would go to the larger better-equipped ones on the lower decks. As he walked away, a shadow came from the restaurant, it was Lisa. She walked up to the screen before it had time to reset and saw what he was searching for and where he would be. She smiled wickedly and bit her thumbnail, her imagination conjuring wild thoughts.

THIRTY

The gymnasium was large, with enough equipment for thirty to fifty people. It was one of four, but Lisa surmised Steel had chosen this gym because it was closest to his room – or rather she hoped it was. Lines of bike machines sat next to running machines. There was a small area at the back for the free weights, and in the middle of the floor space stood a numerous amount of top-of-the-range weight machines. Given the lateness of the hour, it was quiet, giving Lisa perfect opportunity to sneak in unseen.

Lisa moved quickly and quietly with purpose through the area, and she was alone except for one of the gym staff, teaching some young busty brunette how the equipment worked, so they never saw her enter. Lisa looked around quickly to make sure she had gotten there before Steel. Lisa smiled at the thought of what she was about to do. Next to the gym was the sauna room, this had white tiled walls and wooden slat flooring on which six small wooden cubicles were set in two lines of three. Each was large enough for ten people to sit comfortably, the doors a smoked brown colour making, it hard for others to peer and stare inside. Lisa was taking a risk, but that just exited her more. Lisa was a rich girl who never really had to work for anything, nearly everything was on a silver platter, but Steel was different. She knew she would have to work to get what she wanted from him which made this exhilarating. As Lisa sneaked in, she checked the thermostat to make sure it was on. Lisa began to curse as all were off for the night, then as she approached the last one in the far corner, she grinned broadly as it registered hot. She peered inside, but the steam and smoked glass made it difficult to see anything. She looked around before trying the door handle, all the while her gaze fixed on the entrance to the sauna to ensure nobody but Steel was coming in. As Lisa reached, she felt something sharp, and she looked down to see the handle was broken, she peered inside again just in case. Then she saw what she believed to be a glove near the bottom part of the glass. As she looked closely, she noticed the glass had been slightly cracked as if someone had tried to break the glass of the door. Lisa rushed through to the gym area to find the instructor.

"Help, for god's sake, there is someone trapped in the sauna." The instructor turned around from his lesson and rushed over quickly towards the next room. The instructor followed her direction and tried the door to no avail. Crouching down, he peered inside, hoping to catch a glance at what she was screaming about. Then he saw it, and there was a hand lying flat near the door, he grabbed the handle only to find it broken. Sweat began to cascade down his brow in panic.

"Oh god I can't believe this," he mumbled as he tried to use his nails to get some sort of grip to pry the door open.

"Can't you call anyone?" Lisa yelled at him, he stopped and grabbed for his radio and called for assistance.

"Hello this is Derrick in gym three, I need the doctor and some engineers, we have someone stuck in the sauna, the door is broken so tell them to bring crowbars." The woman at the other end of the radio responded to his alarm and told him to sit tight. The radio went quiet, and he knew he had done his part. He looked at the thermostat, which read it was below the standard 194 Fahrenheit and looked slightly relieved.

"It's not hot enough to kill whoever is in there, they have

probably just passed out," said the instructor. Lisa looked over at him in disbelief.

"You worried about her, or your job?" Lisa growled. He looked away and said nothing. All the time Lisa had the vision of Steel being in there gasping for breath on the floor, her heart pounded in her chest as they waited for assistance.

It was a good ten minutes before the doors of the gym swung open, and the doctor and two engineers with pry bars rushed in. The engineers immediately got to work on the door. Sounds of metal scraping on wood filled the room as the two men attempted to get some leverage on the door. Lisa gasped as she turned at the sound of a familiar voice. There in the doorway stood Steel in his gym wear, looking alarmed at the situation.

"What's going on?" He asked, as he rushed over to help. His eyes caught a glimpse of Lisa, who was wearing only a bathrobe over a towel and sandals. Steel moved over to her, hoping she could explain the situation, and later why she was there.

"What's going on, Lisa?" She rushed up and hugged him for support.

"We found someone in the sauna, and I feared it might have been you," He smiled to comfort her, his hand rested on her cheek making her eyes close at his gentle touch.

"OK, I think we got it, you ready doc?" Yelled one of the engineers as the pried the door open, as they did so a massive cloud of hot steam was released, covering the helpers as they dived for cover.

"I don't understand, the temperature gauge said it was below normal it shouldn't have been that hot in there," the instructor said, looking once more at the circular gauge.

"Tell that to her," the doc knelt by the shrivelled naked remains of a woman as he spoke, his words full of remorse and pity for the poor woman that lay before him. As Lisa turned and saw the remains of the woman and just stared at the desperate look on the woman's face.

The woman lay on her front, the skin on her body hung

loose and saggy as if it were a suit that was too large for her. Her outstretched right arm was reaching towards the door. Her fingers, bloody and raw as the flesh of her fingertips had been scraped away to the bone and nails that had been ripped apart and shattered from scraping something hard. The look of sheer despair was obscured by the skin of her face that sagged as if it was made from melted wax that made it unbearable for all to see. Lisa screamed then buried her face into Steel's chest while he held her close. Steel looked over to the body and then at the door. Bloody scratches gouged into the wooden frame with bits of fingernail fragments protruding from them, the glass on the door had been hammered by something but with not enough force to break the smoked glass.

"How long do you think she has been in there, doc?" Steel asked, still holding the whimpering Lisa to him. The doctor looked up at Steel and shrugged.

"Hard to say, hours I would say, let me get her back to the med lab, and I'll see what I can find." Steel nodded and led Lisa away, just as Brad walked in.

"I heard there was an accident, is my fiancée, OK?" Brad looked up at the pair with fierce eyes. "Hey, why the hell are you here with my girl?" Brad lunged forwards and ripped her out of Steel's arms. Steel backed off and raised his hands in a slow-down motion.

"Look Brad, I just got here OK, so calm down," Brad growled and swung at Steel who just leant at the middle to avoid the punch. Brad swung several more times. Each time Steel continued to avoid the hits.

"Brad I can do this all day, in fact, its good exercise but it's not the time or place," Steel announced as he caught the next punch in a vice-like grip. "Now behind me we have a dead woman, so, you need to take your girl away to comfort her because she found her, OK?" Brad nodded and turned to Lisa, who just shook her head at brad and ran off crying. Steel turned back and walked back to the doc, who was busy examining the body.

"Any ideas doc?" Steel asked, crouching down next to the doctor.

"It's ok boys I got it from here, Mr Black will assist me," The engineers just saluted and made their way out.

"Suits me fine doc, I need to leave before I lose the rest of my appetite anyway," said a bulky engineer, as he swung the crowbar over his left shoulder. Seeing they were alone, the doc pointed out a bruised area on her back.

"Someone broke her back?" Steel noted and looked back to the doc, the doc tilted her right wrist.

"See the burns on her hand?" Steel noted them then looked around the room, there in the corner by the door lay a stone from the sauna's stone pile. "She tried to smash her way out with that stone, my god it must have been red hot?" Steel said, with a painful look on his face. The doc nodded but gave Steel a curious look as Steel looked around the small cabin.

"The killer put her up there on the top shelf where she would get the most heat; I figure she was unconscious to start with but woke up," Steel stood up and walked through the scene. "She crawled down after realising her back was broken and passed the stone pile, picking up a stone she made her way to the door and started to bang on the glass," Steel stopped and looked around, playing things out as the doctor watched him mesmerised at his deducing method. Steel looked up, excited. "She was banging on the glass to get attention to start with," Steel shot down towards the door and pointed out the first few scratches. "When she realised no one could hear her, she started to panic and then tried to break the glass. Unfortunately she either lost grip of the rock or found it to be useless and cast it away, either way, she resorted to clawing." Steel looked down at the open-mouthed physician and smiled. "Sorry, too much TV." but Steel could see he wasn't buying it.

"How are we getting her back to the med centre?"

The doctor smiled, "Unfortunately we have to wait for the captain, after that I'll go and get a gurney, and we will take her using the service elevators," the doctor explained. Steel nodded with an uncomfortable smile on his face.

It didn't take long for the First Officer to come down and see what had happened.

"Where's the captain?" asked the doctor. The officer looked at the doctor as he stood over the remains of the woman.

"He is indisposed at the moment; he asked me to see what had happened. So, what's your theory then doc?" The first officer stood there, his arms folded, awaiting the verdict.

"Well, the doc reckons the door was broken before she went in, obviously didn't notice it, went in, but while she was in there, she tripped or something, and hurt her back. Made it to the door to try and get out and well…" Steel pointed with an open palm as if to offer the conclusion; the first officer looked over to Steel with utter disdain.

"And who might you be Mr……?" Steel could see he wasn't interested in either Steel's name or the fact there was a dead girl in a sauna. Steel noted the man was playing with his fingers of his right hand nervously, he was either missing his next fix, or he was just upset about this whole thing, and he just wanted to get out of the room and throw up.

"I am…." Steel said, as he started to answer the first officer's question but swiftly got an evil look. " – just leaving," Steel finished, as he began to walk away. The first officer held Steel in a look of contempt as he walked away to the weight benches.

"I need to get her back to the medical bay," The doctor's words became quiet.

"OK, do it quickly and quietly, I'll tell the captain and we'll shut this room off, for now, say we are doing repairs or something," The first officer stormed away, passing Steel, who was sitting on a weight bench waiting for the doc. The man didn't stop, just gave Steel a look as he went. Steel stood up and walked back towards the doc. "Wow, he wasn't the entertainments manager, was he?" Steel laughed, the doc looked up and smiled.

"I have to get my gurney and a bag if you can wait here?" The doctor said. Steel smiled and shrugged.

"I have been hanging out with stiffs all night, and least this one knows when to shut up," Steel shrugged. The doc gave him a quick smile.

"Thanks for helping," said the doctor. Steel nodded. "Is there anything I can get you?" the doc continued. Steel's eyes lit up at the offer.

"Her fingerprints would be great," Steel said, with a broad grin.

THIRTY-ONE

McCall awoke and peered at the alarm clock through half-open eyes. The electronic beep of the alarm was abruptly ended as she reached over, slamming a hand onto the off switch and waited for the second alarm to sound before she stirred. McCall rolled back over and stretched off the stiffness of a good night's sleep. The night before, she had relaxed by staying up late with a bottle of red and an old movie. Unwillingly, McCall forced herself out of the warm, comfortable bed and made her way to the kitchen to switch on the coffee machine she had prepped the night before. McCall clicked on the button and then rested her head on her arms as she leant on the counter next to the machine as she waited for the sound of the motors and heaters to activate into a chorus of a whirring sound. Still half asleep, she made for the bathroom to soak under the shower's warm embrace. As she entered the bathroom, McCall looked into the mirror and stared intensely at herself.

"Oh well, here we go again," she said to her reflection, as she stripped off her t-shirt and shorts and climbed into the shower.

After her morning ritual of breakfast in front of the TV, she headed to the precinct. Her normal stop off at the ME's office to play catch up had to wait as Tina was on call. In the bullpen, McCall found Tony and Tooms discussing the Knicks game the night before and Jenny was out working on her mugging gone wrong. McCall smiled. Jenny was doing well as McCall knew she would, the girl just needed guidance and a kick in the ass.

"Morning guys , hard at work I see," McCall joked, making them turn around to greet her as she sat on the edge of Tony's desk. "So where are we with these cases?" McCall asked, before taking a sip from her coffee through the safety lid of her take away cup.

"CSU got a trajectory of the bullet and found that the shooter was in the East River," explained Tooms as he rocked in his chair. Tony moved back in his chair, so he was almost sitting next to Tooms, so he didn't have to keep turning around to talk.

"It appears my vic decided to chew on a .45 after a deal fell through." McCall smiled as she saw the confused look on his face.

"But?" She said, expecting him to come out with something. Tony looked at her and smiled.

"However, something felt off, so I am checking some things out." McCall nodded in appreciation of their finds.

"So, what you got?" Asked Tooms, sipping coffee from an oversized mug.

"I have got an expert electrician who supposedly electrocuted himself while doing a menial job; I have no trace evidence to show anyone had done anything to cause it, apart from the fuse box, which was wiped clean. This was a stand up guy, good job, family, no debts. No, this is definitely a weird one," McCall said, with uncertainty in her voice. Tooms saw the frustration in her eyes.

"What did the 7/11 owner say?" He asked, hoping it may jog something. McCall shook her head as she stared at her own board from afar.

"He couldn't say, he was in Boston at the time, and he had given my vic the key to the shop the day before. Anyway, I have got footage from his workshop and hope that brings something to the table." She paused, then turned to the two detectives.

"Nice job, guys." She stood up and walked towards her desk; she wished that she had as much luck with her case.

Tony picked up his victim's file and flicked through personal and financials trying to see a pattern in his day-to-day life. Bill Foster had been married for three years to Brenda who worked in a salon part-time; they had been working on their first child. After he had left Cartwright Global, Tony had gone to speak with her at their home. From what he could tell, they were still in the honeymoon phase and everything was going well. The apartment was large which reflected he earned well, but it wasn't extravagant, or over the top, it was a home. The place was on the upper side, which meant he had to travel many subway miles each day. Apart from that, nothing stood out. She confirmed he was a bit preoccupied with this new deal, but he never seemed anxious or upset, the fact was she had the impression he was excited about the deal.

Tony stood up and moved to his murder board, where he started to fill in some of the blanks. Tony turned towards his desk as his phone began to ring and rushed over to pick up the receiver.

"Homicide, Detective Marinelli speaking," he was slightly out of breath from the leap he had just made from the board. It was the Tech Unit, they had looked over the footage from Cartwright Global and had flagged the person he was talking to before he took his life.

"That was Tech; they're bringing up the footage from Cartwright Global. Apparently there's something we need to see," Tony said, tossing an M&M into his mouth. Captain Brant, who just walked out of the elevator and heard what Tony had said, walked over to the group.

"Well, I hope it's good news; god knows we could use some right about now." Tony put the receiver back on to the cradle and looked at the board. "What the hell made this guy do that to himself and why inside the building, he could have just gone up on the roof and done it or jumped?" Tony shook his head as he flicked through the notes in Bill Foster's file, he stopped for a moment then hurried through the pages again, scanning each line.

"What's up, man? You look like you lost something?" Tony shook his head to Tooms's question then slapped down the file on to the desk.

"Where the hell did he get the gun?" Everyone in the group turned and looked at Tony, "He never registered for a gun – ever. So, where the hell did it come from, and why did he have it there?" The elevator doors slid open, and a Chinese woman got off and rushed over to Tony with a laptop cradled in her arms.

"I need to show you this," she said, her voice was soft and shy. Everyone got up and headed for the small briefing room where a sixty-five-inch monitor sat on a stand in front of a six-foot table.

"What you got for us Susie?" Tony asked, all excited at the hope of a break in the case. Susie Lee was tall, and her slim Asian figure was draped in a baggy T-shirt and jeans. She stood in front of the stand and plugged in the cable from the back of the set, plugged it into the laptop, and then set the laptop on top of a holding tray that was attached to the stand.

"OK, you ready?" Everyone nodded as they all took seats and waited for whatever had made the tech giddy. She brought up the video from the downstairs lobby of Bill Foster's workplace and fast-forwarded it to the time Bill went to the lobby, then let the feed run. Everyone one watched as Bill Foster came off the elevator and walked towards a row of seats. The tech moved the mouse and zoomed in on Bill just as another man approached him, the man was taller and had a larger frame than Bill. Even though the footage was in black and white, they could see he had dark hair and wore a dark suit with a coat draped over his left arm. As the two men spoke the conversation became heated, Bill turned to walk away but the man grabbed Bill's arm and pulled him back.

As Bill turned angrily, the man held something up, a piece of paper or photograph, this made Bill stumble backwards slightly as if his knees were about to give in. The man walked towards Bill and passed him something from under his coat, something that glinted for a second. The man patted Bill on his shoulder then casually left the building, leaving Bill to slowly return to the elevator, and out of sight. Everyone stood up and moved towards the large monitor, McCall spun round to the tech.

"Please tell me you have footage from the elevator?" The tech woman smiled and moved the mouse to bring up another feed to show inside the elevator, with Bill standing with his back to the wall, looking down at the floor. Suddenly he reached inside his jacket and produced the .45 revolver in his hands.

"That's where he got the gun from, the guy in the lobby." She turned to the tech who was now wearing a huge grin.

"You brought a blow-up of our guy, didn't you?" The tech pulled out three different-angled photos of the man, even though none of them were directly facing the camera, they could still get a good description, and the sketch guys had something to work on.

"Oh Susie, I could kiss you," McCall said, all excited as she rushed out, leaving the guys standing there, slack-jawed, as their imaginations ran wild.

Outside in the bullpen, they heard a phone ring then McCall's voice as she answered it. Her words were muffled by the noise of the everyday chaos of the department floor. Moments later, McCall came back with a puzzled look on her face.

"That was Tina; she wants us all down there, something about all our cases."

As the three detectives entered the bleak corridors of the ME's office, they saw Jenny leaning up against the wall of Tina's cutting room, texting.

"I see you got my text?" Yelled McCall, making Jenny look up and quickly stow her cell away.

"Yeh, so what's the big news?" Asked Jenny, wide-eyed and excited. McCall smiled oddly back at her.

"Don't know, she wouldn't say, just that we should all get down here." They entered together to find Tina in her office, dancing as she sat, to some nineties tune that blared from the radio, McCall smiled deeply at the sight of her friend having a good time. Tina looked up, embarrassed at being caught in the moment.

"Hi Tina, you said it was important, so here we are. What you got?" Tina glided over the body of Bill Foster, the tune still in her head as she went. She pulled back the sheet to show her findings to the group.

"OK, so CSU found fragments at all the scenes and compared them, some of them too degraded but they were able to determine that they were all shot by the same weapon," Everyone looked shocked, faces like carp, as their mouths fell open in surprise.

"What do you mean everyone?" Asked Tooms confused.

"Oh, apart from your crane man, his was a .338 that's definite, they found that out by using computer simulation and stuff, all too complicated for me thank you very much," Tina said, waving her hand about in a vogue dance motion. McCall sat down against the stainless-steel side tables.

"And Jane Doe?" McCall asked, with a curious look on her face. Tina nodded.

"Her too I am afraid, the gun left wasn't a match to anything, it was just a plant to send us off, hoping we would call it a suicide and move on," Tina shrugged. McCall nodded, taking in all the new data.

"Anything else?" McCall asked. Tina nodded awkwardly.

"Yes, Steel sent me a print from an accident victim on his cruise," Tina could see the veins in McCall's temple begin to throb in anger.

"Why did he send it to you and not me?" McCall growled at the thought of being left out; she suddenly turned to Tony, "Has he sent you anything?" she asked just out of anger, but not meaning anything towards them. "Sorry," she said, realising everyone was staring. "So what did it come up with, dancing girl, showgirl?" McCall asked. Tina shook her head slowly, not wanting to say in McCall's present mood.

"Dead girl," Tina replied, getting the confused look, she knew she was going to get.

"What do you mean dead girl, what dead girl?" McCall asked, confused at the statement. Tina cringed before she spoke.

"You know those false prints we found on Jane Doe?" Tina started to say. McCall's mouth fell open.

"No, you don't mean Jane Doe had her prints, but why?" McCall looked down at her feet as she swung her legs back and forth, as she thought. "OK, so we have a gun that connects nearly all our victims and a print that connects one of our vics with Steel's ship." Tooms could see her mind working, and then she looked up suddenly and jumped down from her perch. "OK, first Tony, go and see the face-makers, see what they can do with the photos of our mystery man, then get them into circulation." McCall turned to Tina. "Jane Doe, did you get dental and DNA samples?" Tina nodded and pointed with her thumb to her office.

"Got them back there under lock and key, why?" McCall looked over at Tooms.

"Tooms run the print on Steel's dead girl and any information on Jane Doe through all services including Interpol and MI6, just in case either of them wasn't from the States. The women are connected somehow. Let's just hope we find out how." Both men headed for the door. "Things have just got interesting now," Announced McCall, with a cunning smile.

"What makes you say that?" Tony asked, as he spun round to ask her, inquisitively.

"We are now all working the same case." She replied.

Everyone had left on tasks, leaving McCall and Tina alone with radio still playing tunes from the nineties. "How you doing?" McCall asked, sitting back on the table behind her; Tina had a sparkle in her eye.

"Well, I took your advice, and I got some "counselling." McCall gave Tina a bit of a Mona Lisa look.

"Too much information, but spill," She said, laughing like a teenager in a schoolyard.

THIRTY-TWO

Back at the precinct, the fresh leads had given everyone the boost that they needed. For too long, it had seemed as if they were hitting a brick wall in the cases, but now those walls were coming down. The four detectives grouped around Tony's and Tooms's desks while they worked out their strategy; each had their case files to hand while McCall stood in front of the blank side of her murder board.

"OK, so it all started with Jane Doe, she was found on Monday at fifteen Hundred. However, Tina puts TOD at around midday." McCall had written JD....1200 hrs on the board in blue marker.

"Karen Greene was next, she was mugged in the alleyway at around midday," Jenny looked up from her notes in utter surprise. "That can't be a coincidence...could it?" She asked as she watched McCall go through the notes on Donald Major and Tooms and Tony did the same for theirs.

"Our killer only kills at midday, what – he does it on his lunch break?" Tooms yelled, unaware of what he just said. He looked up at Tony and McCall who were wearing the same look of enlightenment.

"Why not? Makes sense really," Tony added, as he watched McCall's expression change to a meaningful one as she rushed to the mobile map board.

STUART FIELD

"What's up, girl?" Asked Tooms, wondering where this was going.

"Donald Major was killed in the 7/11 near Alphabet City on East 4th street." McCall placed a red pin on the map board then turned to the others.

"Uhm, Karen Greene was in the alley off of spring street," Again McCall place in a pin.

"OK, next," she yelled with excitement, with a pin at the ready.

"Well, Jane Doe was found at the hotel at the junction of Hester Street and Bowery." Playfully McCall placed in another pin then grabbed another, her fingers poised ready to stick it in to place.

"Bill Foster was at Spruce Street." Tooms threw down his file, angrily.

"Yeh, and Jon Barr was in Brooklyn Piers, hell the only reason we got it was because they didn't want it, and Barr's wife complained, and she lives in New York," Tony said. McCall couldn't help but wonder about something.

"This John Barr, did he always work there?" Tooms looked in his notes and looked up with a blank look on his face, almost as if he had seen a ghost or something.

"No actually he worked most of the time abroad; in fact, he had just finished some work in the UK helping to build some ship or something." McCall turned around towards Tooms,

"So why was he at those docks?" Tooms shrugged.

"Don't know, maybe he needed the cash?" McCall shook her head as she looked at the board.

"No there has to be more to it than that, look everyone who has died has been led to this area, why?" Tooms stood up.

"Yeh, but Barr was in Brooklyn, not New York let alone the area," McCall smiled.

"Yes, he was, it wouldn't take much to get as close as you could in a boat, take the shot, dump the weapon in the river and be back before someone missed you." McCall stood back slightly and outlined with her finger. "Everything is confined to this area of lower Manhattan. We need to find a central point.

If this person is indeed committing these murders on his break, then they must be using public transport, be it a cab or the subway." Everyone nodded in agreement. "We have a face to go with our search, or part of one anyway," Tooms added, rocking in his chair while he twizzled his pen between his fingers.

Captain Brant came out of his office and approached the team who seemed as excited as he had seen them in awhile.

"What's up with you guys , don't tell me you know who did it, so we can all go home, and I can get the commissioner off my back?" He seemed almost disappointed as McCall shook her head with an apologetic smile on her face.

"Sorry Captain, however, we have figured out a few things." Brant sat on the edge of Tooms's desk and folded his arms ready to receive the briefing.

"OK, all of the deaths occurred in lower Manhattan which means whoever carried this out is in that vicinity. We know all the deaths occurred at around twelve midday, which means our killer has a day job in that area." Brant nodded with a look of been impressed with their theory,

"Do you have any suspects?" McCall smiled, confidently.

"We found a shot of a man who was the last person to see Bill Foster alive, and now if anyone else from the other companies recognises him, it's a good chance it's our man." Brant stood up his stern face now had a hopeful look on it.

"Good work, people, keep me in the loop." Then he headed back into his office to answer the phone that had just begun to ring.

McCall sat on the edge of Tony's desk and picked up the lidded thermos cup.

"OK, even if we find this guy, we still have to prove he had something to do with it, any good lawyer would argue that it was circumstantial he was there, and they would be right, hell for all we know he may just have business with them, and that's all." She swung her legs as she thought, her eyes fixed firmly on both boards. McCall jumped off the desk and stood up straight.

"OK here's the plan, everyone goes back to the places of work of each vic, once the likeness comes in. Find out what their last jobs were. These people are connected by something, something worth killing them for." McCall walked over to her desk and started to unpack the large cardboard box that lay on her desk. Inside were the items she had gotten from Donald Major's workshop. Blueprints, files and a couple of notebooks was all she was able to take, without looking suspicious. She sat down and started to go through the things, especially the notebooks, to see if anything pinged. Jenny walked up to her and picked up the folded blueprint,

"What's all this?" she asked, looking at the blue document quickly, then placing it down.

"This is all from Donald Major's workshop. I figured something might tell us what he was doing. We have the feed from his cameras, so we can see if anyone had been there, and the best part is that we can see if anyone goes there now." Jenny smiled at McCall.

"Nice, hope it brings something." McCall nodded as she flicked through one of the notebooks.

"Me too, me too." Jenny wandered back to her chair and picked up the Karen Greene file as she sat. She opened it up and laid it flat before her, leaning onto her folded arms as she read. Every so often, she would look up and around, smiling to herself as she scanned the room. She looked up at the television set that was on a bracket above the captain's office.

"Well folks, it appears there is a storm coming and its coming in from the east coast." Jenny smiled as she sat back in her chair and watched the satellite pictures of a mass building up in the ocean. She reached over and picked up her cell phone and pressed to speed dial someone. As she waited for someone to pick up, she scanned the room, but her attention always landed on McCall.

"Yes, it's me – we may have a problem." Jenny said, her eyes scouring the room.

* * *

As the afternoon sun burnt brightly, McCall made her way back to the electrical firm where Donald Major had worked. She had phoned ahead to make an appointment with the CEO in hope he could shed some light on a few details. McCall had parked not far from the entrance to save time; on the off chance she had to get back to the 11th quickly. McCall entered the large lobby and was instantly met by a tall pale woman in an all-black suit. They shook hands, and she beckoned McCall to follow her. The woman spoke very little, but she gave off an aura of power and control, like an old headmistress with a cane. The ride in the elevator was the quietest and most uncomfortable McCall had ever experienced. Her eyes kept darting to the woman, who just stood there as still as a statue. Even though she was in her early forties, she dressed as stiffly as she looked, with her hair tied up into a bun at the back, and shoulder padding in her jacket, at least McCall hoped it was padding. The elevator doors opened, and McCall released the breath she had been holding as she stepped off. The woman walked before McCall at a pace that would have made professional speed walkers blush in shame.

She was led to a large conference room with a massive ebony wood conference table with fourteen black leather chairs and large panelled windows that showed a fantastic view of the city. William Brown sat at the far end of the table with his back to the world outside, while he typed something on his tablet.

"Good afternoon Detective and what do I owe the pleasure of your visit?" His words sounded distant as if he had other things on his mind, but she brushed it off as he did have a company to run, despite the goings on around him. However, he seemed pleased to see her, despite the tone.

"Can you tell me what Donald was working on last?" Brown smiled, and looked up from his work.

"No, I am afraid I can't." McCall pulled out one of the chairs and sat directly opposite him.

"Can't or won't?" her words were sharp and directed to hit the sore spot.

"My dear Detective, first off we work under a code of

discretion when required, besides, the client asked for him and no questions asked, the money for his services were, shall we say, enough to warrant that only he knew what was going on," Brown said. McCall frowned.

"So, you have no idea if it was illegal or not?" McCall asked. Brown stiffened at the accusation.

"Detective, in this company, reputation is everything; if we take on disreputable clientele we might as well shut down. No we have a policy that if our workers get a hint of wrongdoing they are to bail and inform us. Besides, Donald was the sort of man who would never have taken a job that was not legal." McCall gave him an angry stare.

"So, it never bothered you that, whatever his last job was, it might have gotten him killed?" Brown looked at her, shocked and confused.

"I thought it was an accident, and they said it was faulty wiring or something." McCall shook her head.

"Think again, now what was the job?" Brown looked genuinely saddened by the news, the sort of look you couldn't fake straight away.

"I am truly sorry, Detective I really don't know, and if I did, I course I would tell you regardless. My god, someone killed Donald, but why I don't get it?" McCall nodded, satisfied with his answer.

"I found Donald's workshop and some plans. I wondered if you could take a look and figure out what he was working on?" William Brown sat back and smiled.

"I am sorry, Detective I am just the CEO. It was my father's company. I am good with business, not electronics," He paused and leant forward to press the intercom button on the three-pronged device that sat in the middle of the table. "But I know someone who might be able to help." As he pressed the central button, McCall heard the voice of his secretary, Susan.

"Yes, Mr Brown?" Her voice was chirpy and cheerful.

"Susan, can you get hold of Simon Roberts and ask him to come here please?" he released the button and walked to a small steel trolley that held bottles of water. "Can I offer you a drink, Detective?" He asked, offering a bottle to her, McCall rose and took the small bottle from him and smiled.

"Thank you." He just smiled and sipped from the open mouth of the bottle.

"The contract for his last job, how was it done?" McCall asked then took a sip from the cold water. William Brown thought for a moment.

"I got a call, someone wanted a job doing, requested Donald personally which is not unusual as he was a hell of an electrician. They arranged a meet…" Brown looked into space for second while his memory went over the facts. "Two weeks before the job was due to start. Then on the day of the meeting, one guy turns up. Nice guy, … Jones, I believe he said his name was. Yes, that was it, Mr Jones, anyway they came into here in fact to take the meeting." McCall gave him an odd look.

"Alone, was the meeting recorded or anything?" Brown shook his head.

"No sorry, it's all part of the "confidentiality," McCall and Brown said at the same time.

"Yeh, yeh I get it," McCall said with a disgruntled look. They both looked over at McCall's cell, which lay on the table next to her leather-bound organiser. It was signalling she had a new text. McCall touched the screen to retrieve the message. It was from Tooms, he had sent an attachment, the picture from the sketch artists.

"That's Mr Jones," McCall turned slowly and held up the picture for him to get a better look.

"Are you sure?" Brown nodded, while he took another mouthful of water.

"Yeh, that's him." McCall grinned.

"Got you now, you son of a bitch," McCall quickly sent a text in reply informing Tooms. *The man goes under the name of Jones.*

When Simon Roberts arrived, McCall had already flattened out the massive blueprint ready for him to examine. He knocked and shyly entered. He was tall and thin with a pasty complexion and brown curly hair. He wore brown, thick-rimmed glasses, his dress sense had the sixties look to it, even though he was thirty-two. At first glance, she was expecting Scooby doo to come in with him, but she forced a smile away.

"Simon, this is Detective McCall of the NYPD, she's here about something Donald was working on, could you take a look?" The man walked up to McCall and shook her hand. His palms were cold and sweaty.

"Mr Roberts, I found these in Donald's workshop, do you know what they might be for?" Simon leant on to the table with both hands supporting him as he looked over the blueprints. He shook his head, then he looked up with wide eyes and an awe-filled smile.

"I have no idea what this is, but it's a work of art, may I take it away to study it?" McCall smiled a sarcastic smile.

"I would prefer this not to be out of our site, do you need any special equipment or something?" Roberts shook his head and gave her a confused look.

"Good, in that case if you want to study it, you can do it down at the station, I don't have time to babysit the blueprints. If that's alright with you, of course, Mr Brown?" McCall added, swinging round towards William Brown. He smiled and raised his hands.

"Anything you need, Detective, if it will clear things up fast – for poor Donald of course," Brown said, with an almost sincere look on his face. McCall smiled and packed the blueprints away and headed back to the station with Roberts in tow.

THIRTY-THREE

After having a late breakfast, Steel spent the rest of the morning at the internet café checking the news headlines of the New York Times webpage. He had read of the tragic deaths of Donald Major, the suicides of a woman in a hotel who was yet to be named and Bill Foster, who had taken his own life at work in the Cartwright Global building. His eyebrow rose as he read another day's column about the tragic accident, *Tragedy as dock worker John Barr falls to his death*. He worked the mouse furiously, searching for more *Accidents*. Steel soon found it when he spied a page telling of the mugging gone wrong and the shooting of Karen Greene. He sat back in his chair and sipped the hot tea, the aroma of *English Breakfast* filled his nostrils. His head was spinning with facts, who were these people and why did they stick out in his mind? Was it because he had made no headway in finding out any more about the ship or indeed, why he was here? So he had to find something to fill his curious mind? He looked up casually at the day, and the time Karen Greene was gunned down. *Karen Greene, aged thirty-four, was gunned down by muggers on Tuesday at around twelve o'clock. Police are asking for witnesses*. Something twigged in Steel's mind, something he had read while going through the others quickly. He scrolled back and made a note of the day and the time the people died. He sat back in his chair again and looked at the piece of paper in his hand. Each one had died consecutively in the week starting with Donald Major, who was an electrician, on the Monday. Also, each one had been died around twelve o'clock midday, coincidence?

Captain Brant had been right, the shit had hit the fan over there, but there was nothing he could do. For all he knew, his instincts had been wrong, and he was being sent on a wild goose chase. However, things had happened while he had been here, and that, there was no denying.

Steel leant back and flexed his muscles underneath his black shirt. Before breakfast, he had done a good two hours, workout in the gym, mostly to make up for missing his workout the night before, and it helped clear his mind as he blew off steam. Now he was feeling the effects in his tightening muscles as he stretched in the chair.

He looked around outside the café at the wandering groups of people, all completely oblivious at the goings-on of the past couple of days, but then was it a case of I don't know, or I don't care? He smiled, shook his head and then got back to work. He had to find out why the engineer boy had died and was Jane Doe from the sauna involved. He remembered the captain's conversation below deck of how he was the last one to see him. Steel looked blankly at his empty teacup and at the tiny traces of black tea-leaves at the bottom. He had heard that the boy was an understudy to one of the chief engineers on board. If Steel could find him, maybe he could fill in some of the blanks. Steel wiped his history then ventured out into the sea of people and made his way to the elevator that would eventually take him to the lower decks. All the while, on the lookout, to see if he could catch a glimpse of Tia. He had checked her room, but it looked as if nobody had been there in a while. He knew she was on the ship, but where on the ship was the question. The only feasible theory was that the Stewarts had her held up somewhere for the time being; why was also a mystery. They were far from Vigo now, so whoever tried to kill her is long gone. Steel reached the elevators, pressed the call button, and then leant against the wall next to the polished doors. Moments later, the doors slid open, and he stepped into the quiet of the steel box. Just as the doors were closing, he caught a glimpse of Missy and her new friend Antony Bishop walking arm-in-arm together in the swell of the crowd. "Interesting," Steel thought, as he pressed the button for deck three. From there, he would have to walk down to engineering, and the cargo holds, as he had no security pass to use the elevators on those floors.

THE ENGINEER'S restroom was empty except for the tall, strange, thin man. He sat at one of the tables sipping tea from one of the cups from the drinks area while doing a crossword puzzle. With his pale completion, he almost looked ill, with his thin form and the black pants and black turtleneck that he was wearing. He was alone, and that's how he liked it; if someone came in, they would hurry out again to his great delight, even the giant hulks of men were afraid of him. He sat with his back to the wall and one eye on the entranceway, yet he was cautious about things that may happen by accident.

Jim Docket walked in, oblivious that he was not alone, as he walked to the coffee machine. He picked up the glass vessel that contained the strong-looking liquid and poured himself a mug full, his hand shook as he lifted the jug filling the mug, almost losing the coffee before it reached the drinking vessel. His mind was adrift with thoughts of his lost protégé. He never saw the body of the young lad. He couldn't bring himself to look upon him, not like that. He wanted to remember the boy as he was, bright and enthusiastic. He slid the coffee pot back into the machine and turned towards the seating area. He stopped and stared straight into the strange man's eyes. Anger grew within as Jim saw the man just sitting there, looking up at him as though nothing was amiss.

"You," Jim's voice growled like an angry grizzly, as he approached the man with both fists clenched, ready to do some hurting. Even though Jim was not a young man, he could still do some severe damage with his fists, and that's exactly what he wanted to do at that moment. The strange man didn't move; he just sat there, looking up at Jim with large bloodshot eyes. "Why did you kill him, he did what you asked, so why?" The man face changed to one of confusion.

"Whatever do you mean?" replied the strange man, his voice full of high and low pitches, like nails on a chalkboard. Jim roared at the denial of what he had done; his only thoughts were of putting the man through the wall. "Mr Docket, I never did anything to the boy, apart from scare the daylights out of him. When he left me, he was very much alive and screaming." The man smiled slightly at the memory of the boy running out of the cargo hold.

The man stood up, closed the musical pocket watch, and placed it into his black vest, his form towered above Jim's, but he didn't have the engineer's build. His thin form looked unable to lift the coffee cup, let alone be a danger to anyone. He went to leave the room, his movement slow and deliberate, then he stopped and turned his head slightly.

"I thought the boy's death was an accident; I heard he had tripped and hung himself?" the man could feel Jim shaking his head.

"No, I spoke to the doc, someone had staged it like that." The strange man turned to face Jim.

"Why would you think that I had killed him, Mr Docket. What possible motive would I have?" Jim looked away for a second, his mind going through the questions; he only wanted just one answer that was good enough for him to rip the man apart. But he couldn't find one. Annoyingly, the man was right, he had no reason. "Mr Docket, my business is discretion – until it is necessary not to be. However, I have to be discreet here. If I were going to do something, trust me there would have been no body and a note would have been found, telling how he couldn't take it anymore." As Jim looked into the man's eyes, he knew he was telling the truth. This man was evil, of that Jim had no doubt, and that alone said that this man would do things to resolve problems in a way he didn't want to think about. "No Mr Docket, I didn't kill your friend." the man paused and looked into space for a moment before turning back to face Jim.

"But it would be interesting to find out who did?" Jim's stomach turned as the man's look held a grimacing look of evil. This was the look of a man who was seeking revenge, not for the boy, no, someone had upset his plans, and he wanted blood. Someone was going to pay, and Jim couldn't think of anyone better to do it.

Jim sat down and sighed as he felt his pulse beginning to slow to a normal rate as the strange man left the room. With a shaky hand, he lifted the coffee cup to take a sip from the brew. He looked up, over the rim of the cup, and saw a man leaning on the opposite wall with his hands in his jacket pockets.

"Sorry about your friend." Said the man. Jim spat out a mouthful of coffee at the sudden shock at seeing someone there.

"Who the fuck are you and how the hell did you get in here?" The man smiled.

"My name is Antony Black, and I walked here." Jim looked up at him, and then at the door, which was shut.

"OK, Mr Black or whatever your name is, this is for crew only…." Jim looked in surprise as Steel walked over to the chair opposite Jim and sat down.

"The boy worked under you, didn't he?" Steel could see the man's pain written over his face. Jim looked stunned for a second, how did he know so much? Was he the one who had killed the boy?

"I asked you to leave Mr," Jim growled, his words vibrated at the back of his throat, giving it more power in the tone.

"The boy was tortured before he died. Why?" Steel's eyes fixed onto Jim's as they sized one another up.

"Now how would you know that, may I ask?" Jim's expression was bitter and full of accusation. Steel's eyes looked sorrowful.

"Because I saw his body, someone had used a taser on him. What had he done or seen?" Steel asked. Jim shook his head, images of the boy crept into his imagination. Steel could see the man was in no state to be messed around; something else had stirred his emotions and quite recently. Steel stood up and walked over to Jim, and he offered his hand. "I am truly sorry about your friend, I work with the NYPD, and I want to find who did this. I just want to help. I am trying to find out who killed the boy and the woman in the sauna." Jim looked confused.

"I thought what happened to the woman was an accident?" Steel shook his head as he crossed the room and poured himself a coffee.

"No, she was murdered. Someone broke her back and left her in there. I am waiting on the doc, but I reckon she had been in there pretty much all day." Jim's face screwed up at the thought of the woman boiling to death slowly.

"Who would do such a thing?" Steel sat back down and took a sip from the coffee.

"The same person who wanted your boy out of the way," Steel replied. Jim Docket looked down at his coffee, his mind awash with too many facts. "Before the boy disappeared what was he doing?" Jim smiled as he thought back on that morning, the boy practising his knots, then his smile faded as the thought of the thin man wiped out the happy thought.

"We were in here practising knots. Then Mr Bloody Williams comes in and gives him a package. "Take it to the captain" he says , "Straight there and straight back," he says." Jim shook his head, trying to think of a reason why he had been killed. "I asked Mr Williams about it, and the strange thing is he didn't know anything about it" Steel saw the look of confusion creep over Jim's face.

"What did he have to take to the captain?" Steel asked as he was just about to take a sip from the hot brew.

"A box or something, didn't look like much though," Jim shrugged, after putting his cup down to show a rough diameter with his hands, "It was about this big and made of black plastic or something, didn't really get a good look at it. The lad got it from Williams, and he was gone quick as you like, he was." Steel nodded as he took in the facts. Jim Docket looked at Steel up and down as he sat there drinking the hot coffee, his gut told him that this stranger was OK. "You work for the NYPD huh, so you're a cop or something?" Steel smiled.

"Something is a pretty good description, yes," Steel replied. Jim turned and looked down to the floor beside him as something caught his eye. He smiled fondly and picked up the book of knots that lay on the floor next to him.

"Funny, the lad was getting quite good at these, he was, would have made a damn fine sailor, he would." Jim looked back to where Steel had been sitting, only to find an empty seat and an empty coffee mug. Jim crossed himself twice and drank his coffee, nervously.

THIRTY-FOUR

McCall arrived back at the 11th with Simon Roberts. She led him into one of the briefing rooms where he could work in peace. Roberts thanked her and got to work. His eyes were wide with excitement at being a consultant for the NYPD. McCall crossed the bullpen floor and headed for the break room, on the way she passed her desk and got her porcelain mug from the bottom drawer. The floor was busier than normal with phones ringing off the hook at the desks of detectives, who were out in the field, and other detectives darting here and there, trying to do twelve things at once. As soon as McCall entered the break room, the bitter smell of their new brand coffee filled her nostrils and she let out a sigh of contentment. She poured a cup and savoured the aroma; she hadn't had a coffee all day which made this smell all-the-more special. McCall opened one eye to see Tony and Tooms coming in, brandishing their own mugs, ready for a refill.

"Hi, guys " McCall was pleased to see them and would have been even more pleased if they had gotten somewhere with their cases.

"Hey McCall, any luck with those documents you found?" Tooms sounded as hopeful as she had.

"No, not really, I brought one of the electro wizards back with me to see if he can work something out." McCall pointed with her head towards the briefing room and the man inside, who sat with his head in his hands studying the plans. She shrugged, then filled their mugs with the hot coffee. "And you, how did you guys get on?" Tony shook his head as he put milk and sugar into his brew.

"Nothing, all we got was that they all died on the Lower East Side of Manhattan, nothing we didn't already know. We did a cross-check, but that just led us to a park," Tony shrugged.

"There goes your lunch hour theory," Tooms said, with a shrug. McCall leant against the counter and took a slow sip, her thoughts a million miles away, calculating.

"We're missing something – we have to be. Just that one bit of the puzzle." She looked down at her jacket pocket as it began to vibrate with an incoming call. She placed her cup down and took out the cell, it was Tina. "Hi, what's up?" McCall just listened as the ME asked her to come down and to bring the others. McCall placed her cell away and looked up at the two detectives.

"Saddle up, Tina has something she wants to show us." She turned to look at Jenny, hard at work at her desk, "All of us."

The detectives entered the corridors of the ME's office like a scene from a western with McCall in the lead. McCall smiled as she caught their reflection in the glass of a door at the bottom of the long corridor and the theme from The Magnificent Seven popped into her head.

They found Tina standing over the body of Bill Foster as she made her examination. She didn't look up she just gave a friendly wave and got back to speaking into the Bluetooth headset as she made her notes. The detectives took up positions around the room where they could, as they waited patiently for the ME to finish. After around ten minutes, Tina looked up as she pressed the off button the headset.

"Glad you could all make it," she smiled. "OK, so suicide guy didn't commit suicide." Tina said to their surprise.

"What do you mean, he didn't commit suicide? We have a witness who said he went into his office alone and upset and then heard the shot. There was no one else in the room, so how can you be sure?" McCall didn't doubt Tina, just the evidence they had. Tina picked up Bill Foster's right hand.

"Now we know that he was a righty. However, due to a small accident on the squash court two weeks ago, he wasn't able to write his own name. I got his records from his GP, and he confirms he wasn't able to do anything with that hand." Tina could see the look on McCall's face.

"Shouldn't he have had a –," McCall started to say. Tina smiled

"– A bandage or cast, yes he should have had. However, whoever did this, removed it to throw us off. Well, tried anyway," Tina said, proudly. McCall looked the body up and down, hoping for some revelation in her thoughts; then she looked up at Tina.

"Did Trace find any prints on the gun or GSR anywhere?" Tooms asked. Tina picked up the file and opened it to look for that particular reference.

"There were traces of GSR on his right sleeve and hand; fingerprints were a match to our vic," She closed the file then placed it back on a pile. "But they only found prints on the trigger and grip," Tina said, with a broad grin as she saw the look on McCall's face.

"It was an automatic wasn't it?" She asked, looking up at Tony, who nodded in response.

"Yes, 1911 custom. Why?" Tina and McCall looked at each other, both of them grinning.

"Who cocked the weapon? There should be prints on the top slide when he cocked it, also no prints on the magazine or rounds. Who wipes the prints off a gun you are just about to commit suicide with? No, I don't buy it. The weapon was a plant. Tina's right; this was no suicide; just another loose end being tied up." Tina smiled at McCall as she took off her safety glasses.

"That's not the only reason you're all here." McCall could see that twinkle in Tina's eyes, the sort of look that says, "This is about to get weird." Tina walked over to a work-surface that held a stack of files in trays that were marked up: *DONE, PENDING, THIS JUST IN.*

"So why are we here, you found something that linked them all?" McCall asked, in hope of some sort of break in this case. "They were all killed by what appears to be the same weapon," everyone looked at her strangely, as if she had gone mad.

"How is that possible, are you trying to tell me that someone killed Bill Foster and left the gun to make it look like he killed the others, then shot himself?" Tooms said, a puzzled look on his face. Tina shrugged, her look was one of disbelief in the facts that she had.

"The GSR was on his left hand, so it is possible he did take his own life, but the others I am not so sure of unless he was standing close up, but we didn't find stippling or powder burns on the others, so they weren't shot up close," Tina continued. Something didn't sit right with McCall, the evidence was all wrong. McCall jumped down from her perch.

"OK, everyone go back to where these people worked and show the photograph of our mystery guy, see if we get any hits. Tony while you are there, speak with the secretary again, see if there was something she missed or just isn't telling us." Tony put his notebook away and headed out.

"Tooms, speak to the local boat hires, see if anybody took a boat out that day to go fishing," McCall said, making Tooms stand up straight like a robot who had been activated.

"You got it," he bellowed, and headed for the door. McCall looked over at Jenny and smiled.

"Jenny, go back to the motel where we found Jane Doe, flash that picture, check traffic cams, anything that will tell us where she came from and if our mysterious Mr Jones was anywhere near," Jenny gave a quick friendly salute and pushed through the double doors. Tina looked down at the remains of Bill Foster.

"McCall, what the hell is going on here?" Tina asked. McCall smiled and shrugged, she had little to go on. Her only lead was the mystery guy who could just turn out to be just some poor man in the wrong place at the wrong time. She smiled broadly, as she looked into space, her thoughts wandering elsewhere. Tina noticed the look on her face and gave a subtle cough.

"Something you want to share?" Tina asked, knowing what that look meant. McCall looked up, shocked for a moment by the break in her daydreaming.

"Wha…I was just thinking Steel would have loved to have been part of this mystery," McCall admitted. Tina nodded, her face painted with a mischievous grin.

"Talking of mysteries, how was your date with Doctor Dave?" Tina almost purred as she spoke the words. McCall gave her a false grin and headed for the door.

"You know where I am if you want to share" Tina yelled, as McCall pushed through the doors.

"Bye Tina." Her tone, full of sarcasm, echoed through the corridors.

THIRTY-FIVE

Tia May sat in her room while the Stewarts took down her account of what happened in the restaurant in Vigo. It had been a long day and all she wanted to do was shower and crash into bed. Their questions began to wear at her, she had no idea who had shot at them or why. They sat facing the cabin door on chairs they had found around the suite, notebooks and bottles of water lay on a large coffee table just before them. The debrief felt as if it had gone on for hours and Tia was getting bored and tired of answering the same questions. She looked at the door for a brief moment, half expecting Steel to walk in with that boyish smile on his face, she didn't even know if he was alive. The last she had seen of him was when he bundled her into a taxi, which had brought her away to safety. Tia was no rookie, but she had never taken fire like that, looking down to see her hands were still shaking from the ordeal.

A sudden knock at the door made them all freeze. Bob raised a finger to his lips to signal for them to be quiet, and slowly he drew his Glock from the kidney holster beneath his blazer and lifted it so it was next to his face in the quick aim position. He slowly inched forwards to the door and looked through the small fish-eyed spy hole, only to find the corridors empty. He shrugged and put his weapon back into the safety of its holster. He walked back to his seat and picked up the note pad once more.

"OK, just to run through it again…" Tia shot him angry look, she was tired, and her eyes were burning from fatigue.

"Look Bob, no matter how many times you ask me, it will still be the same story," she closed her eyes and masked them with her hand, her thumb and fore finger resting on her temples.

"Sorry, look it's been a really long day, can't we pick this up later? I just want to sleep." Tia said. Jane smiled, sympathetically.

"Sure, I can't see any harm in that; I think we have enough facts about what happened." Tia smiled and was about to thank her.

"The facts about what happened, really. I would love to hear what those are, because I am still trying to figure out what did happen." They all turned to face the bed where they found Steel sitting comfortably with his elbows on his thighs and his hands clenched together in front of him as he leant forwards.

"How did you…?" Bob looked confused as his view switched between the door and Steel's position on the bed, Steel smiled taking pleasure at Bob Stewart's agony.

"Don't worry about it, plus if you are going to pretend you're not there, may I suggest you don't talk really loud then go suddenly silent, oddly, it doesn't work." Steel said, lying down on the bed and testing it by gently bouncing. Tia grinned and looked away, hoping Bob and Jane had not seen her.

"What do you want Mr Black?" Bob asked, annoyance still rang in his voice. Steel stood up and walked over to Bob, who remained in his seat.

"I want to know what the hell is going on for a start. Ever since I have been on this tub I have been shot at, roughed up by a guerrilla in a hotel room, been followed by a hot, but creepy waitress. So, what's the story, Bob?" Bob Stewart stood up slowly, his gaze followed Steel's form almost as an intimidation movement.

"Sorry Mr Black, it's a need to know basis and you don't

need to know," Bob said, with a smirk. Steel felt his muscles tense as he restrained himself from putting Bob through the wall. Then his gaze fell towards Tia who was sitting next to Jane.

"Are you OK?" his voice was soft and full of concern, she smiled and nodded silently.

"She is fine, thank you for your concern, now if you would please leave, so we can continue with our…. discussion." Bob raised his right arm as if to point the way to the door. Steel made his way to the door with Bob in close pursuit, suddenly Steel stopped and turned.

"Why were they at the restaurant?" Steel asked, Bob and Jane looked confused. "your guys should have done a risk assessment on the meeting place," Steel continued. Bob shrugged.

"We got our orders and she went to meet with another agent, so what?" Steel nosed up to Bob who was at least a foot shorter.

"You have no idea where we went, do you? You just took it on orders, and you sent her," Steel growled the words.

"We had orders that the building was secure, and she was too…." He stopped, realizing he was telling Steel everything. "I don't have to explain anything to you Mr Black, so if you would kindly…." Steel grabbed him by the lapels of his jacket, lifted him off the ground, and slammed him against the wall, winding the terrified Bob in the process.

"That plaza was a kill zone, someone either messed up or they set you up. Frankly I don't care if you guy's kill each other, whoever the other side is. What I do care about are the innocent people who got killed because of it." Steel could see Bob wanted to say something. "If you say anything about collateral damage, I swear I will throw you off the fucking balcony and I will take pleasure in watching the sharks feed on you." To the side of him, Steel heard the sound of the hammer being drawn back on a pistol. He turned his head slowly and stared into Jane's eyes. What she saw in those eyes made her tremble in fear; her hands began to shake as she pointed her Sig at Steel.

"You may want to put that pistol down before you shoot

him instead of me, personally, I think you would do the world a favour, but still," Steel said. Jane Stewart carefully put the hammer back with her thumb and holstered the weapon. Steel smiled gently then released Bob's collar, dropping him to the ground.

"Someone sent your people to that plaza, why?" Steel growled. Jane sat down hard and looked up at Steel.

"Tia said that she received a text saying to go to that meeting spot, we never sent such a message." Steel nodded as he took in the facts.

"And the other agents, did they get the same message?" Steel asked. Bob nodded, as he rearranged his blazer and tie.

"Our network is linked, so everyone working on a job gets the same information at the same time, saves time," Bob explained. Steel pondered the problem for a second, who were these people who could tap into a government network and access the agent's cell phones.

"I have to call this in," Bob sat down as he took his cell from his blazer pocket. Steel reached over, took it from him and tossed it onto the bed. Bob looked up, stunned and angered at the display.

"What the hell are you doing, Mr Black?" Bob stood up and glared at Steel, who just pushed him back into his chair.

"If you were thinking about calling the office, you might want to find a secure line; obviously yours have been compromised," Steel said with a grin. Jane stood up and took down a small aluminium case, and then using the digital lock on the catches, she opened it. Inside were cell phones unused and with the batteries unfitted, taking one out, she assembled it and tossed it to Bob. Tia looked over to Steel, her face longing for him to stay but she knew he wouldn't.

"So, what do we do now?" Tia asked Steel with a longing smile.

"Carry on as normal. I for one am going to dinner, I'm starving." Tia gave him a warm smile.

"Me too, I'll see you there," Tia said, then kissed him softly.

"I am sure you won't be missed for one evening, we have

work to do," Bob sighed. His tone was like a strict parent. Steel grinned and looked into Tia's sparkling eyes.

"Oh, but it's what you will miss, everything that is said or done. Every little curious look that someone makes. No, there is too much out there, and if we miss one little piece, we might miss something important." Steel explained. He turned and left through the door, leaving Tia staring after him, her eyes capturing that last look of him before the door clicked shut. Jane turned to Bob, who was on a burner phone waiting to be connected. She noticed the curious look on his face as he looked at the balcony door.

"What is it?" She asked.

"How the hell did he get in anyway?" Bob asked, looking around the room. Jane rolled her eyes at the question.

"Really, now you ask?"

THIRTY-SIX

Steel returned to his room. He knew that the Stewarts would never give anything up, not intentionally anyway. As well as learning Tia was OK, he learnt that the Stewarts had no idea that an unknown party had compromised them. In Steel's past, he had worked with agencies of all descriptions all over the world. He had come to realise that they were alike, and they were, in fact, more trouble than they were useful – to him anyway. To them, everyone was the enemy.

He showered and changed into his black tuxedo for another engaging night of false pleasantries and laughter, another night off for what he saw to be full of lies and deception. He grinned at the prospect of his brain being taxed by strangers' chatter about how good their lives were and seeing through the charade. He took the jacket out of the closet and slipped it on over his black shirt and black waistcoat. He stood for a moment in front of the long mirror and made sure everything was in place. He leant forwards, checked his teeth and then combed his hair to the side with his fingers. Steel saw the reflection of the clock in the mirror; it was almost seven. Steel smiled to himself, and headed for the bedside cabinet and took out the cell phone. He held it up flat towards the light so he could see along its flat glass surface to see if the double-sided tape had collected any prints. He almost seemed disappointed at the lack of tampering.

Happy the cell was secure, he typed in the code to unlock the sim card and sent a quick message to McCall.

HEADING OUT TO SEA TONIGHT SO I'M NOT SURE ABOUT CELL RECEPTION, SO THERE MAY BE NO CONTACT, SEE YOU ON THE OTHER SIDE. STEEL.

Steel watched the hourglass symbol spin round slowly before disappearing, then a message telling him the message had been sent came up on the screen. He closed down the cell completely and tucked it away again. Steel was now alone, and he would have no contact with anyone until the ship neared the US.

Happy faces filled the captain's dining room, laughter and music drowned out conversations and made the perfect excuse not to be heard by unwelcome ears. Steel walked in casually and stopped near the entrance. Looking around, he took in the room for a moment, his eyes scanned the room like a bird of prey, watching for something or someone out of place. Steel moved over to the plan and was pleasantly surprised to see he was back on the captain's table, and he grinned as he saw with whom he was sharing a table. The band started to play a slow waltz, which Steel had learnt meant, *Take your seats for dinner*. He glided over towards the table to find most of the dinner guests already seated. At the table, there was the Studebakers , the Metcalfs , The Dawsons and the large frame of Martin Goddard.

"Good evening" Steel greeted them with a smile, which they returned readily as he took his seat next to Missy Studebaker. The table was abuzz with conversation when he had first arrived, but then it became more of a silent hum of whispers.

"Hope you're not talking about me?" Steel said jokingly, as he placed the napkin on to his lap. Albert Studebaker leant in towards Steel and gestured for him to come closer, which Steel didn't mind, as Studebaker's wife was between them.

"We heard that the captain is bringing some real big shot to the table tonight, don't know what his name is though." Steel smiled and sat back into his chair as the wine waiter started to pour a full-bodied red into his glass. He had thought it strange that three seats were vacant and now he knew why. From out of

STUART FIELD

the corner of his eye, Steel caught a glimpse of Martin Goddard's huge bulk; however, it was Goddard's open-mouthed expression that made Steel look over to him. He was looking behind Steel and towards the entrance. Steel turned slowly to catch the elegant form of Tia May in a strapless electric blue dress. Steel could see she was enjoying the hungry eyes that were undressing her and in truth, he couldn't blame them, she was a picture of loveliness. Steel stood up as Tia approached her seat between Albert and Martin.

"Good evening Miss May, glad to see you could make it after all," Steel said. Tia took her seat as a waiter assisted her with her chair.

"Oh well, you never know what you may miss if you never go anywhere, wouldn't you agree Mr Black?" Tia said with a grin.

Steel smiled as he placed the napkin on to the table and picked up the wine glass. As he took a sip from the wine, Steel made note that he had not seen Grant for some time, in fact, they had not crossed paths since he had come back on board. His eyes scoured the room for any sign of the journalist but found nothing; with an almost concerned smile, he hoped that Grant was OK. The change in music meant it was eight o'clock and everyone stood as the captain walked in with another man. The captain waved at the many people as if he were some kind of hero or statesman. Captain Long stood at the head of the table, and the stranger took the place next to him. The stranger was around six foot one with thick black hair that glistened with hair products. He had a face that could have been on a fashion magazine and blue eyes that sparkled in the candlelight. He stood upright and straight-backed as if to make himself more prominent, and he had an air of arrogance about him that swayed the women but made the men want to put a knife in his chest. With open arms, the captain beckoned everyone to sit, at which the orchestra began playing a waltz to open the diner, which muffled the sound of chair legs on carpet and the clang of glassware against cutlery and crockery, as people took their seats. Steel took note of everyone's reaction to this new face, he just sat back and watched as everyone sat in silence, their eyes measuring up this new addition to the table.

"So, everyone, I would like you to meet a…um, an acquaintance of mine, Mr Anthony Blacke." The table had a different air to it. Steel looked over towards Tia, who had a strange, confused, almost upset look on her face. Behind the captain, Steel saw the waitress from before, who nearly lost the two wine bottles she was carrying. At that moment he knew Tia and the other women had mistaken him for the man who now sat next to the captain. He was somehow relieved that he was no longer the target of people's infatuations, but also felt a little used by Tia, *but what a way to be used,* he thought.

Steel felt the mood shift as wine glasses were re-filled and conversations ensued like a stuck recording as each of the dinner guests talked endlessly about their lives before the cruise - all except Steel, who just sat there and observed the goings-on around him. He was still amazed at how, each time he heard the same tale, it never changed. He looked around mainly to see Tia's reaction to this Anthony Blacke. She sat calmly and broke a smile when she felt it necessary to do so, but otherwise there was something dark, hidden in her eyes. The table was captivated by Anthony Blacke's stories of how he was a self-made millionaire and how one of his pastimes was to bring aid to countries in need around the world. Steel sat through several courses, listening to the self-absorbed tales, the man had charisma there was no shortage of that, but something about him bothered Steel. Blacke looked over at Steel as he was laughing with the others and found Steel just smiling pleasantly, in a way that made the newcomer nervous. Blacke picked up his wine glass and took a long sip, his eye contact held fast by Steel's cold blue eyes that stared at him, searchingly.

"So, Mr Black, what are the chances of meeting someone with almost the same name?" Said the man called Blacke, his voice was deep with a New York accent. Steel cracked a smile.

"Yes, indeed, what are the chances?" Steel's words were slow and drawn out, almost sounding inquisitive as to the question. Antony Black was an old alias Steel had used many years ago when he had done some black ops for an American Agency. Steel still had the credit cards and passports, and the background sight was still active, just in case he had to do something like this. Steel wondered, was this a coincidence or was this Anthony Blacke just as fake as his Antony Black was?

"So, Mr Black, or May I call you Antony?" Steel gave a slight hand gesture to say *Please do* which made Blacke smiled in acceptance. "What do you do for a living?" Steel eased back into his chair and smiled broadly; he had wondered when or if he would get to him. Steel picked up his wine glass and took a small sip from the glass, the earthy bouquet from the wine tantalised his senses, but he was in no mood to savour the wine.

"Oh, I am just some guy that made money from my parents' death, spent some time in the army, but it didn't agree with me. Now I just go around and enjoy life," Steel explained, as though his story was just like everyone else. Blacke nodded, almost appreciating his story.

"And what brings you on board, just the thrill of being on a big ship?" Blacke asked, before taking a sip of his wine. Steel could see he was fishing for something.

"No, the thrill of being on the maiden voyage of the largest cruise ship," Steel replied with a childlike grin. Blacke sat back in his chair and stared at Steel for a moment, his eyes measuring this man up, almost as if he were categorising him into friend or foe.

"So, Antony, how are you enjoying the cruise so far?" Blacke asked, his eyes still unsure about Steel's role. Steel nodded as he took a mouthful of the creamy dessert; he swallowed hard and wiped his mouth with the napkin.

"It's great; I hope the rest of this trip is as exciting," Steel answered, as he leant back into his chair. Blacke grinned as he took another sip from his glass.

"How did you find Vigo? I hear the restaurants are to die for there?" There was a clatterer of glass and metal as Tia dropped her dessert fork, knocking over a water glass. She smiled with embarrassment as Alan Metcalf quickly picked up the fallen glass and attempted to mop up the spillage. Tia apologised for the incident, her face red from blushing. Steel looked down at Alan Metcalf's right hand and the bandage on it.

"That looks nasty, Alan, what happened?" Alan looked over to his wife, who gave her husband a quick look.

"Oh, it's nothing, just me being clumsy, that's all," Alan smiled falsely, which Steel returned with a fake smile. Steel looked back at Blacke, and he knew then that another piece had fallen into the puzzle, but he feared it wasn't the final one. Steel's view shifted as he looked around to see if anyone else had noticed the subtle hint, but the others went about chatting obliviously, all except for Antony Bishop, who just sat there looking nervous and fidgety. Steel couldn't make out whether that was because of Blacke or Missy.

Guilt takes on many expressions. Some sweat profusely and look nervous, others can't make eye contact in case they give something away, and there are also those who are overconfident, thinking they can get away with whatever it was they had done without been caught. However, the only two who didn't display anything were Tia May and the Studebakers . Steel knew he was sitting in a den of vipers, but only one could bite. He looked up at Blacke who was talking to Susan Metcalf, his eyes fixed like a hawk moving in on its prey.

THIRTY-SEVEN

McCall sat at her desk, flicking through the case files on her desk. She had the feeling that all these deaths were connected somehow, but she didn't know how. The bullpen was even more chaotic than usual, the department was short-staffed and spread thinly, due to a UN meeting over the illegal arms sales in Africa and the Middle East, where each department had to give up some of its people to help with security. McCall looked up at the clock. The hands showed it was nearly five and soon she would be soaking in a tub with lots of bubbles and a glass of red. Her daydream was shattered by her desk phone ringing, shocking her slightly.

"Homicide – Detective McCall." The other end was quiet except for the sound of a woman sobbing.

"Hello, is there someone there, are you hurt or in danger?" Tony and Tooms looked up and she waved a hand to alert them; Tony picked up the other phone and dialled for a trace.

"Ma'am, I can hear you crying, are you hurt? Just talk to me, please. Say anything," Tony said with a calming, but urgent tone. There was silence, then a quiet voice of a woman sounded over the handset.

"Detective, its Susan Hay, we met at Ultra-tronics," She sounded terrified and alone.

"Yes, of course, you are Mr Brown's secretary," McCall

attempted to sound warm and comforting, hoping to make Susan feel safe, so she could calm down. "OK, Susan what's wrong, where are you?" McCall could hear Susan's breathing starting to slow down and become calmer.

"Detective we need to talk, there's a Bistro near Grand Central Station on Pershing Square, meet me there." Each word was almost a whisper as Susan talked.

"OK, it will take me about fifteen minutes to get there, just wait for me OK?" The phone went dead in McCall's hand, and she looked up at the other two, standing there open-mouthed.

"Trace has got her at that address now." Tony put down his receiver and then started to put his jacket on.

"OK, by the sounds of things she wants to come in where it's safe, so the plan is: Tony you get to be wheelman, Tooms you play lookout. I go in, we chat; I convince her to come in. We pick her up, get her back here and see what she has to say. I am guessing she has seen something reference Major's accident and she can't keep it to herself." Tony and Tooms stood there, ready.

"Cool, let's go," Tooms said, as he cracked his knuckles. Jenny looked over with her cell phone in her hand.

"CSU has something for me, or do you need me to come as well?" McCall shook her head.

"No, we got this. You get to CSU, it might be a big break and god knows, we need one." Jenny smiled, and went back on the phone as she watched the others head for the elevator. As the elevator doors began to close, McCall caught a glimpse of Jenny putting on her coat, her cell phone tucked underneath her chin as she struggled with the garment. McCall didn't want her there, Jenny was new, not to the force but as a detective and McCall had a bad feeling about this pickup. The last thing she needed was someone ending up in a bag. McCall smiled as she saw that Jenny was wearing red V-neck top and black boots and trousers.

"Besides, you know what happens to the new security officers on Star Trek when they're on away missions?" McCall joked. Jenny shot McCall a puzzled look, the joke going wide over her head.

THE RUSH HOUR had set in, but fortune had favoured them as they made their way to the Bistro. They were around ten minutes late, but McCall knew Susan would wait for her, Susan had something important she had to share, and she wouldn't disappear until she had said it. Pershing was its usual nightmare at around five o'clock, and Tony had just found a parking spot behind one of the tour buses. The sun was still high, but the surrounding buildings cast a soft shadow. Tooms and McCall exited the vehicle and made for the café. The place was large with plenty of seating space inside, McCall left Tooms outside while she went in to find Susan Hay. The noise of the traffic from the Park Avenue Viaduct was dulled as the doors closed behind her with a sucking sound from the vacuum seals. McCall looked around and found Susan in a far corner, away from the windows and doors. McCall smiled softly as she saw the look of relief on Susan's face.

"Thanks for coming," Susan said, looking around the room every time someone new came in. McCall sat next to her, she felt better with her back against the wall rather than facing the door, and if something were to happen, it would take too long to turn, assess, and then react.

"So, what's wrong, has someone threatened you?"

Susan gave her one of those looks, "And then some," Susan said, as she was about to take a sip of coffee from the large cup. She held the coffee with both hands, but her hands were shaking so much, the liquid was splashing over the sides. McCall smiled and rested a hand on top of hers and gently forced the cup back onto the table before she burnt herself. McCall nodded and smiled, trying to be comforting.

"Why don't you start from the beginning?" McCall said. Susan smiled and nodded.

"Well the other day, when you came in asking about Donald, I did some checking. He had been working for a company on a big job, a massive job really, from what I could see." McCall took out the small recorder and switched it on.

"Do you remember the name of the company?" McCall could see Susan thinking hard before shaking her head.

"No sorry, it's gone. Anyway, after the job, Donald was asked if he could do a quick on-the-side job in the seven eleven. Apparently, the other guy who was meant to do it was off sick. Well, Donald, being Donald, said he would do it." Susan took a careful sip from the hot coffee before clearing her throat and getting ready to continue. McCall looked puzzled for a second before realising something,

"Your boss, Mr Brown said he knew nothing about the other job," McCall said with a curious tone. Susan shook her head.

"He was the one who sent him apparently, said it was a favour for a friend," Susan said. McCall snarled.

"That lying piece of – OF. We have to get you back to the precinct and into safety." McCall stood up and looked down on to the scarred face of Susan.

"You can't protect me; you know that. They will find me, and well I'll be another one of your mysterious cases," Susan said, with fear in her eyes. McCall got onto her radio and informed the other two she was ready to come out. Tony raced forwards and into an empty space which a bus had just left.

"OK, I am in position," Tony replied, his hands gripping the wheel, ready to go as soon as they were clear and in the vehicle. Tooms looked around the street and the buildings on the other side of the viaduct.

"We're clear here," his voice grave and serious.

"OK let's go," McCall motioned Susan to get up and come with her. They walked quickly towards the door, adrenaline pumped through their veins. For McCall it kept her pumped and ready, for Susan it was new and terrifying. As they neared the vehicle, Susan turned and looked at the table they had left.

"My Bag, I need my bag." McCall turned to look at the table but was pushed out of the way by a large fat guy with an attitude. As McCall spun to the ground, the window of the shop door exploded, and people began to scream.

"Shots fired, shots fired," She heard Tooms yell down the police radio, McCall looked up and over to the door and the clear view where there had once been a smoked glass pane. She crawled to where Susan lay and found her lying on her front in a pool of her own blood; Susan had taken a shot to the chest with a high-powered rifle, which had left a large hole, the size of a squash ball, in her back. McCall looked over at the large man who also lay still and no signs of breathing. She crawled over to him and found a large hole in his left arm were the round must have entered.

"You guys OK?" She asked over the radio,

"Yeh we're fine, and you?" McCall ventured out low and steady until her back was against the engine block of the dodge, next to the other two.

"Where's the girl?" Tooms asked.

"She took one to the chest," McCall said, shaking her head.

"Damn it," Yelled Tooms, he looked around as the sound of the cavalry approached.

"How the hell did they know, McCall?" McCall shook her head slowly as she looked at the body of Susan Hay.

"I don't know, but I have a good idea."

THIRTY-EIGHT

It took around fifteen minutes for the place to be shut down and cordoned off as much as possible. Behind the cordons, people with cell phones stretched their arms high to try to get a photo of anything they could show off to say that they were there. CSU quickly set up the targeting laser to pinpoint a location of the shooter's nest, while Tina carried out her initial exam to get the bodies shipped back to the morgue as quickly as possible. The tall, thin CSU tech yelled over to the captain and pointed to the ninth floor of the building opposite, the captain turned to the SWAT commander, but they were already leaving.

"Go find that room, I want this son a of a bitch," The commander nodded and moved out. Tony and Tooms rushed forwards, only to be stopped by the captain, who held them back with his hands on their chests.

"And where the hell do you two think you are going?" Tooms pointed over the road towards the building with a lost look on his face.

"We were just going to...." The captain gave him a stern look.

"You were just going to what, Detective?" Brant said with his arms crossed firmly across his broad chest. The two detectives backed down knowing Brant would never let them in there, not with a possible trained assassin in there. "SWAT can handle it; it's their pond now. You two just sit your asses down, drink some coffee until you are released." They nodded, and Brant gave them a little smile and walked towards McCall and Tina, who were kneeling by the bodies.

"McCall, you OK?" Brant asked, normally it would be a greeting to Tina and asking about the case. However this was different.

"No, not really, I just had two people shot in front of me, one of whom was a witness." McCall was angry, Brant could see that, but he knew it was directed at whoever did this, not him.

"What's the story with the big guy?" Brant pointed with his head towards the large overweight man who had pushed McCall out of the way. McCall didn't know whether to be still annoyed or grateful the man had shoved her; then it hit her.

"He pushed me out of the way, that bullet was meant for Susan and me," McCall said, the realisation that it could have been her lying there, and not him, hit hard. Tina moved over to the male victim and lifted the sheet that covered him from the view of the camera-wielding jackals.

"His name was Simon Watts, thirty-four years of age," Tina said, tossing his wallet to McCall, who looked through it to try and find any more information on the guy.

"A couple of credit cards, some loose bills and a driver's license," McCall took the license out and searched for the address. "This guy was a bus driver, he lives in Brooklyn, I'll get in touch with Brooklyn PD when we get back, and they can take it." Captain Brant nodded as he looked down on the sorry looking man.

"Doc, I can only see the entry point, is it possible the round is still in there?" Tina looked up and smiled "It's more than possible. I am hoping his guy's soft tissue has preserved it for us." At last, the captain had something to smile about.

"OK, we wait for SWAT to clear and contain, then CSU can sweep while we take a look round, I doubt it, but hopefully he has left us with something," Brant said. McCall thought for a moment then a look of realization came over her face.

"I need to get back to Ultra-tronics and see Mr Brown," McCall said, with a desperate look on her face. Brant looked over at McCall.

"Why, do you think he's involved in any of this?" Brant asked. McCall nodded, as she looked at Susan's body lying in a pool of her own blood.

"He was the one who sent Donald Major on that last job at the 7/11; she was afraid of the guy, that's why she came to us, he killed her on my watch," McCall explained. Brant looked outside and waved Tony and Tooms inside.

"I want you two to go to this Mr Brown's place, bring his ass in if he's there. The man has some explaining to do," Brant growled. The two detectives knuckle punched each other and headed off; Brant turned to them, "And hey, take some back up with you, just in case." Tooms saluted playfully and they headed off. "And McCall, I suggest you take some uniforms with you as well," Brant ordered. McCall smiled, thoughtfully.

"Concerned about my welfare sir?" Brant smiled.

"No, his."

THE SOUND of police sirens filled the busy streets, the noise echoed through the avenue of mile high buildings. The Brown's residence was in Larchmont, a large oversized house on a long driveway, surrounded by trees and miles between neighbours. The evening sun was beginning to set, turning the clear blue sky a dark cherry red and the treetops seemed to glow as if they were on fire, Tooms had to admit the sight was breath-taking and a little eerie. Driving up to the house, they found it unlit and quiet. Both detectives got out of the car and immediately drew their weapons. Behind them, four uniforms parked up and joined them. Tooms motioned for two of them, Officers Dunleavy and Short, to take the back and the others to follow. Tooms waited a couple of minutes for the two uniforms to get in position before banging on the door. His fist hit hard on the large wooden door, causing it to open. Tony looked over to Tooms, who just had a startled look and nodded. Tony and the others already had their weapons held up ready to fire as they crept in.

"NYPD, Mr Brown, come out with your hands up," Tooms voice echoed through the Victorian styled walls. Polished oak flooring and skirting filled the main entrance and half-wooden panel and white plaster covered the walls. They stopped in the entrance to get their bearings; Tooms clicked his fingers, getting the attention of the others, then using two fingers of his left hand he pointed at Officer Marks then at his own eyes. Then Tooms directed him towards the kitchen entrance, which was down the hall at the end. Marks nodded and moved out. Tooms did the same for Shaw and pointed to the right and the public rooms. Tony nodded up towards the stairs and Tooms nodded once for OK. As Tooms broke left towards the dining room, Tony headed for the upstairs via the staircase that ran against the right wall of the entrance. Burnt umber shards of light filled the rooms through the ornate windows, breaking up the shadows. The men cautiously moved deeper through the house. The estate had seven bedrooms, all of which could conceal the hiding Mr Brown.

Officer Marks entered the kitchen through the double-hinged door, which squeaked as he slowly nudged it open. Inside, it was almost black, forcing him to take out his flashlight in his left hand and cross it under his pistol arm for support. The bright light cut through the dark, illuminating parts of huge modern kitchen but casting grizzly shadows in others. He was a tall well-built man with very short hair; beads of sweat began to form as he moved through the massive working kitchen. He didn't know what to expect, all he knew was he was looking for this guy Brown. The brief was short and to the point, take Brown by any means necessary but alive. Marks kept to the corners, his back always to the wall; he could hear his heart pounding in his ears as he swept the room with the light. He stopped and began to relax, "There's no one here, rooms clear," Marks yelled, before blowing out a lung full of air he had been holding. He was just about to relax when a clatter of metal against metal came from a corner he had almost missed; he shone the beam towards the noise and a ginger cat ran away from the disturbance.

"Thanks a lot, you fuckin' stupid cat," Marks laughed, trying to get his breath back. The beam of the flash hit the kitchen floor and lit it up as though it was day light. Bloody paw prints marked the cats escape; Marks lifted his flashlight and pistol and followed the trail. He stopped and listened to what sounded like water dripping into a pan. Slowly he moved forwards towards the sound, the tap, tap, tapping grew louder. His hand began to shake making the light distort his view. He edged around the corner where the sound was emanating from, the tap, tap, tap became hypnotic in a terrifying way, he wanted to know, but his imagination told him otherwise. He moved the flashlight round and found a washbasin on a far wall. He moved towards it and saw, on the side of the work surface, what appeared to be some plates stacked up with what seemed to be ketchup on them. A medium sized pan was in the basin, which was catching the water from the leaky faucet. He reached for the faucet to stop the dripping. His outstretched fingers almost at the handle, when his radio crackled from feedback, scaring the already on edge Marks almost to death.

"For the love of…" He calmed himself, secured the faucet, and smiled at how foolish he had been as he picked up one of the dirty plates. He placed it down and turned around casually, holding the flashlight up to look at the rest of the small area. He froze as the light illuminated something in the shadow. There was a large wooden kitchen table where the servants could eat or take breaks. Slowly he moved forwards toward the table. The heavy smell of copper filled his nostrils as he approached. His flashlight flickered as the batteries began to give up on him. Marks reached the table and pulled two spare batteries from the small pouch on his belt. As he fumbled in the dark, Marks began to curse the timing of the batteries fading. Slipping the cover back on he switched it on almost, blinding himself at the sudden brightness. He smiled and stuck the flashlight under his arm as he stowed the dead cells back into the pouch. The beam lit up a large area to his front as he leant against the dining table. The smell was strongest behind him, causing him to turn slowly. On the top of the thick oak tabletop lay naked a man in a pool of his own blood; razor wire was wrapped loosely round the body to allow movement. Marks's face cringed at the sight, but he couldn't take his eyes of the brutal sight and moved in closer. The light picked up the shape of the two electrical cables that ran from the wall mains to the table. The long, thick cable spiralled its way along the floor to the large kitchen table, where it ended in a pair of crocodile clips that had been attached to either end of the coiled steel wire. From what Marks could make out, someone had passed a current through the wire, causing the butler's body to shake and convulse as the massive voltage passed through the wire and through the poor soul wrapped within. The small razors slashed him deeply and made long gashes in the flesh of his body.

Marks stared into what was left of the man's screaming face, the look of horror burnt into Marks's mind and he screamed and dropped his flashlight as he ran from the kitchen, not registering when he collided with the heavy fixed furnishings. He had seen something that made his stomach churn, something that would probably give him nightmares for the rest of his days.

Marks came sliding through the kitchen door and out into the blissful light of the main hallway, there he found the others equally disturbed by what they had discovered. Tony sat on the bottom two steps of the staircase, his head between his knees, trying not to vomit. Tooms took out his cell phone and dialled the captain. "Hey Captain, we found Brown. No sir we can't bring him in, he's a little pinned down at the moment."

THIRTY-NINE

Captain Brant arrived on the scene with CSU and Tina. Tooms had requested that the ME's Office bring more than one meat wagon, which made his stomach turn at the thought of what they may find inside the house. As they pulled up the long driveway to the house, Brant saw Tony and Tooms sitting on the front step with the four uniforms, each wearing a sickly look. The two detectives stood up as Brant approached with the others in tow.

"OK Detective, what have we got?" Captain Brant asked. Tony looked over at Tooms, then back at the captain.

"Follow me, and I give you the tour. Oh, if you have just eaten, I suggest you stay here," Tony said, then swallowed hard, trying not to think about what was inside the house. Tina shot a look at the CSU team leader.

"What the hell is in there?" Tina asked. The CSU tech shrugged as they went in. Tony led them down the corridor of the main entrance towards the kitchen; the lights had been put on to ensure not to miss anything or be surprised by anything for that matter. As they reached the swing door to the kitchen, Tony stopped and turned.

"Officer Marks found the butler when he came into here," Tony said, as he stopped for a second, as though he was bracing himself before entering the large kitchen. As they all walked in, the first thing they noticed was the red paw prints on the tiled floor. Tina shivered at the prospect of what lay behind the dividing wall.

"The butler was tortured, why we don't know," Tooms said, as they turned the corner and immediately came back round to catch their breaths.

"What the hell was that?" Ask the young CSU tech. Tina walked around slowly, followed by the others. They looked down at the butler's shredded body with revulsion at the bloody sight before them.

"So, doc what do you make of this?" Brant shook his head, unable to conceive a reason why anyone would want to do this to a person. Tina looked back at the captain as she put on a pair of blue examination gloves.

"This guy was tortured; from the look of the cuts I would say they shocked him around five or six times," Tina explained. Tony shook his head as he looked at the blood-soaked corpse.

"We found a tub of salt on the counter, and it's all over the floor as well, they put salt on to him," Tooms said, holding his hand over his mouth. Brant looked over at Tony.

"How do you know he was the butler?" Tony pointed at a pile of torn clothes that had been tossed into a corner.

"There was a wallet amongst all that. His ID says he was one Evan Sanders, and he was originally from New York State." Tony showed a clear evidence bag with the brown wallet inside it. Brant nodded then looked back at the mangled mess that used to be the butler before looking up again at Tony.

"You made it sound like there was more" Brant's soul froze when he saw the expression on Tony's face.

"Yes, sir, there are." Tony turned, and they all followed back the way they came.

"We have to go to the games room." Tony's words were horse, his mouth dry from fear. He stopped at the door, the two officers who stood watch seemed pale and sickened.

"This is where we found Brown and his wife, or what was left of them anyway." His words were almost a warning shot for them, but Brant couldn't fathom how much worse could it be after seeing the butler. Tony opened the door, and they all entered; first, they saw Brown. He was sitting in a chesterfield armchair, his hands lay on top of the armrests with one kitchen knive in imbedded in each hand pinning him to the chair; two twelve-inch nails kept his feet from moving off the floor. His clothes were bathed in blood from where they had shot his knees out. He had died slowly; they had made sure of that. Then they saw Mrs Brown, the woman had been pinned down on to the pool table, her chest lay on the fabric, and her lower half hung loose. The long tiebacks for the curtains had been linked together, then her wrists were bound, and the other half fastened to the legs of the table. She had been raped several times, and he had been made to watch before they killed him, but they had made sure she died first from the puncture wound in her kidneys. The men who had done this were paid killers. Brant couldn't believe anyone would have someone this sick on a payroll.

"How did Brown die?" Brant looked over at Tina, who had given Brown a quick once over.

"They cut his tongue out and fed it to him," Tooms said. Brant looked confused.

"And that's what killed him?" Tina stood up and turned to the captain.

"Yeh, well it also had a little help, they put a lot of broken glass onto it." Brant winced at the thought.

"Ouch." Tina smiled softly, and nodded.

"Yeah, it would have cut all of his throat and stomach to pieces." They all turned as they heard someone enter the room. It was McCall. After dispatch had informed her of the murders at the Brown's residence, she decided that this was more important than the electrical company was. Her face turned white at the sight before her.

"I don't get it, why kill them like this, it makes no sense." Tony was chewing on gum to take his mind off the coppery taste that filled the air.

"Maybe it was a warning to anyone else that was going to

talk or mess up, who knows." Tony faced McCall, wearing a confused look.

"What others?" McCall looked around the room.

"Whoever did this is connected or has the cash to pull it off, that means an organization or wealthy person." Brant was angry that another valuable piece of evidence had been taken away, he stopped and told everyone to stop. The room froze at his words, and he wanted to say to them he wanted these men found no matter what, he wanted to say that everything stops, and this was priority. However, he stopped before he said anything. "Edwards, Blake" the two detectives turned towards the captain.

"This is your case, everyone back to the precinct OK let's move." McCall seemed shocked.

"What's wrong?" Brant tapped the side of his head with his right index finger.

"They are trying to do it again; every time we get close, they throw something. Normally I would have called this as a priority, but it's not. What you are working on is, this is just another roadblock which means someone is getting nervous." McCall smiled at his cunning, and she just hoped he was right.

FORTY

Steel had excused himself from dinner and was standing on one of the open decks, feeling the need for peace and time to think. The ocean breeze was cold and refreshing against his warm skin, Steel loosened his tie and popped a top button, letting the crisp wind find its way past the open shirt. He leant against the balcony and looked out across the expanse of crashing waves and smiled. This was the most tranquil he had been all day, and it felt good. In the far distance, the sky looked dark and foreboding, they were heading for a storm either tomorrow or the day after and it looked like a bad one. Steel closed his eyes, letting himself drift away as the cool breeze blew past him and across the decks. Steel opened his eyes and looked up at the towering side of the ship and the thousands of balconies that seemed to cling to the side, his mind was beginning to clear of the noise and complicated facts that came out at dinner. It was as though a vale had been lifted from his eyes and he could once more see clearly.

Jane Doe must have been a passenger, so where was her room? Find her room then discover her name and purpose.

The information desk was in the centre of deck twelve, next to three elevators and a couple of vending machines for the guests to use after closing time. Sandy Shaw was the pretty little redhead who had lucked out and was on the nine till three-shift, but she didn't mind as it was quiet and it gave her chance to catch up on her induction exams for the police department when they got back stateside. She had a large stash of books and folders hidden under the counter out of sight, and she kept it to one book maximum, just so she could easily put hide it if someone came. She did not see Steel as he approached, nor did she see him as he leant on the counter, his head resting carefully on his hands as he watched her reading one of the manuals. He must have waited a good ten minutes before letting of a small fake cough making her look up with a start.

"Oh, sorry sir, how may I help you?" Steel smiled, as she hurried the book away before straightening herself out. Before, Sandy had been startled by his presence, but now she lost herself in his large blue eyes and confident smile.

"If there is anything I can ….do for you, please don't hesitate to ask." She smiled, as she rearranged the desk. Steel looked at her with an awkward smile.

"I am, looking for someone, a woman," Steel said. Sandy grinned.

"Really, anyone particular?" Steel felt this next part would be the most awkward to explain.

"The woman who was killed in the sauna, I need to find her room." The smile fell away from Sandy's face as she backed off slightly. "Sorry, I had best explain, I am working with the NYPD, and I just happen to be on vacation. Well, to be frank, I don't think it was an accident, so I want to investigate her death." He saw her eyes light up at the thought of a real investigation happening and she was part of it.

"Have you got a name?" Steel leant on to the counter looking down at her and taking in her sweet perfume.

"Sorry, I don't know her name," Sandy looked up and cracked a smile from the corner of her mouth.

"I meant yours, I am Sandy," Steel stood up straight with an apologetic look on his face.

"Sorry, I am Antony Black. That's ANTONY, not

ANTHONY and it's Black without the E" Sandy looked up at him, slightly confused, until she saw the computer's search programme gave two men with a similar name.

"Oh. OK, now I see. What are the odds, ah?" Steel shrugged and smiled falsely.

"Yes, what are the odds."

"Do you have any cameras in the gym area?" Steel asked, leaning a little closer, so as not to throw his voice. She shook her head.

"No, we're not allowed for obvious reasons, but I can get footage from the corridor if that will help." Her smile was warming, and her large brown eyes seemed to sparkle from the reflections of the ceiling lights.

"That would be great, if can I get the footage from two nights ago until today?" Sandy made a note of it on a yellow post-it and stuck it to one of her books, so she didn't forget.

"I don't know how to thank you." She smiled; this time, she had glint in her eye that looked purposeful.

"I get off at three, and you can buy me breakfast. Pick me up at the Irish Bar at around half past." She reached out her right hand to shake it, taking it gently he laid a soft kiss on the knuckles.

"Until then," he said, before turning and heading for the set of stairs opposite the desk leading down to the next deck. Sandy sat back in her chair and started to fan herself down.

"Wow" she felt giddy with excitement as she drank the small bottle of water dry. "Wow" she repeated to herself.

STEEL HAD RETURNED to the internet café and decided to find out as much as he could about Mr Anthony Blacke. The café was almost empty, apart from the twelve people checking e-mails or kids checking out some kid's web site, but then it was around two in the morning. He found his usual spot, sat himself down, and began to log on. He looked up as one of the board waiters came over and asked him if he required anything. Steel ordered a large coffee as he thought he might be there for some time.

Page after page Steel read; how an eight-year-old Anthony Blacke was made an orphan after a car accident took away both his parents. He studied business at Yale and eventually made a name for himself buying and selling. He had a motto, "If you want it, I can get it," Blacke moved round the world, rubbing shoulders with royalty and presidents. He was a rich and powerful man and to Steel that made him dangerous. Steel knew all too well the higher up the food chain you were, the more you thought you were untouchable and above everything.

He read through the articles as he sipped the coffee he had just been given, every now and then looking up and scanning the room for anyone new or suspicious. He looked at his watch, hoping to have more time there; it was quarter past two in the morning. He would stay until half-past then go back to his room and quickly change, ready for his rendezvous with Sandy at the Irish Bar, which at first he thought was strange, because it would be closed for the night. But he shrugged it off as just being a central meeting place where everyone would know. Steel sat back in his chair and took a sip from the large coffee mug as he waited for the next page to upload, his mind wandered back to the way Sandy looked and that cute smile she had. Something on the screen caught Steel's eye, and it was a page on how Blacke had been selling weapons to both sides during the gulf war of 1991 and several other conflicts since then, this man was big in arms trading throughout Mexico and the Middle East.

Steel leant forwards and read the page further, taking in as much information as possible. He sat back in his chair as his mind buzzed with questions, but the main one was: What was Blacke doing on this ship? He couldn't afford to print it off just in case someone could trace the last print made. He took a pen from his pocket and wrote down the website's name for later, for now he had to get back to his room and get ready for his date.

Steel finished what he could of the coffee and stood up after wiping the history of his visit, and he had enough time to get to his room and be at the bar to meet Sandy. He hoped there was something on the tapes that would reveal who she was, or better still, who killed her.

The decks were mostly quiet as people were tucked up in their beds for the night, only the odd person who'd had a bit too much holiday cheer, stumbled back to their cabins, ricocheting off the walls as they went. As he reached the elevator, he felt the presence of two large men behind him and he said nothing, just stared into the reflective surface of the control panel to his left. The men were both around six-four with quarterback builds. The doors slid open, and they entered, Steel made for the back, and the two giants each leant against the sidewalls. Both men wore black suits with white shirts and black ties; both men's hair was short with to-the-bone cuts on the back and sides, one was blonde and the other had a darker tone to it. Steel figured the man had some Hawaiian or some other exotic region in his blood. They all stood in silence while the blonde one, who stood nearest the panel, pressed for the sixteenth floor.

"Could you press number twelve please," Steel asked, but the men just smiled, and Steel knew he wouldn't be getting off on his requested floor anyway. He smiled back politely, somewhat intrigued about where he was going and who was at the end of it. Sure, he could have made for the door next time it opened, but the chances of one of them having a taser or other means of rendering him unconscious were probably very high, and he wanted to be awake for when he got to wherever they were heading.

As they travelled up the decks, other passengers got on and off, but the whole time Steel stayed in his position, not moving, just making himself ready for any sudden moves. Sure, the men were big, a lot bigger than he was but with his military training plus the training from Mr Lee, he knew he could take them down, but he was dangerously curious. The LED display read 18 as the doors opened and the two men got out and waited for Steel to follow. Steel smiled and walked halfway out of the door.

"Please, after you, I insist." The blonde man raised an arm

as if to usher Steel down the corridor, Steel's smile faded as he rushed forwards making sure he had a good distance between them and him. The floor was mainly comprised of massive suites for the super-rich, some of which had conference rooms and small home cinemas. They made their way to suite number fourteen where they stopped, and the large half-cast man knocked on the door. A fresh-faced brunette in a red business suit opened the door.

"Please come in, and you have been expected. Please follow me." Steel obeyed her request and followed the woman with the gyroscopic hips, all the while making a note of the layout of the suite. The place was huge. From what Steel could tell, it was a three-bedroomed apartment with a seating area and a large office with an adjoining bedroom. The two guerrillas stayed outside, ensuring they would be undisturbed by any unwelcome callers, while the woman led Steel further in until they reached a large desk in what appeared to be the office of whomever he was supposed to meet. The room itself was large with maroon coloured walls and dark stained wood furniture; two brown leather chairs stood in front of the desk and behind it there was a heavy-looking red leather office chair. As they stood there alone, Steel looked around and smiled at the woman who was now standing just off to the side of him, her face was pale and with a stern look upon it. She just nodded upwards as if to say, "Face your front," Steel maintained the smile and turned back slowly. To his left, two wooden doors swung open and a man walked out, yelling at someone in Russian, not even registering Steel's presence.

The man was huge. He stood around Six-six with a large bald head that seemed to glow as the ceiling lights reflected off it, which sat upon broad shoulders but the man appeared to have no neck. His frame was large and bulky, but it seemed more body mass than fat. Steel smiled to himself as the more he looked, he couldn't help but think this man was the real like Kingpin from the comic books. The man shut the doors to what appeared to be a bedroom, and Steel felt a draft from it when the doors opened, which meant he had a balcony view. The

Russian turned after venting a fiery breath and turned with a smile.

"So, at last, the mysterious Mr Black." Steel seemed almost shocked that he had some sort of reputation, he had tried to keep under the radar, that was for sure, but he was lost as to why this man was looking for him.

"Or may I call you Anthony?" Steel sighed with relief, this man had the wrong guy, but Steel had a split-second decision to make. Come clean and tell him he wasn't who he thought he was and miss probably a lot of info or pretend to be Blacke. The flaw with the last plan would be, if they found out he was faking, he would be dead. Steel shrugged and smiled as he raised a hand like a schoolchild wanting to pose a question in class.

"Hi, um sorry to interrupt, but I am not who you think I am. My name is Antony Black without the E. sorry." The large man drew back his massive hand for a second then burst out laughing at the situation. His laugh was more of a loud bellow which brought the two goons rushing in.

"I must apologise, Mr Black without the E, my men are useful in so many areas, but reading evidently is not one of them." The man extended his hand once more and Steel shook it.

"No hard feelings ah?" Steel felt the vice-like grip on his hand.

"Oh, of course not. Anyway, I have got a hot date for tonight so if you'll excuse me?" The man let go, leaving Steel to shake off his hand to re-establish the blood flow to his fingers.

"Have a good night," The man yelled as the woman showed Steel to the door, then started to yell in Russian at the two goons.

The woman shoved steel out of the door, and the door slammed shut behind him.

"Charming," He said aloud. He looked at his watch; it was nearly three o'clock, and he hoped Sandy would wait. Steel looked back at the doors, his mind starting to calculate. Who the hell was that and why did he want Blacke?

Steel made it back to his suite; he needed to change out of his tuxedo and into something a little more presentable. The door clicked open as he placed the card in the slot. As he opened the door, the lights came on, revealing Sandy lying in his bed wearing nothing but a sheet.

"Good morning," She said, kneeling, holding the sheet around her.

"Good morning," He replied, taking off his jacket and throwing it onto the sofa as he walked up to her.

"I hope you don't find me forward, and it's just been a long day." Steel smiled as he drew her in close and looked into her sparkling brown eyes.

"Oh, don't worry. It seems everyone one wants to pick me up today." He pulled her in close, and they kissed passionately as she ripped open his shirt.

"Well if this is breakfast, I would love to see what you have in mind for lunch," She purred as they fell on to the bed and he reached up and dimmed the lights.

THE SUN HAD JUST BROKEN over the horizon, and the cloudless sky was starting to lose its starlit veil. Sandy hadn't stayed, in fear of being discovered by her colleagues, but she had left him with a good-bye gift. Steel got up slowly and stretched off, and he looked at the bedside clock that showed six o'clock on the digital display. He hadn't had much sleep but then the brief moment with Sandy had refreshed him. Steel got up and showered. Steel wanted to hit the gym and get a good workout before breakfast. He picked up the CD case and tapped it as he thought about the night before. Who was that big Russian? He smiled at the thought of who may know. He took a sip from the coffee he had made himself before he had showered and looked out across the ocean. He hoped today would be full of answers as he had far too many questions. Steel had gotten into his black sports gear and headed out towards the gym where Jane Doe had been killed, some may have thought it callous, but he knew it would be quiet and it gave him chance to take a look, undisturbed.

The gym was bathed in an orange glow as the rising sunburnt with a fiery red, and the large windows gave a fantastic view of the balcony area where people could sunbathe after their workout or sauna. Steel walked in to find himself alone which suited him fine, he picked a CD from the pile of music and chose an album from a rock band and placed it into the machine then waited for it to play so he could adjust the volume. The music blared out, filling the room with the 90's tunes. He had done around twenty minutes on the running machine before heading to the bench press. Steel changed the weights, so he was pushing around hundred and twenty kilograms. He had gotten through his first set of ten reps when he felt the pressure of the bar grow heavy.

"Need a hand with those?" Came a gravelly voice. Steel looked up to see the blonde Russian grasping the bar, the look of pleasure painted on his face. Steel locked his arms at the elbows, but he felt the immense power of the brute bearing down on him.

Steel felt the weight being lifted and he knew what was coming next, Steel put his feet on the edge of the bench for leverage and got ready. As he felt the bar come up further, he let go and pushed off, sliding off the bench enough for the bar to miss his head as it came crashing down. Steel rolled off the rest of the bench and knelt, ready for the next attack. This would be hard as it was two hulks against him. If it had been normal guys, not a problem, they were all vulnerable with weak spots, but these were mostly muscle, but Steel had speed and agility on his side. The one brute who had been standing watch, growled with anger and ran over, his head ducked down and his arms out to the sides ready to catch their prey, but Steel just rolled out of the way and returned to his battle stance. The dark-skinned Russian stopped on his heels and turned, his face full of rage at missing his target. The man ran forwards straight at Steel who was waiting, and the floor shook under the thunderous impact of each step the man took. The Russian's eyes were firmly fixed on Steel, who knew he probably wouldn't make the same move twice. The man was huge but not dumb. As he neared, Steel fell backwards onto his back and made a timely double kick upwards into the man's groin. The brute stopped and slid down to his knees, his hands firmly on the injury. Steel watched as the man went cross-eyed then crashed to the floor. Steel had a second to move before the other used the barbell as a hammer, the wood splintered where his head had been. The brute growled as he watched Steel roll to safety next to the bench of free weights, the brute took a firm grip on the barbell as if it were a sledgehammer. Steel looked around for anything he could use to even things up. He reached behind him and took hold of a pair of ten-kilogram weights and swung them at the Russian as he approached, the sound of metal hitting bone filled Steel's ears as he landed a punch to the man's middle, then his jaw. The dark-haired brute just smiled and spat the small amount of blood that filled his mouth. The big Russian grinned, showing off five bloody gold teeth that glistened menacingly in his muscular head. The Russian rushed forwards, swinging the barbell like a shot put as he came, laughing like a maniac as mirrors smashed and fire extinguishers burst, flying around the room like crazed torpedoes. Steel dived out of the way just as the other Russian was getting to his knees. There was a sickening crunch as the dazed Russian took the swinging weights direct in the jaw, blood and teeth erupted from the man's mouth before he once more crashed to the floor. The dark-skinned Russian looked over at his colleague and screamed like a crazed animal.

"Nicolay," the brute had murder in his eyes as he suddenly turned towards Steel who was now crouched by the glass sliding doors of the balcony, ready for what he expected to be a fast and brutal attack. The man threw the barbell to one side and charged at Steel like a maddened rhino, his head down and nostrils flared. Steel placed his hands on the floor and extended one leg to enable him to spring to one side quickly. Steel waited as the crazed Russian ran full pelt at him, the sound of thunder echoed through the gym as the man's feet impacted hard upon the wooden floor. Just as Steel could almost feel the man's, breath on his skin, he pushed off to one side and rolled to safety. Shocked, the brute turned to see the shape of his opponent crash through the glass and disappear over the side. Steel ran over and slid across the floor towards where the brute had gone over, and found the panicked Russian hanging by one arm, gripping one of the metal railings of the balcony. Steel leant on the railing and looked over with a face of false concern.

"Morning, lovely day to just hang around" the Russian looked up somewhat confused.

"So, it's kind of obvious who sent you but why?" the Russian shook his head and screamed something in Russian. Steel smiled and waved.

"OK, I can see I have disturbed you, so I'll just go and leave you in peace." The Russian's eyes bulged with fear as he watched Steel disappear from view.

"No, please. Do not go, please." A loud metallic thud as the nozzle of a fire hose slammed against the hull wall next to his head caused him to look up somewhat confused at the gesture. Steel looked back over the side, looking slightly irritated.

"Hi, sorry to bother you but if you wouldn't mind grabbing the sodding hose so I can get you back on board that would be great." He smiled and disappeared again, leaving the Russian to grab over with his free hand for the thick, round hose. Steel anchored himself against the weight bench he had put between the doorframes and was pulling up as he felt the strain. After several heaves and pulls the Russian's mighty fingers appeared on the balcony top rail. Steel let go of the hose and ran forward to try and pull the Russian's massive frame over. Reaching over, Steel was able to grasp the man's belt and pulled him up as the Russian pulled himself up. With a crash they both lay there out of breath, every muscle ached from the workout. Steel stood up and looked down at the man who was looking over at his fallen friend, and the Russian smiled as his colleague began to stir and move his arms slowly.

"Your friend will be fine," The Russian looked back towards Steel and nodded in acknowledgement. Steel returned the nod and walked out, leaving the Russian to tend to his friend. The big Russian looked up to see an empty room, and he smiled and shook his head. The big Russian didn't know who Mr Blacke was or why the boss wanted him out of the way, all he knew was he was not just some office guy making a quick buck, no this was something different, something dangerous.

FORTY-ONE

McCall and the others had returned to the precinct. Detectives Edwards and Blake had the Brown case, and they would need all the luck in the world to solve this one. CSU had found nothing; there was no trace evidence or prints at the scene. It was as though the killers had worn protective clothing of some sort.

Brown had known something, after all, it was Brown himself who had sent Douglas Major on the last job at the seven-eleven, so he was involved up to his eyeballs. However, Susan, the secretary? She had worked something out. Unfortunately, she'd not shared the information before they'd taken her out. Susan had worked out that Brown had sent Major. The question was, what else did she find? McCall was hoping that Tech could find something on the feed from the workshop. After all, that was his workplace, his sanctuary. If McCall had found it, who was to say that nobody else could have?

The more she looked at the murder boards, the more the cases didn't make sense to McCall. All of the original victims had nothing in common. Their lives never interceded at any point. Family and friends had confirmed that they had never seen any of the other victims before and their jobs were so different there was no chance of a crossing of paths. The only thing that joined three of the victims was someone used the same gun on them, McCall stretched off, her eyes fixed on the row of boards. She was feeling tired and worn out, but she wasn't ready to give up on them, she and the other detectives were the voices of the victims, they would speak for them and find justice.

THE MORNING SUN brought a cool breeze with it. The teams had finished late and had awoken eager to make a fresh start with rested eyes. All except McCall who had been there all night, at two in the morning she felt like going home then realised: What was the point in going home? Breakfast had been courtesy of the delis down the road, and the gym's shower had revitalised her slightly. McCall moved over to the map board, a clear plastic cover paper on which several large circles had been drawn, depicting mile coverage, five miles up to thirty. This was to show a central point where the killer might be or at least coming from, going off McCall's theory. All of the killings had been on the Eastside, all of them within miles of each other except for the John Barr, the crane guy, but he had been shot from the river somehow.

"All of the crime scenes had one thing in common," she thought, as she stared at the board, "They all have easy access to and from the subway." McCall looked at the board again. Was that it? The subway was the killer's means of transport? It was quicker than using traffic, and they didn't have to worry about parking. Also, easy to blend in and disappear if you needed to. She smiled and folded her arms as she nodded happily. McCall looked over to Tony's board, and the security cam picture of the man who had spoken to Bill Foster before his death, next to it a sketch composited from one of the lobby staff who had called him "Mr Jones." The photo and likeness had been shown around at the offices and workplaces of all the victims, and all confirmed that Mr Jones had indeed been to see the victims at some point.

Detective Taylor, who had picked up the shooting of Susan, returned with the other officers. CSU had found the room the shooter had fired from using the trace laser, but the room was clean.

"Hey Ron, any luck at the nest?" The small overweight detective shook his head.

"Na, it was a bust. The shooter had used a supply room that the twenty cleaners and fifteen maintenance people used every day, not to mention the hundred-odd workers who would sneak in for a quiet smoke out of the window instead of travelling down the eight floors to the smoking area. The security camera gave nothing up from the elevators, which meant the shooter used the stairs to get in and out." McCall looked thoughtfully for a moment.

"But what about the weapon? It wasn't as if the shooter could walk out into the street brandishing a sniper rifle?" Taylor said, then shrugged.

"Who knows, CSU is checking air vents and dumpsters. Maybe we'll get lucky," McCall said, as she watched him walk back to his desk and start with the paperwork to start the investigation file.

McCall had placed pictures of William Brown and Susan Hay in the victim's column, someone was cleaning house which normally meant they were no longer of use, whatever was going on was happening soon. McCall had resigned herself to the fact that the victims had worked on something or were part of something, their deaths were not random or the work of a serial killer, but the work of a professional. McCall looked over at the board of John Barr, the man was shot from a boat in the Hudson. That took skill as the river was never calm. The boat, which they still hadn't found, would have been thrown about, plus any ships would have seen the shooter or gotten in the way. She shook her head with puzzlement, how the hell did they do it? None of the small boats had been let out, also if they had had a boat, where was it that the killer was on foot?

McCall's eye caught the TV set that hung from the wall next to the captain's office. There were scenes from the shooting at the deli and McCall frowned, the press was all over the story, and she knew it wouldn't be long before they knew about the

Brown's murder. All-in-all their job was going to get harder while the press was reporting every detail. McCall's desk phone began to ring, shaking her back from her brief moment of thought.

"Homicide, Detective McCall." She sat in her chair slowly as she waited for the reply, the cheerful voice of the tech came over the handset.

"Morning Detective, its Toby Lang from the lab, um its reference the workshop feed." McCall felt a rush of excitement but kept it to herself, just in case she was being presumptuous.

"Oh yeh. Morning, so what have you got?" There was an awkward silence, which suddenly made her nervous.

"Yes, well I ran the feed all the way up until today, and well I have found nothing." McCall crooked a smile.

"Yes, I thought that might be the case; it was worth a shot though." The silence came back, and it was short but enough.

"No Detective you don't understand, you went to the workshop, yes?" McCall's stomach turned at what he was going to say.

"Yes, why?" Then she had that sudden feeling as if the stage trap door had just been opened.

"Well Detective, I have not found any clip with you on it, plus there is a clock in the background. It hasn't moved in fourteen hours. It appears the feed has been tampered with, sorry," explained the tech. McCall felt like screaming, but then logic kicked in.

"Can you find out where the feed had been tampered with?" McCall asked, then she heard typing in the background,

"Not sure but I'll give it a go, I'll call you if I have anything," The line went dead, leaving McCall with a bad taste in her mouth. She replaced the receiver on its cradle and sat back in her chair,

"Another piece of bad luck," she thought. "Yes, bad luck seemed to be the thing at the moment," her mind was working out of sleep deprivation, there seemed to be a lot of bad luck lately, probably too much. McCall scanned the room with her eyes as she sat with her hands behind her neck, every time they find a lead, it's ripped away from them. One thing was for sure, they had a mole. She stood up slowly, her eyes looking at everyone suspiciously as she headed for the restroom, before shaking her head and dismissing the theory.

"No, that's a stupid idea," She muttered to herself, heading for the full coffee containers. She looked out across the men and women who sat working tirelessly and smiled. If there were a mole, it wasn't any of them. She looked at the empty chairs of her three colleagues and filled her cup with the freshly made brew. They were out there trying, as she was, to tidy up their cases, to find that missing part to make things fit. McCall ran back to her desk just as her desk phone began to ring.

"Homicide, Detective McCall…" It was the desk sergeant from downstairs, informing her that he had just gotten a report from two of his uniforms telling him they had just seen Mr Jones going into a hotel on East 34th. She grinned as she took down the address. She stowed the receiver back on the cradle and stood up "Gotcha."

The captain's orders had been simple. Plainclothes only at the front, and tactical units were to stand ready around the back and service areas. Snipers would be in place on rooftops covering the roof and the fire escapes. McCall had left text messages for the three to meet her in a café across the street where she would brief them on the situation. He had to be taken alive, that was paramount, but McCall knew he was not going down without a fight.

McCall was already in the coffee shop when the others walked in; they sat down immediately and leant forwards for instructions. McCall leant forwards to meet them.

"OK, this is what we know so far, two uniforms saw Jones enter that hotel there." McCall pointed over towards the red brick, four-story building over the road.

"Someone is finding out what room he is in and if he has guests. When the word is given, we meet the others in the lobby, but for the moment we sit tight until we are called," McCall's words rang with authority. She knew her stuff, years of tactical training had given her some insight. The others nodded to show they understood, Tooms and Tony gave their usual knuckle bump.

"I need you guys to go to your cars and get ready, listen to your radios for the word to be given." The others nodded and stood up, "Listen, we don't know what to expect up there so everyone, be careful, OK?" Tooms just smiled as they left. McCall watched them walk out separately and shivered as though someone had just walked across her grave. She had a bad feeling about this whole set up and she feared that someone wasn't going to make it out.

Mr Jones lay on his bed in his black suit, listening to the silence. The room was a flashback from the '70s with gordy green patterned wallpaper and orange armchairs. He preferred to think in the quiet, also he could hear anyone coming up the hallway along the creaky floorboards. Nearly all of his targets had been erased, but there was still one he had to find. Things had moved too quickly for his liking, but it couldn't be helped. He swung his legs around and sat on the edge of the bed; the sun bled through the slits in the blinds, lighting the room slightly. He wiped the sweat from his brow and stood up, walking towards the bathroom. He turned on the faucet and let the cold water run through his fingers before cupping his hands and splashing the refreshing water onto his face. He looked up into the mirror; he looked old, he thought, this job had done that to him. There was too much at stake and losses were inevitable, the job was nearly over, and then he could go home. Jones was a tall man with a slim build, and his black hair was short with a side parting on the left. He looked into his own brown eyes in the mirror and searched for what was left of his soul. This was his last job, one way or the other this was his last. He walked back towards the bed to find his cell vibrating across the bed; he sat down and picked up the cell and pressed the icon for the mail. The mailbox had one message *You're blown, get out, now.*

FORTY-TWO

McCall picked up her cell as it danced across the table next to her coffee cup. She saw the ID was from her friend a CSU.

"Hey, old man, what's up?" Jim Burke was an old friend of the family and the head of the CSU Department.

"Hi kiddo, look we found a hidden camera in the Brown's place, in fact, it was directed straight at the front door." McCall began to get excited.

"Have you seen the footage yet?" She asked, her tone now sounded worried.

"No, not yet. Why what's wrong?" It was a simple question, but she felt the answer might be too complicated.

"Look don't do anything or say anything to anyone about it, OK?" Jim noticed her worried tone and knew if she was asking such a thing, there was a reason. "Look you have to trust me on this, just put it somewhere safe and forget about it until I get back." Jim bit his lip; he had been in the job a long time and had never done anything against the principals of the job. However, after the incident at the morgue he could see how she could be worried.

"OK kid, you get back here, and we'll watch it together, hell, I'll bring the popcorn." She smiled and listened to the other end go to a tone as he hung up. She feared that if someone found out she wouldn't just lose the evidence, but someone could get killed this time. The earpiece from the radio crackled as someone was getting ready to send a message,

"All teams prepare to move in figures ten." The radio waves buzzed with acknowledgement at the order. McCall stood up and left a five-dollar bill next to the half-drunk cup of coffee, as she crossed the street others started to move in, hugging the corners of buildings as they moved towards the entrance.

The doors of the hotel swung open, and McCall strolled in with the others behind her, the sight was awe-inspiring as the four came through, wearing their vests and weapons ready. There was something dangerously erotic about the way McCall looked in her tight-fitting bullet-proof vest, and leg holster, and the fire in her eyes made her look all the more passionate. The owner of the hotel looked up from his small pocket TV set as he leant on the counter and gasped at the sight, the gum from his mouth fell out onto the register book.

The hotel wasn't the Ritz, but it was clean and tidy, even if the decor was a flashback to the Nixon era. The owner was a large man with black hair and a bad comb-over, his thick-rimmed glasses and Hawaiian shirt fitted in well with the feel of the building as though he too was lost in time. McCall strolled up to the captain who was standing next to the long wooden reception desk, "McCall." His words sounded happy to see her, even though his face was hard and unwelcoming.

"Captain, do we have a room number?" He nodded, "214, and he's alone." McCall took out her custom Glock and cocked it.

"Yeh, but it doesn't make him all that less dangerous," McCall growled. The others responded by making their weapons ready.

"All units get into position and remember we want him alive if at all possible." McCall's earpiece picked up the return sound offs, she was ready and so were the others. They waited for SWAT to take point, as this was their territory now. These guys were good, after the last incident on the EISENWOLFF their training had been stepped up, and so had their equipment.

"OK guy's you have the lead, we're just here for show," The team leader laughed at McCall's comment.

"Right guys let's do this by the numbers and remember our target is well trained, so no heroes , OK?" The team let out a "Hooha" and set off up the stairs. The elevator's power was cut, and the stairwells had been secured to limit any movement through floors, the only way out was through them. McCall and the men of team one moved quickly up the stairs to the top floor, they had the element of surprise, or so they hoped. As they got to the fire door on the fourth floor, the team leader held up a clenched fist to say stop. He reached down and tapped the lead man on the shoulder twice. The man then opened the door slowly and edged out his corner shot weapon. This was a tactical weapon extension that was hinged in the middle, ideal for shooting around corners. To the front of the weapon was a Glock 17 with an extended magazine. To the rear next to the trigger, the gun had a small monitor that showed images from the camera on the front.

"How are we looking son?" Asked the leader.

"We seem to be clear sir," replied the man, leaving the weapon trained on the corridor.

The leader pointed to two of the team members and used his fingers to indicate for them to proceed. One of them had a shield with a small window at the top while the other clung to his back like a well-armed parrot, his M4 assault rifle held ready, and its laser sight held fast on the doorway of 214. As they made their way down, they stopped just short of the door, and the shield man knelt and held the ballistic shield steady. The team leader then motioned the others to follow except for the door guard and the detectives. McCall wanted to be up there, but she also knew the drill, these guys had armour, and they didn't. The other team members took cover on the other side of the doorway as part of their drill while a SWAT member with some charges moved up to the door and placed the charges on the door near the lock and hinges. He turned to the leader and nodded before taking his place on the other side of the doorway.

"Command, we are good for breach over," McCall heard over the earpiece.

"Rodger that, breach now." There was a loud explosion as the door was blown off its hinges and propelled across the room, the team members entered quickly with the shield man first to take any incoming fire. The sound of static was the only noise to come over the waves; the detectives looked at each other confused and irritated.

"Maybe they're dead?" Tooms shrugged, McCall shot him a disagreeable look, which just made him smile wider.

"Command, the nest is empty; I repeat the nest is empty. Our bird has flown. Over." Silence while command thought about the next move.

"OK, roger that, move and sweep, teams two and three do a floor by floor, check the elevator shafts, air ducts, everywhere. The teams immediately split off and headed for their directed tasking, the detectives ran after them, but McCall stopped halfway down the poorly lit staircase. Tooms, who was in front of her, halted suddenly and looked back at McCall, who was looking up at where they had just come from. "Come on, we are going to lose the others, McCall." She just stood there, staring at the door as it slowly closed.

"How did he get out so fast?" Tooms looked puzzled at the question,

"What do you mean?" McCall turned around to face Tooms, who was panting from the adrenaline rush.

"There was no way of knowing we were coming, so how did he get out so quickly, he couldn't use the elevators because they're all locked down, he couldn't use the fire escapes because we have snipers on them. So how did he get out?" Tooms shrugged, he saw her point, but everything was covered.

"Beats me, you got any theories?" McCall smiled, as she lifted her wrist to speak into the microphone on her wrist.

"Command this is McCall, I am going back to the nest, we

have to check something out." There was a crackle of static before the command post got back with an answer.

"OK but proceed with caution," came back a voice. McCall looked down at the polished steel slide of her custom Glock, she thought back to the day she had gotten back to the station after her shooting and Steel had given her the custom piece as a welcome back present. She smiled at the memory and her grip tightened on the pistol grip. She looked at Tooms, who just nodded and held his service up with both hands, gripping it tightly. McCall noticed the silence first as they re-entered the corridor, the deafening silence that could make the slightest noise sound like a symbol in a brass band. They edged slowly down the hallway to room 214; smoke still rose from the wooden doorframe from the shape charges, the smell of burnt wood and paint filled their nostrils as they continued inside. Even though the room was searched, it was a brief one, and the teams had been looking for a man, not a secret hiding place. This time, McCall and Tooms had time to do a thorough search, and if they didn't find him, they might find something else. McCall would search, and Tooms would cover just in case of any sudden surprises. They were alone in this, the others were either doing a door to door or checking any other route out.

"Command, this is McCall, we are back at the room, starting to do a sweep now." The sound of static buzzed in her ear for a second.

"Roger that, keep us apprised of your situation." McCall nodded to Tooms, and they started in the bathroom. The bathroom was small but had all the usual amenities, McCall looked up at the ceiling to check for hatches, only to find white concrete. They moved out into the bedroom area and began to do a sweep of the room, starting with the wardrobe: All of Jones's clothes remained in the suitcase, possibly just in case he had to move quickly. The room was clean.

"Okay McCall, it was a long shot but we ain't found zip. Let's get the hell out of here and get to the others." McCall nodded as she took one last look at the room. They relaxed slightly and headed for the door. Suddenly, they stopped as though they had just been frozen, and looked up. They both slowly held their weapons tightly and brought them up, aiming at the ceiling

"Neighbours?" Tooms asked, not taking his eyes off the tiled ceiling,

"Doubt it, this is the top floor, above us is maintenance room and storage." The roof above them creaked from something moving above.

"Rats?" McCall shot Tooms a look of disgust.

"God, I hope not, or our guns are useless." Tooms tried to break a smile, but he was busy holding his breath with anticipation. Silence followed, just the noise from the traffic below filled their ears,

"Maybe it's gone?" McCall shrugged, but kept her gun trained on the ceiling.

"Maybe, but…." The ceiling exploded into a cloud of dust and polystyrene fragments as something dropped down, McCall covered her eyes but just caught a glimpse of Tooms flying across the room and crashing into the closet. Jones had dropped down and, in the confusion, had time to windmill kick Tooms and leg sweep, McCall. As she crashed to the wooden floor, her head hit hard, and then she saw darkness. Jones stood up, looked at the two downed detectives, and smiled.

FORTY-THREE

Tooms awoke, blinked, he was finally awake. He felt giddy and disorientated. He had the taste of copper in his mouth. Tooms spat and watched as a pool of blood hit the rug. Tooms groaned as he felt his body hurt all over. He knew he had to get up, check on McCall. As went to get up, he was suddenly pulled back by something and he felt as if his arms were made from lead. He looked down to see that he had both hands handcuffed to the radiator behind him, he tugged at his shackles and grunted. His mind was full of clouds, and he was beginning to get the feeling back into his body as his system began to waken. In his blurry vision he made out someone in front of him, the silhouette was more masculine, and he figured it was Jones.

"Where's McCall?" Tooms yelled, as he struggled to keep his head up, he gave his head a quick shake and tightly squeezed his eyes shut. As he opened them, his vision started to come back. McCall was on the floor at the far side of the room, lying still. Tooms growled, as he feared the worst for her. Tooms sat handcuffed to the radiator that was fixed on the back wall opposite the doorway, which was now covered in debris from the ceiling.

"OK, so what now pretty boy?" Tooms looked over to Jones, who was sitting on the bed, tapping his chin with a long thin-bladed dagger. He saw Tooms look over to McCall's limp body and then looked back with a smile.

"What the hell did you do to her you son of a bitch?" Jones tutted and stood up slowly.

"How touching. Actually, I would be more concerned about yourself," Jones said, with a menacing grin. Jones listened to the chatter on the radio he had taken from McCall. "I don't have much time before they start to look for you, so I had better be quick." Tooms's eyes widened.

"Better be quick with what?" Tooms asked, nervously. Jones grinned and started to come towards him slowly, living off watching the big man squirm. But Tooms was struggling to get out so he could smash the guys face to a pulp. Jones knelt in front of him and started to pick chunks out of the floorboards with the tip of the blade.

"So, you finally came for me, nice job giving the others the slip." Tooms gave Jones a confused look, which made him uneasy,

"You have no idea, do you?" Tooms shook his head with a vacant expression on his large face.

"Man, I have no idea what the hell you are talkin' about, what I do know is when I get out of these cuffs your momma ain't gonna recognise your sorry ass." Jones heard movement behind him, but he didn't need to turn around to know it was McCall.

"Awake at last, Detective, good we have only a few moments before they come for me." Jones put the blade up against Tooms's heart, a small trickle of blood meant he was too close for anyone to shoot. McCall was brandishing her Glock 23 back up, but the 40 mm round would push Jones into Tooms if she fired and he knew that.

"So, what do you want, safe passage out of here, a million bucks – a bullet in the fuckin' brain?" McCall asked calmly. Jones smiled, still looking at Tooms's heavy, sweat-drenched face.

"Now, now Detective, we both know I am not getting out of here alive, and even if I did, I would have an accident in prison." McCall edged round to try to get a better look at the situation.

"Put the knife down, and we can all walk out of here alive, all of us." Jones shook his head.

"No, I am afraid there are people who would like me out of the picture, so I think I will pass." McCall looked at him strangely, even though he wasn't facing her, she could tell that there was something wrong. Tooms's eyes widened as he saw McCall slightly lower her weapon, McCall was still wearing her radio, but her custom piece was on the bed, just lying there. The sound of static was then followed by the captain's order to fall back to the room, McCall and Tooms had been missed.

"Look, come in with us. We can protect you," Jones turned slightly to catch a glimpse of her face, he smiled at her tenderly.

"Oh, you have no idea who you would be protecting me from, do you?" His eyes were gentle, and she instantly knew something was off.

"I can see why he picked you, Detective; he would be proud." McCall saw his eyes move over to the doorway and his grin broadened as he dropped the knife and held his hands up.

"Well Detective, this has turned out to be a real HEEL of a day wouldn't you say?" he smiled and shot a glance upwards.

Six shots rang out, the bullets ripping through his flesh and casting eruptions of body fluids into the air. The shots were precise and accurate; he took one in each shoulder and one in each leg. The final two hit him in the heart and the last impacted between his eyes throwing his lifeless carcass to the side of Tooms.

"No," McCall screamed and ran for Jones's wounded body, but it was too late, he was gone. She spun around and ran towards the door; she wanted answers from the shooter. Her face filled with anger as she approached, but she stopped suddenly and stared blankly at the figure in the doorway, Tony stood there with his pistol drawn.

"You guy's okay? We got orders to come and look for you," Tony said. McCall just stared at him in disbelief.

"Why did you shoot, he had his hands up?" Tony looked at her blankly.

"Shoot who? I just got here, I heard shots and feared the worst." McCall's gaze fell down to Tony's drawn Glock, he felt a cold shiver run down his spine, and he began to back off slightly.

"What is it you think I did?" McCall looked over to the bloodied body of Jones who was slumped against the blood-splattered wall next to Tooms.

"Oh shit, look, I didn't shoot anyone McCall you have to believe me, look take my gun." Tony went to release the magazine from the housing and draw back the top slide when Jenny and the others came bolting into the corridor.

"McCall, what the hell is going on here?" Yelled the captain, then he saw the scene.

"Did you shoot him?" McCall shook her head before her eyes shot to Tony.

"Detective, do you know anything about this?" Tony felt like a child who was being blamed for something the dog had done.

"Sir, I heard shots, so I made for the room, when I got here, I saw …well this. I never fired a shot, let alone killed anyone." Captain Brant's eyes searched Tony's. Brant could usually tell if someone was lying, but he just wasn't sure about Tony. Brant turned to see CSU coming down the corridor.

"You know the procedure, give your weapon to CSU for trace so we can clear this up." Tony nodded and headed for the techs who were just getting ready, laying out boxes, getting evidence bags, and document pads ready.

"Sorry," Jenny apologised as she backed out of a room down the corridor from the crime scene into Tony. Jenny dropped the boxes she was helping a young CSU tech carry.

"You okay?" They said in unison, then laughed together.

"Sorry, my fault completely," Jenny said, rescuing the boxes and she was just about to pass Tony his gun that had fallen with the collision.

"Stop Detective; he has to hand the weapon over to CSU so no other prints, okay?" She nodded at the captain to say she understood. Tony smiled at her.

"Thanks anyway." Jenny smiled back.

"Oh, it was nothing really. I am sure you would do the same for me." Tony picked up the weapon and headed for the CSU team to hand over his weapon. The captain walked over to McCall who was standing in the doorway, watching the commotion in the corridor.

"You okay Detective?" She looked up at him and tried to make a smile, but she couldn't.

"No, not really, he said he didn't shoot anyone but...." Brant's eyes squinted.

"But what?" McCall shook her head.

"No, it's nothing. Just been a long day, that's all sir." He smiled and nodded.

"That it has, but you'll have to go back to the precinct and give a statement to IA reference the shooting." McCall smiled as she heard someone cough behind her, she turned to see a growling Tooms, who was still handcuffed to the radiator.

"Oh, don't mind me, please. I enjoy been chained up next to a dead dude that's bleedin' all over me." McCall let out a small chuckle, then took out her handcuff key from her pocket and walked towards him. The captain followed close behind and looked down at Jones's twisted body.

"Ok, you two so what made you come back here anyway?" Asked Brant who was looking up at the hole in the broken ceiling.

"I had a feeling he was too professional to do what we thought he might do." Brant helped McCall get Tooms to his feet and watched the large man pat the dust off himself.

"Well I am glad you're both alright, get yourselves cleaned up then get back to the precinct." As he watched them leave, his gut churned. Something wasn't right here and he hoped ballistics could prove Tony's story.

FORTY-FOUR

The sound of the waves crashing against the massive hull was dulled out by the music from the bars on the seventh deck. Steel leant on the cold plastic-topped balcony rail of his room and looked out across the darkness of the night sky, the usual array of sparking starlight and glowing moon had denied them this night, as if someone had turned out the heavenly lights for the night.

He wondered about the two gorillas that the giant Russian had sent after him in the gym; they were under an order, that was plain to see. If it had been personal, he was sure they would have been more brutal, and it wouldn't have been one on one. No, the boss had sent them to get him, but why wait and why did he think that he was Blacke? Steel closed his eyes and let the cool breeze sweep across his face and the sounds of the ocean fill his ears. He loved the ocean, even though he wasn't a naval man; it was a source of great power but also of great serenity.

Steel opened his eyes and moved into his room, where one bedside light broke up the darkness. Moving past the bed, he took a small leather jacket off the back of the dresser chair and slipped it over a strange turtleneck that had the look of neoprene rather than wool or polyester. He wore all black so he could fade into the shadows; he needed to put away Black and become himself once more.

HIDDEN STEEL

They were now in the open sea, and only a few days remained, he had the feeling that things were going to start to reveal themselves and he had to be ready, ready for anything.

THE CAPTAIN'S cabin was bathed in darkness; where normally the light of the moon would create pools of light through the small portholes, now there was only darkness. The sound of the captain's snoring filled the room with loud vibrations as he slept soundly and deeply. His many years at sea had taught him to sleep anywhere, "Get it while you can and where you can" His old mentor used to say. In between snorts, he would mumble about something then return to his chorus.

Suddenly, he opened one eye and scanned the room, not moving or stopping the snoring is if trying to conceal the fact he was awake. He sat up slowly, his eyes squinting trying to pick a shape or anything out from the pitch black.

"Who's there – is …is that you? It can't be time yet, surely?" Tobias Long gasped as his desk light was suddenly switched on and he found Steel sitting on the edge of his desk. Long's face creased up in anger as he pulled himself up quickly and went for an old African walking stick that had a concealed blade within, but Steel was quicker, and he shot up and grabbed and tossed the alarmed captain into his office chair. The captain and the chair slammed into the back wall next to his desk; Steel before him, ready to push him back into the leather captain's office chair the moment he tried to get up out of it.

"Black, what the hell is the meaning of all this, get out before I call for security to put you in the brig." Steel just stood there, sideways on to the frightened captain,

"Captain, my captain, you seemed surprised to see me but not surprised that someone should be here, who were you expecting and what isn't it time for?" The captain began to sweat heavily, aware of his obvious blunder.

"Nothing and no one, I will ask you again sir to leave my cabin before I call…" Steel leapt forwards; his hands gripped the cushioned armrests, and his face stopped inches away from the captain's.

"I should be interested in knowing who you would call," Steel said, backing off slightly. "The boy, what did he bring you, and before you start, I know he brought you something, so don't try to deny it." Long's face was filled with remorse and a touch of fear, but it wasn't fear for himself.

"I can't tell you anything; they have my family. If I talk, they die," Captain Long said, his words were heavy. Steel sat on the desk and prepared to listen.

"I have friends who can help, you know," Steel said. Long cracked a smile.

"The police you were talking about? No, they would investigate, and that would be the end of it," Long shook his head as he spoke. Steel smiled.

"No, other friends," Steel said, his tone was serious. A shiver ran down Long's back at the thought of such people, agencies with no titles because they shouldn't and don't exist.

"Captain Long, something is or will happen on this ship, and I have to stop it." Long stared at Steel for a moment with curious eyes; this was not the same man at dinner. This was not the rich man going through life without a care.

"Who are you?" Long asked. Steel smiled at the question and put on a bedside light.

"Oh, the importance of a name, funny how it's only important after the shit has hit the fan." Steel sat back down and looked down at the captain through his sunglass-clad eyes. Long shivered at the full sight of this man in black who gave off an aura that you only found in nightmares.

"The lad was here, and he was told to deliver something to me, something that had to be kept safe. The key they called it." Steel frowned slightly.

"They, who is they?" The captain swallowed hard and shook his head.

"They never said, I just had a letter delivered the day we were setting off, it just said that they had my family and that they would kill them if I didn't do as instructed." Steel nodded with understanding.

"So where is this key now, your safe?" Tobias Long shook his head.

"No, a special compartment I had made, just in case." He knelt and went under the desk; Steel heard the sound of wood against wood as the captain prised open the compartment.

"Oh my god it's gone," Long yelled, after banging his head on the desk as he came up. "The box, it's gone." Long wandered around like a lost child in a mall until Steel shoved him back into the chair. Long began to rock back and forth in his chair. Steel got up and moved to a large wooden globe that sat next to the desk. Steel opened it to reveal a drinks cabinet. He poured a large rum and passed it to the captain, who took the crystal glass with two shaky hands then took a large mouthful which seemed to relax him slightly.

"Captain, who else knew about the key and the hiding place?" Steel asked. Long took another drink before shaking his head.

"Nobody, especially the hiding place, hell it wasn't even on the blueprints," Long smiled at his own cunning.

"So, who else may have known about this key?" Then Steel stopped and thought for a moment,

"Captain, when did Anthony Blacke first join the ship?" Long looked puzzled at the question.

"We picked him up at Vigo along with his cargo." Steel's mind began to process the new information.

"Captain, who the hell is Anthony Blacke, and I swear if you lie to me, I'll push you through the window." Long looked at the portholes that were at least two feet in diameter and smiled.

"You idiot, you couldn't push me through there it's too narrow, hell you would have to chop me up first." His laughter fell away as Steel removed the blade from the African walking stick and slammed it into the desk, just missing the captain's fingers. Long looked up, frightened, into the disturbing face of Steel.

"He's an arms runner, buyers and sells to anyone; in fact, the cargo is part of a deal that was set up. That's why he's onboard, to meet his buyers." Steel put the blade back into the walking stick scabbard and stood up.

"Buyers – as in more than one, he's having an arms auction on your ship, you silly bastard." Long gave Steel a sheepish look.

"Captain, what I don't get is if the boy did as he was told, why did they kill him?" Tobias shook his head; the look of guilt made him look pale.

"I don't know it doesn't make any sense." Steel looked thoughtful for a moment before turning back to Long.

"This cargo of Blacke's, where is it, and what is it?" Long thought for a moment.

"Well there are ten sizeable military-grade boxes, around three feet by three feet, you'll find them in cargo area B. Just look for a sign that says KEEP OUT. Steel switched off the bedside light, and the corner fell into darkness.

"Mr Black, what are you going to do – Mr Black." Long rushed for the light switch by his bed but tripped and fell over something, he reached up and switched on the light, revealing he was alone. Long looked down to find his pillow underneath him, and he sighed in relief.

Steel ventured down to the lower decks to try to locate this cargo hold. Deck 2 was filled with storage rooms and cargo holds, in the centre of the deck lay the crew's canteen that sat long and proud. This broke up the area between the two masses of storage and cargo holds. Below that was the massive engine room and logistics rooms.

As he made his way down the tight corridors that separated the holds and the think iron hull, he checked for signs of shields displaying warnings. Steel stopped as he stood in front of one door that held a large sign depicting the very words Long had uttered. As he smiled and went to reach for the door handle, he snatched his hand away, and he turned to face the voices that approached him slowly from the right. Next to the door in an alcove, was the door to a cleaning closet. Steel quickly got in and closed the door quietly so as not to draw attention to the sound of a door closing. At the bottom of the door was an air vent to allow the fresh air to clear the smell of chemicals in the room, this also made it excellent for Steel to listen out for the approaching men. Footsteps echoed down the iron avenue as the men approached, Steel could hear them laughing and joking as they came down. He smelt the stuffy air as he nestled himself close to the vent. The men stopped just outside the door of the cargo hold he had just left, and another voice greeted the men.

"The storm will hit at around four o'clock or sixteen hundred to the more educated among us." The voice was scrappy and deep in places; Steel had the feeling he had heard the man's voice before but couldn't quite get it.

"The gas is also in place to send the passengers to a nice sleep for around thirty-six hours, and everyone will be told to stay in their cabins or somewhere safe indoors and avoid windows." Steel listened with interest as the plan began to unfold before him.

"We get our stolen gear and get off, the passengers wake up none the wiser, and everyone's happy. So, I want everyone ready to go at four o'clock; we rendezvous in the captain's dining room then." The other men said their "Yes sirs", and then Steel heard the three move off in opposite directions.

Steel looked at his watch, and the hands showed it was nearly four in the morning.

"They're going to hit tonight," Steel cursed. He had to worn Tia, he didn't know where she was, but he had a reasonably good idea.

FORTY-FIVE

McCall, Tooms and Tony had been seated in separate rooms to write their statements. Tony had been escorted downtown by a couple of IA goons before McCall and Tooms had had the chance to speak with him properly. They had agreed to write the truth as it may be the only way to get Tony out of suspension or jail. If their stories faltered, IA would become suspicious and rip their stories to pieces, making things worse for him and them. Most would argue that if Tony had shot Jones, he had saved Tooms and McCall but instead he denied it. If his weapon were proven to be a decisive match Tony would go down for a long time. McCall hoped he was telling the truth, but she saw no other way it couldn't have been him. She looked up at the large clock above the elevator and sighed at the lateness of the hour, it was now nearly two in the morning, and she could feel the last coffee beginning to wear off. There were lots of things with the situation that McCall found off; firstly, the shooter was a crack shot, who had managed to get pinpoint hits with a pistol from over thirty-five feet in quick bursts. McCall was the best shot in the department when it came to the handgun, but that was better than she could do on a good day. If he had shot Jones, why deny it? Things didn't add up for McCall, and she started to feel Tony had been set up.

She sat in a small briefing room with a little, pasty looking man who had a brown suit and mousy coloured hair. He sat there and watched McCall write down her account of the shooting, starting from when they re-entered the room. She finished it, signed it and then stretched off the hours she had spent on the most uncomfortable chair in the world.

"I take it we're done, Detective?" She smiled at him, making the pasty man turn away quickly with embracement and head for the door. McCall stood up and made for the open door after him, but a tall, broad-shouldered female IA officer was waiting.

"Detective, you're not to leave until our Lieutenant has interviewed you, understood? Also do not discuss this with anyone and that includes Detective Tooms," said the large female IA detective. McCall smiled falsely and headed for the desk. She sat down hard in the chair and rested her head on the large jotter pad. She was tired and just wanted the comfort of her bed, but that was not going to happen for a while.

CSU and ballistics would not be ready until at least mid-afternoon, depending on the caseload they had at the lab. Tony's jacket and shirt had been taken in to check for Gun Shot Residue or GSR as everyone called it. The mood of finding the killer had suddenly been swept away by this tidal wave of sorrow for Tony. McCall watched him as he talked to one of the IA officers calmly, while the officer was yelling, trying to get under Tony's skin, hoping to make him lash out or say something incriminating. McCall took out her cell phone to see if she had any messages, especially from Doctor Dave, but the display was empty of new mail.

"Who are you phoning?" asked the IA investigator in a brash tone. McCall looked up with her eyes, but not moving her head. McCall gave a menacing gaze as she looked up at the female IA officer. The woman backed off slightly but held her straight back form.

"I was texting with the local media, and I thought they could use a good story," McCall lied. The woman's mouth fell open but slammed it shut as McCall sat back in her chair and smiled.

"Don't worry Cassandra, the detective is only playing with you, why don't you see how the others are doing?" Said a tall man who was standing behind McCall. The woman nodded and left, but shot McCall a scowl before she did. McCall stood up and grabbed her coffee cup, she had the feeling she was going to be here a while so she may as well top up her caffeine levels. The tall man followed.

"I guess you're the Lieutenant?" He nodded and flashed a smile as they entered the break room. He was around six-three with broad shoulders and short black hair. He wore a grey suit with a white shirt and a blue tie. A strange combination, but he made it work. McCall tagged him as being in his mid-forties with timeless skin and chiselled good looks. He looked more like a guy from a commercial than an IA lieutenant, at least he was a pleasant change from the ghoul she had been speaking with earlier.

"So, how are you doing, Detective, must have been a hell of a night?" He watched McCall pour herself a cup of coffee and he smiled at the unfriendly attitude.

"May I?" He asked, picking up a mug. She shrugged as if not caring what he did.

"It's a free country," McCall replied. He shook his head, smiling as he poured a cup of the aromatic smelling brew. McCall smiled as he took a taste of the coffee and watched his face savour the flavour.

"What the hell is this?" He asked, as if he had never had good coffee.

"A colleague gets it sent in, he couldn't handle our coffee, so he got this, and it will do me I suppose," She lied as she took a sip and felt her soul lift with the taste. "Look Lieutenant I am tired, I had a hell of a day yester…" She looked at her watch which read just after three, "Sorry today, so if it's OK, can I please go home and get some sleep?" The Lieutenant smiled as he sipped his coffee.

"My Name is James Green, head of the IA unit," He said with a comforting smile.

"Sam McCall, but I guess you know that already?" She laughed. Green shrugged, keeping his expression.

"We have your statement; we will text you with the interview time. Go home, get some rest," He replied with a smile before taking another sip. McCall could feel his eyes sizing her up, why, she had no idea, and at that moment didn't really care. McCall shot him a brief smile before dragging herself out and to the elevator.

"What a woman." The lieutenant said, shaking his head, and smiled.

McCall was awoken by her second alarm. She had slept through the first one. The morning sunshine was unable to break through the thick drapes in her bedroom that remained dark and tranquil. She turned over and checked the time with a half-opened blurry eye, it was around six in the morning, and she didn't have the energy, or the will, to crawl out of the comfort of her bed.

McCall had showered and changed and was now heading towards the morgue. Something Jones had said was nagging her. McCall had phoned ahead to see if Jones had been processed yet and smiled to know he hadn't, she had convinced Tina to wait until she had gotten there. McCall burst through the Cutting Room doors to find Tina sitting on one of the side worktops, waiting patiently for her. "Morning, Tina" McCall smiled, as she handed over her coffee.

"Good morning, heard you guys pulled an all-nighter last night," Tina said, with a concerned look. McCall tried to smile but couldn't bring herself to, in light of the circumstances. "How's Tony doing?" McCall shrugged in response.

"I don't know he was kept separate from us the whole time, like he was a mass murder or something." McCall just stared at her coffee cup, unable to think straight as her brain was still waking up.

"So, what was so important that I couldn't slice this little charmer up?" Tina asked. McCall shook her head to bring herself back to the land of the living.

"What? I am sorry, I got around an hour sleep last night." Tina smiled in response to her friend's plight. "There was something he said last night that was bugging me. He said. "A reel HEEL of a day, with a big emphasis on HEEL," McCall explained. Tina looked up at McCall.

"You think he hid something in his shoes?" McCall nodded with a childish grin on her face.

"Where are his clothes?" Asked McCall, Tina pointed to several brown bags that hadn't been sealed yet on the opposite worktop. McCall put on some surgical gloves and pulled out the left shoe to examine it. The shoe was plain and ordinary with no hidden compartment in the heel.

"You know you have been watching too many Bond movies, not that I can blame you," Tina laughed, McCall scoffed at her bad luck on the first try. McCall picked up the second shoe and twisted the heel, the sound of metal hitting ceramic tiles echoed through the cutting room, the two women just stared at the key on the floor.

"I think I know where this is for?" McCall remembered, as if it had just happened, the way Jones spoke those last words then looked up briefly. McCall reached down and picked up the key. She looked it over to see if there were any markings, it was a blank key.

"Thanks, Tina, I owe you one." Tina smiled coyly as she watched her friend leave. Tina smiled and picked up her scalpel.

"Good morning Mr Jones, let's see what you have to say, shall we?" Tina smiled and slit the corpse from the sternum downwards.

FORTY-SIX

Steel waited some time, in the storeroom, until the coast was clear, hiding himself away in a darkened corner so he could sleep for a while. He made it back to the passenger decks and was heading for a small restaurant which was located opposite the Irish Bar. It was now ten o'clock in the morning, the blazing sun had risen high in the blue heavens and it was already getting warm. Steel sat himself down and picked up a menu card from the top of the small round table. He was hungry, and he needed time to think, he looked up as a young, skinny-built waiter with long hair and an attempt of a moustache under his large nose, asked Steel for his order. Steel ordered the BLT and a coffee. As the waiter left, Steel pondered over things in his head. The deck was almost empty as many people were outside or at one of the many restaurants, but Steel wanted quiet, and this seemed the perfect place.

He thought about the large Russian and why did he think that he was Blacke also why did he send the goons after him in the gym afterwards? The waitress who kept appearing, how was she involved, and who was she working for really? Steel's concentration was broken with the arrival of his coffee. His eyes caught the sight of the swirling liquid, the restaurant in Vigo came to mind, who were the men who had shot the place up and why were they shooting at Tia and the other guy? Steel waited for around ten minutes before his order arrived on a large thin plate that held a massive portion of the sandwich. The time passed slowly, and it gave him time to strategize. He had to find Tia and the Stewarts , he had to let them know what the hell was going on, so they could get some sort of back up on board.

As he sat contemplating his next move, he caught a glimpse of the waitress. She had not seen him, but he had definitely seen her. She wore an all-in-one burgundy catsuit that left little to the imagination. At first Steel thought it was lack of sleep, so he took a mouthful of coffee, but there she went, heading for the elevators. Steel stood up quickly as he saw her talking to the blonde goon from the gym. Steel pulled out a twenty-dollar bill and left it as he made off for the elevators. As he approached the set of metal doors, his eyes firmly on the LED display which showed the floors, the other set of doors opened as if to welcome him. Steel waited with his foot in the door well to stop them from closing, and Steel smiled as the other elevator stopped at deck sixteen, she was off to see the Russian.

He took the elevator up to sixteen and got off. As he stepped off on to the floor, the feeling of déjà vu crept over him. The corridor was empty, but he could hear voices in the rooms as passengers started to awaken. Steel needed into get to the Russians suite and find out what was going on. His best bet was the bedroom that was situated next to the office. He got to the corner of the corridor that led to the end and the Russian's suite, but the two large goons were standing there with folded arms. Steel peeled back around the corner to rethink his plan as the normal route appeared to be not an option, so he had to be creative. As he started to walk back, a young Hispanic woman with a cleaning trolley trundled passed him,

"Hola," Steel said, greeting the woman.

"Hola," she replied with a smile then stopped at the first door she came to and knocked.

"Good morning, housekeeping," there was no reply, so she used her card to enter. Steel pivoted on his heels and turned, just in time to see her head into the bathroom with a small radio playing Spanish music. Steel saw his chance and headed for the balcony door and opened it, only to be met by a gust of heavy sea breeze. He slid the door back almost closed and stood for a moment looking at the black clouds forming in the distance, before him the maelstrom of what was to come. The wind was for the first time blustery and unkind, Steel looked up to the heavens and shrugged.

"Really, now?" He said, making a joke with God. Steel got onto the balcony and jumped from one railing to the next one; as he landed he fell into the area and rolled as the wind from the ocean fought against him. He looked over and saw he had two more to go before he reached his goal. He leapt for the next one. just as a massive gust blew, making him fall short. He hit the side and slid down, his hands grasping for the barred railings. He hung there, almost sixty feet from a watery death and clambered up slowly until he was at the plastic railing on the top. Pulling himself up and over, Steel stopped for a breath, then, with his hands on his knees he looked over at the last one and just ran for it. Steel ran, then at the right moment, leapt up and used the safety rail to boost his jump. He flew long and true, landing perfectly on the other side before rolling towards the bedroom door. Luckily, the door was slightly open to let some fresh air in to circulate and freshen up the room. Steel crept in like a cat on the prowl, his body low but agile. At the entrance to the office, Steel opened the door slightly so he could get every word.

He could hear voices in the background that began to get louder and clearer as they came into the office area, he couldn't see their faces, but he had a good idea who was who. As much as he could tell, there were only two voices, that of the large Russian and the other he imagined was the waitress in the catsuit.

"Yes, Mr Vedas, he told us to be in the smoking lounge at three o'clock." Steel tried to find a keyhole, but the locks had twist bolts.

"And what of the Americans have they been dealt with concerning the death of Anishka?" Steel looked puzzled.

"Who the hell is Anishka?" Steel thought to himself.

"No, not yet, they have so far given us little opportunity to act, but our sister will be avenged," said the woman. The more Steel listened, the more it sounded as if they were moving around the room, and he hoped that none of them needed this bedroom.

"What of Mr Black? The contact asked that we get rid of him and yet he bested two of our top men and saved one of their lives in the process. Are we sure he is with the Americans?" There was a moment of silence.

"We can't be sure of anything, sir, we just have to be ready." The woman said, in a husky Russian ascent.

"Okay one thing is clear, and that is we need to get the merchandise before THEY or the Americans do." Suddenly Steel realised this was bigger than he thought. Blacke was running an arms auction with the CIA and FSB, and whatever he was selling wasn't handguns or cookies.

Steel waited for a while longer before looking at his watch. The hands showed it was nearly noon. He looked up as he heard Vedas yell to the others.

"Come, I am starving. We go and eat now before meeting with that idiot Blacke." There was a click as the door was secured behind them. Steel smiled at his good fortune, as he didn't fancy going the way he had come. Slowly, he slipped into the office area and moved quickly towards the door until he saw the laptop on the couch. Steel looked around then rapidly walked over to the laptop. Steel pulled out a USB drive from his jacket and started to download any files he found. The files were in Russian so he wasn't able to decipher them straight away. When and if he had time, he would go through them but now was not the time nor the place. The screen flashed as the download was complete. Taking the drive, he put back the computer and slipped out of the door into the safety of the corridor. Blacke was having a meeting at three, and the men from down in the storage mentioned a gas would be released at four o'clock. Steel had to get to that meeting and stop whatever trade was about to happen. He was alone, and that's just how he liked it. Steel headed for the elevators, he had to get back to his room and see what goodies he had collected from the mercenary in Vigo. The doors opened, and he stepped in casually,

"So, where you headin'?" asked a kindly old man next to the switches.

"Oh, the belly of the beast, but number twelve is fine, thank you," Steel replied, with a smile.

FORTY-SEVEN

McCall made her way back to the hotel where they had found Jones. Crime tape still blocked the doorway of room 214. They had replaced the door mostly to keep undesirables from taking souvenirs from a crime scene or taking cell snaps of where the body of Jones had lain. The air was thick, and the smell of too many people in one spot still lingered, as if the walls had absorbed their scent.

CSU had finished their sweep hours ago and was on the way back to the lab to carry out their investigation, but McCall wasn't interested in the room. As she reached the doorway, she strolled past it and headed for the stairwell to the attic. At the top of the stairs, two doors faced each other, one was for the fire escape, and the other was for the attic. On the red-coloured door, a large sign warned of no trespass and employees only. McCall produced the key she had found in Jones's shoe and tried it in the lock, the dull metal key slotted effortlessly into the lock and, with a turn and a click, she was inside.

Inside was dark and the sound of her shoes echoed throughout the empty building. McCall took a small flashlight from her pocket and searched for the main switch. The switch was a pull handle on a breaker box, she pushed it down and watched the strip lights flicker on, one by one, revealing a large room with map boards and murder boards, personnel files were

HIDDEN STEEL

broken down into the groups of people as if each one was a case file for Jones. He had locations marked and timetables showing what they did as routine. He had studied them until he had a pattern in which to kill them.

"Oh my god," she said, in awe of the room. She put on her surgical gloves as she moved around, trying to soak everything in.

"Why go to all this trouble, unless it had to look like an accident," she thought to herself. McCall took out her small camera and started to make photographs of as much as she could. She wanted something she could study later and something on file, in case any of this should go missing. McCall looked over and found an old desk with a load of files stacked neatly in piles. McCall moved over to it and sat in the office chair. The old wooden chair creaked with age as she sat on the faded brown leather cushioning. She noticed one file explaining how all her victims were connected to something called *OPERATION UNITY*. She sat back and started to read, the more she read, the more everything came together. McCall had a feeling this whole damn mess was to do with a ship, considering that most of them worked around ships or shipping, but she didn't know how they were connected or why. In the file, McCall found a list containing all their names. Karen Greene was the recruiter of thirty-six personnel who would start on a ship that was due to sail three weeks before. Donald Major had done some specialist electronic work on the ship, and John Barr had been on sight during the final build and helped install some specialist equipment, John Barr was a welder as well as a crane operator. Even though she now had more than enough proof that Jones had contact with each and every one of her vics, something didn't sit right. McCall worked her way through the piles of different coloured files until she reached one that made her stop, the front cover merely said NYPD HOMICIDE. With a shaky hand, McCall opened it slowly, expecting to find a hit list. Instead what she found was enough to make her slam the file shut and push it away from the desk. McCall thought for a moment, rocking in the chair and looking at the door. McCall felt she had to do something but now, more than ever, she wasn't sure who she could trust. She picked up the file and placed it in the small of her back, underneath her jacket. With a sigh, she took out her cell and pressed the speed dial for the captain.

"Sir, its McCall. I went back to the crime scene, and I think I found something, we need CSU back here." She powered the cell down and placed it away and waited for the captain and the techs to arrive. She knew she had only a few minutes before this place became a circus, only a few minutes to find something else that confirmed the mole's identity.

She continued to look through the files for information, something more about this Operation Unity, but came up empty. McCall walked over to the boards and the faces of the victims, pictures of them laughing and just going through life oblivious of their fate. It was obvious they had been pressured into whatever they had done, be it a good pay check or coercion. She looked at one picture of Donald, who was hugging his wife before he went to work, her hand rested on the picture as if she was memorising that moment. She smiled and moved on, hoping to find something in the pictures that might reveal what they had been working on. McCall stopped and looked around.

"The Browns , where the hell are the Browns ?" She felt a presence at the door. It was the captain who was just standing there with his mouth open.

"You have got to be kidding me," He said, making her turn.

"Sir, I didn't hear you come in." She felt shocked at his sudden presence. He walked up to her, still taking in the contents of the room.

"Sorry, Detective, what were you saying before about the Browns ?" Brant asked. McCall stood and pointed at the boards in front of them.

"Sir, I don't think he killed the Browns . If you look, he has done everything with precision so far and then to do a messy job at the Browns? No, I don't buy it. Someone else is involved." Captain Brant nodded in agreement.

"He could have paid someone else to do it," Brant said. McCall shook her head.

"No, this guy had some sort of sick code, every one of his victims never suffered," she explained.

McCall reached into her pocket and took out her cell. There was a message from the precinct telling her she had to be ready for the interview at one o'clock. She closed her cell down and put it back in her pocket.

"Bad news?" Asked the captain, McCall shook her head.

"No, just the station letting me know my interview is at one," McCall said, placing the cell phone back into her pocket. Brant looked over at her and smiled.

"Just tell them what you know, nothing more nothing less, this is just a standard procedure, you know that," Brant said with a shrug. McCall had a strange look on her face as if she felt it wasn't this time.

"What's wrong Sam?" He asked, seeing the look. She wanted to tell him about the file but she couldn't, not yet.

"It's nothing, sir, just been a long week that's all," she lied, then walked over to the door, stopped, then turned, "Sir I have to go and get ready for IA." He shooed her off with a flick of his hand.

"You go, I'll wait for CSU, just remember it's just procedure, nothing to worry about. As she rushed down the stairwell, she began to feel Steel had been justified in not telling about his past with anyone, the reason he stuck to the shadows. He had warned of a mole in the precinct, and he was right.

FORTY-EIGHT

Dark clouds hung over the ocean like a fearsome beast, flashes of light emanated from within as the raw power of the heavens was about to be unleashed upon the ocean below, as the massive liner cruised slowly towards the blackened maelstrom. Even the gigantic leviathan rose and fell, carried on the monstrous waves that carried them on their journey. The speakers throughout the ship gave a quick tone to alert the passengers of an announcement.

"Ladies and gentlemen, due to adverse weather conditions, we request that everyone please remain in their cabins until further notice, thank you." The message was then translated into several different languages before the chime sounded again and everything became silent throughout the corridors and hallways.

Everyone obeyed the captain's request, all but a handful of people who sat in the smoker's lounge. The room was large with the capacity to seat over a hundred people, the floor had thick expensive carpet throughout, heavy-looking leather chairs, and couches sat round oak coffee tables in groups. This looked more like a gentlemen's club than a smoking room; at the back along the left wall sat a long bar with a huge mirror that filled the wall behind the thick carved oak and brass bar. To the right, a large panoramic window displaying the starboard side of the ship and the dark foreboding skies.

Tia looked out across the chaotic horizon through the large windows. She watched as the rain began to fall in sheets off marble-like droplets that hammered against the thickened glass. Flashes of light illuminated the dark foreboding clouds. Below, the waves, started to grow in size and intensity; some of them were larger than a small house. The storm was upon them.

Opposite the entrance to the room was a nestle of six armchairs surrounding an oval oak coffee table which held a silver champagne bucket and six flutes. Facing the door sat the Stewarts red-faced and angry. Jane checked her watch and then continued to tap the leather of the arms of her chair. Bob turned to her and gave her a look of disapproval, which made her stop. Tia watched them in the reflection of the glass. The dark backdrop made it easier to see the room in detail. The door opened, and they all looked over to see Anthony Blacke stroll in, accompanied by the waitress in her maroon velvet catsuit that glistened as she walked, followed by Vedas in a grey pinstriped suit and a burgundy cravat. The Stewarts snarled at the sight of the new company.

"You said you would sell to us" Growled Jane, Blacke nodded.

"Yes, and I said the same thing to them." He pointed to the two Russians as they sat opposite them. Blacke walked to the table and checked the label on the Champagne, which was a 1970 Dom Perignon and smiled appreciatively as he opened the vintage bottle.

"Now that we are all here, we can get down to business?" Blacke announced smugly, as he sat in the chair that was at the head of the table.

"Now everyone is here due to an invitation to procure some lost merchandise, now the game here is who has the deeper pockets. So, shall we play?"

Everyone shot up out of their seats as Missy and Albert Studebaker walked in as if they were late for something they were invited to. Blacke remained seated as though nothing was amiss.

"Okay folks, let's get some buying done shall we?" Blacke shook his head as he grinned at the whole ridiculous situation.

"Mr and Mrs Studebaker, I am afraid you have the wrong room, this is a private gathering, and well it's probably out of your league." Blacke smiled, showing his bleached white teeth, Albert sat in one of the free chairs that were next to Vedas and got his pay check out and placed it on the table.

"Mr Blacke, my wife and I recently sold some stock which we made a handsome profit on, so you see I have five hundred million spare in my account, just doin' nothing." Blacke's eyes lit up as he put down his glass and opened his arms as if he were a long-lost friend.

"Welcome, Mr Studebaker, welcome." Tia rolled her eyes and continued to stare out into the dark.

"Do you know what's for sale?" Tia asked, her gaze focused on the reflection in the window. Albert shrugged and sat back into the chair, causing the leather to give an almost moaning sound as he did so.

"Don't know, don't really care as long as I can make a profit." Blacke had a cunning smile on his face as he listened to the large man's gripes.

"So, is it hot, the thing that's on offer, is it hot?" Studebaker asked with a drooling lust. Blacke sat right back into the chair.

"Oh, my dear sir, hot isn't the word. The cargo we have, well it will blow you away." Suddenly Albert was feeling nervous. Sweat began to build upon his forehead as he realised he had walked into the wrong party.

STEEL HAD MADE it back to his suite and pulled out the black bag he had gotten from the shooter in Vigo. He had only briefly looked inside before, but now he needed to know if there was anything useful inside. He looked at his watch, the face lay next to his palm, it was ten minutes past three, and he had to get to the smoking-room that was on deck eighteen. The bag that doubled as a rucksack was fastened together by zips and buckles, he opened it and smiled as he began to lay everything out to get inventory of what he had to work with. He laid down the leg holster and pulled the Glock 41 from the rigid plastic holster. Pressing the small catch next to his thumb, he released the magazine and then pulled the top slide to the rear. He caught the hollow point .45 calibre round as it was ejected from the open barrel, Steel laid both the round and the weapon down beside the holster.

Going back inside the bag, he took out a small combat knife, seven full magazines for the Glock and his smile widened as he pulled out a silenced Heckler and Koch UMP or Universal Machine Pistol. Steel laid it down after checking the thirty round clip was full. Inside the bag, he had another five stick magazines for the .45 calibre machine pistol. Steel strapped the leg holster onto his right leg and the knife's sheath to his belt. Taking up the weapons, he stowed them securely. He was as ready as he could be. His goals were simple, find Tia and get her off the boat then find Blacke and find out what this is all about.

Steel looked at his watch. It was now a quarter past. He had to get to the smoking room before the gas was released throughout the ship. He moved quickly out of his room and headed for the elevators, knowing he didn't have to sneak around as everyone would be in their rooms. Steel thought it brilliant in a devious way that the best way to ensure everyone got the gas was to confine everyone to their rooms. He also felt some admiration for the planning as it would have taken more planning than the D Day landing to pull this off.

Steel pasted through corridors until he reached the elevators. As he went to press the call button, he saw the numbers on the LED display were counting upwards, someone was coming. Quickly, he headed for the fire axe behind the plated glass and, using the fire extinguisher next to it, smashed the glass. Steel ripped the axe from its mount and hurried over to the doors and, with a massive swing, the blade of the axe imbedded itself into the metal. Steel used this to pry open the doors. As he looked down, he could see the approaching elevator hurrying upwards. Steel knew he had to time it right or whoever was inside would be alerted to his presence as he got on top. Steel held the doors open with his hands as he looked down, one leg dangled ready to step on to the box as it came past. His timing had to be perfect, or he would be dead. Steel closed his eyes and listened for the sounds of its approach. Then he stepped off the landing and on to the elevator. As he crouched down, he exhaled deeply and got himself together. Moving over to the maintenance hatch, he opened it slowly and looked down.

Inside, two men, wearing all black with combat vests on and plenty of guns, stood by the door. He had to be quick. Steel opened the hatch carefully then quietly dropped down behind them. The first man he kicked in the back so his face met with the door panel and he fell to the ground, unconscious. The second man was quick to react and brought his machine pistol round to fire, but Steel had forced the weapon against the man's chest as it sprayed bullets into the door. The two men struggled against each other until Steel head-butted the man then brought his knee up to the man's crotch. As he fell forwards, Steel ejected the stick magazine and smashed the flat end against the man's left temple. Steel moved back into the corner to catch his breath before taking the rucksack off his back and laying it down. Steel took off one of the combat vests that the men was wearing and put it on. Checking the pouches, he found more magazines for both the pistol and the machine pistol. In a small bags, strapped on the men's hips, Steel found some gas masks. He patted one of them on the head and strapped the mask to himself and stowed the other in the bag.

Steel smiled as he stripped the men of their armaments and ammunition. Reaching over, he pressed the button for deck eighteen, and then continued to fill the bag.

Steel removed the left leg holster from one of them and strapped it on, he stood up and adjusted the straps. He smiled as he thought that, for every bad guy he took down, that was more ammo. The doors opened on the eighteenth floor, and Steel edged out and checked the corners. As he scanned the floor, his eye caught a glimpse of a possible hiding place for his new pals, the ladies restroom. He smiled a wicked grin.

FORTY-NINE

McCall entered the cutting room doors to find Tina dancing around whilst she spoke to someone on her cell. McCall smiled and leant against the doorframe with her arms crossed as Tina laughed a false laugh and spun around like a ballerina. Tina turned, stared McCall straight into the eyes and froze.

"Oh yes, captain, yes I understand, yes sir. Well, I have got to go now. See you later." Tina hung up and put her cell away as if nothing was wrong.

"Wow, I didn't know you and the captain were such good friends," McCall joked, knowing full well that was Tina's mystery man.

"Anyway, Detective, your Mr Jones was a very interesting customer." McCall walked over to her usual perch and hopped up on the counter.

"What do you mean, what did you find?" McCall lifted the sheet that covered Jones's face,

"Well to start with, your boy has had a lot of surgery and not just once, this guy had changed his face several times, and I do mean changed." Tina pointed to the cheeks and the jaw area "All of his teeth are implants, so no chance of dental and also his fingerprints have been surgically removed. His facial features have been altered as well, cheeks, nose, chin. Well you get the idea." McCall nodded.

"Just like someone else who paid a visit." Tina and McCall looked at this strange man on the slab, at first glance he was Mr Average, Mr Every day.

"So there is no way of finding out who our mystery boy was?" Tina threw over a file to McCall.

"I found some plates and pins in him, many in the the legs and arms. He was Staff Sergeant Luke Powell of SEAL Team-Three. He disappeared after an operation went wrong and the team were taken out. It was a set up to get the team there and take them out. There were only two survivors, Staff Sergeant Powell and Sergeant John Steel."

McCall's mouth fell open, Steel had said a bit about his past but never about that, as far as she knew he left to join the PD. She looked down at Powell's body and shook her head, still thinking back to that day in the hotel.

"I don't know what to make of him, a killer with morals?" Tina shot a look at McCall.

"What makes you say that?" McCall picked up a hint of anger in Tina's voice.

"He could have quite easily killed both Tooms and myself, but he didn't. When he put you in the freezer, he phoned all of us to ensure someone found you." Tina could see her point but refused to, as far as she was concerned, whoever shot him did the world a favour.

"Any more good news?" McCall joked, but Tina wasn't smiling.

"The ballistics came back from the gun Tony gave. It was the weapon used to shoot Jones – I mean Powell – you know what I mean," Tina said, stumbling over her words. McCall looked up from reading through the report on Powell,

"So Tony was the shooter, why would he lie?" McCall said, puzzled. Tina looked uneasy as she shifted from one foot to the other.

"It was also used in several other homicides," Tina explained. McCall felt faint; Tony was the mole?

"What homicides?" McCall forced the question out, and her mouth felt dry and sickly.

"All the shootings you are investigating were done with the same weapon. Somehow someone has been able to replicate the same ballistic signatures in two guns," Tina explained. McCall sat silent for a minute.

"So, what you are saying is if we caught two people with two guns that fired the same, we couldn't do a damn thing because we can't prove which one was used to kill someone," McCall growled, now she was angry. Not just at the smart son-of-a-bitch who was screwing with their case, but because Tony could be a mole and she had no way of proving which was the murder weapon. Tina nodded; her sorrowful look said it all. McCall took a deep breath and closed her eyes for a moment, letting all the new information wash over her, calming herself before she became blinkered by the facts.

"Did we get any prints on the weapon, the one Tony gave up I mean?" McCall asked, her eyes remained shut awaiting the answer, Tina searched the notes.

"Yes, prints found on the slide and the grip." McCall's eyes opened, and she smiled.

"Was that it, nowhere else?" Tina rechecked the report and shrugged.

"No, just there, why?" McCall swung her legs like a schoolgirl.

"Get CSU to dust all of the weapons again and include the magazine and bullets please." Tina made a note of it.

"What are you thinking, he was set up?" Tina asked, excitedly. McCall shrugged with a grin on her face. "I suppose next you're going to say Powell never killed anyone, it was someone else," McCall looked up at Tina with a strange look as if the penny had dropped. "Uh uh, no way, don't you even think it," Tina said, the smile falling from her face. McCall ran for the door.

"Thanks, Tina, if you get anything else I'll be uptown," McCall shouted back. Tina sneakily took out her cell and pressed the dial icon and waited.

"Hi, it's me again." She laughed.

As McCall rode the elevator upwards, she pulled out her cell. She paused before going through the contact numbers. McCall was about to make a call, a call she hoped she would never have to make, to speak to someone she hoped she would never have to talk to again. She found his number under the code "ASSHOLE," she pressed the dial button and waited while it rang. Part of her hoped he wouldn't be there or pick up, but she needed information, and he could get it.

"Agent Bryce, can I help you?" she closed her eyes as the sound of his voice brought back so much anger in her.

"Bryce, its Sam….McCall, we need to talk," There was a silence. She hoped the sound of her voice had made him fall off his chair, but she wasn't that lucky. "The place, fifteen minutes." The line went dead, but that suited her, talking to him made her skin crawl. She put her cell away and breathed out a long-drawn breath. "Alex Bryce, god I hope it's worth it."

FIFTY

The huge ship cut through the giant waves like a child's toy at bath time. Even though its massive tonnage held it firm, the powerful waves heaved it upwards on the back of Poseidon's steeds. The blackened clouds above flashed with power, releasing bolts of white streaks that turned the heavens an eerie purple.

They were approaching the eye of the storm and the wrath of nature, as the ship remained true and steady. The passengers and some of the crew hid themselves away in their cabins as they felt the vessel heave up and down. The ship had been locked down, and anything breakable had been made secure as much as possible. Shops, bars and restaurants were closed until the all-clear was given. Captain Tobias Long stood on the bridge of his ship, watching the heavens give a terrifying display of raw power. "How are we doing number one?" The tall officer walked over to the captain.

"So far, no casualties, the ship is taking it in her stride. Passengers and non-essential crew are in their quarters as you instructed." Long smiled as he took out his cell phone and sent a text.

"Excellent number one. Thank you." The officer looked at the captain strangely, the way he said thank you sounded more like a goodbye.

. . .

STEEL LOOKED AT HIS WATCH, it was quarter to four, and he had to get to that room. He moved down the corridor quickly with the silenced .45 calibre Glock held up ready to take out any of the mercenaries if necessary. He moved the weapon in a sweeping motion as he went, covering the area. Then as he turned the final corner, he saw two large men standing by the door, Steel smiled and holstered the weapon.

"Hey buddy, this is a private matter so scram," yelled the bald one of the two. Steel kept smiling as he approached.

"It's okay fellers I am expected," the man shook his head disapprovingly and stuck his hand out to stop Steel's approach. "Really?" Steel frowned as the man went to take a swing.

Tia had joined them at the chairs, she could have remained standing, but her feet were killing her from wearing the black high-heeled shoes. Blacke had lit up a huge Cuban he had produced from the inside pocket of his black suit and was busy making smoke rings. Soon, the air was thick with the musty smell of the hand-rolled leaves.

"So, when do we start business, Mr Blacke?" Asked a nervous Albert Studebaker, Blacke turned and looked at him and just smiled before inhaling once again from the cigar.

"What if we are disturbed, someone could walk in and ……" Blacke shook his head. The large American's nervousness was making him suspicious.

"Don't worry, as you heard, all passengers and crew are to stay in their quarters, also Mr Vedas has two large gentlemen guarding the door. Trust me, Mr Studebaker, absolutely no one is getting into this room."

The doors burst open and one of the guards flew in, landing next to a white concrete pillar, the other was dragged in by the collar and dumped next to his unconscious partner.

"Mr Black, what in heaven's name are you doing?" Ask Bob. Steel stood before them, the machine pistol held tightly in both hands.

"Everyone against the window, move." Everyone stood up

with a look of complete surprise on their faces and started to move.

"This is your doing; you made all this happen." Tia's eyes were red from the build-up of frustrated tears as she yelled at him. Steel looked down at his watch. It was five minutes to. Steel cocked the weapon and opened fire, spraying bullets indiscriminately at the windows.

The Group dove for cover as the large window exploded outwards sending broken shards out into the wind. Steel released the empty magazine from its housing and let it drop to the ground, taking out a fresh magazine from the ammo pouch on his left leg he clicked it into place and ran over to the window.

"Everyone, move closer to the window," He yelled over the wind that howled past them and into the large room. They all looked up at the speakers as a strange voice squeaked on to the microphone.

"Ladies and Gentlemen, on behalf of the new crew I bid you all a good night and pleasant dreams." The group ran towards the broken windows as a strange green cloud began to seep out of the air ducts, but the blustering wind carried the knockout gas to the back of the room where it dissipated.

"OK, will someone tell me what the hell is going on here?" yelled a red-faced Albert Studebaker, Steel just looked around to see if he could find the storm shield controls.

"What the hell you looking for boy?" Albert yelled over the howling wind,

"The storm shield controls," Steel yelled. Everyone looked blankly at him.

"The what?" Tia shouted. Steel moved closer to them all so they could hear.

"The storm shield was created for all the larger windows to help protect them from adverse weather conditions; it's a bit like the roller blinds that rolled down like a garage door. It will keep the storm out but let fresh air at the same time," Steel explained. The group separated, looking for the controls. As they split off, Steel turned towards the door in time to see two mercenaries come through the door. The men rushed in and were suddenly surprised by the forceful wind that was blowing furiously through the missing window. Steel ducked down behind one of the large leather couches and got ready. The men moved in slowly, trying to figure out what the problem was.

"Control, yes that alarm was set off in the smoking lounge. Yeh, you should see it, the whole damn windows gone." Said the one mercenary into the intercom in his gas mask.

"Where's the shield control? By the bar, OK roger that," said one of the mercs. Steel looked into the large mirror to see the men's position, and then he caught a glimpse of Tia disappearing behind the bar. He had to get to them without making a scene.

Steel moved silently out of cover and across the room, luckily the noise from the wind would mask any noise of footsteps. He moved from cover to cover, ensuring he was not in the view of the mirror. The men fought against the blast of the storm's wind, which minimised their movement. Steel moved up to the man at the rear and held him in a neck lock, cutting off the oxygen long enough to render him unconscious. Slowly he lay him down and moved to the next one. Steel was almost upon him when something crashed at the back of him, causing the mercenary to turn around.

"Would sir like anything from the bar?" Steel joked, as he kicked the man in the chest with a straight leg kick. The mercenary shot backwards and raised up his machine pistol, firing it as it swept upwards. Steel dived out of the way in time and waited for the click of an empty magazine. He dived back around, hoping to catch the man before he could reload. The mercenary threw the weapon at Steel, hoping to distract him. Steel batted away the weapon and came straight for him. The men locked and exchanged punches and kicks before Steel grabbed the man and rolled, throwing him far across the room towards the open window. Steel rolled back over so he was now kneeling and sprung up and ran at the mercenary who had spotted his weapon. Steel ran forward towards the man and then leapt at him using a double-footed kick; the man staggered backwards from the impact but shook it off and started running forwards. The gasmask covered the man's expression, but Steel imagined that he was snarling underneath the rubber. The mercenary reached behind him and drew out a large combat knife; Steel saw the light reflect off the blade as he moved it slowly ready for the next attack. Steel grabbed one of the magazines from his leg pouch and held it tightly; the two men circled the room, each waiting for the other to make the first move. The mercenary sprang first, swishing with the blade, trying to get a piece of this new foe but each time Steel caught him with a jab to the upper thigh or the arm. The man swung again but was met with two swift stabbings to the eyelets on his mask then a kick to the middle. The man stumbled backwards; dazed he ripped off the mask and growled at Steel.

Steel never saw Blacke pick up the gun from the unconscious mercenary, but he did feel the first round passing by his ear as it took flight into the mercenary's leg and middle. Steel dived for cover as Blacke just kept on firing until Steel got up and snatched it from him. Steel rushed over to the dying mercenary.

"Who do you work for and why you are here?" The man mouthed words, but no sound came out until his eyes stared into nothing and his lips stopped moving. Steel turned around towards Blacke and made for him.

"Its okay everyone you can thank me later," Blacke said smugly. Steel grabbed him by the throat and threw him to the ground.

"What the hell do you think you were doing?" Blacke looked shocked then it changed to anger.

"I just saved your life, and this is the thanks I get." Steel grabbed him by the lapels and lifted him up, so they were face to face.

"I wouldn't have been in that situation if you hadn't have knocked something over, now would I? I needed them alive so I can find out what the hell is going on and, as for saving my life, I doubt it." Steel threw Blacke to the side and headed for the second mercenary, but he was also dead. A trail of bullet holes reached up from where the mercenary had started to shoot, and ended in the other's side and head. Steel kicked one of the coffee tables, sending it up in the air.

"Just great Blacke, thanks very much." Yelled Steel as he headed for the bar and the control panel. Finding the switch, he activated the shutters and watched them come down and lock off at the bottom, the room was silent for the first time in what seemed like ages.

Steel moved over to the first mercenary and started to take his ammo and anything else that may be useful. Steel found his shoulder radio, but it was shot to pieces.

"So what's with the private party?" Steel asked, as he checked the second man.

"I don't know what you mean?" Blacke announced, trying to look innocent and failing badly at it.

"You're all here for a private meeting, CIA, FSB and the rich couple, so my instincts tell me you guys are having a sale, so what's on offer and I bet I can offer the best deal." Vedas moved to the bar and put a bottle of vodka on the counter and started to pour himself a shot into a small glass, while the others sat on the chairs, drained from the experience.

"So, Mr Blacke, how are you involved in all of this?" Blacke shook his head and waved his hand.

"Not me sorry, don't know anything about this." He lied, as he sat down and crossing one leg over the other.

"That's strange because you're obviously selling something, and those mercenaries are looking for you because you stole something from them. So, want to try again, or shall I just throw you outside where these guys can find you, and they can just go on their way?" Tia shot Steel a puzzled look.

"What makes you think they will just leave?" Steel smiled slightly

"They used knockout gas, that means they want everyone alive; they just want to get their stuff, and get out without a trace, killing everyone is not on their agenda. These people prefer anonymity." Steel looked at Blacke with angry eyes.

"So, Mr Blacke, what did you steal from these people that

want their belongings back and your head on a plate?" Blacke said nothing, he just sat looking at the shattered window.

"Does any of you know what you're buying into?" They all shook their heads.

"We heard that he had found some sunken cargo from a ship that went down in New York around a month ago. The ship was supposedly smuggling weapons, so naturally, when we heard the Russians were interested, we jumped on board." Jane shrugged as she let it out, Vedas looked up shocked "That is the same for us also." He looked at Blacke who was now looking sheepish; Steel turned and laughed.

"So, no one has any idea what is in the cargo. He's played you all," Steel said, the smile fell away from his face and he looked at Blacke. "You have no idea what's in the cargo, do you?" Blacke looked around and then to the floor before shaking his head.

"No, there is a digital lock on the cases, and I didn't have the key." Steel sat down on the arm of one of the leather armchairs.

"So how were you going to show the merchandise if you couldn't get into it." Then he thought back to the captain.

"The boy gave something to the captain, something that got him killed. You found someone with a key didn't you, and then you got double-crossed, wait, who's idea was it to do business on the ship?" Blacke thought for a moment then looked up at Steel with wide eyes.

"It was the contact, the one with the key, damn they took me for one million on this." However, Steel didn't care; he just wanted to get them off the ship and to safety.

"So Mr Black…god, this is getting confusing," Albert stuttered. "Look Tony what's our next move here?" Steel smiled at the large American.

"Well, I am going to find out how I can get you all off this tub and figure out exactly what it is that you're bidding for and what they want," Steel said, rechecking his weapons. Albert smiled at the thought of getting off the ship.

"So when you're ready, we can go," Albert said. Steel smiled and gently pushed him down into his seat.

"I am going alone, I can move quicker and quieter," Steel looked around at Blacke, who just looked away. "All of you stay here and barricade the door, don't let anyone in." Jane Stewart looked confused.

"How are you going to get in to tell us it's safe?" Tia sat back in her chair and took a sip from the champagne glass.

"I wouldn't worry; something tells me he has had a lot of practice getting into places," Tia said. Steel stopped at the door.

"The cargo, where is it?" He never turned, he just waited with one hand on the handle.

"The cargo hold, can't miss it, the door has a 'do not enter' sign on it. ," Blacke replied. Steel nodded and left. The door made a sucking sound as it broke the rubber seals. They just stared at the door, wondering if he was coming back for them.

FIFTY-ONE

The sunshine was warm, wisps of cloud filled the blue sky, and a gentle breeze softened the warm air. Central Park was full of those who just wanted to get away from it all and lounge in the sun on the soft grass; joggers passed by, in their efforts to stay in shape for that up-and-coming holiday. The only sound was the noise of the park, dogs barking, children playing, the odd new musician trying to sell his latest album. The park was a place of peace and tranquillity, a place where even the noise of traffic seemed to be phased out by the park's serenity.

McCall sat on the stone bench opposite the Victorian steps of the Bethesda Terrace; she looked upon the almost aged sandstone steps and the underpass. McCall sighed fondly at the memory of her first encounter with Steel, how she had chased him, but lost him in the crowds. That too was a warm day, but as she looked up at the approaching figure the smile faded, this was one memory she didn't need. "Thinking of us?" She looked up with dead eyes and glared at the CIA agent. The agent was tall with broad shoulders and brown hair that made him look too pretty. He sat down next to her and took off his sunglasses to clean them.

"Thanks for coming," She said, her focus on the point where she had found Steel.

"Thanks for asking me here, how long has it been now… five, six years?" She didn't answer, she wanted something from him and causing a mess wouldn't get her anywhere. She pulled out a surveillance picture of Jones; she didn't want him to know he was dead, not yet. She had a card to play, and she didn't want to show her hand.

"This guy one of yours?" Bryce took the picture and looked at it for a second.

"Can't say but I could do some digging for you if you like. Maybe give you the answer over dinner tonight?" McCall never faced him. She knew if she looked him in the eyes, she would probably shoot his smug ass.

"Call me at the precinct, and you know the number." McCall got up and walked towards the steps. She wanted to put some distance between them. Bryce leant back on the sandstone bench and took in the rays with a broad grin on his face.

"Well, well, well. Samantha McCall."

SHE WALKED BACK to the precinct from the parking lot and took the elevator up to Homicide. McCall was still seething from the encounter with Bryce, she knew he would try something tonight, but she wouldn't give him a chance. As the elevator doors opened, she saw the Lieutenant from IA in the coffee break room, and she smiled to herself. True, this was the guy trying to get something on Tony, but she found him cute. She grabbed her cup from her desk and walked in.

"Morning," her voice was soft and playful.

"You're late, Detective," he said the words, but his tone didn't mean it, she saw the corner of his mouth curl upward into a secret smile.

"Sorry sir, I had a last-minute thing with a contact." He nodded and smiled,

"So, shall we?" He stretched out his right arm, edging her to lead the way to the interrogation room across the way, he could tell something was bothering her but just put it down to the stress of the past couple of days. As McCall entered the interrogation room, she felt the anxiety that all the people she had ever brought into that room had felt; that cold shiver as you instantly felt guilty as soon as you passed that threshold. The walls seemed closer, and the back wall two-way mirror seemed more menacing from where she was sitting. The mirror was a brilliant scare tactic, a person could lie to another person easily, but to do it when you were looking yourself in the eye was a bit more difficult for some. He took out a pen from the leather-backed folder and opened it up to reveal a lined note pad of A4 size and arranged his paperwork, which involved photographs of the scene. McCall saw one that was from where Tony had said he was standing, and she tilted her head slightly to try and steal a look while he wasn't looking or so he wanted her to believe, she smiled and just took a photograph. He smiled broadly.

"I guess you have been doing this too long, Detective, sorry." She smiled back and then looked down at the photograph, her brow crinkled as she studied the shot.

"What's wrong?" He asked, leaning back in his chair. McCall looked up and threw down the photograph on to the pile of paperwork.

"Nothing, just curious. Never saw it from that angle, mine was a little too close for my liking." The lieutenant broke a smile of understanding, then leant forward.

"OK Detective, this is just a standard paperwork exercise we have to carry out after a shooting of this kind." He switched on the two stick microphones that sat in the centre of the table, then adjusted his jacket, making McCall smile.

"I thought this was radio, not television or are you just making yourself look nice for me?" He looked up at her and smiled, somewhat embarrassed.

"Sorry, right then, Detective, in your own words what happened," The Lieutenant asked. She smiled back.

"In my own words, we entered the hotel hoping to surprise a suspected killer and instead we ended up wearing his ceiling and Tooms nearly had heart surgery, then, as in the movies just before he is about to tell me something, someone uses him as target practice. How's that for in my own words?" McCall took a sip from her coffee and leant back on the back legs of the chair. He looked down and flicked through her statement.

"So you wake up and find your partner cuffed to the radiator, then what?" McCall put the chair back on all four legs and put the cup down.

"He has taken my main piece off of me but left me my backup which I thought was odd. Anyway I have the guy in my sights, but I don't have a shot, I shoot and Tooms has got a heart problem." The lieutenant put his pen down and reached for his coffee.

"Go on." McCall looked down at the photograph, her eyes fixed but not on the picture but on the moment.

"We start talking, don't really remember about what, my head is still a bit fuzzy, I just get the impression something is wrong. Before I can learn anything, the shots come." The man leant forwards.

"And that's when you saw Detective Marinelle shoot the suspect and possibly save Detective Tooms's life - is that how you see it?" McCall looked at him and smiled smugly,

"Yes and no!" the lieutenant looked up shocked.

"What do you mean 'Yes and no'?" McCall leant forward, her elbows resting on the table

"Yes, the shooter did save our lives, but NO, I didn't see who the shooter was, I was over here when it happened." McCall pointed to a point on the forensics map of the room.

"You were out of the line of sight, so you only saw Detective Marinelle when you ran forward to see who was doing the shooting." McCall sat back and slightly, enjoying the look of disappointment on his face.

"Sorry to burst the bubble," McCall said as she stood up. He reached forward and grasped her arm.

"Detective, we aren't done yet," He growled. As McCall retook her seat, she felt something was eating at him.

"What's wrong?" She asked, leaning forward and covering her microphone.

"OK, five-minute break," He winked before closing down the evidence tape and then heading for the break room. As they entered, he closed all the doors to the room then sat away from the window.

"You found something didn't you? You don't think he did it, but you have got to go through the motions," McCall said quietly, she looked to the side as though going through things in her mind. He nodded slightly.

"I saw what you saw in that photograph, Marinelle was too far away. I checked on his scores, he is good but a marksman with a pistol he isn't, unless he has been bluffing it all these years. Also, where he was when you found him, there was no way he could have shot then run back to that position in time. We found the shell casings near the door, he was at least twenty feet beyond that," the lieutenant explained. McCall smiled.

"You think he was set up?" She asked. He nodded as he pretended to drink from the empty cup.

"You saw the report from ballistics?" He asked. McCall looked around before answering.

"Yes, and I am still confused. How the hell did they swap weapons? Was the chain of custody broken? If not, that means we are looking at someone on the inside," McCall whispered. The lieutenant nodded with a twinkle in his eye, McCall felt like screaming out.

"You're not after Tony officially are you, you're after the mole?" He looked slightly shocked that she knew about it, but then he also would have been more disappointed if she hadn't have known anything.

"The problem we have is that the gun was used in another shooting," he explained. McCall nodded.

"Yes, it was used to kill Bill Foster in his office, we know," McCall said, as she sat back in her chair. He shook his head.

"No, this was before that, in Britain around ten years ago. It was used to kill some Lady Steel and her daughter in law." McCall just sat there opened mouthed.

FIFTY-TWO

Steel moved through the lonely corridors quickly and quietly. The plan was not to encounter or engage the mercenaries. He usually would be, after taking them down, but he had no idea of their number of countermeasures, he didn't want to find that they had the ship rigged to blow, with nearly seven thousand unconscious passengers and staff aboard. He needed to get down to the cargo hold and find out what he was dealing with. Also, he knew that the gas was probably being pumped through, using the ships air conditioning unit which was near the engine room. Steel was wearing one of the masks he had taken from the mercenaries in the elevator; this had a full-face screen, which gave him perfect full view rather than lenses, which had many blind spots. Steel had found that most of his routes included going down long corridors, so he decided to take the long way, elevators were also out as they would draw attention. He was on the eighteenth deck, he needed to be on the second. As he approached the twelfth deck, he looked at the wall map and this showed the back stairs, which would be easier to move around than the large public staircases. He would have to navigate his way through the *London Lounge*. This was more of an upper-class bar that could seat five hundred people. It was filled with shelves full of books, leather armchairs, the furnishings were oak, and the carpet was thick and expensive. The table lamps and the odd standard lamp that filled the gap between bookshelves dimly lit the room. Steel moved in low, using the large furnishings as cover as he went. As he neared the middle of the room, he stopped and listened. He heard voices that were muffled by their masks, and he knew it had to be mercenaries. He had a plan, and the exit was in sight. As he passed by one of the couches, he saw four men standing over a pretty cocktail waitress.

"Come on, boys, get her on that couch, and let's have some fun." Yelled one of the mercenaries, laughing as he struggled with his belt. Two of the men picked her up and threw her onto the sofa, so her top half lay over the back. The one mercenary finally unbuckled and dropped.

"Ok boys I am going in." He turned at the sound of someone falling down, only to find the two onlookers grasping their throats, maskless.

"What the!" He yelled through the restricted respirator. He looked up to see a man in a gas mask holding something, he went to scream not to shoot, but the taser's remote shockers found their mark in the exposed flesh of his crotch. The man fell, twitched, and convulsed in agony as the many thousands of vaults buzzed through him. Steel caught a glimpse from the respirator on the ground; a reflection on one of the lenses alerted him to the danger behind. He rolled just in time as the fourth man swung two steel batons at Steel's head, which missed but contacted a table lamp, dashing it into pieces. Steel landed in a crouched position, ready for the man's next move; the mercenary had two flick extension batons and he knew how to use them. The man raced forwards, twirling the batons like two propellers as he went, hoping to gain the most coverage. As he neared Steel, he changed tactic and swept with both rods at the same time, causing Steel to fall backwards, the thick pile catching him as he fell. Then the mercenary span round and, with both rods together, smashed down on to the carpet below where Steel's head had just lain. Steel rolled to the side, then came back pushing the rods out of the mercenary's hands. With one swift movement, Steel thrust a straight palm upwards, so the man's throat met with his open grip. The mercenary stumbled backwards, holding his throat, and Steel grabbed the batons and stood up. Shaking off the attack, the man stood ready and drew out a long machete-type blade from a sheath behind him. Steel held the batons tightly, and he stood ready in a half-crouched position. The mercenary rushed forwards, screaming into his mask, slashing with the blade, but Steel just couched as the blade came overhead and he swept the man's legs with one stick, the other smashing into his throat. There was a brief gurgling sound, then silence. Steel took off the backpack and stripped the men of their ammo and weapons. True, he couldn't use them all, but he could deny the enemy a resupply. However, his main thought was that he didn't need some poor kid finding one and taking out his family because he thought it was a toy. Steel made for the back stairs when he noticed the touch-screen information panel on the wall. He typed in *Security Room*, and a 3D image came up, showing the location of the room. Steel needed that room, the mercenaries could track movement throughout the ship using the security cameras, so he had to make them blind after he had located all of the hostiles. The room was at the middle of the floor he was on, but the simplest way was through a kid's playground, *"The Adventure House."*

The playground consisted of three rooms that had a jungle scene. Each room had plastic palm trees and bushes and a rope bridge system that zigzagged its way across the twenty-foot square rooms. The wood and rope walkway expanded over a vast pit filled with blue coloured foam balls the size of tennis balls that gave a water effect. The lights were low and dry ice crept across the fake water below. The noises of the jungle echoed through loudspeakers and things flew out under control of the computer-controlled birds and bats.

The six men of Delta Squad were placed at their locations and given their orders. To hold and contain the area. The men were good, some of them ex Delta or some other special forces. They were there for the promise of a good payday and easy money. The men had been broken down into three teams,

Delta-One, who was concentrating on the first room down to Delta-Three, who had the last room and exit. The men of Delta-One had never met before the job and were from different parts of the world. One of them stood on the bridge, watching the entrance near his new colleague, while the other stood at the door, watching his old buddies play racquetball, using the coloured balls and a flick out baton.

"So, sweet deal we got her hu?" The other man just shrugged.

"No habla ingles" The British mercenary just flicked his hand and strolled over to near the entrance.

"Yeah whatever, you ignorant fuck," he left the man laughing at his friends in the next room as they failed to hit a single ball. As the South American mercenary watched his friends, he never noticed the figure loom out of the plastic ball filled pool and grabbed the other man, dragging him over the side of the handrails, and into the three feet depths of the pool. The South American laughed and clapped as his friends shouted muffled curses at him jokingly, the one facing the door who was the pitcher reached down to get some more balls from the pool. The bridge was only an arm's length from the top of the surface, making it easy pickings for his overlong arms. He stood up and got ready for the first pitch, looking over to the doorway he saw their colleague had gone but thought nothing of it. He stood ready in a pitching position, his arms locked in, as he mockingly got ready to throw the first ball.

"Are you ready hombre, I will pitch you out of the park." They both laughed. The batsman nodded over to the doorway of the next room to where team three stood.

"What do you think those guys are doing?" The batsman shrugged.

"Not having as much fun as us, I guess." One of the men from team three appeared at the door; a large man from Austria held his H&K machine pistol tightly with both hands and watched for a moment. His towering form just stood there, not moving, as though he had just become stone.

"Hey, hombre, you want a game?" Joked the pitcher, the

man just turned and left, leaving the men laughing. As he left the room, a fake thunderstorm was erupting inside. Flashes of light mimicked the lightning – or so he thought.

The lightning flashed in all of the rooms as the fake storm arrived. The lights flickered the regular lights shut off, giving the illusion of the jungle storm. The large man turned to look at his colleague who was kneeling on the bridge, his weapon ready as they both sensed something was wrong; someone had played with the settings to the room. The Austrian held the weapon up into his shoulder and crept around the corner keeping low, the flashlight attached on the gun let out a beam of light like a searchlight of a ship or lighthouse. The men were gone; nervously, his gaze locked onto the door awaiting for someone to try getting passed him. He backed away towards his friend on the bridge until he reached him.

"Die Männer sind nicht mehr da." he froze for a second.

"Did you hear me? They are gone, the other men are gone." He turned to see a tall man with guns all over him and a full-face mask instead of the two-eye piece that they all wore. The Austrian went to raise his weapon but felt the sting of the taser as the two-conductor pins imbedded into is bare arms. The man fell and convulsed as the volts passed through his body. Steel had decided to use two taser? guns on him, he didn't need the big man to shrug it off as he didn't have time, time that was running out.

FIFTY-THREE

Steel made his way out of the funhouse, brushing off bits of blue foam from his clothing and gear. He had collected some more equipment from the men and had placed it into the bag. Looking around, he smiled as he found another information board. Moving quickly, he stood in front of the panel and pressed the information button. The screen changed, and a set of options came up, of which one was *LOCATIONS*. Typing into the search menu, he asked for the location of the security room. The screen changed into a 3D map that showed present location with a red dot, and the location required with a blue one. He studied the map and saw it wasn't that far away; it was just down the corridor and was on a cross junction to two halls. He readied the UMP machine pistol, he had to be ready for anything. Steel looked back on the playroom he had just left and bit his bottom lip as an uncomfortable feeling came over him. So far, it had been easy, probably too easy.

The corridors seemed clear as he moved down slowly; he would stop and listen for voices or footsteps. As he neared the junction, he stopped and knelt with his back to the wall. He could hear voices just around the corner, one of which he thought he recognised from somewhere. Not wanting to risk sticking his head out, he neared the corner and took in the conversation.

"Are you sure it's now on board?" Asked the familiar voice.

"Yes sir, the locator has it in cargo hold number seven on deck two." There was a pause, and Steel thought he heard the sound of a shoe, tapping.

"And what of our Mr Blacke, any sign of him yet?" Steel suddenly became worried about the safety of the others, Blacke would get them all killed for something he had done.

"Not yet sir, but there are a lot of cameras. Unfortunately, none are in the rooms." The younger voice spoke confidently.

"Very good, stay on it. At the first sign of him, call it in. Oh, and Hawkins, would you be as kind as to ask the captain to bring the box to me, please. Tell him I will meet him in – cargo hold number seven was it, Charles?" Steel heard nothing from the other man, so he presumed that he had just nodded in reply. Steel listened as another voice confirmed the man's request and was followed by heavy footsteps. Steel's grip tightened around the forward grip and the pistol grip of the machine pistol as he heard footsteps approaching from the way he had come. Next to him was the cleaner's closet, the door had been left ajar, probably when they got the warning to go to their rooms. Quickly, he dived in and secured the door. The vents at the bottom of the door gave some light but more importantly, noise carried quite nicely through it. A single set of footsteps marched past on the way to the security room. Steel waited anxiously for a moment before venturing out. Using a small mirror, he had found in the closet, he angled it around the corner to get a view of the split corridors and the door for the security room. Under the mask, Steel frowned at the situation, the hallways were empty. Then he had a thought, why have guards remained conscious while everyone was unconscious? Steel drew back the mirror quickly as he heard voices approach the security room; he had to get in there fast and locate the other mercenaries. The main thing for Steel was to get the others to safety, especially Tia.

* * *

The clock in the Homicide Department showed it was two in the afternoon as McCall stepped off the elevator. After the interview, she had gone to the range to take her frustration out on a couple of targets, plus she never really had time to check out the custom Glock 17 that Steel had given to her on her return to duty. After obliterating the centre of the targets, she smiled, impressed how accurate the thing was, even without having to move the green dot sights.

As she entered the bullpen, the smell of freshly-brewed coffee carried her to the restroom, as she ventured there, she couldn't help but notice the empty desks that usually were full with detectives, her gaze fell upon Tony's desk and she wondered what fate would befall him. As she entered the room, her cell vibrated to alert her to a text. Drawing out the phone, she noticed a text from Doctor Dave asking.

"Is tonight good for a dinner date?" She smiled and replied.

"Can't wait, say around nine." The cell buzzed and a smiley appeared on the display. Switching it off, she placed it back into her pocket, and she poured herself a fresh cup and savoured the scent of the unique Jamaican blend. She looked up over the rim of the cup to see Captain Brant ushering her into his office with a delicate head tilt. McCall walked out and placed the coffee on to her desk on the way to the captain's office.

"Tony is on suspension until the proceedings are done with; they have enough to warrant jail time." McCall's face fell at the news.

"Is there anything I should know, detective?" Asked Brant, as he noticed her secretive look.

"No sir, everything is fine." He nodded disbelievingly and went over to see how the tech was doing. McCall looked at the clock and realised that Steel would be coming into harbour in around twenty hours. The sound of the elevator made McCall look over to see the ragged-looking Tooms heading for the break room. She followed him in and shut the door,

"How you doing?" McCall asked. He smiled.

"I'll be ok, heard about Tony. Man, that sucks," Tooms groaned, McCall nodded and moved in closer.

"I think that Tony was set up, don't ask me how but he was, and our friend Jones. I think he was watching those people, not trying to kill them," McCall explained. Tooms gave her a confused look.

"Where you gettin' this from?" He asked, while McCall poured him a coffee.

"I went back to the hotel and found a hidden room in the attic, that's when I found this," McCall said, handing Tooms the file she had found. He flicked through it in silence, his hands shaking as he turned the pages.

"Who else knows about this?" He asked under his breath.

"Nobody, at the moment you're the only one I trust," McCall admitted. He nodded and passed it back to her,

"You need to keep that safe, nobody can know of it – not yet," Tooms whispered. She thought for a moment and smiled.

"Don't worry, I know of the perfect place," McCall laughed.

FIFTY-FOUR

The security room on the Neptune was around eight feet square with twenty thirty-inch monitors covering its dimly lit walls. Each screen was broken down into twenty smaller screens that displayed a specific area that the security cameras patrolled. Inside, a mercenary sat at the consoles, scanning with his eyes the multitude of screens, and exhaling deeply with boredom. As he rocked backwards and forwards in the padded office chair, he noticed the small, three-drawed desk cabinet and smiled. Leaning over, he began his search, hopeful to find the obvious bounty.

"Oh yeh, that's more like it." He yelled, pulling out the men's magazine from the bottom draw. There was a click of the door opening as he viewed the middle full-length picture of that month's hottie,

"Hey man you're early but what the hell." He spun round in the chair and patted the masked man on the shoulder and headed for the door.

"You know we can take those damn things off now but hey your choice, man." He laughed as he left.

The figure sat at the controls and searched all the decks quickly, suddenly stopping as it caught a glimpse of the smoking-room. There,t Tia and the others were sitting. Using the joystick, the figure zoomed in on Blacke. The figure panned out on to Tia and, using a cell it took from the combat vest, sent a text to Tia. The figure got up, headed for the door and turned, just in time to see Tia look at the text message.

Tia looked out across the fantastic sight of the bright sunshine and calm waters, a rainbow so deep in colour it could have been solid, the calm after the storm. They had raised the storm shutters to get rid of the bodies as Steel had suggested. If someone were to find them, it was better they weren't found with dead mercenaries littering the floor. She closed her eyes as the cool breeze caressed her skin.

"So, what now?" Albert Studebaker yelled, as he paced up and down the room.

"He told us to stay here where we would be safe, so we stay," Jane spoke calmly, slightly irritated about what she had just said in Steel's defence. Tia walked back to the chairs and sat down with the others. As she reached for the glass of water she had been drinking, she heard her cell buzz in her small purse. She took it out and read the message. Shocked, she stood up quickly.

"We have to go now." She showed the message to Jane who had rushed forwards:

TIA GET OUT NOW, GO TO CARGO HOLD. THEY ARE COMING.

STEEL STOOD at the door of the security room, his heavy breathing fogged up the sides of his full-faced mask for a brief second before clearing. The room was dark, only the sparks from the broken monitors and computers lit the room. Someone had been in and destroyed everything. Steel used the tactical lamp on his machine pistol to search the room but found no bodies. Someone had done this, but it wasn't the mercenaries, it was someone else. Why was another mystery he didn't need. Suddenly a broken message came over the headset of the radio on his shoulder.

"Command be advised, target is in the smoking-room on deck eighteen, is not alone. Other guests are armed and dangerous." Steel felt a shiver of panic come over him. He had to get to them before the mercenaries did or it would be a massacre. The mercenaries were expecting a gun battle so they wouldn't hesitate to use grenades before entering.

Steel moved quickly down the corridors towards the elevators, this time he could move freely. The cameras were out, and they were blind; however, even though he was dressed like them, he still had to be careful. All it would take is someone not to recognise him as not one of theirs or to ask questions, and the game would be up.

STEEL MOVED QUICKLY through the maze of corridors, he had avoided using the elevators, as he knew that someone would be watching them, a single sole using them could be seen as suspicious and he didn't need the attention. Steel felt lucky he had only ventured from deck twelve and not the cargo hold. As fit as he was, it was still a hell of a journey.

As he entered the corridor of the smoking-room, he expected the worst. He froze as he noticed that the door was slightly ajar. Holding the weapon tightly, he used the suppressor to nudge the door open. Inside, the cool breeze played with the pages of the magazines that lay on the coffee tables. He moved in slowly, the weapon still high up into his shoulder, ready to fire. He breathed out slowly as he saw that the room was empty. Looking round, he had mixed feelings of anger and relief. Why had they left and where the hell had they gone to? Steel moved back to the door, and as he stepped out of the door, he saw the numbers flashing on the display panel of the elevator, both of which were coming up. He closed the doors quickly, and dived into an alcove just passed the elevators.

The doors of the elevators opened almost in sequence, the two teams moved forward quickly, and quietly, their weapons held up ready. No words were spoken, only flicks of the hand or pointing of fingers were used to issue the commands; these were highly trained and worked as one. Two men stepped forward, each carrying long armour-plated shields, behind them were two men with weapons ready. The team leaders knelt at either side of the doors and, using their fingers, counted down from three. As the team leaders made a fist to signal zero, the breaching parties entered, firing as they went; cushions and glassware exploded as the amour-piercing rounds ripped through the smoking room.

"Room clear." The six men yelled in unison. Moving in, the rest of the team members rushed in to ensure it was clear. The two team leaders moved in slowly and waited for the report.

"All clear Sir." One of the mercenaries yelled over, the leader of Team-One raised a thumb then pressed his throat mike.

"Command this is Team-One, the bird has flown, I repeat the nest is empty, and the bird has flown. Over." There was a brief pause before the radio crackled with life.

"Roger that, all teams report back to command, we have a situation. Team-Three has gone dark, and the crow's nest has gone blind. Out." Steel had sneaked in behind them as they had breached and he hid himself among the other mercenaries. He was within earshot of the two leaders, but far enough not to be recognised by them.

"Wow, the boss is going to be pissed, Blacke is in the wind." The leader of Team-Two said, as he shouldered his weapon.

"You got that right. After that bastard ripped off the bosses, I am surprised he had the balls to show his face anywhere." The leaders called their men back and moved back to the elevators. Steel fell back and hid behind the door at the last minute. As much as he would love to follow them to see where command was, he had other things on his mind. Steel saw the rear guard disappear onto the elevator. He took off the respirator and breathed out heavily, then took in deep, refreshing gulps of the clean sea air.

"The cargo, what the hell is so damned important about this cargo?" Steel thought, as he moved to the bar, poured himself a large whisky, and then downed it in one. He knew where he had to go next. Even though he wanted to search for Tia, he didn't have time to play hide-go-seek. Everything revolved around the cargo, and he wanted to know what the hell it was. If he could use it to his advantage, great - if not, he could at least see to it that no one got to it. He put down the glass and shook off the tension from his muscles, before heading on out. He got to the elevators and noticed they had both stopped on deck three. He smiled as he forced the doors open, the stale air, filled with the tang of hot metal and burnt oil and grease, filled his nostrils. Taking off the bag, he opened it up and started to look through the equipment. Smiling, he took out a strange device that had two wheels fixed on top of each other and a handle on the side. This had one purpose. Steel smiled broadly, as he put the rucksack back on and took a deep breath.

"OK, time for some fun." He said under his breath, as he leapt for the elevator cable.

FIFTY-FIVE

McCall was downstairs in the precinct's gymnasium, kicking the hell out of a punching bag. She needed to let off some steam before going home. It had been a long case for everyone, and the signs were beginning to show. Maybe that's what the mystery person behind this wanted, to split the team, string everyone out. They had already succeeded in making everyone thin on the ground with the break-in at the morgue and the series of murders all over New York. Tony had been sent home on Administrative leave, but was told to report in every hour by I.A. They wanted him out of sight, out of mind, while they investigated.

Her fists smashed into the bag in quick succession, her mind a torrent of questions. Who had shot Jones and how was he involved? What connected the victims, and why did they have to die? She spun around and kicked high, making the bag move to the side with the force of the impact.

"Glad it's not me," came a voice from behind her. She looked over and scowled at the man who was standing on the gym steps.

"Bryce, what the hell are you doing here?" McCall said, her voice full of anger and tension.

. . .

McCall showered and changed quickly before meeting Agent Alex Bryce upstairs. She found him in the restroom, helping himself to a cup of coffee and she paused before entering. Her eyes looked him up and down; he hadn't changed a bit in over five years. He was average height and build with mousy-coloured hair that was kept in place by too many hair products. His expensive-looking grey suit glistened with newness. She shook her head as she looked at him and all she could think about was how much she wished he had been the punch bag.

"What's up Bryce, I thought you were going to call with the information?" McCall said, as she walked in. He looked her up and down with a grin of approval.

"What? And miss how good you look? Not on your life. You look good, Sam," Bryce said. She looked at him with distaste.

"So what you got?" McCall cut straight in as she noticed the large brown envelope in his hand. He lifted it and shook his head.

"Uh uh, sorry, this is for the captain," Bryce said with a childish grin. McCall rolled her eyes and led the way to Brant's office. McCall stopped and turned around suddenly, raising a hand to stop him.

"You wait here," McCall ordered. He faked a sorrowful look and sat on the edge of the desk in front of Brant's office. She knocked and entered.

"Sir, I had to call someone for some information on Jones," McCall admitted. Brant's face fell as he looked outside the office to see Bryce's smug face smiling at him.

"Why in the name of God did you call that asshole?" He looked up, saw in her eyes the pain, and knew if she didn't have too, she wouldn't have.

"Has he got anything?" McCall nodded to the question.

"He says he will only give it to you," Brant growled at the thought of being anywhere near the man.

"OK, Sam, give me a sec, gotta make a call," Brant said, picking up the phone. McCall stepped out and took Bryce back to the break room.

After ten minutes, McCall noticed Brant appearing outside

his office. He beckoned her over while wearing an angry look on his face. McCall hurried over, concerned at what the call had been about. Bryce followed, still wearing his smug grin.

"Ok, let's see what the asshole has got," Brant said, his words were sour.

"Captain Brant, it's so great to see you again" Bryce smiled.

"Pity, I can't say the same, ok, what you got?" Bryce stuck out his bottom lip and tried to look distraught. Brant snatched the envelope that Bryce handed to him. Brant read the document then looked up at the smug-looking agent.

"You have got to be kidding me," Brant said, shocked at the document,

"What is it?" McCall asked, taking the document from him. She read it, then looked up with a shocked expression on her tired-looking face.

"This is a warrant; you want all documentation on the case?" He smiled and raised his hands to the side.

"Sorry, but it's a federal case now." Brant smiled as he ripped up the warrant. Bryce looked shocked at the demonstration.

"You can't do that, that's a federal warrant," Bryce said, shocked at the display. Brant nodded as he threw the bits of paper at him.

"Yes, a warrant that your superiors knew nothing about. In fact, they were shocked to learn that you hadn't mentioned that Agent Jones was in our morgue," Bryce went to leave but found two huge uniformed officers behind him.

"Agent Bryce, we have some questions regarding agent Jones before some nasty looking men come to take you back to Langley, for a chat." Bryce's face fell into a look of despair. He knew he had nowhere to run. They had gone into one of the interrogation rooms for some privacy, McCall knew she had him and breaking him would make her feel a little better. He sat on the chair opposite the mirror and looked around quickly.

"So, agent Bryce, how long had you and agent Jones been tailing these people?" McCall slapped the pictures from Jones's attic onto the table. These were pictures of their everyday lives, shopping, working and socialising. He looked down at them and shrugged,

"What makes you think we worked together on anything?" He smiled briefly, his eyes constantly on the room, as if he didn't want to make eye contact with her or the mirror. McCall leaned forwards and opened another file containing security camera stills of him with Jones.

"Well if you weren't working together then why have I got camera footage of you and Jones meeting with several of the victims before they died?" Bryce leant back in his chair, despite his *don't give a crap* attitude. Small beads of sweat had started to form on his forehead.

"What was the mission? Why kill them?" McCall asked. Bryce looked up, shocked at the insinuation.

"Kill them, we didn't kill them we were…. he was supposed to look after them, that's the truth," Bryce yelled. McCall smiled as she watched him squirm.

"Look, we got word that something big was going to happen, someone was recruiting people to put some sort of operation together. Someone was blackmailing these people into doing the things they had done," Bryce admitted. McCall sat back in the chair and listened.

"Your electrician, he had to install some kind of electrical network and security stuff into something, we didn't know what, just it was a big job. The recruiter had to get some permits for people to work on a liner or passenger jet," Bryce said, as he leaned onto the table. "The crane guy was also a welder; his job was to install some tanks or something." McCall watched him as he sat there; she noticed the beads of sweat start to accumulate on his forehead as he kept looking at the elevator.

"Go on, what was the job that was so secretive?" McCall asked. Bryce shrugged.

"I don't know, look our agent in London said she had gotten a tip, some major terror organisation was planning something big, then about three weeks ago she disappeared . We had everyone looking for her, but now she was gone. At first, we thought she had been taken out by the group she was tailing,"

Bryce said, before taking a sip from the bottle of water that McCall had brought in for him. He looked up at McCall and, looking into her eyes, he saw thunder. "We thought we had lost her for good until she turned up at your city morgue as a Jane Doe," McCall sat back, gobsmacked.

"She was one of yours, but why the dress up?" McCall asked, her words bitter. Bryce shook his head.

"She only did that if she had to be someone; you see Sam, agent Carrol was a chameleon. Her job was to take the place of other people and blend, whether for information or wet work," Bryce admitted. McCall drank from her bottle as she sat back into her chair.

"Did any names come up, anything that might tie everything together?" Bryce took out his cell and searched through his messages until the right one came up.

"Callan Industries, she found some…shall we say discrepancies with the company," Bryce smiled. McCall felt the colour drain from her cheeks, she knew that name, but she couldn't place from where. She stood up and quickly excused herself as she ran to her desk. Frantically she searched her desktop and the draws.

"What's up McCall, you lose something?" Asked Detective Rodriguez, who was sitting at the desk in front of hers.

"Yes, a post-it or bit of paper, it had a name on it," McCall said frantically. Pablo Rodriguez checked his desk and found a dirty looking yellow post-it, stuck with the pile of others.

"Guess the janitor thought it was mine and put it on my desk, here." McCall reached over and took it while giving him a grateful smile.

"Oh, thank God, thanks, Pablo." McCall looked at the note then up at Pablo. The man was average height and build, but he had a presence about him that mostly read. *Don't mess with me.* Her eyes were stern.

"Pablo, can you check this out for me please?" His smile was warming.

"No problem Sam, but you owe me a beer," Pablo winked. She cracked a smile that faded as she turned and saw Bryce inside the interrogation room. She straightened herself out and went back in for round two.

"So why did you want our investigation files, so you could go to the big boss and say it was your handy work?" Bryce scowled at her as he drank.

"It wasn't like that," he said, trying to sound honest.

"Really, because you're very good at it," McCall said. Bryce suddenly had a look of someone who had just been slapped.

"McCall, look about the thing…I am sorry," Bryce started. McCall gave him a venomous look and walked out.

"You can go now Agent Bryce thank you for your help," McCall said, standing by the open door with her arm extended as if to usher him out.

McCall walked into the break room and just stood for a moment, resting her arms on the tabletop, her head down as she sucked in the air to try and calm herself down. There was a knock on the door, and the captain walked in, his large frame rested against the counter next to the coffee machine.

"You okay McCall?" She stood up straight and turned to face him, her eyes bloodshot from emotion, but there were no tears, not for him.

"No, not really," she smiled softly as Brant pointed a thumb at Bryce as he was heading for the elevator. McCall shook her head.

"No, not for him, for Steel. He tried to tell me something, but he got me so mad I couldn't listen. He tried to warn me about Callan Industries," she said. Brant nodded.

"OK, so, what ya going to do now, Detective?" Brant smiled. McCall nodded and returned the smile.

"Go and find out what is so friggin' special about Callan Industries," she laughed.

FIFTY-SIX

Steel had made it to the lower decks unnoticed by the mercenaries. His plan had gone wrong, but it remained the same, get them off the ship so they couldn't be used as leverage against him. Below, the vessel was full of dimly-lit corridors with shadowy corners that gave the white iron walls an elongated effect. Steel knew exactly which room he had to search; he remembered the door with the large *Do Not Enter* sign on it. Whatever was inside was worth killing for; the engineering kid had found that out with deadly consequences. He moved slowly making sure he kept to the doorways and alcoves, his machine pistol held ready and its skeleton stock firmly imbedded into the arch in his shoulder. The thumping heartbeat of the mighty ship vibrated through the thick walls, making them carry the echoes of each heavy thud; the notice was almost hypnotic but also made it impossible for him to hear anyone sneaking upon him.

Steel stopped and knelt on one knee as he strained to listen to the sudden noise coming from one of the rooms. Slowly he crept forwards, his weapon made ready, but with the safety catch on, in case it was one of his group. As he drew near, he saw it was the cargo hold he wanted, and the door was slightly ajar. The voices that emanated from within were both familiar

STUART FIELD

and welcoming to his ears. It was the survivors from the smoking room.

"OK, so Blacke wanted us to meet him here, do we know why?" came a voice from the shadows. Steel smiled as he recognised the angry voice of Albert Studebaker, who was hidden behind a group of crates that had been stacked up, creating a wall that ran parallel with the wall of the entrance. Inside the room, crates and boxes had been stacked up; one pile ran along the west wall creating a kind of staircase to the roof. Both sections of stacked containers seemed to encase an open area in the middle of the room.

Anthony Blacke walked towards the others that were standing in front of ten large military-style cases, each one measured around two feet square. He stopped, and his eyes widened as he saw the weathered cases.

"I think there has been a terrible mistake, we need to get out of here, it not safe." Blacke moved towards the shadows of the dimly lit room, looking around as he went as if he were expecting someone. There was a muffled cry out then Blacke slid across the floor, halting just in front of the others.

"You're not going anywhere Blacke; get your arse back there," came an angry voice. Everyone looked over to the shadows and gasped as they saw Steel walking towards them, still partly bathed in darkness.

"Black, what the hell is going on?" Yelled a red-faced Albert Studebaker.

"What?" Blacke and Steel asked in unison, Albert went to speak and shook his head in confusion.

"Not you – him," the large American thrust a fat finger towards Steel.

"Why don't you ask him. After all, we are all here because of his cargo; by the way, do you know what it is yet?" Steel asked, curiously, as he edged back and rested his back against a column of huge steel crates with stamps for South America on them.

"So, what's in the boxes Blacke. Weapons, diamonds, the ark

of the covenant?" Steel asked. Blacke stood up and brushed himself off.

"I…. I don't know?" Everyone looked blankly at him. Vedas crunched his knuckles in preparation of giving him a good beating. Steel smiled and shook his head.

"OK, let me get this straight, you have no idea what is in these boxes, but yet people have died over them on the off chance there is something worth having?" Steel said, fighting back the urge to either laugh out loud or cave the man's skull in. Blacke nodded, shamefully.

"They came off a ship that was smuggling arms out of New York, on a salvage operation. I found these boxes and thought they were sealed up pretty tightly so whatever was inside was safe from the elements. Hell, I thought it was firearms, sell them off and well you know." Steel nodded, with a disappointed look across his face.

"So why don't you just open it and find out?" Steel looked over at the silent Blacke, and his mouth fell open in surprise.

"You can't open it can you? You were hoping one of these could open it for you, weren't you?" Steel said, leaning back on the wall. He smiled callously. Blacke backed away from the others as they shot him a look showing how much they wanted to hurt him.

"The captain, he had the key. I found him online saying he had a strange key and wondered if it belonged to anyone. The picture showed a long device that seems to fit the lock," Blacke said, as he pointed to the cases that the group were leaning against. Suddenly, fearful of their contents, the group shot away from the boxes and stood far away from them. On the front of each case was a gap that looked as if something was missing. Steel looked down at his watch and stood up straight.

"We can finish this later, for now we have to go, the lifeboats are on deck five on the outer corridors, we have to move as one. When we get there, we get off the ship." The group got themselves ready to move out and started to line up behind Steel in single file; Vedas grabbed Blacke and made sure that the conman remained in front of him.

"Please you go before me, I really insist." Vedas's words stung with venom. As they edged out into the corridor, Steel checked both sides before moving out.

"Tony, why bring us down here if we have to go up again?" Steel stopped and looked around at Tia; her large glistening eyes were like deep, dark pools in the dim light.

"What are you talking about? I told you lot to stay upstairs," Steel said, confused. Tia looked panicked as she showed the text message to Steel.

"Tia, I never sent that," Steel said. His heart suddenly went into his throat. There was the sound of the metal door being opened at the end of the long corridor, making them all turn towards the sound.

"Quickly in there," Steel whispered, as he pointed towards another cargo hold next to the one they had left. Moving quickly, they dived into the room and Steel slowly closed the door. Just as he heard the entranceway door squeak open, metal ground against metal on the heavy door hinges as it was opened and closed. The echo of heavy footsteps travelled towards them as the stranger approached. Steel had not fully closed the door, as he needed to hear if the stranger was going straight on or stopping off. He needed information before he could act.

"Yes, I am nearly there. Of course, I have had the key for ages, courtesy of some Russian spook. What no, no everything is on schedule. How're things at your end?" Steel made out a heavy Irish accent on the man who was now laughing at whatever the caller was talking about. Steel lost the rest of the conversation as the stranger entered the cargo hold that they had once occupied.

"Everyone stay here, no matter what, OK?" Everyone nodded apart from Blacke, who was being held at the back of his jacket collar by Vedas. Steel smiled and shook his head at the amusing sight of Blacke, who looked like a lion cub being held by its mother.

Steel edged out into the corridor, the weapon ready. As he approached, he saw the door was fully open, and he could make out the sound of electronic beeps, like the sound of a keypad being used. As he moved into the room, Steel stuck to the shadows and kept low, he needed to find out who this was and what was in the cases, not to have a gunfight. Edging around the corner of one set of stacked crates, Steel saw a hooded figure in front of the crates that Blacke had pointed out earlier. There was a click as the lock was released and the figure opened up the crate, and Steel was unable to see what was within, as the military crate was at shoulder height. Knowing he had one chance, Steel decided to make his move.

"OK, put your hands up and interlock them at the back of your head and turn around slowly," Steel ordered with the barrel of the UMP machine pistol pointing at the stranger's chest area. At this close range, Steel knew the .45 calibre rounds would tear the man apart, even if he had a vest on. The figure began to turn when Steel heard a noise behind him. Steel tilted his head slightly towards the sound in the hope of making it out better. The stranger used the chance and kicked upwards, but Steel caught the man's foot and threw him forwards into a stack of small cardboard boxes, the sound of breaking crockery was drowned out by the sound of gunfire from behind Steel, who dived for cover.

"Stop shooting you, idiots. You'll hit the crates," Yelled a voice from the doorway, Steel reckoned it was a mercenary sweep team, who were looking for Blacke.

"OK, move in and sweep," The voice commanded; Steel watched as he saw the figure use the arranged crates on the west wall like a ladder up towards the ceiling with curiosity. The figure stopped and pushed one of the ceiling panels which opened up into a maintenance hatch. Quickly, Steel put on his respirator and fired some shots after the figure. Steel heard the yells for him to put down his weapon as the team moved around the corner, on hearing the gunfire.

"What the hell is going on?" Yelled the team leader, as he ventured in and saw what appeared to be one of his men on his knees with the others surrounding him. The leader pushed the others out of the way to get to Steel.

"Report." He yelled.

"Well, sir..." The one mercenary started to speak, but he suddenly froze as the leader pointed a .50 calibre Desert Eagle pistol at him.

"Not you, him," the leader said, looking over at Steel. Steel stood to attention before speaking.

"Sir, I followed a hooded figure down here from the games room. My squad was taken out, but I somehow managed to get free from the bonds. I followed him here, and I was about to apprehend the intruder when I was interrupted. The intruder got the drop on me, but I got some shots off when I was detained by your men, Sir," The large team leader nodded slowly.

"So, you were part of Team-Four then?" The leader bluffed.

"No sir, Team-Three had the games room, I got stuck with some South American who wasn't exactly talkative," The leader smiled as he knew precisely who Steel was pretending to know.

"OK this intruder, what did he look like and where did he go?" Steel pointed up towards the hatch, he had a hoodie and jeans, and he went up there, it looks like a maintenance hatch or something." The leader smiled and patted Steel on the shoulder.

"So what was he doing here, did you see?" Steel pointed round to the crates, the leader froze for a second then made his way to the open casket.

"Command, this is Team-Five we have a situation," Steel heard the crackle of static in his earpiece, then a voice answered up.

"OK five, send report and LOCSTAT." The leader, who was now acting nervously, pressed his throat mike again.

"We are in the cargo hold, and the merchandise is not in the nest, I repeat the merchandise is not in the nest." There was a brief silence then the voice came back over the net.

"All stations, this is Command, mission abort. All call signs, make your way to extraction point Bravo. We are taking the lifeboats. Command out." The mercenaries headed for the door and Steel hung back, pretending to limp.

"Are you OK soldier?" asked the leader, Steel gave the thumbs up.

"I'll be fine sir. You go, I'll be fine." The leader stood there with a proud look of admiration on his muscular face and left.

"What a dick," Steel said under his breath, as he watched them leave. As the last one passed through the entrance door at the end of the long corridor, Steel went back for the others.

"Is everything alright?" Missy asked, while wearing an innocent look on her face. Steel shook his head, an angry look on his.

"No – they're stealing our ride."

FIFTY-SEVEN

McCall rose early the next morning, to the sound of bird song and the faint sound of the dumpster trucks making their early morning rounds. She climbed out of the comfort of her bed and put on her running gear as she decided to go for a run before work, to blow off some steam. McCall found the morning fresh air and quiet would help her to think. The roller coaster ride of the past thirteen days had begun to wear everyone down. To some people, the killer had been caught, and the case was closed. However, Tony was in trouble, he was being framed for not just Jones's death but anyone that they could tie the gun to. As he struggled to protect the victims, Agent Jones had found something out, and he had been silenced to keep it hidden. These people were clearinghouse and they would use any means necessary to keep everyone in the dark about what was truly happening. A cool breeze clung to the air, and everything had a bluish tint, as the sun had not broken the horizon. She loved this time in the morning, as everything seemed still and tranquil. Shopkeepers and deli owners got their places of work ready for the masses of New Yorkers on their way to work. It had seemed as though she had been running for hours as she stopped for a breather. McCall looked down at her watch, it was four o'clock, and she knew she had enough time to get home, shower and get to the precinct in time for her shift. In the distance, she watched the sky turn a strange purple as a blood-red sun began to immerge. As she watched the wondrous sight, she couldn't help but have a bad feeling about the day. Something was in the air, and it wasn't good.

As McCall got off the elevator, she noticed she was almost alone in the bullpen, some had decided to make a late start, or they were off on a canvas. Unfortunately, McCall's victims were not the only bodies that had dropped, and the Homicide Department was stretched. She sat down at her desk and logged in to her computer. Taking a sip from her thermos mug as she waited, McCall looked round to see who was there. Tooms and Thompson hadn't arrived as of yet, and Tony was sitting at home, probably going nuts. The sound of the elevator made her turn round to see the bright-faced electrical engineer from Ultatronics, heading towards the briefing room with an arm full of books and a laptop.

"Morning, Detective," he said, with a Cheshire cat-like grin,

"Morning," McCall replied, just as he disappeared inside the room and shut the door. She smiled at the sight of him getting excited about trying to crack what was on the blueprint, she felt someone looming over her, and as she turned she saw it was Pablo Rodriguez.

"Morning Pablo, so did you find anything?" The Mexican made a face jokingly "Well yes and no, you see we checked the company and its bogus, the website, everything, just gone. The building they had rented was paid out for the full year using cashier's check, so that was a dead end." McCall felt like screaming at the news of the dead-end so early in the morning. She looked at him and knew something was wrong by the mixed smirk and disappointment on his face. "We did find security footage in that floor space," McCall's eyes widened.

"And did it show anything?" The man waved a beige coloured file.

"Are you sure you want to know." McCall looked at him, somewhat suspicious of what he was asking.

"What was in there?" she thought out loud. McCall reached out an uncomfortable hand and took the file from Pablo. McCall folded back the top cover to reveal the photographs inside; she looked up in shock and gazed into Pablo's saddened eyes.

"Who else knows about this?" He shook his head as if it had the weight of the world on his shoulders.

"No one, just us. But shouldn't we tell someone?" McCall looked around the room that was beginning to fill up with the oncoming shift.

"No, we keep this to ourselves, for now. I think something is going to happen, and we need certain parties in play, just in case." Pablo smiled and nodded in agreement.

"Okay, McCall we do it your way." McCall smiled back and mouthed a thank you as he left her to her thoughts. McCall put the file into the lockable drawer of her desk and sat back in the chair. As she rocked back and forth, she stared hard at the colleagues in the room; she now knew who the mole was, what she didn't know was, were they alone?

FIFTY-EIGHT

Deck five was filled with shops and boutiques with a garden area running down the middle. To look at it, anyone could have imagined that they were in an English village or a small European town. In the daytime, the light from the large windows above the shops gave it that "outdoor feeling." On the outside of deck five were the lifeboats. Twenty huge yellow vessels, capable of holding around four hundred people, clung to the side of the ship like limpets. The entrance to these was nestled in-between the stores, ten large metal bulk head doors sat in alcoves on either side. As Steel and the others approached the double doors to the floor's entrance, he raised his hand to stop them. The doors looked plain with two porthole windows, but each one was thick steel that could contain water or fire. The doors were automatic, and Steel couldn't risk them opening at the wrong moment. Taking off his rucksack, he opened up one of the side pouches and took out a small monitor that was attached to a long snake-like camera. He smiled at the others and gave Tia the monitor, as he edged the camera up to the window.

"Do you see anything yet?" asked Jane Stewart, impatiently.

"No nothing, just an empty room," Steel said. Jane went to rush forward, but Steel put his hand out to stop her. "Nobody goes through this door until I say so, got it?" He gave everyone a cold stare.

"Look we've beaten them to it; I say we go in and get the hell off this tub. These things are built for over a hundred people so there will be enough food," Albert Studebaker paused as he looked at the large Russians.

"Maybe?" The Russians returned his comment with an angry glare. "My point is its safe; there are no bad guys here." Steel looked at the feed and shook his head.

"Nobody leaves this spot until I say," Steel said, as he took out another radio from the bag, put it on channel four then gave it to Tia.

"Okay, listen in. When I give the all clear, come in one at a time and stick to the corners. If anything goes wrong, I will meet you all in the cargo hold," his eyes scanned the faces of the survivors, each one held a different look, anger, frustration. Sorrow.

"And what if they come down there, you have all the weapons," Bob Stewart grunted in disapproval of Steel's plan. Steel reached into the bag, pulled out the spare silenced UMP machine pistol, and handed it to Tia with a smile.

"What about ammo?" Bob asked. Steel shot Bob an unpleasant look, making him step back nervously.

"We have plenty of ammo; dead guys don't need it," Vedas said. Steel looked up at Vedas and nodded in approval.

"You know Mr Vedas; I am beginning to like you," Steel said with a smile. Vedas grinned back, showing his gold-capped teeth at the back of his mouth. Steel walked over to Tia and kissed her gently on the forehead before disappearing through the automatic doors. She gave a worried smile, almost as if she knew that this may be the last time she would ever see him.

Steel kept to the corners as he manoeuvred his way along the dimly lit mall, Victorian-style streetlights gave off a comfortable light that also gave enough shadow to the store's entrances, which were in the windowed alcoves; these were perfect for cover and observation.

The group huddled around the small monitor as best they

could as he moved down towards the first doorway. They watched him move quickly and stealthily like a snake after its prey. Steel suddenly stopped and disappeared from view.

"What's wrong?" Jane asked, trying to catch a peak but only managing to make the door slide open as she broke the sensor's beam.

"Someone is coming, so if you could not draw attention to yourselves that would be great." Tia shot Jane a look as she backed off slowly with a shameful look on her face. Tia angled the camera again, but this time they saw the groups of men patrolling down the mall towards the life raft entrances.

"Gentlemen, we need to ensure nobody leaves with our cargo, so to that end we will each take a life raft," Yelled a voice down the long mall. Again, the voice seemed strangely familiar to Steel, but he couldn't place it. The only thing on his mind was to take out the man just two stores down and take his life raft. Steel had a clear view through the stores' windows however the mysterious leader was too far away for him to get his eyes on him.

"OK here's the plan. I am going to take out the first guy, then wait for them all to get off. That way you guys will be free and clear to get off safely," Steel's words seemed reassuring to everyone, smiles of hope-filled the group's faces as they watched with bated breath as they could see Steel begin to move out of his hiding spot.

The group watched in horror as the mall was suddenly enveloped in flame and flying debris. The noise was like thunder as a multitude of explosions ripped through the deck, the group flew back as the shock wave of the blast slammed against the double doors, buckling them slightly and smashing the safety glass. The bulkhead doors had been rigged with explosives to prevent anyone from leaving. There were no screams from the men, who were now just charred remains. Tia screamed for Steel, but heard nothing back; only crackling static filled the airwaves.

"I think this is what Mr Black would consider as "Something going wrong" Vedas said, with a shrug. Jane looked up at the giant Russian with a frown.

"You think?" Jane said. They knew they had to move and get to safety. Once there, they could work out a plan. Tia looked around.

"Where the hell is Blacke?" Tia screamed over the noise of explosions and roaring flames. Everyone looked around, puzzled.

"I bet that slimy bastard has an escape plan," Growled Jane. Tia shook off the moment and stood up.

"We have to go it's not safe here. If he survived that, then he will be looking for us at the rendezvous point," Tia shouted to the others. The group, who were still in shock over the incident, nodded in agreement. Tia wiped the tears from her eyes and headed for the stairwells that lead down to the lower decks. She gripped the weapon tightly for comfort as she turned and looked at the buckled door, then headed down, back into the belly of the ship.

The room was full of smoke, burning trees and park benches, the windowless shops gave the mall a war zone look about it. The silence hung in the air like the blanket of smoke, but it was soon broken by the crash of a large bookshelf being pushed up and over. Steel stood up shakily from the ordeal, his black clothes covered in grey soot. He had managed to get some shots off into the glass doorway and slid in just as the explosion hit. The shockwave had sent the heavy wooden shelving crashing down on Steel, saving him from the flying debris and flames. He coughed out a lung full of dust and reached for the shoulder radio. The broken device had a piece of glass and wood embedded in it. Steel groaned and ripped it from the shoulder pouch on his vest and tossed it aside, as he looked over at the damaged door he had come from. He smiled as he knew that they would have done as he asked, there they would be safe.

He stepped out cautiously, and the smell of barbequed trees and mercenaries was enough to make anyone gag, but he had smelt worse. He looked around at the carnage as he made his way to the first door, the metal was slightly blackened from the blast but seemed undamaged. Steel moved closer to examine the door. The handle had been destroyed, making it impossible to open, and four charred, square outlines had been embossed into the white metal.

"Shape charges, why the hell would anyone put shape charges to face the wrong way?" He thought aloud. He stood up and looked around, only to see the same thing on the opposite doors. Someone wanted them or something to remain on the ship. He looked down at his watch, it was midnight. In twelve hours, they would be in New York, and whatever was going to happen would happen then. He didn't know exactly what had been in those boxes, but he had a reasonably good idea. The rules had changed, but the game stayed the same. Stop whatever was going to happen and save the survivors. As he ran back towards the double doors, the blonde-haired Mr Williams watched Steel disappear.

"Gentlemen it would appear not all of our guests are napping, find Blacke and bring him to me," said Mr Williams. Deck four was a lonely deck, and this was home to the crew quarters and the main lobby and check-in point. The lobby was dimly lit with tree lights that illuminated the great palm trees and the few ceiling lights, and shadows caressed every corner, making it eerie and unwelcoming. The stairwell door opened slowly, and a figure crept out and hid in the shadows. In the distance, the sound of men's heels tapping on the marble floor broke the silence of the deck as someone was running for cover. Slowly the figure broke from the cover of the shadows, motionless it listened to the footsteps disappear, and then slipped back to the safety of the darkness.

Two men sat and argued in the poorly lit kitchen next to the captain's dining room. Grant and Martin Goddard sat at the staff's table with a plate of what was the dinner from the night before. The cold beef slices still held their flavour and tenderness.

"So what are we going to do Grant, do you want to answer me that?" Grant looked up at the sweating man and smiled.

"Look we made it past the gas and hid from those lunatics, we could make it to the lifeboats of rubber dinghies and get the hell off of here," Grant said. Martin thought for a moment then nodded as he nervously bit into the meat.

"OK sounds good," Martin agreed. Grant smiled at his escape buddy as he filled the glasses in front of them with water.

"Or, you could come with me and join the rest of the group?" They turned around startled as Steel stepped out of the shadows.

"How did you find us?" Grant looked round to see if there were others with him.

"If you're going to run at least take your shoes off, you make too much damned noise," Steel said. Grant smiled and shrugged as Martin shot him a disappointed look.

"He has a point," Grant laughed.

STEEL MOVED QUICKLY with the other two following close behind, stopping only for Steel to check around the corners. Steel was hoping that the explosion and his own antics had thinned the mercenaries' numbers. As they reached the heavy door to the cargo bays and engine room stairwell, Steel raised a hand and told them to get back.

"OK, you guy's stay here, once I am in shut the door behind me and don't open it until I say," Steel ordered. The two men looked at him puzzled, but nodded as if they had a choice, as Steel opened the door he moved in quickly, keeping low into cover as sparks flew off the bulkhead as someone opened up with bursts of fire.

"Hold your fire it's me, Antony Black," Steel shook his head as he had a good idea who was shooting.

"Prove it," Jane Stewart yelled back, Steel shot a confused look in Jane's direction.

"OK, I am coming out, hold your fire," Steel edged out, but

was forced back by the stray rounds that were impacting off his cover.

"What the fuck are you doing?" Steel heard Bob yell at her.

"He moved too quickly, sorry," came back a voice. Steel growled as he heard the pleasure in her voice.

"Tell you what, we do that again, but this time, if you shoot, I shoot and believe me I don't miss," Steel yelled. There was a brief silence followed by a woman's scream.

"It is ok, Mr Black, you can come out, she is how do you say – indisposed," Vedas yelled back. Steel edged out and moved down the darkened corridor. He stopped and looked around the corner to find that Jane Stewart was being held by both arms by the two Russian gorillas. Steel grinned widely and walked over to the others. He bowed to Vedas who returned the gesture.

"Glad to see everyone made it safely," Steel then shot a look at Jane as she dangled a few feet above the floor. "Well, almost everyone." He smiled at Jane who returned the sarcastic smirk.

THEY MADE their way to the staff's cafeteria, which separated the cargo holds, the long dining room could support five hundred of the thousand workers aboard the ship, large ceiling strip lights made sure the room was brightly lit. Large industrial refrigerators held cold drinks, and an open kitchen with a large hot plate system was situated at the north wall by the entrance.

They all sat down at a group of tables. Steel made sure he was facing the door.

"Glad to see you again, Mr Black," Bob said genuinely, as he shook Steel's hand.

"I brought some more guests to the party, hope you don't mind," Steel gave a loud whistle, and they all watched hesitantly to see who the mystery people were. With a metallic grind, the bulkhead door opened, and gasps of relief filled the air as Grant, and Martin Goddard walked in. Steel looked around.

"Where's that snake Blacke gone?" Steel asked. Tia shook her head.

"He must have bolted after the explosion, and he will be

going for the lifeboats," Tia said, with a disappointed, but somehow relieved tone. Steel shook his head.

"No, he won't. The doors are sealed from the explosion," Steel explained. Grant looked confused.

"What explosion?" Everyone looked at him, shocked.

"You never heard anything?" Bob asked. Grant just shrugged.

"We heard a loud thump, but that was it." Jane looked weirdly at the two men, her eyes full of questions.

"How did you get past the gas?" The two men looked at each other and smiled.

"Believe it or not, we went out for a smoke, and that's what saved us," Grant admitted, Martin nodded to confirm Grant's story.

"Well, there's a smoking advert you'll never see," Steel's words made Tia giggle as he opened one of the bottles of water Vedas had gotten from the fridge and tossed his way.

"So, how did you guys escape?" Grant asked, his words slipped away as everyone watched Steel stand up and start to walk towards the cargo hold that had been so troublesome.

"What is it?" Missy asked, her tone gripped with anxiety, Steel raised his hand to make everyone stop.

"Wait here," He ordered futilely, as he knew that they would him follow anyway out of interest. Steel entered slowly and just stood at the mouth of the wall of crates and boxes.

"Kill the lights, will you?" Steel asked. Tia found a switch next to the door and killed the lights; they all looked as an ominous red glow emanated from behind a group of long crates.

"OK, that will do," Steel called over, acknowledging that the lights could go back on.

"What is it?" Missy asked, shaking with fright. Steel walked carefully over and stopped at a safe distance to investigate the glow. Slowly he moved back and turned to run back to the others.

A metallic scraping sound from above made him stop and look up; someone was coming in. Steel rushed back, telling everyone to get back with hand signals. At the doorway, they all peered in to see one of the mercenaries climb down from the opening, but the man was too short for the drop and, as he fell, he caught the edge and dropped towards the crate which Steel had been investigating.

"RUN" Steel yelled. The explosion ripped through the room as if the metal caskets were made of paper. The wall divide disintegrated into deadly metal shards. The survivors ran for cover, diving into rooms and locking doors in the hope of slowing the fiery beast down. Jane ran past several open doorways as fear had gripped her. She tripped, and as she turned, she saw the maul of the black and red flaming beast coming for her, she screamed and closed her eyes. The noise roared like an angry mythological beast. Tia covered her ears and screamed as if to drown out that dreadful noise. She felt the heat against the door even though she was feet away. Tia stopped screaming, and everything went dark as she passed out from the shock.

Tia dreamt of bluebirds in the park on a sunny day. She could feel the warmth of the sun against her skin, the sound of woodpeckers tapping on the trees as she sat on the soft grass. She looked over at the trees as the tapping of their beaks made more of metallic noise. A little blonde-haired girl in a red dress walked up to her and started to call her name. Tia looked strangely at the girl, who began to poke her with a stick.

"Hey get off," Tia sat up and looked around in the darkness, flashes of orange light illuminated Missy's sweet face.

"Oh, good, for a moment I thought we had lost you," Missy said with a grin. Tia cleared her throat.

"What happened?" Tia asked semi-consciously.

"The crate the man fell on was rigged; well, that's what Mr Black thinks anyway," Missy explained. Tia struggled to get up but felt weak from the sudden loss of adrenaline.

Missy and Vedas helped Tia up and into what was left of the corridor and took her to the others. Tia looked at the back wall where the explosion had cleared a horrific unobstructed view of what Steel had seen before.

Sparks flew down from broken power cables like bright orange raindrops. Intermittent flashes from bursts of electricity lit up the darkened lower sections and the faces of the scared passengers. Their wide, unblinking eyes were glued to the electronic counter as it flickered with every change of the countdown. A man knelt in front of them. Even though he was dressed all in black, his broad-shouldered back was made visible by the emergency lighting above the doorway and the intermittent flash of blue light from the broken power cables. The man used his hands to search for a way to switch off the timer, in case there was another way other to switch off the device.

"Can you stop it?" Asked a tall, blonde woman. The man remained silent, lost in his task, the rest of the world was oblivious to him, as though he was the only one in the room.

"Hey, the lady asked you a question," barked a large American, but the man knew it wasn't personal. The American was scared but acting bravely, mostly for the sake of the ladies – or himself.

"Please, Mr Black – can you stop it?" The women asked again, the man they all knew as Mr Black stood up and walked towards them. Mr Black was tall, and his rugged features seemed more handsome as the flashes of light illuminated one side of his chiselled face. He wore all black, and he wore it well.

"I need the code, but we have time" he lied – hoping it would reassure the people. He turned and looked at the timer that read 04:45:36. "I have to find the actual device and hope to stop it from there." He turned and started to walk away but stopped; he half turned towards them and waited for a moment as if pondering his next move. "Oh, and by the way, the name isn't Black its Steel, Detective John Steel." There was a large burst of sparks from the cables, making them shield their eyes, as they looked back to where Steel had stood, they saw only the empty passageway.

FIFTY-NINE

McCall had been to see Tina at the morgue and they'd had their daily chat. This time there was a lot she was holding back, there was a lot she just couldn't say. However, the conversation traversed to the usual conclusion as Tina strove to get the low down on her time with Doctor Dave. However, the conversation was cut short by a text message from Tooms, "*Get your ass back here as electro geek has something.*"

As McCall stepped off the elevator, she made a beeline straight for the small briefing room.

"OK, so what we got?" The tech looked up from his computer and smiled as she entered.

"Your boy reckons he has got something," Brant seemed lost, like a child who had come across algebra for the first time.

"This Detectives, Captain, is in a word genius," said Roberts, the computer tech.

"Great, what the fuck is it?" Tooms barked, causing McCall to crack a smile. Roberts adjusted his glasses and grinned in marvel at the machine in front of him.

"This is a multi-binary unit with a multiphase control system," he explained. The room fell silent, and mouths fell open.

"It's a what now?" Tooms asked, as he sat down suddenly.

"It's a control system for multiple devices, but this has a

split-second reaction time, it also seems to be linked to something like a special warning device, an infrared beam, for instance, something like that," Roberts continued. Brant looked at McCall who also wore an edgy look.

"Do you know where it would be used?" Asked McCall, who moved slowly to look at the outstretched blueprint that lay on the long briefing table.

"Judging by the size of the area you are looking at a stadium or somewhere with a large surface area. It's all controlled by a central unit, a computer or mainframe of some sort," Roberts explained with admiration in his voice.

"Any idea what it's for or where it is?" Brant asked. Roberts stood up and searched through his notes.

"No, not really, just one name did come up though," Roberts explained as he searched further through his notebooks. McCall turned slowly and shot the man a look. "The name was Neptune, whatever that is?" Roberts shrugged. McCall looked over to Brant, who had the same puzzled look on his face.

"What the hell is Neptune?" Brant yelled.

"It's a new British-American venture, the largest cruise liner ever constructed and it's due to come into New York at around four o'clock this afternoon," A young uniform informed them all; the captain looked shocked and amazed.

"How the hell did you know all that?" The uniform pointed up to the television set on the wall that showed aerial footage of the leviathan.

"My god, look at the size of that thing," Tooms muttered, under his breath. All of them stood and watched. McCall walked over to her desk and sat down hard into her chair, the colour drained from her face.

"McCall, what's wrong?" Tooms rushed over. She looked up at him with distant eyes.

"Steel's on that ship," Brant walked over and shook his head in disbelief.

"Come on, how could you know that he could be on any damn cruise ship. What makes you think he's on that one?" She looked up at the captain, and a smile broke from the corner of her mouth.

"Because it's a doomed cruise ship and he is a magnet for trouble," McCall shrugged. They all looked up at the TV set and watched more footage.

"Well, Detective if your right we better get ready," Brant said, heading for his office. Tooms looked confused.

"For what, Captain?" Tooms asked. Brant turned and faced them and smiled.

"The shit to hit the fan and a lot of dead terrorists is my guess."

Steel had left the others downstairs in the safety of the crew's cafeteria. They would have questions when he got back, but for now he had to find a way to the lifeboats. His plan was simple: If he couldn't go through the doors he would go in from above. The silent corridors seemed surreal, almost like a bad nightmare. The air was musky from the lack of fresh air being pumped in from the air-conditioning units. Steel made his feet impact on the ground a little harder to break the unbearable silence of the ghost ship. Slowly he edged up the stairwell to the doors that led to deck six, his weapon held shoulder high and braced into his shoulder ready for any surprises. The door slid open as he approached; carefully he made his way in, checking corners and listening out for chatter or footsteps. The silence was everywhere and the shadows hung in the alcoves of the doorways of the rooms, like strange beasts ready to pounce. The thick plating below his feet muffled the *thump, thump, thump* of engines.

Deck six was mostly comprised of the bars and restaurants which were situated at the centre of the deck, with an elaborate open-spaced walkway full of tables and benches that had been fixed to the iron flooring. The walkway, unlike the others, was free of flora; this was the party floor that wound itself from entrance to exit. On the outside of the deck with the dimly lit corridors lay the smaller cabins which only took up one side, all of which were facing the ocean and all had balconies. Steel went to the first room and forced the door. Inside, a family lay huddled together, sleeping, with a look of contentment on their faces. He thought it was fortunate that no one had any idea what was going on. He moved quickly towards the balcony and slid open the sliding door. The drop to the deck was substantial, plus he needed a way back up, just in case his plan failed. Running out into the corridor, he searched for the cleaners' room where they kept the extra bedding and cleaning equipment. Earlier, he had taken notice that each floor would have one, just in case it became necessary. Steel smiled, as he found the cleaning closet not too far down the corridor. With a massive kick he was in. Steel stood for a moment and grabbed around half a dozen sheets from the metal shelving. Then, as he hurried back to the balcony, he began to tie the sheets together as he made a rope from the white linen bedding. The smell of starch crept up his nostrils as he bound the ends together then securely attached one end to the balcony top railing.

He climbed down effortlessly and was checking to see if there was any blast damage on the way. Steel turned and headed to one of the massive lifeboats. The enormous yellow beast was at least thirty-foot-long with a small window on top for the pilot. Steel ran forwards and peered inside one of the windows, then stepped back, so his back was on the wall of the ship, a look of complete shock on his face, which then turned to anger. He ran down to two more of the craft, and each one was the same. His gaze fell upon the ship and his lips curled in an animalistic snarl. He wanted to find Blacke. He had questions, and Blacke would answer them.

SIXTY

Antony Blacke was dirty and frightened and looked around at the slightest sound. He had made it to deck five in the hope of getting on board one of the lifeboats and disappearing into the horizon. He wanted this nightmare to end so he could go back to his old life. He coughed as he inhaled a strange mixture of smells that he wasn't familiar with. Blacke looked around at the sight of the devastation but paid it no heed; he was only interested in the bulkhead doors that led to his salvation. Blacke's smile faded as he saw the blackened edges and the damage on the door. He froze for a brief moment that seemed like forever to him. As he looked at the handless door, all his hopes of escape melted away. He screamed and ran at the door, smashing it with his fists and begging for it to open.

"You could always try open sesame," Fearful of the voice, Blacke stopped but didn't turn, beads of sweat cascaded down his body, and he could feel his legs beginning to fail him. Blacke dropped to the ground and turned to face his pursuer.

"Oh, Tony. Thank god it's you," Blacke wore a fake smile etched into his smug face. Steel grabbed him, lifted him up and threw him to the ground next to a heavily burnt carcass of one of the mercenaries.

"See that, that's the work of your precious cargo," Steel growled. Blacke looked to the side, and as he realised what the blackened twisted shape was, he scrabbled away quickly to the other side on all fours.

"I didn't know what was in the cases, I swear," Blacke insisted with tears in his eyes. Steel grabbed him and pulled him up to his feet then threw him towards the other exit. Blacke looked over at the door nervously.

"Where are we going?" Blacke asked, his voice broken with fear.

"For a drink and some answers, now move," Steel ordered. Blacke heard the distinctive metallic clatter of a weapon been held firmly, a sound he had heard all too often.

As THEY MADE their way to the Irish Bar, Steel had time to think. They were taking the elevator up to the deck. They were taking the elevator because he was sick of skulking around and hiding, and if they wanted him, he would rather face them head-on. Steel thought back to McCall's cases like the crane op and the electrician who had had the "accidents", his mind ticking over as the hypnotic knocks of the elevator, as it travelled upwards, filled the large cabin. He thought about all of McCall's cases and how they had to be linked by something, probably to this ship. Steel looked over to Blacke as he cowered in the corner of the steel box and he knew that this devil of a man didn't have all of the answers, but he had enough.

As the elevator stopped, the doors slid open, slowly, revealing another quiet lonely mall. Steel grabbed Blacke and shoved him towards the Irish Bar. Blacke smiled as they saw the door was locked up with a closed sign hanging from a plastic sucker. Blacke looked a Steel and smiled.

"Oops, it's locked, what now tough guy," Blacke sneered. Steel looked up at the door and smiled at Blacke.

The front door swung open with a loud crash, fragments of glass and wood sprayed across the polished wooden floor, followed by the body of Blacke.

"Now, it's open," Steel laughed. Blacke looked up at Steel with contempt and fear. Steel grabbed Blacke's slightly cut arm and led him towards the bar. Using zip ties from the combat vest, he secured Blacke to the highly polished brass railing that ran the length of the bar surface. Steel went behind the bar and poured himself a large whiskey. He downed it in one and shook off the taste of the cheap tasting malt.

"Ok Blacke, tell me about the boxes and what was in them, and don't try to lie to me because I don't believe for a minute you had no idea, in fact, I think you handled the inventory deals for that ship that went down," Steel said. Blacke smiled at Steel. In a way, he felt some admiration for this strange man behind the bar.

"Why are you on the ship making the sale? It doesn't make sense," Steel said. Blacke shrugged.

"It was the safest place for everyone, international waters and all that," Blacke explained. Steel nodded and poured another drink, but this was for Blacke. Steel placed it on the floor next to Blacke, who just shot him a confused look.

"What, there's a straw in it," Steel joked. Blacke bent forwards and drank the nasty tasting spirit,

"So, why are the bombs on the lifeboats?" Then Steel watched as Blacke suddenly looked over in complete shock, Steel smiled.

"Someone set you up. You didn't know what the plan was. You just brought the stuff onboard?" Steel shook his head and laughed slightly at the irony of his situation.

"I swear I didn't know, look someone arranged this whole thing. I bring the stuff on board, and it gets sold off. It was meant to be a fifty/fifty split, and they said it was okay, and nothing could go wrong." Steel looked over at Blacke with dangerous eyes.

"Who arranged everything?" Steel asked. Blacke swallowed hard at the question.

"Look they're on board. You have already met. I am sure they didn't know all this would happen," Blacke said hysterically. Steel felt the rage build up within him.

"The name, who was your contact?" Blacke opened his mouth, but instead of words, there was a roar of thunder as eight shots rang out, each round hitting Blacke and the bar. Steel brought up the machine pistol to bear and opened up on the flashes of the pistol's muzzle flash. The firing stopped, and Steel leapt over the bar and headed outside to see if anyone had been hit. As he approached a small group of plant pots. Steel found the empty 9mm and a small blood trail, he had hit whoever it was but not fatally. Steel turned and rushed back to find a Blacke who was hanging by the zip ties on his hands. Several of the hits had been lucky and hit him squarely in the chest. Whoever it was, they were a bad shot and desperate. Steel stood up and headed out towards the stairwell. He had to get to the bridge to see if the lifeboats could be released from there. If so, he could prevent the devices reaching the city and most of all he would prevent the deaths of the sleeping passengers. Time grew shorter by the minute, and so did the distance.

STEEL MADE his way to the bridge, hoping to find the release for the lifeboats there. He used the elevator as it gave him time to think and take stock of his equipment, as it travelled upwards towards the nineteenth deck. Steel looked over to the brightly lit LED display and noticed he was approaching his destination, and he had to be ready. He crouched behind the wall next to the door and awaited automatic fire as the doors opened, but only silence greeted him. He slowly peered round to see an empty floor. He slid out of the elevator; he hugged the walls as he made for the bridge. The corridors were quiet and barren, as though he was the only person on the ship, only the soft rattle from his gear broke the lingering stillness.

The door to the bridge was a heavy-looking wooden door with a brass plaque with the words 'Bridge' inscribed into the highly polished metal. The way in was through a digital keypad to the right of the door. However he didn't have the code, but he did have a key. Steel stood back and aimed at where the door hinges would be and opened up on the door, splinters of wood filled the air as the .45 calibre rounds shredded the door. He stood back and kicked the door, sending it crashing the bridge's floor. The room was almost dark, but the lights from the monitors and flashing lights of the computers lit up the faces of the unconscious crew; Steel looked around and found a panel near the pilot's console that read *Autopilot engaged*. The console had been smashed so the command couldn't be disengaged, Steel rushed around the room looking for the controls for the lifeboats but was not surprised that the captain wasn't there. Searching the back wall, Steel found the emergency release control for the lifeboats, a small monitor above the control just read *Error* in heavy red font. Someone had made sure that the ship would remain on course and deliver its deadly cargo. Steel cursed the situation and pulled his cell from his vest. He only had one bar but it wasn't enough to get a message to McCall, and he had to find a way of getting through to her.

McCALL SAT WITH THE ELECTRICIAN, who was still looking at the blueprints, trying to figure out what use the set up would be for.

"It appears there are several devices that are busing a set signal from a singular device," Roberts pointed to two rows of ten blocks, in the centre was one smaller box. "This could be controlled by infra-red or Blue-tooth, wi-fi. But in any case, this is a central hub, and this is the control unit." McCall nodded, then looked down as she felt her pocket vibrate; taking the cell from her pocket McCall checked the caller ID. The display read number withheld; an unknown caller. McCall paused and pressed the green accept button.

"McCall, Homicide," she said, hoping there wasn't another case. There was a crackling noise coming from the loudspeaker of her cell, and then his voice came through clearly.

"McCall, its Steel, look there's a slight problem with this ship," Steel's voice held a playful but concerned tone to it. She smiled, playfully.

"What's up, there's no more champagne?" She waited for him to laugh, but he didn't.

"No, I was thinking more of the explosive devices hidden in

the lifeboats. Look I am calling from the bridge, and it's been smashed up pretty badly. I will try and find a way to stop or at least slow this bastard down," Steel said. McCall's face fell as she ran into the captain's office.

"McCall, what the…?" Brant yelled, as she barged in without knocking.

"Sorry sir, but I have Steel on the phone, you need to hear this," Brant looked up, concerned

"Steel you're on speaker, the captain is here as well." There was a pause before he spoke.

"Hi Captain, look there are some bombs hidden in the lifeboats on this ship, it's due to get into the city at around four o'clock, you have to stop this ship if I can't get them off. Sir, this ship can't be allowed to get there," Steel's voice had lost the humour. Brant looked at McCall, confused.

"How bad a device are we talking Steel?" McCall could feel the tension in Steel's voice as he replied.

"Sir, the devices are red mercury, the stuff was used in fusion bombs in the former Soviet State. Each one has the explosive power a thousand times greater than normal explosives." Brant looked over to McCall; sweat began to form on his massive head.

"How many are we talking about?" Brant was fearful of the answer; he closed his eyes as Steel spoke.

"Twenty sir, there are twenty. Look I have a plan. I am going to try and get the lifeboats off, but if I can't…" Steel didn't need to say anything else. There would be no other option.

"Understood, good luck," Brant said. McCall looked over to the electrician in the next room and realised what the plans were for.

"Steel we have some blueprints from one of the cases, the tech here who has been studying them says that there is a central unit that is controlling everything, like a relay or something. You need to find that, and you should be fine and don't get yourself killed, ok?" There was no reply, just the sound of static. He had hung up on them. He wasn't ready to say goodbye. Brant picked up the receiver of his desk phone and dialled a number.

"McCall get next door, try and figure this thing out. I have got to call in the feds and the commissioner." McCall nodded sternly and ran out, closing the door behind her. Brant watched her leave and smiled softly until a voice on the other end greeted him with a "Hello." Brant sat down, preparing himself for the news he was about to give.

"Commissioner, its Captain Brant, sir we may have a situation."

SIXTY-ONE

Captain Tobias Long sat at his desk in his room; the only illumination was from the bright sunshine that beamed through the two portholes. He sat leaning on his elbows as he stared at the picture of his family while he cradled a bottle of Jack and a crystal cut glass. Tears of remorse flowed freely down his rose-red cheeks and collected on his white whiskers.

"I am so sorry, please forgive me," He cried into his glass, as he took another hit of the golden liquid.

"Sorry for what, Captain?" Tobias spun around, brandishing a 9mm that had lain next to the photograph and pointed it at Steel.

"How the hell did you get in here?" Long asked, shocked he had not heard the man enter.

"Sorry for what, Captain?" Even though Steel was wearing his sunglasses, the captain could feel the anger in his eyes, burning him,

"Sorry you have put everyone in danger? Sorry you sold out and got a kid killed?" Long looked puzzled for a moment,

"What do you mean put everyone in danger, I was just meant to cause an accident on the ship, run it aground or something, the passengers would never know the truth." Long said, confused. Steel nodded as he looked around the room. He saw there were no air vents, just an air conditioning unit attached to the outer wall.

"They would never know because they would be asleep. That was the plan," Long continued. Steel looked at him with a curious glare.

"Whose plan was it, and who designed your room, Captain?" Long shook his head in confusion; the mix of questions and alcohol were not going together. Long raised the weapon and pointed it at Steel.

"What do you mean put everyone in danger?" Long asked again. Steel smiled and in one swift movement snatched the automatic out of Long's grasp and threw it out of one of the open portholes.

"My dear Captain, this boat is a floating bomb, when we get to New York a lot of people are going to die, so, tell me what you know," Steel growled. Long stared into nothingness as the shock of what he had been a part of became painfully clear.

"I was told to take the ship to New York and scuttle it, some people would be making a lot of money if the ship failed, I was given the box to hold by one of the men, and he said it was to be kept safe. The man had designed the room, so he knew of the secret compartment that you had seen earlier, he never said what it was for, just that it should be hidden well until he asked for it." Long looked at the photograph that showed a woman and two girls standing side by side, the picture looked a couple of years old from the fading on the paper. "I just wanted them to be proud of me, think I was a hero." He looked back at Steel and straightened himself out,

"Okay Mr Black, how do we stop this thing?" Steel smiled for the first time. He looked like the man he should be. "Can you slow the ship down, when I was on the bridge, I noticed it was on autopilot, but the controls had been disabled." Long smiled broadly.

"That I can do, look, lad, you go sort out those damned bombs, and I'll handle the ship," Long said, with a proud roar. Steel turned to walk out but stopped suddenly without turning to look at Long.

"The lifeboats, can they be deployed manually?" Long thought for a moment, his head still cloudy from the heavy drinking.

"Yes, on the support arm there is a lever, a sort of emergency brake release if you will. But it is on top of the arms under a panel." Steel nodded in appreciation of the information and walked out the door.

As Steel walked towards the stairwell, he knew what he needed to get the job done. The hardest part would be to tell everyone what had happened. The situation was volatile, and he needed them to trust him, but that was going to be difficult. So far, everyone had lied, including him. As he headed down, he planned the route that would have to take him past the Irish bar, as the elevator was too dangerous. Moving along the corridors, he moved quickly but cautiously, there were still mercenaries on board, and he didn't have time for a firefight. Steel reached the entrance doors to the fifth floor, and he peered through the entranceway into the quiet. Steel rushed forwards, ensuring to use as much cover as possible. He stopped by an entranceway to catch his breath. He was tired. The last hours had taken their toll on him. He hadn't slept or eaten for hours. Looking through one of the pouches he found a candy bar he had put in there, just in case. Ripping open the package with his teeth, he spat out the loose end and feasted on the sugar bomb. He felt the sugar surge through his body, making him slightly giddy for a moment. Then he stood up and got ready to move. The room started to spin from the glucose injection, and he thought he had imagined music playing. He steadied himself until everything stopped moving, then he heard it. From the Irish Bar someone was playing music. Steel gripped his weapon and moved towards the sound like a moth to a flame. Inside was dark, and the music was playing softly in the background. Steel walked in the past the body of Blacke, who was still tied to the bar's brass railing. Then Steel looked closer. Steel noticed someone had pushed cocktail umbrellas into the flesh of his face. Steel stood up without a wince and carried on towards the back of the room where he had noticed someone sitting in a corner booth, wearing a large fedora hat.

"Good afternoon Mr Steel, so glad to see you again." The man looked up, slowly, and Steel felt an unbridled rage as he recognised the man as Steven Brooks, a man he had encountered months before. He was a cold, calculating psychopath, but this ship incident didn't have his mark. Sure, he wanted to put a bullet into the man, but he also wanted answers.

"Please sit, drink something," the man known now as Mr Williams insisted. A goon dressed in black placed a bottle of water and two glasses on to the table then left. Steel took no notice of the man, but he registered the noise of his heavy footsteps and ascertained where he was going.

The thin man opened the bottle and poured out two glasses of the gas-filled water. Steel looked at the glass then back at Williams. The man smiled as he went to take a sip from his own glass and stopped.

"What, really?" He placed down his own glass, grabbed for the glass before Steel, and took a sip before putting it back down.

"See I am all right...." Brooks grabbed his throat and pretended to choke grasping his throat with both hands, then falling sideways on to the benches long leather seat. There was the sound of laughter as Brooks crawled back onto his seat. Steel just sat there and watched as the clown got back up again.

"I see you haven't lost your sense of drama," Steel said, as he drank from the glass.

"I see you still haven't found your sense of humour," Brooks said, with a hideous grin. Steel's eyes were fixed on the man, and Steel wondered how Brooks was involved in all of this, how THEY were involved.

"What do you want Brooks?" Steel asked. Brooks clapped excitedly, his broad grin almost reaching both ears, his face was long and pale, and his blue eyes looked cold and full of madness.

"You see John, that's what I always like about you, straight to the point. No dilly-dallying around. Oh, and it's Mr Williams now, time for a change I thought," Williams said proudly. Steel nodded in some sort of appreciation of the mad man's comment. "I would like my explosives back." Steel sat back in the chair, all the while the machine pistol was pointing at William's middle.

"They're on the lifeboats, be my guest they're all yours," Steel grinned. Brooks smiled

"See, you have got a sense of humour. No, no, you see I would rather they were intact and not ready to vaporise Manhattan. Bad for business you see, call me picky if you will," Williams said. His voice was like fingernails on violin strings. Steel laughed as he realised why he was still talking to this lunatic.

"You want me to bring you the devices; you have got to be joking," Steel said, standing up and heading for the bar to grab a proper drink. Brooks smiled but with a childish look on his face that made him look even more menacing. Steel returned with the bottle of bad whiskey and two glasses and set them down.

"Look it's simple, you bring me the devices and I tell you who arranged everything – after I have properly thanked them, of course," Williams grinned showing off a set of pearly white teeth. Steel took sip from the whiskey. He felt as if he had no choice but that which was being offered one. Either way he had to disarm them if he could, what happened to them after that wasn't his concern for the moment.

"Tell me, why is everyone on board? This business could have been done anywhere, why here?" Steel asked. Williams sat back and crossed his arms. He could see that Steel was tired, tired of the whole damned business.

"Tell you what John you have a guess, and I will fill in the blanks if you're close," Williams said with a cat-like glare. Steel didn't have time, but he knew he wasn't getting any answers otherwise.

"Whoever arranged this, heard about the red mercury and thought the only way of getting it on board was the deal," Williams smiled with delight.

"Go on," Williams insisted. Steel looked around the room, as if he was searching for some kind of inspiration.

"Both the Americans and the Russians said they had no idea what was in the cases. I believe it was a need to know basis. Their governments set them up, probably told them their orders were just to retrieve the items." Williams sat back in his seat and revelled in Steel's detection skills.. Then Steel looked up, a startled look on his face.

"Whoever did this needed both parties because they could blame each other if any remains were found. They also needed you onboard so if anyone connected to your organisation were found, that would be it, your organization would be discovered and made public. Someone is after your organisation, someone is after SANTINI," Steel said with a grin. Williams's face scowled at the very idea but started to clap.

"Well done, all you need is the name of that person and their partner in New York," Steel looked up at Williams and growled.

"What partner?" Steel said. Williams stretched out a hand.

"The explosives for the information, and oh yes, I have files you require, if you wanted to go down that road. Personally, I would take them to a pig farm or something," Williams nodded. Steel went to reach but stopped halfway.

"I deactivate them; the rest is up to you. " Steel said. Williams crunched together and gave himself a little excited shake.

"Ooh, I must say working with you is wonderful, all the rest are boring, apart from McCall." Williams winked then shook Steel's hand. "Well John, it's been marvellous to see you again, and I wish you well. Oh, by the way, how is that fat clockmaker, has he boinked Mrs Studebaker, yet? Should have a chat, he does wonders with timepieces and stuff," Williams giggled, his laugh was erratic, with high and low pitches. Steel turned to see the last of the men leave. He stood up and made for the stairwell, he was running out of time, and Steel had a clockmaker to find.

Steel had made it to deck two and the heavy bulkhead door

to the engine room and cargo hold. He paused for a moment and gathered his thoughts. He had much to tell them but recent events had probably shattered all hope of them trusting him. Beyond, lay the long corridor of the cargo hold and the first defence against any intruder, someone would be lying in wait, guarding the entrance way. He knocked three times. The heavy metal made a hollow thud with each impact from his fist. Slowly, he opened the door and waited for a second.

"It's me, Steel." He sucked in a breath before moving slowly through the half-open door hoping Jane Stewart wasn't on guard. He smiled in relief to see the massive form of Vedas, trying to hide behind some boxes for cover.

"Ah, Mr Steel, my friend, it is good to see you once more," Vedas suddenly frowned and shot a look towards the dining area. "Many people are mad at you, big time." Steel shook the man's massive hand.

"Good, then this will make things easier, come on I have to talk to everyone," Steel said. Vedas looked back at the door.

"What about mercenaries they come." Steel shook his head as he walked.

"They're no longer a problem," Steel said, his voice excited. The buzz of conversation echoed along the white metal corridors like a strange humming sound until they grew near. Albert Studebaker cut his laughter short as he looked up to see a pale-looking Steel stood behind them. The rest of them turned to see what the American was looking at and the room fell silent. Without a word, Steel made his way to one of the sizeable glass-fronted display fridges and took out a small bottle of water. All of them watched as he downed the first bottle, and then proceeded to finish off another.

"So, Mr Steel, the lifeboats are ready to go, I take it?" Studebaker asked, as he sat up in his chair as if he was trying to make himself larger. Steel looked at them all as they just sat there, staring at him with hopeful eyes. He reached into the refrigerator and pulled out another bottle. As he turned back, his eyes met with Tia's. Her look was one of horror at his appearance.

He was dirty, and his clothes held small long cuts showing bloody scratches underneath. The man looked as if he had been in a war zone, but no one seemed to care.

"How is everyone doing?" Steel asked, as he took smaller, more controlled sips from the bottle.

"We are fine. Thank you. Now what's with these damned lifeboats, when can we get off this tub?" Steel glared at Studebaker.

"The lifeboats are out of the question, and each one has an explosive device on it, so it's not recommended you try," Steel explained. Grant spat out a mouthful of coffee.

"The mercenaries, they rigged the lifeboats to keep us here?" Bob said. Steel shook his head as he looked around the room, carefully trying to get a read on all present.

"No, it was someone else, whoever planned this whole trip, the person who got you all here. The mercenaries are here to get them back," Tia looked up at Steel with sad eyes.

"They want you to get them back?" He nodded, then shrugged.

"Well, I had some time to kill before we hit the port," Steel joked.

"So, what if you don't, what then?" Jane Stewart asked, in a defiant tone.

"Then a lot of people die, and I can't let that happen," Steel said, then turned to Vedas and smiled.

"I need some strong backs, can your men assist me?" The two men from the gym stepped forwards and folded their arms.

"We are ready. You tell us want you want. Da." The men smiled, broadly, and Steel laughed to himself as he tucked the water bottle into a pouch on his vest, as he noticed that one of them had no front teeth.

"Ok fellas let's go." As they headed off, Steel stopped and looked over at Martin Goddard.

"Say, Martin, you said you were good with clocks and electrical stuff, right?" Martin nodded, cautiously.

"Yes, why?" Steel smiled.

"I need your help, I'll tell you on the way," Steel said. Grant stood up, angrily.

"And the rest of us, do you expect us just to sit here?" Steel turned and shot Grant a curious look.

"You're safe in here, just stay here until I call you and pray we pull it off."

As the massive liner cut through the water, the warm midday sun blazed down upon the cold waters. The cloudless sky showed no sign of the storm which they had passed through as though it had never happened. However, the silence of the vessel and the battle-scarred decks showed otherwise. Steel and Martin Goddard had made it up to deck five using the elevators. Steel knew he had free access and that Brook's men wouldn't get in the way. If they were there, it was to observe and nothing more.

"Ok, Mr Steel we are here, what now?" Martin asked, as he stepped off the elevator. The sound of safety catch being released made Goddard freeze and slowly turn around, Steel stood there, holding the UMP machine pistol at hip height, the barrel facing Martin.

"What in god's name are you doing, man?" Goddard barked, somewhat confused at the gesture.

"So, Martin, where is the control unit, and why did you set it?" Goddard looked shocked,

"How did you know? Look, it was meant to be for an insurance scam, the ship has an accident then the company goes under. It was meant to be just the lifeboat falling off that was all…that's what I was told anyway." Goddard sat down hard on one of the benches near the elevator.

"Did you set the charges?" Steel watched over him, but he knew just by looking at his sorry state that he was no killer.

"No, I just finished the work someone else had started, set up the wireless connection and the activation unit." Steel remembered what McCall had said about the central hub.

"So what sets them off?" His voice had softened but still held that tone of authority.

"The radar, it's fixed to the radar. Whoever puts in a point and when that point is achieved, it activates." Goddard sat with his head in his hands. Steel looked at his watch, it was now two o'clock, and the clock was ticking, just not in their favour.

"Come on, Martin, you can save the people on this ship and those in New York." Goddard looked puzzled as he stood up.

"What do you mean Mr Steel, why would anyone be in danger? I thought you found the charges that would destroy the lifeboats." Steel turned and shook his head, a look of sorrow etched across his rugged face.

"Do you know what red mercury is, Mr Goddard?" Martin went pale as he slumped back down on to the bench below him.

"They told me…" Goddard started.

"They lied, and when this is over, you can tell me who hired you." Goddard stood up and shook himself off, the thought of all those people, Missy. The notion that he may have caused her any harm because of them sickened him.

"We have to get to the bridge, but what about the ship how are we going to stop it?" Steel smiled as he received a text on his cell.

"Oh I wouldn't worry about that, someone else is dealing with that." The two men raced for the elevators at the other end of the deck; from there they would be closer to the bridge. However, Steel felt uneasy, one of the group had to be the perpetrator, the master mind. Question was, which one?

SIXTY-TWO

The two giant Russians were on their way to the elevators. Steel had given them instructions to go to the elevators near the engine room and wait. They had been there for at least twenty minutes before the elevator came down and the doors opened. To their surprise, the captain stepped out and grinned at the men. "So lads, have you ever smashed up and engine room before?" The men grinned and shook their heads in anticipation of the next order.

"Well, it's your lucky day." Captain Long giggled as they ran down towards the engine room.

As they arrived at the engine room, Long sent a text to Steel, after a short while he looked down at the simple reply.

"Roger that." Before Long opened the door, he handed the Russians each a set of red plastic ear defences and smiled.

"You'll need these, believe me. Now when we get in, you stick with me, yes?" The two men nodded as Long put on his ear defence and stood by the door.

"Welcome to hell, boys." He opened up the door and the roar from the seven marine diesel engines and the smell of oils and lubricants filled the air, as well as the potent waft of hot metal. Long took the two men down to the lower floor where the pistol arms were busy pounding like some mechanical beast trying to get away from them. Long pointed to the arms and showed the men roughly what to do as he mimed the action of them swinging sledgehammers at the control arms to damage them. With large smiles, Long could see that they understood. His intention was to slow the vessel, not stop it, not if Steel had to get the lifeboats off at a safe distance. As the men got to work, Long ran up to the power grid for the fifth floor, he would wait for the signal then cut the power. He didn't know why and he really didn't want to know. All he could do was watch as his ship was being destroyed before his eyes and he was helping to make it happen.

GRANT PACED UP and down to the annoyance of the others. He was scribbling in his notebook as he went.

"Can't you sit down and do that?" Yelled Jane, angrily. Grant looked over to them, wearing a troubled look on his face.

"Don't you find it odd we never went with them?" Everyone just stared at him as if he had gone mad.

"How do we know Steel didn't set this whole thing up? You think about it, since he has been on board it's been one thing after another. How do we know he isn't getting off the ship on one of the lifeboats, ah?" Missy tutted and rolled her eyes.

"Because there are some kind of bombs onboard, silly." Grant sat down and leant forward.

"And who told you that?" He sat back and grinned as he saw the looks on all of their faces, all except Vegas who just stood at the entranceway and scowled at Grant. However, Grant felt too good to be bothered about the big Russian and started to jot down ideas in his leather-bound notebook.

"If there was no danger from the mercenaries, why keep us cooped up here? No, if you ask me, something is going on. He has lied to us before, why not now?" Grant looked around the room to see the look on their faces, and he could see the anger welling up inside them.

"What do you suggest we do, Mr Grant?" Bob Stewart spoke softly, trying not to be heard by Vedas.

"We overpower the Russian and head for the lifeboats, then

get off this ship." They all nodded in agreement, all except Tia who was now sleeping in the corner on a makeshift bed.

As they neared the bridge, Martin Goddard stopped.

"Look, someone else has got here before us." He rushed towards the splintered door and stopped before entering,

"You better go first, just in case whoever did this is still here." He turned to face Steel who had a naughty schoolboy look on his face.

"Oh, never mind, I hope you didn't break anything." The large man said as he entered, the bridge was as Steel had left it. The midday sun flooded through the polarised glass, lighting up the large room. Goddard headed for the guidance control and the radar system. Kneeling, he patted his pockets as he remembered about the four securing screws holding on the panel.

"What's wrong?" Steel asked, seeing the man looking perplexed.

"Do you have a screwdriver or something I can use to get this panel off with?" Goddard suddenly jumped to the side as Steel rammed an eight-inch combat blade into the top of the cover and, with a screech of metal, prised it open.

"Will that do?" Goddard smiled nervously at Steel as he lay on his back looking up,

"Yep, that should do it." Martin got up and started to disengage the radar so the activation device would be inoperative.

"How long do you think it will take?" Steel asked, looking at his watch.

"Twenty minutes, it's not like yanking all of the wires out you know, it has to be taken apart, or it will set everything off anyway." Steel nodded and headed for the door.

"I have to find a way to get the lifeboats off this ship while you're doing that, good luck Martin." Martin smiled at Steel.

"You too, my friend, for all our sakes."

STEEL HAD MADE his way down to deck five using the elevator. As he travelled down, he stopped and listened for the first time at the silence, the soothing quiet. He closed his eyes and just let himself drift off for just one moment. He took out the bottle of water, took a small mouthful, and swilled it around his mouth to get rid of the dryness. The metallic knocking as the metal box hurried past floors was almost musical to his ears, for a long time he hadn't stopped and just took a moment to let his brain recuperate. The elevator stopped with a small jolt, and the doors opened. Steel knelt quickly and held the weapon ready. Even though he had a cease-fire with the organisation, he didn't have one with the person who had orchestrated this whole thing. The fifth floor was empty, but the potent smell still lingered in the air.

He moved quickly out of the elevator towards cover. Taking out the sat phone he dialled McCall's desk phone. He needed to find the control unit she spoke of and fast. It took several rings before she picked up.

"McCall, Homicide." Steel smiled at the sound of her voice. It was soothing and hopeful.

"Hi Sam, it's me. Okay, I am on the fifth floor near the damned lifeboats so what am I looking for?" McCall took the cordless handset and moved into the briefing room where the tech was busy figuring things out.

"Ok hotshot, he's on fifth what is he looking for?" The young tech placed his finger on the small box drawing.

"There should be something in the middle of the room, around about where the fifth lifeboat is." Steel ran down, counting the doorways until he reached doors five and fifteen, he stopped and looked around at the empty space.

"Did you find it?" Asked the tech. His voice was sounding anxious as he looked up at the clock.

"Find what? There is nothing here, are you sure you read it right?" The tech nodded to reassure himself and McCall.

"Yes, you can't miss it. It's something large and square." Steel looked around the large empty space.

"Oh, you can't miss it, its large and…." Steel looked straight up and swallowed hard.

"Oh-oh," Steel said.

"What do you mean, Oh-oh. What's wrong?" McCall and the tech looked at each other puzzled at Steel's words.

"Steel, you okay?" Steel walked towards some service steps in the gap between two shops.

"Um, I think I found your thing and yep it's big." Steel clambered up the ladder and headed along the service walkway until he made it back to where he had started. In front of him, held by four long metal arms, was a large Victorian-style four-faced clock. The gold and brass encrusted timepiece stood around six feet square.

"Steel, you still there, what is it, what did you find?" Steel moved towards the nearest arm and prepared to run across the long beam.

"It's a clock, a bloody big-arsed clock. So, genius, what do I have to do?" McCall looked down at the tech who was looking through his notes.

"If you can disable the connection you should be fine." Steel looked at the handset as though he was looking at the man himself.

"Should be, define 'Should be'." McCall shot the tech the same look.

"You will be, once the connection is broken, the devices should be disarmed." Steel held his breath as he prepared to dash across.

Below him, he heard footsteps as Captain Long, and his new helpers came rushing over. Steel leant over the side and called down to get their attention.

"Captain, good to see you again, how did we do?" Long looked up to see the tired-looking Steel.

"Ah, Mr Black, we have damaged enough so she will crawl and not run, and the power is off in this section."

"Good, okay Captain, we need to get those lifeboats off as soon as I take care of that clock." The three men looked at the shimmering timepiece.

"What do you mean 'take care of?'" Long asked, but somehow didn't want to know. Steel shrugged.

"I don't know yet, but I think you will know," Steel laughed.

Tobias Long grinned; he had a fair idea of what the signal might be.

"The doors are stuck so you will have to get to them from the floor above." Long gave Steel a surprised look.

"And you couldn't have mentioned that before?" Long growled. Steel shrugged and just looked apologetic.

"Ok we'll take care of the boats; you just get rid of that damned clock." The four men headed off towards the stairs and the sixth floor.

Steel looked at the long distance he would have to go, the arm stretched for around twenty feet before it ended in a platform for engineers if they needed to work on the clock. Light blazed through the high-density windows above the heavily damaged shops and lifeboat entrances lighting up the room below. Steel looked over to see the captain and the oversized Russians climb down from the sheet rope he had used earlier. He was glad they had found the room open and bothered to investigate the option. As Steel watched, he could see the captain explain with hands and feet what he wanted.

"Hit the top of the arm support," he remembered the captain saying.

"A massive impact registers that the ship is sinking. A failsafe in case the electronics fail." He looked over, set his mark on the clock, and began to run.

Sparks flew as rounds ricochet off the pipe, sending Steel back to the walkway.

"I can't let you do that Mr Steel, you'll kill us all. I know that you set this whole thing up, you used us, and you used Tia." Steel looked over the edge to see Jane Stewart holding the weapon he had given to Vedas, and he worried about the man's safety.

"What have you done with Vedas, and where are the others?" He yelled, as he tried to work out a plan to get over before it was too late.

"Oh, don't worry about Mr Vedas he'll be alright, and the

others are on the way up, they sent me to clear a path for them, just in case." Steel laughed to himself.

"Well, this couldn't have gone any more wrong." He looked at his watch. It was now three-thirty, time was ticking, and they were still moving.

SIXTY-THREE

The news coverage never told of a hostage situation on the cruise liner, nor mention a device that could vaporise anyone near it. The footage was on the good news of a unity of two countries. McCall rushed over to the window as three black hawk helicopters flew over, followed by three F-22 Raptor fighter aircraft. To the public it was an air display to welcome the ship, but McCall knew it was a two-option deal. If Steel managed to do it, the SEAL teams in the black hawk would secure the ship; if he didn't succeed, the Raptors would send her to the bottom, and it would be swept under the carpet, people in dark offices probably already had a plausible cover story. Brant came up next to her, and so did Tooms.

"Don't worry, Detective, that crazy son-of-a-bitch will pull it off." She smiled without facing him.

"Yes, I know, but we have another problem." She handed him the file she had gotten from Jones's loft, including the pictures that Pablo had given to her. Brant looked through it, and his face began to crease up in anger, McCall turned to him and took the file.

"When this is over, I will need a closed interrogation room." Brant nodded.

"Don't worry, you have it, but we need to keep this tight. Only we know." Tooms nodded in agreement.

"Let's just hope we do get to finish it." Tooms lent against the window and watched the helicopters disappear into the glare of the sun.

THE CLATTER of metal hitting the tiled floor filled Steel's ears, and he knew Jane had just done a magazine change.

"Jane, I don't know what someone has told you, but I am trying to stop millions from getting killed." The sparks flew from the side of the walkway miles from his location.

"Liar, you're the one who wants to blow up the ship." Steel didn't have the time for a gunfight or a slanging match, reaching inside one of his pouches he pulled out a grenade and pulled the pin.

"Sorry, Jane but it's for the best." She watched something fall from the walkway and watched it roll across the floor until it stopped close by, her eyes widened as she realised what it was, but it was too late. A loud explosion and a blinding flash was the last thing she saw.

Steel smiled as Jane was engulfed in a cloud of green smoke from the smoke grenade; he could hear her coughing and spluttering. He used the chance and ran as if the devil himself was ready to take him. He reached the clock and searched for a panel or opening, he found it underneath one of the clock faces. The two-foot-long cover had a grip on either side, quickly he ripped it off to display a counter like the one in the storage room. The unit was enclosed and inaccessible. Steel cursed his luck and looked around quickly for other options. He saw the bolts holding the platform on to the arms, took out two grenades, and pulled the pin on one of them. Running over, he released the safety lever and watched it fly. Each one had a seven-second fuse. Taking it, he placed it onto the joint knuckle and ran for the other. After doing the same there, he ran as fast as he could, all the while counting down the seconds as he went. By the time he had gotten to zero, he was over halfway across. The explosion seemed louder inside, pushing the already damaged safety windows into the midday air. There was a creak of metal as the arms gave way on one side causing the clock to swing like a giant pendulum towards the portside wall. As heavy gold and brass slammed against iron, the sound inside was like being in the bell of Big Ben. The shock wave was enough to dislodge the boats on that side, leaving the starboard side for Long and the Russians. Smoke, fire and fragmented metal lay across the deck floor. Jane stood up after being thrown across the room by the explosion. The loud ringing was all that she could hear; her eyes were red raw from the smoke. As she moved across the debris, she saw an LED display that lay next to a charred body. She bent down and dusted it off, the symbols sent a shiver down her spine. "00001."

THE SURVIVORS STOOD near the helicopter-landing pad as the black hawks took turns to drop off their cargo, they all watched as the teams abseiled from the mighty gunship transports on to the deck and ran forward to take up positions. A large black officer walked towards them. He was a broad-shouldered man with a flat top and he was chewing on a fat cigar as he approached.

"I am Captain Osborne of SEAL Team-Four. "Which one of you is Jane Stewart?" Jane stepped forward and showed her CIA badge.

"What's the situation?" He asked, as the teams rushed past them and Military Medics moved up to inspect the survivors.

"The threat has been eliminated along with a good man." She said, with a sorrowful look on her face. The officer said something into a throat microphone, and the teams dispersed to their tasking.

"We will make sure the ship is secured while we get you guys to safety." His mouth fell open as the three Russians stepped forward,

"Goddam, we may need a boat for you guys," Vedas laughed. He stopped and looked around.

"Where is Mr Steel, he didn't make it?" Jane shook her head as a tear rolled down her cheek,

"I am so sorry Vedas, he died in the explosion. It was all my fault, I should have listened." The large Russian snarled as he looked at Grant, who was busy with his notebook.

"Nyet Jane, it was not all your fault, and you did listen, just to the wrong man." A smile crossed Vedas's face as he thought he saw a figure, all dressed in black, swimming for the shore.

"Come, Jane, we will drink, to say thank you and farewell to our crazy friend," he said, pulling a bottle of vodka from his pocket and laughing . Jane went to say, "No thanks," but shrugged and grabbed the bottle.

"Ah, fuck it," she said, taking a massive hit from the bottle.

McCall stood outside the interrogation room, psyching herself up to go in. This was no ordinary box. This was the one for the hardened criminals, the ones they knew would take ages to break. Brant stood with her, "You sure you're up to this? I can take this piece of garbage if you like." McCall shook her head. "No, this one's mine." The solid steel door screeched as she opened it, the noise echoed around the long thin room. The room itself was around twenty feet by twelve feet. A table was placed in the middle with a single small light that hung down from the ceiling, while the rest of the room was in shadow. This room was made to stir emotion, mainly fear. It hadn't been used since the days of Hoover and his novel way of getting information. To the side, there was a small two-way mirror which hardly showed any reflection at all.

McCall walked in but said nothing. She made sure the chair legs ground upon the concrete as she moved it backwards. The mole had been in the box for a good five hours, no drink, no food, and no phone call. She sat down and opened up the file and arranged the different photographs around the long table. McCall sat for a moment taking in the silence, her eyes scanned the person at the other side of the table, and she leant back in her chair.

"So, tell me, who do you work for, and what was with the whole evaporating New York thing?" The mole said nothing.

Bathed in shadow, the mole just sat there motionless. "Who do you work for?" The figure sat there, unchanged. "Look I can tie you to everything, so do yourself a favour, and do a deal, you hand over the top brass." McCall leant forwards and banged the table with a clenched fist. "We have enough to bury you."

"You have nothing" The voice was heavy, and gravelly, McCall smiled at the challenge. "We found a street camera that puts you at the scene of Douglas Major's electrocution. Then there are the shoe impressions left at the scene of Karen Greene. At first we couldn't place them until you left the same print here accidentally the other day." McCall could feel herself starting to enjoy this, she was taking them apart, and there was nothing they could say to get out of it.

"We found out why so many people wanted the office of Bill Foster. It wasn't the view, it was the hidden executive bathroom that CSU found behind the bookshelves. Guess what else they found? There were droplets of water, but when they examined them, they found them to be sweat. When they ran it, guess whose name popped up?" McCall could feel the hate from the person opposite. She could feel their need to leap over the table and shut her up.

"The best one, and this had everyone baffled, was the shooting of John Barr, we couldn't figure out how you did it. We thought about a boat on the Hudson, but trying to keep that still to take a shot? Not a chance, but then CSU found another scrape on the crane. The round had fallen short, or you had moved accidentally. Either way, the bullet ricochet off the flooring and shot up, making it look like he had been shot from the river. My guess is, you couldn't believe your luck when he fell." She saw the figure move uncomfortably.

"We found the sniper's nest you used by the East River bikeway, a nice little nest just on the river bank, a hell of a shot, but not for you." She opened another file. "You spent four years as a Delta Force sniper, lots of medals and awards for sharpshooting." McCall slammed the file shut and leant back in her chair.

"You used the same weapon on the secretary, Oh, by the way, we did find the weapon in the trunk of your car, sorry."

She smiled and shrugged as she showed a photograph of the sniper rifle.

"In the case of Detective Marinelli, well that was simple. You were seen at ballistics the day it was compared, which isn't unusual, granted, but you offered to pick up the weapon as you wanted a rush on it and the tech was busy. Hey, who would think twice about you?" McCall leant her arms forwards, outstretched, so they grabbed the edges of the table. "Your plan to frame Detective Marinelli had gone south. In addition, we have CCTV footage of you at the victim's work and homes, courtesy of Agent Jones. He was on to you, and you had him killed." The silence persisted, and McCall could feel the tension from the suspect.

"You had a partner, you were here, and they were on the ship. If this went off, it would be a major disaster and the public would want blood. So, you gave them the Russians , the CIA and the organisation. The question is, what would you gain, both you and your partner would be dead, so again, who are you working for?" She watched the figure adjust its seating position, and that was the point she realised they were not going to talk. McCall stood up and packed the file away.

"You will talk, if not to me then someone will make you." The silence remained, McCall saw she was wasting her time and stood up.

"A shame what happened to your friend," He said, with a callous grin. She scowled as she could see him laughing,

"He was one of us, you son of a bitch," McCall said, with venom. His laughter filled the room, and she needed to get out.

"Is someone else coming around to visit? I don't want to get lonely," he laughed. McCall turned around to face him.

"Oh, I am sure you'll make lots of friends where you're going." She jested.

"Like whom, your dearly departed Mr Steel? I heard he got incinerated, stopping the devices. Nothing left but ashes they say." Lieutenant James Green leant forward into the light, wearing a smug grin on his face. "You have nothing, Detective, and I am not talking." McCall smiled.

"Maybe not to me, but you know what they used to call Steel in the service? The Phoenix." McCall knocked on the door and watched it open. Behind her, Green felt uneasy, as though someone or something was behind him. Out of the shadows, a hooded figure emerged and as the door slowly closed behind her, a scream of utter terror pierced the air, the door closed and silenced the chilling sound. Brant looked down at her.

"Are you sure we just did the right thing sir?" Brant looked at the door and started to walk towards the elevator with McCall.

"What? Leaving him alone with Steel? By the way, why did the survivors say he was toast?" McCall shrugged.

"I guess it was a thank you, just like they never revealed his name, just left it as Antony Black." The elevator doors slid open, and Tooms and Tony stood, holding the doors open.

"Glad to see you back, Detective." McCall smiled as she saw the group back together.

"Glad to be back." Tony looked down the dimly lit corridor.

"Odd thing is, I hope he takes a long time to talk." As the steel doors slid shut, they all looked down that long dark corridor, and no words were spoken, they just looked and dared to wonder what was happening in that room.

SIXTY-FOUR

Grant sat at his computer in the local coffee shop; his fingers flew across the keyboard as though they were possessed. He was typing up his exposé, the tail of the CIA and the Russians mixed up in a plot to blow up New York. Sure, he didn't have all of the facts, but he could fill in the blanks. This would be his masterpiece, his Mona Lisa. The waitress poured him another coffee without asking. She knew him too well to ask. If he was writing, just keep them coming. He stopped for a moment to take a brief break. He looked out of the window and out into the street, he felt the warm morning sunshine against his skin, and he closed his eyes to take in the rays as they caressed his flesh.

"Why Mr Grant, fancy meeting you here" He looked up to see the startling beauty of Missy Studebaker. He stood up and offered her a seat; she sat down opposite him and grinned that innocent smile.

"So, what brings you to Queens, it's a bit far out for you, isn't it?" He sat back in his chair and called the waitress over.

"Oh, nothing for me, I just saw you in the window and just thought I would stop and say hi." She giggled like a fourteen-year-old.

"So, are you writing that article you were working on?" He nodded as he took a mouthful of coffee.

"Yep, everyone should know the truth about what happened, I am going to tell it all, and who knows I may get Pulitzer out of it." She giggled again, but the black Ranger Rover parked outside, beeping its horn, caught her attention.

"Oh, I am sorry, hubby is waiting. It was very nice to see you again, Mr Grant and good luck." They shook hands, and she stood up, the light reflected off her golden hair, making it glow.

"Look after yourself, Mrs. Studebaker." Missy walked out of the coffee shop, turned, and waved just as she got to a blacked-out vehicle. Grant noticed a man get out of the driver's side and open the rear passenger door for her. Grant peered out of the window to get a better look of the driver, but the suns glare shone off the car's darkened windows, almost blinding him. He smiled and shook his head.

"Na, can't be," Grant looked back towards the car; he could have sworn that the driver looked the spitting image of Alan Metcalf. He sat back down and drew his attention back to his computer screen. Out of the corner of his eye, he could see Missy had left her purse.

"Damned stupid woman." He thought, as he reached to pick it up.

As the Ranger Rover headed down the street, it stopped at a set of lights. A massive roar like a lightning strike filled the air as, in the distance, the coffee shop was engulfed in a massive explosion, which was enough to send the cars parked next to it into the air. The vehicle's rear window wound down, and a woman's voice simply said.

"It's done, the story is buried. No, there are no more loose ends. Understood, yes we can lie low for a while, let them forget about us before we strike."

Dear Reader,

We hope you have enjoyed reading Hidden Steel from the John Steel thriller series.

There are many more novels to follow.

If you have a moment, please feel free to leave a quick review, because your feedback is always important.

Best regards,

Stuart Field and the Next Chapter team

ABOUT THE AUTHOR

Stuart is an ex-soldier who was born in the West Midlands. He has served in Bosnia, Kosovo, Iraq, Germany, Canada, Cyprus, and the UK. Stuart loves to write but admits he has little time to read as his brain keeps churning out new stories. When he does so, he finds a good thriller just the ticket. He loves to travel and tries to incorporate some of the places into his stories. Stuart has been writing since 2014 and has already written six books of the John Steel series as well as other works, yet to be published.

Stuart loves to sit in cafes and watch the world go by. "The world is our inspiration; each person has a story, just waiting to be told through our words," he says.

He works and lives in Germany, working security, but finds danger in his writing. Born in the seventies, he grew up with Bond, U.N.C.L.E, Star Trek, Mission Impossible and other great shows. All were having an impact on stirring up his imagination as a child. At school he loved to read The Hobbit, The Lion, Witch and the Wardrobe and other great fantasy classics. He loves the works of Sherlock Holmes, Lee Child, Michael Connelly, Jeffery Deaver to name a few.

Stuart lives with his wife Ani in the north of Germany and enjoys the cities, the culture and obviously the odd Currywurst.